A PARANORMAL JOURNEY by

# ARGENT AMOS

Design and distribution by Bublish, Inc.

ISBN: 978-1-647045-58-6 (paperback)
ISBN: 978-1-647045-57-9 (eBook)

# Prologue

Three long stretches of electrical conduit, curved in the shape of goose necks, hung over a four-by-eight sheet of cracked and delaminated, whitewashed plywood. One tube had barely visible wires hanging from its hollow; the other two shone dim, low-wattage, incandescent amber light from two exposed bulbs that resembled the bulbous eyes of an interstellar being.

In the late evening, drizzling fog of Humboldt County, California, the lamps strained to illuminate reddish, six-inch-tall block letters, a few of which were dreadfully misaligned as if they had been painted by a bumbling half-witted cartoon character. Attached to a denuded tree trunk at the edge of a secluded state highway, the announcement read: Scully Brother's Fuel.

"Weird-ass place," a bulky silhouette mumbled in the dark.

With the flowing dexterity of a symphony conductor directing the music to a Viennese waltz, he smoothly slid two large black hands around an oversized steering wheel and maneuvered a seventy-eight-foot semitruck combination into a leisurely left turn.

Then, creating a perfect relationship with the steering tires of the large three axle tractor and a narrow slit of driveway, he inched the heavy front suspension off the asphalt and crept onto the broken rubble of a potholed parking lot that in his beams appeared as if it had been hit by a heavy meteorite shower.

He quickly doused the lights as a courtesy to any dozing truckers who might be backed in under the redwood canopy. One hand steering, the other on the shift lever, his head rocked like a wooden dummy as the entire rig, tractor and reefer trailer bumped onto the rutted property, violently pitching his torso and the wheeled box behind him in all directions.

Successfully jockeying the entire eighteen wheels as if they were a team of mad oxen, his load of forty-three thousand pounds of trailered junk cardboard followed its leader through too many water-filled holes. He finally pedaled to an abrupt stop.

Sitting in foggy darkness, except for the blur of light over the shabby sign and a mushy half-moon, he pulled the yellow knob that set the truck's parking brakes. Pop! A valve behind the dashboard momentarily interrupted the clattering diesel engine. The noise was followed by the familiar reptilian sounding hiss as the pressure in the air system locked the tractor's brakes.

He stared dumbly at his fuel gauge resting firmly on "E" with its solid red warning light. Shutting the rig down, he waited motionless as the big motor slowed to a stop in unison with his over-revved brain and hammering heart. When man and machine were in total silence, he exhaled with a long sigh that had been buried somewhere between his solid stomach and broad chest.

"Done," he said aloud.

Outside the rig, the murky void was thick and sodden, but in the distance, about a hundred feet farther to the rear of the parcel, he could barely see the outline of a wood-sided structure with a dimly lit upstairs room that suggested the image of a late-night reader or internet client.

Grabbing a tube of self-defense spray not much bigger than a roll of breath mints, along with a small, folding, military-style survivor knife—the only two defensive weapons most states allowed a commercial driver to carry—he gently opened the heavy driver's-side door. The interior light lit up the immediate area as if he had started a bonfire.

"Shit!" he said, as though he was scolding an onlooker, convinced that a stadium of gawkers had to be watching.

With one hand inside his sweatpants pocket clutching the tube of pepper spray, he climbed down quickly from the mechanized monster and gently shut the massive door trying to pretend he didn't hear it latch. He was then greeted by dead silence, except for faint cracking sounds as the steel and iron of the engine cooled and contracted. Standing perfectly still, he counted the five seconds it took for the insistent timer on the computerized lamp system to shut the light off.

He was unofficially a nighttime intruder, but he needed fuel. Moving stealthily in the dark, his soft, slip-on Skechers were quickly soaked in cold, muddy water that reeked of rotten eggs. Irritated, he squished and stumbled over broken asphalt, finally reaching a barred door. In a small dusty window, faded orange fluorescent letters offered a common, thankless apology:

SORRY, WE ARE CLOSED.

A modern Union 76 diesel pump sat in front. It was dead, the digital screen black. There was no other visible signage on the property, but both the forsaken building and the shadowy, socked-in property seemed to issue an unwritten, ominous warning: NO TRESPASSING.

The guy didn't really want to care, but he knew that the veiled message suggested another much more personal statement: THAT MEANS YOU, BLACK BOY.

"Ain't that 'bout a bitch," the guy said aloud, as if anyone was there to listen. "No fuel's pure-ass booshit," he said, unwilling to admit that he was disgusted with himself for failing to stop and buy fuel one-hundred-forty miles sooner at one of the many truckstops in Ukiah.

His heavy eyelids felt like mudflaps. He needed sleep and he needed fuel. He knocked. Nothing. He knocked again. Dead silence, except for his own labored breathing. Then, scanning the lot as best he could in the fog, he looked for a house, maybe also with a light on.

Again, nothing except a night black redwood forest that combined with the unoccupied property offered only bad vibes, an odd sense of dread to be more precise, maybe a threat, but mostly the familiar feeling of losing control, and then being penalized for his own stupidity.

At first glance, the remote spot might have been viewed as a long-haul trucker's paradise. There were no glaring fast-food signs, convenience store bright lights, or loud rhythmic electronic rock music that would keep a dead-tired highway hauler wide awake all night.

The roominess of the property also prevented the usual assortment of ham-handed drivers from making bad decisions trying to back into tight spots where they could wipe out some working stiff's headlights or grill. And any half-drunk smart-asses would also have enough space to stay up all night, race their engines, and rap their exhaust stacks without creating a donnybrook.

But there were no parked rigs, only a few abandoned log carrier frames on flattened tires, their massive steel stakes wishing for former days of hauling big timber. These chassis had been dropped at the rear of the lot, where piles of broken riprap met a jumble of underbrush and a tight vertical grove of dark-trunked redwood trees that looked like the legs of many giants.

He quickly slipped back to his tractor and popped the door open, forgetting again that the interior light would illuminate him and the rest of the world as the area burst into a golden blaze. "I'll be damned!" he said aloud, as he scrambled inside the security of the truck. Deftly shutting the door, he locked it, rechecking the button and latch twice.

Again, he nervously waited for the light to time out, as if he was an aquarium fish anticipating the net. Finally falling on his bunk mattress, he focused his burning eyes upward at the bottom of the empty bunk above.

Only a few seconds passed before he impatiently snatched his mobile phone, sat up, and attempted to find a signal that might lead him to a fuel map and a working diesel pump somewhere close by. A familiar nothing. Dead internet also. He was fuel dry and alone in the Northern California redwoods in a nighttime foggy drizzle.

It had been a long day, beginning in the predawn blackness of an Oakland truckyard, where he had hooked an empty reefer trailer and then run for thirty-four miles in heavy traffic to Milpitas. There he maneuvered the rig through the muck of a vast open-yard shipping facility that forwarded spent paper and cardboard for recycling.

That shithole was in the lowlands where the San Francisco Bay had once lapped the shore, but was now a marshy landfill consisting of a county-subsidized recycle center, a garbage dump, and a thoroughfare for massive Pacific Gas and Electric towers and cables that brought power from the central part of the state to the urban sprawl of the great Silicon Valley, where masters of the tech industry did their best to rule the world.

The shipper hosted a constant, chaotic stream of trucks and trailers that clashed and competed with one another like mechanical dinosaurs, each attempting to be first in line, or first on the scale, or first at a dock, or first to flirt with the cute, too-young Mexican girl in the scale house, or first out the gate, or first back on the frontage road. *First* was all that mattered.

The forklift operator projected a common superior attitude that spoke to drivers from all stations of life. "If you be good, maybe you be next, home boy, or maybe not, too, bro'."

He was a neck-and-cheek-tattooed, Chicano kid who seemed to have definite issues with truck drivers. He smugly took his time stuffing several trailers with damp, wired bales of cardboard, while visibly irritable African American men, vacant looking white guys, and big-eyed, young, coffee-colored kids from the Middle East, all worn very thin and irritated from pounding the highways, stood in knee-deep wet trash dodging gulls while measuring the cardboard bales to ensure they would not be held financially accountable at their receivers for any miscount.

After getting through a four-hour loading contest, it had taken the best part of a day to crawl northward through bumper-to-bumper bus, truck, and commute traffic and pilot up the peninsula that connected San Jose to San Francisco, wind through the Presidio Park reserve, and steal across the Golden Gate to reach the suburbs of the Wine Country, and then the Redwood Empire.

For California's several major seaports, cardboard and paper recycling is a massive business. Where a load originates determines if it goes south to the Long Beach harbor or to Oakland in the central part of the state. In either case, it is cross-docked into steel containers for ocean shipment to China, where it is reprocessed and resold mostly as boxes and cartons again.

This load was an anomaly. Its destination was far out of the way from the usual mainstream ocean shippers. Instead of a roundtrip back to Oakland, it was consigned to a forwarder a full day's drive north, in Humboldt County inside the Port of Eureka, making it a wet, winding, many hours ride that landed drivers in the isolated redwood forest, with lousy overnight parking, no rest stops, and too many state cops with too much time on their hands.

The port was known to be no picnic either. A comparatively small harbor, it was sheltered by a natural jetty that in its heyday protected a commercial fishing fleet, but large oceangoing ships never ventured past the breakwater. So, for truckers, there was the possibility of a complicated or risky unloading and transferring process onto a barge or floating dock. That could be a pain in the ass if not also dangerous.

Taking the lousy load had been a difficult decision for other reasons. He had run into legal problems in that area in the distant past. He only ran the load as a favor to his dispatcher with the promise of a better-paying run.

Hauling recyclables into the rural counties of Northern California, coming from the South Bay was what drivers called "a nothin' load." When he wasn't hauling junk freight, he ran for much better money with the temperature-controlled trailer—either forty-eight state food, bottled cold liquid loads, or the discount retailers' steady stream of high priority frozen baked goodies. Sitting in silence with a quiet reefer engine because of the cardboard not requiring temperature control was the only good thing about the run.

Examining outside the windows in the dark, again checking for intruders, either animal, human or otherworldly, he muttered aloud. "Least the damn reefer ain't runnin' an' scarin' up the dead."

He scratched his marblelike scalp with both hands. Then, pulling the heavy privacy curtains shut and popping open his folding table, he flipped on a tiny reading lamp and grabbed one of the many cheap, plastic Paper Mate pens along with a stained, dog-eared spiral notebook that he kept in an old, rumpled leather Coach bag.

A lack of computer experience had cost him his earlier attempts at trying to write a story about trucking. While sitting for three days in a snowed-in Montana truck stop near the Canadian border the previous winter, he lost over sixty pages and $39.00 to a phony data saving system. His bank told him it had been untraceable Russian hackers that were responsible.

Now, his hand and the retractable pen point began to move swiftly across the lined, white pages.

# *One*

# WAR ZONE

A few years short of seventy, Noah Calvin Sowles had been behind the wheel of a big rig for a long while. He started as a driver in his late twenties after a stint in the US Merchant Marines and had evolved over many years into what is known as an owner-operator, a driver who owns his equipment, but because of not being authorized by the Department of Transportation as an actual motor carrier, he leases the rig and himself to an established fleet.

Almost beaten by trucking because of the struggle to maintain consistent income in the midst of cyclic economic downturns, Sowles had progressively become exhausted with everything, starting with life. He felt worthless, but he was good at glad-handing—the art of bullshit—so he was seen by his employer as a solid, good guy. He had no living family and no friends other than a Latino supervisor he joked with. Nobody but Sowles knew that he was an emotionally perforated man. He viewed himself as being a bit like Swiss cheese, solid but full of holes. He was alone, disillusioned, and withdrawn.

Even as a robust, athletic man, five feet eleven, thickly muscled, and two hundred pounds, his image of himself was deprecative. He believed that he was small, timid, and physically weak. He hid this aberration from others, making long-distance trucking a good occupation, as it allowed him to isolate. His negative self-image had also worked to some earlier advantage, as it had kept him isolated from active violence while growing up in one of the worst neighborhoods of Oakland, California, then later at sea and on the road.

In his youth, he had been awarded a blue belt in Tang Soo Do Karate, a tough kickboxing style. This was beneficial for navigating the mean streets as a kid, and later in the labor trades, but he had never been in a street fight, either as a kid or as an adult, despite being challenged by drunken laborers, doped-up teenage hoodlums, merchant seamen, and a few truckers. His style when confronted was always to make some unrelated conversation and then walk away.

That might have been an admirable quality to the peaceniks of the San Francisco Bay Area, but, in his mind, only confirmed his cowardice. He concluded that his passive nature was the result of being raised by a stern, Southern Baptist mother with strict, Bible-based values, and whether or not he believed them, he found himself turning the other cheek. But that even temperament helped him avoid the many violent risks that put African American boys and men from the inner cities into state prisons.

At the age of ten he briefly ventured into petty crime, filling his pockets with penny candy from the neighborhood market. Nothing came of that incident, but in the sixties, when much of the country's Black youth were in family and social crises that often led to disaster, he compensated for his insecurities by stealing trinkets from unlocked cars and participating in the burglary of a bicycle store, in search of a new Schwinn Sting-Ray.

He was arrested but was exonerated by a well-meaning, white juvenile court judge who reviewed his top grades in English and US History and believed that he was not a stereotypical Black hoodlum, but only needed time to mature. The judge was only partially correct. By sixteen, he was drinking regularly until he wrecked an old Ford. He then quit alcohol in favor of experimenting with marijuana.

All of these misdeeds led to further juvenile court hearings and a school psychologist placing a formal statement in his records: *After reviewing the juvenile records and having an interview with Noah Sowles and his mother, I've concluded that Noah is in danger of leading an idle and dissolute life.* Coming from a self-righteous white woman, that statement bored into his heart. He began to turn the corner. He started playing some decent street basketball and went to church when his mother absolutely insisted.

Yet, none of these efforts had helped socialize him or aid him in overcoming his self-doubt. It was the interest in history that finally filled part of the gap. It led him to study the records of US slavery. Without the animosity or reparation views that some Black youths had toward Caucasian America, he became a committed advocate of a Martin Luther King Jr. style of integration.

Other than being skeptical of certain white men's motives, he believed in a racially integrated society that held moderate political and social values. This awareness continued to keep him at a distance from the many racial conflicts that had prevailed in Oakland and throughout the country since long before he was born.

Sowles's hope for racial equality and opportunity was soon shattered by race riots in Oakland and an armed, anti-war protest at the US Army Induction Center, followed by King's murder. Then a few months later when he was ordered to appear for a preinduction physical to determine his draft eligibility for the military, integration in the U.S. made little sense. He knew he was a Black man destined for jungle combat in a mock war orchestrated by white politicians.

At that stage of the Vietnam War and the ensuing anti-war movement, boys who were not gung-ho to fight against the Vietnamese either sought deferments by attending college, getting married, or declaring themselves conscientious objectors or homosexual. Then there were those that simply refused to be inducted and faced five years of federal incarceration. Other than joining a less aggressive branch of US military service, the less impacting alternative was to seek draft counseling resources. These services were prevalent in many college communities.

Sowles's legitimate fear of death combined with a first-hand view of the devastation and suffering that occurred among neighborhood families over the deaths or permanent disabilities of Black boys from his high school led him to the streets of Berkeley to ally with radical protesters against the war.

Through coffee shop postings, he found a young, white, political activist who was studying law at UC Berkeley and worked also as a pro bono draft counselor. The young man instructed him in securing a medical deferment that had been effective for men in World War II and in Korea. He was referred to appointments with pacifistic orthopedists who were active in the anti-war movement. They documented a congenital foot condition known as pes planus or flat feet.

This had worked well for other men in prior generations, but at the physical examination and face-to-face interviews, he was poorly treated, regardless that he was equipped with letters and diagnostic statements from medical specialists. The military personnel were nasty and unreceptive. A few low-grade officers and medical technicians conducting the basic examinations publicly insulted him or smirked when he stated that he was not fit for the leg and foot exercises required as part of the examination. Several other Black draftees threatened to meet him in the street or shouted him down, telling him to join the Coast Guard. The white boys laughed at him, made faces, flipped their middle fingers, and told him that he was dead meat.

When he reached the end of the six-hour-long examination, he was put in a room with a Black, high-ranking officer, who from his questions appeared to have been a psychologist. Sowles was confident as the officer examined his medical records nodding as he read. The good feeling waned when the man cited Sowles's one-hundred-percent scores on basic cognitive quizzes, as well as excellent hearing, eyesight, and overall positive health tests.

When he said that the famous NBA center at that time, Wilt Chamberlain, had flat feet, Sowles realized that the psychologist was not an ally. Sowles was in trouble, but he had been well coached. He defended his inability to run, walk, or march long distances, and complained of burning pain in his arches and legs, all of which the psychologist viewed as malingering.

The man criticized him harshly for being unwilling to serve his country, leaving Sowles speechless. Then the intimidating Black officer slammed the paperwork with a heavy metal, chrome-handled rubber stamp that read: FIT FOR MILITARY SERVICE.

Sowles was then sent to another room, where a group of apathetic-looking young men, representing several minorities were told their classifications and MOS—Military Occupational Specialty. After reading from a long list that started with A, a uniformed white Army lieutenant with a southern twang finally reached S.

Sowles's mind went blank until he heard his name.

"Soo-wells, Noah C., I-A, US Army Infantry."

His stomach rolled. He had believed that the doctors' statements would defer him from what he had been told by anti-war activists would be his death in a foreign war that all Black men had no business being involved in to begin with. He lost his composure.

"You can't take me into no fuckin' army. I got bad feet," he said. "I got the doctor statements to prove it. I want to see a general!"

He ran up and down the hallway repeating this coached mantra, while several young, white military officers watched him in awe. Finally, an older white captain heard the ruckus and came out into the corridor. "Son. Son. Slow Down. What do you need? Son?"

The man was kind. He listened to his concerns and promised him that he would get an appointment with an orthopedic specialist. He was instructed to return the following afternoon and then sent home with a credit chit to get a three-course meal in a cafeteria on Broadway in Oakland as a gratuity from the US Government.

Sowles was appeased, but not convinced. On his way home, he stopped at a Navy recruitment center just in case it didn't work out the next day. That took less than five minutes. A pink-faced, dress-booted, web-belted Chief Petty Officer in starched whites told him that the US Navy didn't want him.

"Yer a marijuana smoker, son," the man said. "I smell it." He escorted him to the curb.

Sowles was highly insulted and worried. The next day, he showed up for the appointment calm and well-dressed. The orthopedist was a white man and an officer, but he was not in uniform. He examined Sowles's plank-like feet, his underdeveloped calves, and his loose knee joints.

In the midst of chatting amiably about possible future plans for college and marriage, both of which Sowles had concluded he had limited skills for, the doctor classified him 1-Y:

REGISTRANT QUALIFIED FOR MILITARY SERVICE ONLY IN TIME OF WAR OR NATIONAL EMERGENCY.

Noah Sowles was free of the Selective Service, Army, Marine Corps, Air Force, Navy, and Coast Guard. He did not have to risk his life for the white man's political war in Southeast Asia. It was a cause for celebration. He drank some cheap wine and got stoned with some older men from the neighborhood and then went home to an angry father.

His father had been a World War II veteran of the Navy, a cook's helper on a destroyer that survived a Japanese air attack. He then became a porter with the Southern Pacific Railroad, and then Amtrak, and worked over twenty years on passenger trains.

"Beatin' the draft," his father called his efforts. "You a god-damned fool nigga," the old man said, scowling. He appeared as if he was ready to spit.

"The service woulda got yo' ass outta these goddamned streets an' got you inta somethin' where's you coulda made a future fo' yo'self."

Sowles reacted. "Like you?" he asked.

"Whachu mean, 'like me?' I served my country on a ship an' worked my ass off on them damn trains fo' yo' mama an' you."

"You a cheatin' Uncle Tom hypocrite!" Sowles said.

"Get outta my damn house," his father said.

Sowles stood his ground. "You sell out yo'self workin' onna train, fluffin' white folks' pillows, shufflin' fo' they drinks, an' waitin' they tables for tips from broke-asses that can't 'ford to fly onna damned jet plane! Fo' what? So's you can play the high life an' spen' yo' money on other women 'sides yo' wife? And what about, me, yo' son?"

Sowles then imitated the old man, stoop shouldered with a big smile on his face and his palm extended. "May ah gets dat fo' ya, suh?" Sowles said. "I can gets it, fo y'all, sho' 'nuff."

The older man raised his hand to backhand his son, but Sowles grabbed his wrist. They tussled, and Sowles pushed his father into his armchair. The old man was angry and miffed.

"A Black man got no damn business fuckin' with the US Government at no time," his father said from his position of safety in his chair. "An' 'specially now with the Black Panthers and white folks stirrin' up all they crime an' anti-war shit!"

"Yo' ass is fulla booshit, ole man," Sowles said. "You ain't gonna never gimme no opportunities 'cept fo' the military, an' you know it!"

His father shook his fist. "Don' matter, boy, you out there fuckin' 'roun with white people will get yo' ass in jail or dead soon 'nuff!"

His father concealed his tears as Sowles stormed out of the house but Sowles saw him wiping his eyes. The old man never forgave him. Sowles later regretted his decision and became obsessed with his own cowardice and survivor's guilt as he saw the many returning Black and white wounded veterans and the special camaraderie they shared. He also never overcame the pain he caused his father, regardless of the fact that the older man had been a failure in his eyes and had been invisible throughout much of his youth.

It had been true that Mrs. Sowles had always assumed the parenting responsibilities while Sowles's father kept secretive alliances with other women. Her resourcefulness had been her faith in Christ. She had tried to communicate with her son within the context of those beliefs, making her position adamant that his obligations were to God and to his father in that order, regardless of his father's sins. Sowles was not willing to accept either concept.

It took years for Sowles to realize that his father's work ethic had fundamentally been correct. Sowles finally admitted to himself that he owed his life and the roof he had been raised under to his father about the time he also recognized the restrictions and challenges that Black men resembling his father endure to even exist and stay alive, not to mention marry and provide for a wife and family on any level.

It became very evident to Sowles that a Black man could not resist the mores, economic, racial, or caste systems of any democratic country and expect to succeed on any level. Either he would have to pursue security or face the streets and ultimately find himself in prison.

It took living in the confinement of a truck to bring him to that realization.

# Two

# YOU DON'T SEEM LIKE A TRUCKER

As is true of most long-haul drivers, including those who own their own rigs, Sowles had mixed feelings about trucking. He liked the sensation of motion and speed, the noisy engine, traveling, the anonymity, the big-boy image, and the risk of danger, but running over the road on long hauls is a dirty, lonely life juggled between the extremes of anxiety and boredom.

The workload requires concentration, organizational skills, and uncompromising courage. It leaves little time or energy for what most people would consider a normal life. The life consists of hammering the asphalt up to 75 hours a week, languishing at loading docks for another few dozen hours, finding the time to locate healthy food, and having the time to eat it, stealing catnaps of three or four hours, two or three times in twenty-four hours on a four-inch bumpy mattress. Added to these obstacles is the loss of personal or shared time with friends and family after decades and millions of mind-numbing miles over US highways and rough, isolated back roads through the lost towns of yesteryear. It all leads to watching oneself age alone and lonely.

Trucking requires an almost sociopathic ability to live without significant relationships, including even acceptable association with other drivers and workers, as there are deceitful deadbeats in the business itself and in its periphery. Angry laborers slave in warehouses. Oddballs frequent the truck stops along with dangerous itinerants, nighttime trespassers, and displaced criminals who also wander the nation's roads, impoverished rural areas and inner cities. These wrongdoers have been displaced or upended by bad legislation, inflation, civil upheaval, or foreign wars. They drift in the fringes of society. Many are mentally ill tramps or thieves. This subculture of marginalized rural and urban males lost in the streets and hollows of the US are similar to that of the many men who drifted after the Civil War and during the Great Depression.

In large part, the trucking industry is only removed from manning a wagon or stagecoach in the western badlands with a team of horses the result of oil, the diesel engine, and one-hundred and forty years of perfecting bearings and gears—except today a single, high-speed accident can end a career in seconds, and, if the trucker is not burned alive from hundreds of gallons of modern volatile diesel spewed onto a hot exhaust manifold from ruptured fuel tanks, a driving mishap causing another person's death can result in a manslaughter charge and long imprisonment.

Unless they leave the industry, many truckers never fully discover their own true character or identity other than that of a truck driver. They vainly attempt to define some other personal individuality but when unsuccessful, the failure is mitigated by overeating, smoking, drinking, yearning for a homelife and any loved one, reminiscing and pining for the past, and thinking about what a guy might still do with his life or what he should have done.

Sowles's self-image was impacted by years of trucking too, but he had also concluded from reading articles written by psychologists that his poor understanding and opinion of himself had begun from having an absent father. Then over time, greater study suggested that the shame and doubt he experienced came from being Black in a dominant and frightening white culture. This disparity combined with being a lost boy in his family then created the conditions for developing a borderline personality disorder. Trucking had only added to the malady.

As he tried to rest inside the rig, vulnerable to what he considered to be a threatening nighttime environment, he wasn't able to shut off his thoughts, fears or memories. The solution was to get the rig rolling, not only to get away from the abandoned fuel station and its perceived threats but because the hum of the highway and sound of wheels spinning against asphalt was therapy for calming worry until that too became part of the anxiety.

That syndrome was a phenomenon that few truckers were conscious of or rationally capable of discussing. Driving a loaded rig, heavy with fuel and cargo at a high rate of speed became a troubled trucker's only relief, but it also created a dangerous cycle of addiction for many long-distance, solo, big-rig drivers. As with any psychological or physical dependence, the highs from endorphins or adrenalin from the weight, motion, and speed came with the risk of overdosing or overdoing. In trucking, that could mean rolling over, crashing into another vehicle or immovable object, or simply running off the road. This threat in itself became part of the addiction. The danger and excitement and relief the driver craved could also potentially end his life.

Under normal driving conditions, without an immediate threat of an accident, the sensual pleasure of a roaring engine and eighteen wheels spinning under a driver's feet was satisfying, regardless that it would also wear off within short hours, to be replaced by apathy, sleepiness, mindless boredom, and depression. Then the driver wanted out of the truck, but once he was out and away from it or even stopped for a short DOT required thirty-minute break, the compulsion to get the wheels spinning again would return, and the cycle of dependency was reestablished.

Longing and craving were replaced by excitement that quickly became mundane and led to depression. Separating from the cycle created anxiety and then recycled back to longing and craving. In cases where drivers lost jobs or lost trucks to accidents or long-term repairs and could not satisfy their craving, many would experience withdrawals. This syndrome could also even include the temporary separation anxiety of having to sleep between shifts, making most drivers chronic insomniacs also as they anticipated the moment they could again roll. Remedies could be in the form of other dependencies. Alcohol abuse, cigarettes, pornography, sexual compulsions, and chronic overeating are often replacement therapies for a trucker when separated from the truck itself or from the sensual effects of the vehicle in motion.

Truckers are compelled to stay in isolation and motion for reasons often removed from income. Sowles was no exception, and he resigned himself to that truth. In his forty years of driving, receiving either good or poor earnings, he rarely even spent any money. Sowles was living in a truck because he had no other psychological choice. It seemed that there was no other place his struggling psyche could survive.

# *Three*

## GIRL POWER

Sowles had learned to assimilate into white culture and not take racism personally, regardless that Western society did not fully extend to him or any other Black person the rights promised by the principles and the laws of the US. His father had alluded to that reality in their final argument but it was proven true for Sowles when he had his legal showdown years earlier in the same area of Humboldt County where he sat in the dark contemplating his empty fuel tanks.

He had been about twenty when he was arrested on a weed possession charge outside of Fortuna, while driving a car with a white girl as his passenger. He became the only Black man in Eureka's concrete and steel-barred downtown jail. He couldn't make bail, so for six months he lived with white, emaciated dope smokers and acidheads, close-mouthed rapists, big-mouth strongarm robbers, and sneaky thieves, and even a guy who stole a tow truck, profitably hauled wrecked and impounded vehicles to police yards, and justified himself in court by saying the crime was better than stealing the actual cars.

A bold public defender with his eye on the Eureka City Attorney's position finally came to Sowles's rescue. The lawyer had been determined to expose the arresting California Highway Patrol officer for busting young kids for possession of marijuana without clear probable cause, specifically those he determined would be easy arrests, either Blacks or hippy long-hairs. The patrolman and the DA had enjoyed several convictions because they had not been properly challenged in court.

The defense lawyer was a former southern gentleman with a sweet and polished charm that easily enabled him to secure a court order from a lower court circuit judge to put the cop on the stand and test his olfactory sense.

First waving soaked rags of Aqua Velva aftershave and gasoline under the cop's nose, the legal comedian, potbellied in a vested suit, took his sweet time firing up several corncob pipes in open court and theatrically paraded around the witness stand blowing smoke in the cop's face. In short minutes, he demonstrated that the cop knew what after shave and gasoline were but he could not distinguish the difference between burning marijuana and numerous other burning odors from common substances. Tea, straw, pipe tobacco, shredded paper, smoldering clove, Bull Durham, and Mexican pot were all unidentifiable to the cop, and because the odor of residual weed smoke had been the cop's "reasonable grounds" for searching the vehicle, the case was dismissed by the very entertained judge.

But the dismissal was temporary. Because the hearing had been held in the lower-tiered Fortuna Justice Court, within weeks of the ruling, the DA appealed the decision to the Superior Court of Humboldt County. For young Sowles, poverty colluded with plea bargaining. He was forced to plead guilty to a DUI.

The toxicology report had read: ZERO ALCOHOL.

The girl's name had been Katy. They had met on Telegraph Avenue in Berkeley during one of many protests over the street people's demands to use a public park for their habitat. In actuality, their civil dissent was just one more reaction to Nixon in the White

House, Ronald Reagan in the California Governor's office, and the Vietnam War.

After smoking a joint together, Katy invited him to ride with her in her flower-decaled, bright-yellow VW Bug back to Humboldt State College, "to party where the real weed was."

"Why not?" he said. After all, she was cute, friendly and seemed color blind.

He had little to do at the time. He had recently avoided the draft on the medical deferment, so his life had consisted of washing pizza trays at a franchise restaurant with a merry-olde-England theme and he was about to get fired from a nighttime gas jockey job working for an Iranian egomaniac who owned a Shell on San Pablo Avenue in West Berkeley. The owner had already taken back most of his previous week's wages because Sowles had been tricked by nighttime cash hustlers who confused him on his money count at the exact time that he closed up the station. The official dismissal was pending one final accounting with the Iranian guy.

Katy had let him drive as the evening wore on. They had smoked weed earlier, but the windows had been deliberately left open for hours. There was no odor of burned pot. The truth was that the cop was a mean white man. He saw a Black kid driving a VW Bug with a pretty white girl on a summer evening and pulled him over under the pretext of a flickering taillight.

Then, as if he had inside information, the cop went straight to the girl's guitar case, where he found a Glad bag with a half-ounce of Mexican weed. He then jostled Sowles, cuffed him until it hurt, slammed him against the black and white, and threatened to shoot him if he resisted.

After stuffing him in the back seat behind the Plexiglas, the cop invited the girl to sit next to him in the front seat. On the nighttime ride to the jail, he chatted casually with her as if they were old friends. She was released. Sowles was detained and booked. He never saw her again.

In the era he was arrested, Fortuna had been a small, wood-structured enclave for itinerant woodcutters or seasonal workers who did local fishing tours. Humboldt County itself had been an esthetically appealing forested community, but typically also a low-income, low-rent, logging area, dependent on regional and national lumber demands. Unemployment would be double-digit until logging, housing, small building, or highway construction ramped up.

Then workers headed for the woods, the corporate lumber and paper mills, and general construction or highway projects, but regular economic downturns had stimulated an underground economy both then and even in contemporary times. The area was well known to be rife with under-the-radar, tax-free activities.

Some of those goings-on are seemingly harmless, such as cash-only private flea markets and garage sales, curbstoning used cars outside of state regulations, and the labor force working for under-the-table money, but the isolated and woodsy geography of the area also makes it convenient for private gun sales, sundry dope deals, and the farming of marijuana.

These economic factors might explain Sowles's encounter with the California Highway Patrol in the early 1970s, as many visionary dope growers moved into Northern California from cities all over the US to grow weed which then also created opportunities for aggressive and even complicit law enforcement.

In the region's recent history, it had also become a tourist destination for frequent pretentious festivals orchestrated to attract highly paid, Bay Area people who would drop big money for veggie omelets, trinkets, and real maple syrup that was made three thousand miles away in Vermont. Yet the underground economy and what had finally become legalized weed farms made up the underbelly of the area.

Katy and the state cops in Humboldt County represented one of a few bitter memories for Noah Sowles, but as he became more aware of discrimination and the lengths that Blacks went to for their survival, he did not disrespect the law as many citizens did when they felt wronged. He was aware that cops held society together and that Black officers could be as discriminatory and tough toward Black arrestees as white officers could.

Even as he yet harbored some discomfort over that early discriminatory experience with the law, in recent years, the heightened visibility of the BLM movement had become a different challenge. He viewed it as a new twist on radical racial segregation, but he also believed it was a necessary undertaking for African Americans to further establish their societal positions. Yet, he was ambivalent with the crusade. He refused to align with the violence of the campaign or support the tearing down of the fabric of society as a solution. Neither was he an advocate of the radical "defund the police" campaign. Instead, he did what he knew to do, isolate in the truck and rack up miles as if nothing outside the truck mattered other than the road, the motion, and the scenery.

Coming to grips with his father's philosophy as a result of his experience in Humboldt County had matured him and forged some fundamental opinions of his own, but a few years later those simple views led him to losing the only woman he had loved.

Sheylinn Watkins had been the striking, light-skinned niece of James Persons, the pastor of the neighborhood Baptist church in East Oakland where Sowles's mother had attended. She had been a junior in high school and he a sophomore when they met on one of the rare Sunday mornings that his mother had been able to convince him to attend. He had an immediate conversion, convinced that God had arranged their auspicious meeting.

Reverend Persons was not eager about Sowles and Sheylinn seeing each other, nor was he convinced of Sowles's new commitment to Christianity—specifically because Sowles declined baptism—but he was happy with a new, young member from the neighborhood's streets. He saw that as step toward reaching the wayward local Black youth, many of whom were making good money in street drug trafficking and could be potential tithers in exchange for a few blessings and a place to call home if the streets got too tough.

As was typical of Black preachers of that era, Persons was demonstrably extreme in his style and mannerisms, but he knew the Bible cover to cover and could apply it theatrically to contemporary life and keep his congregation coming back for more.

"The Lawwwd is unrelentin' in His love for you, mah people. He is yo' brother. In union with him, we are our Father's children, adopted, adopted, I say, adopted as joint heirs with the Lawd to receive the same glory alongside the Lawd Himself. Ahh, yes, I say, ahh, yes."

"Ahh, yes, the Lawd Himself," the crowd repeated, as they swooned to the handsome, charismatic, mustached Black man.

Persons mesmerized his congregation by waving his hands over the crowd of worshippers as they repeated many of his key words.

"It is written in Romans 8. We are predestined fo' this callin'... and if the Lawd be for us, then I ask you here today! I ask! Who can be against us?"

"Amen! That's right! Who can be against us?" the crowd said.

Persons and Sheylinn had accomplished what God and Sowles's mother had been unable to achieve—getting Sowles into the church. He had been invigorated by the messages, and as long as Sheylinn was with him, he would earnestly listen to Persons's orations and sermons.

That changed when Sheylinn graduated from high school and went to San Francisco State University. Sowles's newfound Christian faith was then put on the back burner as he pined for Sheylinn, and yet they remained barely in contact, with only a few casual letters and undefined promises of seeing each other again.

Sowles knew Sheylinn as a sweet neighborhood church girl but when she joined the academicians who supported the extreme political theories of the radical African American segregationists, while ironically supporting white environmentalists, progressives, and anti-war protestors of the 1970s it threw Sowles into another spin.

Any radical cause that created dissent seemed to fit Sheylinn. With her newfound liberal education, she could get a gushing audience anywhere on any campus she attended or visited and if it had been up to her, everyone would have been collectively farming and riding bicycles with baskets on their heads, while she commuted to school in a BMW 3.0CSL coupe.

Sowles developed an urgent need to redirect her and soon became obsessed with a rash plan to make money to create the security he believed he needed to convince her to get married. At eighteen, he quit school in the second half of his senior year, only eight weeks before graduation. He then passed the GED, making vocational training his only immediate viable option other than restaurants or filling stations.

He immediately enrolled in Administration of Justice classes at Merritt Junior College in Oakland, with a plan to join the Oakland PD. It was a short-lived endeavor. The department, in conjunction with the mayor's office, was poorly administrated and had squandered much of the money it had been allocated. That led to internal investigations. The first change was an indefinite moratorium on hiring.

Without giving thought to another police agency, he left junior college with a 3.75 GPA and was back at pizza houses and gas stations until he found an apprenticeship program as a carpenter. But instead of building homes and learning fine carpentry, he was assigned to a labor crew on a three-story commercial project. That ended when he told his Black foreman that stripping second-story concrete forms on slippery, wet mornings or in ninety-degree sun was for slaves working on a pharaoh's temple. He was terminated.

Crashing here and there among the street people and communal houses of Berkeley, but then with the benefit of a shady California unemployment claim, he had access to good job postings, and, as an African American, he easily qualified for a government-subsidized program to train as a third cook for the US Merchant Marines, with a union position on a ship. Within months, he was on a freighter shuttling back and forth between the West Coast, Japan, and Korea. It was lucrative, and, unlike most seamen, he was not a drunk, so he could save money for his plan to influence Sheylinn.

Sheylinn and he remained reserved about their personal goings-on. He suspected that she was dating young white men in school. That vision plagued him while at sea. He was only able to calm himself when she became an aspiring Black history scholar and white people became somewhat of the enemy. But his respite was short-lived. Sheylinn got her BA and moved further away politically and geographically to Sonoma State University, her alma mater's sister school in Cotati, a small-town north of the Bay Area.

Everyone from the head shops on Telegraph Avenue in Berkeley or the Haight-Ashbury section of San Francisco knew about Cotati. Only sixty miles from San Francisco, the one-street, former stage-coach depot and then Greyhound bus stop had become another playground for doped out hippies, Black and white radicals, coffee-shop poets, and revolutionaries. It was infamous for its sleazy taverns and dirty organic restaurants that served as hangouts for providing easy access to illegal drugs and the continuation of the sexual freedom movement that had started in the 1960s.

It was developing as the Berkeley of the north, but unlike UC Berkeley or any of the other University of California campuses, Sonoma State at that time had a low-achieving student body that pursued fast-track degrees in the social sciences or alternative degrees in new age education.

Everything that Sheylinn did or promoted appeared to be in total opposition to the innocent courtship that she and Sowles had shared a few years earlier, the religious training of her uncle's Christian church, and Sowles's plan to sweep her into a marriage. He believed that he had to save her from a radical destiny and maybe even from the actual forces of evil.

When he had worked his way up to second cook and baker and had enough experience, union seniority, and money that he could pick his ships and sail short cruises, he took a few breaks from sailing, bought a sharp, used Volvo P1800, and began regularly visiting Sheylinn in Cotati, sharing alternate weekends together. They soon decided that his income would aid her in getting her master's and a permanent teaching position. They agreed to get married, rented a Thunderbird, and drove to Sparks, Nevada, where he found a white minister who operated out of his home. They then moved into a tattered apartment in an old section of Rohnert Park, an LA-styled, well-worn bedroom community of cheaply built homes that bordered Cotati.

He went back to sea, and she worked on her graduate degree. Because they could only see each other every four to six weeks, they would spend their time together in bed or going out to dinner. This loose arrangement only succeeded for a short while, because, as before, they did not discuss their personal lives, so Sowles was never sure what Sheylinn did when he was away. Then when she got pregnant, he was completely unprepared and uncertain if the child was his.

"How can I be at sea, and you get pregnant?" he asked.

"Don't be a damned Black-ass fool, Noah," she said. "Of course, it's your baby."

"Well then, how can I go to sea while you go to school with a kid?"

"You can't! I can't!" she said.

"Yes, I can. I have to," he said.

"My master's is more important than your lazy trips to Hong Kong to buy cheap leisure suits like you're in the damned Temptations!" Sheylinn said, screeching at the beleaguered Sowles.

"I make my money at sea so you can go to that damned white people's school!"

They argued for the week that his ship was ported in San Francisco. When he sailed, the first port of call was Honolulu. The US mail beat the ship. Sheylinn had gotten an abortion. But that was only her first. Over the next year, while he was home, she got pregnant again. Other than casually informing him of the second pregnancy, there had been no further discussion. She went to a Planned Parenthood clinic and aborted again. Sowles was disgusted but loved her and loathed her simultaneously.

Sheylinn soon got a Master's in Sociology and was offered an assistant professor's position to teach Black women's studies at the college while she was commuting to Berkeley for the PhD program in African American studies. Her views moved further to the left, beyond anything she and Sowles had learned at Oakland High or the First Baptist Church of East Oakland.

She stopped straightening her raven hair and grew an Angela Davis-style Afro. Sowles tolerated the new look until just a few months later, when she cut her hair short to resemble a tribal woman. He was then livid. He told her that "she looked like an angry Black brother at the draft board on his way to boot camp at Fort Ord in Monterey."

She responded by snubbing him and reminding him of their completely divergent paths and political philosophies, his lower "socioeconomic status," having "working-class ideas about integration," and "suffering from a crossword-puzzle education."

They only avoided a more serious conflict by Sowles catching a ship, but it was clearly over. It did not take long before Sheylinn began with a new man, a light-skinned African-American who was a full professor, someone that Sowles had assumed she had previously dated when he discovered photos that she had modeled for to help the guy publish a pictorial book about aspiring Black women of the twentieth century.

The divorce was amicable, but Sowles became chronically depressed. A year later, his father died, and Sowles felt responsible for every contest or disagreement he had incited or participated in with both his father and with Sheylinn, concluding that it was his fault that both were gone. He was left with only his mother to turn to. Adding some of his money to her life insurance award, he paid off the family home for her so she could live trouble-free in her old age.

She was soon afflicted with kidney problems and her blood pressure became unmanageable with any medication. She then seemed to lose her Christian faith and willed her own death. He was devastated that he couldn't save her. He inherited the home and locked it up tightly leaving it exactly as it had been throughout his earlier life.

He was then completely alone. He numbed his feelings with marijuana, while again returning to sea. But ship life had too many people involved: cooks, stewards, deck and engine department personnel, officers, and even a few passengers on the modern freighters. All interfered with an acquired need for total solitude and isolation. He left the shipping union and got a commercial driver's license.

# Four

## THE KNOCK IN THE MIDDLE
## OF THE NIGHT

Setting the pen down, he shook the cramp from his hand. Then, turning off his bunk lamp, he peeled his curtains open and glanced out the window again, fully convinced that Humboldt County had been a very poor choice for an overnight trip.

To put it simply, the place was spooky. The entire property still appeared abandoned, and, as it had been earlier, there was not a flicker of activity, and not even a single headlight on the adjacent stretch of highway. It had also gotten darker as the half-slice of moon climbed higher, often disappearing completely behind a thick, high-altitude overcast and then reappearing as if it played peekaboo. The intermittent, on-and-off moonlight gave the effect of someone taking long-exposed, black-and-white photos with an old 35mm flash camera.

The perimeter of the property was also portentously still. Even the encircled redwood trees that the many rubberneck tourists came to view in the daytime, stood perfectly motionless and unfriendly, like giant guardians or protectors of the secrets of the tribes that had once lived under their feathery emerald-green branches.

Thinking that he would power up and bolt from the disturbing property, he turned the ignition to the on position. He should have known better. It was a mistake. The dash lit up, illuminating the interior with a bright green light. A bell chimed, and all of the exterior running and parking lights activated including the twelve or so on the trailer.

He quickly turned it off. In a few seconds, the truck settled again in silence. He knew that to leave his spot suggested the very real threat of running out of fuel and getting stalled on the shoulder. With an impotent mobile phone and in the dark, the decision to move was out of the question. A lone Black trucker was a fool at any time of night on any lonely two-lane road.

On that isolated California road late at night, he could have any type of risky encounter with anyone, especially the California Highway Patrol. Then he could be jacked up for just about anything. Even a single trailer tire veering over the fog line into the shoulder or a flickering running light could result in a stop and then a long night of paperwork involving a log check, a background, medical card, and driver's license verification, a hundred-and-fifty-two-point tractor and trailer inspection, and maybe even get the cab and his personal possessions ransacked after being cuffed on false suspicion and towed into an impound for $3000.

He had to stay put in the truck until morning. He had slept in the rig many times in risky warehouse neighborhoods and remote gravel lots in areas that were infamous for crime. He would handle his emotions in the redwoods.

He checked the door locks, aware that it was for the third time, and then fumbling with his thick fingers for his heavy oak tire knocker in the eerie light of the fading moon, he secured it in his grip as if it was a Norseman's battle club. Only twelve-inches, it resembled a small baseball-bat but to its credit it also had a heavy one-inch plug of lead concealed inside the tip of the barrel. When tapping a tire, its harmonics told the driver if the tire was low on air. But Sowles knew that its defensive capability was negligible against the threats of the night that can surprise a sleeping trucker.

He closed the curtains again and tried to doze, very aware that he was fearful of the unknown, nervous that he would be awakened by an intrusive knock in the middle of the night. Truckers alone in the dark in remote areas understood, as did sleepers alone in their own homes that to be awakened from a deep sleep by someone pounding on a door in the middle of the night was always frightening. The reaction is to hide under the covers and pretend it isn't real, that it is part of a dream, but more often it is real and rarely good news.

He felt ill. His heart palpitated. He didn't like the vibe of the property. "Who is Scully Brother's Fuel?" he asked himself aloud. Memories and visions of the past in Fortuna and the Humboldt County Jail forced sour bile from his stomach into the back of his throat. His guts rolled, uncertain whether to heave upward or release downward.

He had been having recent problems with his digestion, especially at night while lying on his side. After about two hours, he would be awakened from the liquid in his stomach slipping up into his esophagus, then past his epiglottis, into his trachea, and then into his lungs. It was a feeling of suffocating underwater, choking him and creating a sharp pain in the area of his heart. He would then fly onto his feet, struggling to regain his breath.

"Not tonight, please," he said aloud.

He tried to calm his pounding heart. He had not slept well in years, drifting in and out of feverish slumber with obscure dreams of his father, of Sheylinn, of his mother. He needed some decent food. He needed some good sleep. He needed to wash his face and eyes with fresh, warm water. Instead, he again turned on the reading lamp, nibbled on some peanuts, wiped his eyes with a terry-cloth rag, and then flooded them with Walmart eye drops.

Blinking repeatedly, like the blinds of an old 1940s wartime merchant ship's semaphore lamp, he set the pepper spray, the knife, and the club on his fold-out table, and then made another attempt at sleep.

Finally, he drifted into a series of intermittent naps, but was plagued with entangled dreams of vaguely recognizable events from his past; being lost in Tokyo, needing penicillin in Korea. These melded with odd unintelligible nightmares that had followed him since he was a child and had created decades old dread of the night-time and sleeping that he had only partially overcome as an adult.

He felt as if he was in a fifty-year-old rerun of a Turner Classic horror movie, waiting in the fog for the monster to sniff out his location. Being alone among the massive and foreboding redwood trees with knowledge of the centuries-old California folklore that surrounded the forest only made it worse. He began writing again:

The Northern California swath of coastal redwood forest had flourished in the fog and rain of the region for undetermined eons of time along with the ancient indigenous peoples who believed that the redwood trees were sacred with a spiritual purpose and medicinal value. The tribes reserved and revered the forest for the thousands of years they thrived among the trees.

This peaceful bionetwork changed rapidly with the occupation of the Mexican army, the proliferation of massive Mexican land grants, and the Russian expeditions of the eighteenth and nineteenth centuries when the trees were discovered to be a strong construction material for building large presidios and settlements on the bluffs above the Pacific Ocean and inland expanses.

Within a few generations, the Russian explorers departed, and Mexico surrendered its holdings to the Caucasian populations of the emerging government of California and then to US authority. Then began the quest for gold. With the prospectors came the settlers and developers who demanded durable lumber for mining, homes, farm structures, fencing, railroad ties, buildings, boats, telegraph poles, the military, and for exportation to Europe for shipbuilding.

These East Coast and Midwest speculators and old-wealth European investors sought to extract the full profit potential from cutting, milling, and selling the redwood lumber. These same immigrating populations also began to exhaust the tribal food sources of the inland and coastal fishing sites. The great redwoods and the native food supplies were diminished to near depletion.

Wars and skirmishes over the natural resources ensued between the new Californians and the tribes throughout the region. The native populations were reduced to near extinction, and, in only a few generations, the entire ecosystem approached eradication.

By 1880, the battles ceased, but settlers still feared the natives. Legends began to proliferate that the spirits of the vanquished tribes would reap unending revenge against the reckless intruders and their descendants. Any settler or traveler who mysteriously disappeared anywhere near the redwood forest was attributed to this ghostly theory of vengeful native spirits.

This was only demystified in the early twentieth century, as the indigenous populations had been destroyed or assimilated, and the stories among tribal ancestors were limited to a few eccentric elders among the survivors of small coastal reservations.

But the unique redwood region, unlike any other forested area of the Earth, still remained secluded and mysterious with folklore that reemerged larger with the counterculture of the 1960s and 1970s among amateur anthropologists and soothsayers. Theories that human adult and child disappearances in the redwood region were from extraterrestrials or a thriving Bigfoot populace.

This was never substantiated, and so both the mainstream and underground media wildly speculated on new, more convenient scapegoats for these abnormal deaths or abductions, attributing the disappearances and losses of life to the Zodiac Killer out of San Francisco, who had never been arrested and also to Ted Bundy, until he was jailed and the disappearances continued, and then eventually the Manson Family, who had not confined its misconduct to only Southern California. Again, no substantial evidence existed, and individuals and families with children, and lone children themselves continued to disappear long after those infamous headlining criminals were jailed or deceased.

In recent years, the deaths or disappearances were more aptly attributed to attacks by bears, wolf packs, and mountain lions, or they were simply explained away as lost hikers who had starved, had mishaps, injuries, or falls and had been consumed by the remote environment.

But the mysteries of the region had been revived again with the national epidemic of missing children, and the few bold investigators who sought real answers were not impressed by tales of the spiritual qualities of the redwoods, the spells or the curses of the natives— *That include' me*—Sowles thought, as he glanced out the window into the darkening void of the forsaken property—*I know somethin' else is messed up in the redwoods.*

# Five

## DUST TO DUST

"Noah Calvin Sowles! Child! Don't you be readin' no ghost stories in them comic books. That ain't the Lawd's writin'."

The shrill pitch of his mother's voice feigning anger was enough to rattle the young boy. She believed that there were definite dark influences in the cartoonish drawings and macabre stories that he had been collecting, and she was quick to frighten him with warnings of reprisals from God Himself.

Sowles opened his eyes to his mother's vanishing face. It was morning. He had finally gotten some sleep, but a heavy sadness hung over his bunk. He missed his mother, wishing that she was still alive so he could sit on the couch with her in Oakland in their sweet, one-story house. He longed to see her again fussing over her couch cushions with their embroidered, quaint phrases and dusting her little, ceramic animal knickknacks. He missed the pictures of his father that she kept on her tall, mahogany end tables, photos of the man either in his naval uniform or dressed in a snappy blue suit and tie from when he was the head steward on the Amtrak train to LA.

Sowles would visit the deserted home occasionally, but hadn't been back in over a year. The front and backyards were overgrown, making the home shabby but more so sinister and disconnected in time. Yet, that didn't seem to matter to anyone in the old, crumbling East Oakland neighborhood. When he had forced himself to return to the house, he had been too heartbroken to go near his father's spanking new electric lawnmower, push-roller lawn edger, and garden shears, the few material things that the old man had been proud of.

Sowles hated the house, but refused to sell it for reasons he was wasn't fully sure of. He seemed unable to release his difficult childhood memories, as if he needed to shelter them in the house, and by doing so also keep his deceased parents alive.

But it was also the forty years of memories of the few skewed youthful years he had spent trying to stabilize with his beautiful, sixteen-year-old, caramel-colored Sheylinn that kept the pain alive. If only he could have her again, walking up to the porch to get him for their morning bus ride to school. In spite of them both now well aged, there was still that part of his psyche that believed or at least wished that they could start over, maybe even in his old house.

The sun was shining. He had survived an abysmal night in the truck, but in the light of day, he calculated that he had also survived over fifteen thousand nights without being attacked by bandits or monsters or dying in his sleep. He felt relieved but amazed also that he had lived as long as he had, considering the many nights where he felt that he was losing his mind and suspected that his body wasn't far behind.

He opened a window and filled his lungs full with cool, fresh air. Outside the truck, a shiny dew glowed in the chilly sun on every leaf, bough, and rock it settled on. The redwoods were dripping with sticky water that left maroon-colored stains on the hood of the tractor.

"Get over your booshit, boy, and be thankful it's morning!" he said aloud. Again, he spoke as if he was chatting with an invisible person, maybe the same one he had been grousing at the night before, when his interior light had nearly awakened the forest bugaboos.

Surveying the highway in the light of the early morning, he could see that the property itself was just a simple cutaway from the old two-lane section of US 101. The old wooden building also didn't appear to be as threatening by day as it had the night before. In fact, it was kind of rustic and hip looking, like a trendy, Bay Area gift shop. The sign pegged to the tree announcing the station had its lamps still burning. There was no evidence that there had been any disturbance during the night. Everything was perfect, tranquil, pastoral, and actually quite pleasant.

The new day spoke well of the area. The dark, nighttime redwood trees had relinquished their swing shift and had been replaced by massive, red trunks topped with thick, emerald-green foliage. All were greeting the day with their towering presence, and, just as the natives believed, the trees really did feel as if they offered a curative medicine.

"I was ten years old when my barber gave me those wicked comic books," he wrote in the notebook, remembering that he had read them fervently until he had several nights of dreadful nightmares, where he walked and talked in his sleep, even once opening a kitchen drawer, removing all the sharp knives, and hiding them under the washer.

On another occasion, also while asleep on his feet, he turned on a gas burner on the family's old stove without igniting it with a match. His father had been gone, assumedly on a train. It was only by chance that his mother discovered him in the dark kitchen before both of them were asphyxiated from the unlit vapors.

In the middle of that same night, his mother made him gather the comics. She demanded that he burn them in the backyard the next morning. He made a bonfire in a pit and fed the flames with the thin paper. The gray smoke from *Grandfather's Clock*, *The Attic*, *She Wouldn't Die* whirled upward as if every ghost from the pages had been reconstituted in the smolder.

He didn't receive any apparent blessing or the spiritual reprieve that his mother expected. Other than the sleepwalking ceasing, burning the dismal stories did not eliminate the nightmares. In fact, the act of informal exorcism only created more fear of payback from the spirits he was convinced he had unwittingly conjured up. However, the experience did seem to lead him to an introduction to playing with matches and starting small fires. After that morning of burning his comic treasures, he began a campaign of igniting and melting everything in his toy box.

Remembering that back then, those fires had been his new best friend, he also remembered his mother's voice.

"The Lawd is good, Noah. He loves you just as who He made you, and He protects you to save you from harm so you can do His work."

Her melodious tones rang in his ears. He felt his eyes water as he also remembered the many times that she had offered that same consolation during his youthful struggles, but her words had provided only a little relief back then, specifically because they did come from her, not because he believed that God had any personal interest in Noah Sowles. His real, true conception of God loving him felt foreign, and if he dared to ponder the thought of a protective, loving deity who looked like a bedraggled, long-haired white man, God seemed even a little debauched.

His racing mind and sleeplessness had given him a pounding headache. Both eyes hurt. They had been playing tricks on him in recent years. Often blurry and painful, they forced him to be cautious with night driving. He would often see images that weren't there, people or shadowy figures that lurked along the shoulders of dark, rural highways. Often, he felt they waited for him and then when he passed them, they became mailboxes, signposts, or tree branches, or they rose up like sixty-foot-tall banshees and disappeared into the night shadows. But then he suspected them of following him. He was never without some sensation of being followed or watched.

These unusual reactions compelled him to give some serious thought to the possibility that he was losing his cognitive abilities and not just his eyesight. To be certain that he didn't lose his ability to drive, he had faked his last few DOT medical examinations, thanks to fly-by-night chiropractors at the major truck stops. These tricksters would punch out official DOT commercial driver's medical cards for a flat hundred bucks with only a cursory physical examination. But he knew that scheme wouldn't work forever. He intuitively knew that he needed help.

But he dismissed his concern over his eyes as an allergy as he also seemed to be plagued with a constant itch in the corneas. He attributed that to road dust. Even when keeping the truck windows tight, obsessively changing the filters in his cab, and amassing several small, expensive bottles of eyewash and lubricants, he could not prevent the fine dust from worsening his vision. The powder in the air felt as if it had become an invading army of particles.

In recent years, he concluded that the progressives who were advocating for electric vehicles had not taken into consideration that the elimination of fossil fuels was not going to reduce the dusty mixture of powdered tire residue, sand, concrete, granite, shale, asphalt, trace metals, and airborne topsoil that circulated like a fine ash above the surface of all of the world's highways. He hypothesized that the crud would ultimately kill the flora, fauna, and all colors of humankind and then leave the Earth as barren as the planet Mars.

He snapped his thoughts back into the present. It was time to roll. He opened the door and took a long piss from the steps, chuckling at himself the way a boy does as he watches his urine splash in the dirt and puddle into muddy water. Then, strapping himself in the seat, he started the diesel engine. The motor roared to life, clattering like an ailing washing machine.

He didn't panic over the noise. He recognized the sound as the normal compression of air in the cylinders and the ignition of fuel.

"You ain't no damned foo', Sowles," he said aloud as his two big, brown, yellowed eyes stared back at him from a cheap Chinese-made, Walmart mirror he had over his visor. "You a fine Black man," he said, laughing as he forcefully flipped the visor shut.

Slipping the transmission into gear, he crawled through the lot, bumping and swaying through the same potholes as he had ten hours earlier.

Once on the road, he shifted up through the ten gears and remembered he had not completed a DOT-mandated, pre-trip vehicle inspection on his electronic log.

"Damn, Sowles, you fuckin' up big time," he said, knowing that if he were randomly inspected, the DOT would cite him for failure to record the inspection or would even shut him down for a brief period of time. But in that moment, his need to get away from the property was greater than his fear of the DOT.

He rolled north. Glancing at his speedometer: fifty-five mph, the California maximum for all trucks with trailers. He wanted to ramp it up and get as far away from the mushy, ominous redwoods as fast as possible, but speeding could result in number of unknown and well-known negative outcomes, and even more so in Humboldt County.

"Ashes to ashes and dus' to dus'," he said.

His spoken words rang in his ears as he thought about what it might be like to live in the red dust of Mars.

# Six

# THE SHELL GAME

"Come an' get me, Mama, I'm messin' up 'gain."

He was only a few miles up US 101, when he thought again about his mother and the old horror comics and then reflected on what had really spooked him the night before. He couldn't answer the question. Fear was something that just perched on his left shoulder. It always had, as far back as he could remember in his early childhood.

Recollecting the many past religious admonitions from his mother, there was a modicum of peace in believing that some supreme being might care or look after his life. After all, he was alive, he had a job, actually a one-man trucking business, his parents' home, and a few bucks in the bank. But so, what? God hadn't driven and lived in various trucks for forty years.

Almost instantly, a familiar, scalloped, orange sign came into view: SHELL.

"Well, there ya go!" he said aloud, with an upbeat tone, not conceding to himself that the fuel facility had been only minutes away the entire time he sat worrying the night before.

His mood quickly soured when the fuel price jumped in his face like an arrogant stink: $6.99.9. He frowned at the audacity of the California government, with its high fuel taxes levied for repairing the potholes and washboards on the primary interstate routes and highways of the state. It was common knowledge among truckers that California highways resembled the televised pictures of Baghdad streets during the fall of Saddam Hussein and more recently the roads in Ukraine. But California wasn't alone, in recent years he had noticed a crumbling infrastructure throughout most of the country.

OPEN—TRUCKERS ALWAYS WELCOME.

"Sure, truckers are always welcome at seven bucks a gallon," he mumbled, while thinking that the federal government's blind eye to soaring national diesel costs was even more incomprehensible than California's.

As he entered the truck stop, he felt a tiny sense of relief. His heartrate slowed. He even found himself tapping jovially on the steering wheel to an inaudible beat. The facility was teeming with life. Many of the major commercial carriers that he drove alongside every day were either parked in the yard or at the pumps.

Werner, Knight, Schneider, Swift, US Express, and UPS were parked neatly in organized rows. Several jade-colored, Old Dominion Cascadias towing two twenty-eight-foot trailers sat alongside grand, white, FedEx Volvos with their purple and red-lettered trailers dutifully attached behind. In addition to the big boys, many independents like himself were hooked up to elongated, fifty-three-foot, temperature-controlled food trailers like his, or sleek, white dry vans carrying basic freight. Some were pulled by old Peterbilt 379 long-nosed classics. Other Petes were hosting long, flatbed trailers, stacked and chained with industrial freight or earth-moving equipment.

The usual gang of blunt-nosed Kenworth T680s and their more expensive Peterbilt 579 copycats were in the fuel islands. Representing their patriotic color lines—fire-engine red, white, blue, and bright silver—they sat proudly in their parking spots, their diesel engines thumping.

Newly designed Mack rigs tooled through the runways, all appearing to have been built to resemble a kid's transformer robot vehicle. Most were painted in bright, new age colors and had their hundred-year-old, cocky, bulldog hood ornaments pointing to the wind. They pulled shiny, stainless-steel, bulk food tanks or snappy-colored cylinders for hauling hazardous materials.

Sitting defiantly in the back of the lot in their parking stalls, huffing and puffing black smoke into the air, were a few old, out-of-fashion Freightliner Century and Columbia class rigs. These box-nosed tractors had once been the reliable, fleet workhorses of the industry's smog-free days of the 1990s and early 2000s but had since become leftovers destined for wrecking yards.

Most of the old rigs were illegal in California. Whether licensed in California or another state, they were required to have their engines and exhausts retrofitted for California's twenty-first century climate mandates. Because of the high cost of the modification, some California units in prior years had been given temporary waivers, but unmodified out-of-state tractors were forbidden as non-compliant.

These hangers-on pulled wheeled chassis topped with bolt-sealed, portable, steel shipping containers labeled predominantly in Chinese. The boxes were likely filled with bananas shipped from Central America to California ports for road transport, or gaudy women's shoes, or any other conceivable assortment of imported odds and ends bound for the warehouses of discount retailers.

There were also other old, well-worn rigs that pulled logging chassis like those he had seen on the property the previous night. Or they hauled trailers or hoppers filled with recyclables, trash for waste sites, or fouled landfill earth headed for special recyclers, where it was filtered for its valuable metals.

This single, incidental truck stop cut out of the California woods was one of many thousands throughout the country, representing a variegated cross section of the multitrillion-dollar world of fuel, equipment, tires, parts, the roar of diesel engines, and the men and women who lived in their rigs far from their homes while staying committed to the organized confusion of trucking. Every component was needed for transporting every commodity on the planet.

Not many observers are able to fully comprehend the big picture of the industry, other than certain truckers who have adapted over years to the vagabond life of freight hauling and also own their own equipment and run it as a business rather than simply drive. Sowles had achieved that status, but with burdensome and negligible regulations, high fuel costs and a reckless subculture of ancillary workers in the industry it was a financial struggle regardless of how diligently he worked, so as pleasant as it was to see familiar companies and know that he was an integral part of the industry, he viewed trucking as the equivalent of Coxey's Army or a traveling circus of hustlers, jugglers and unfunny clowns.

Sowles lamented the erosion of trucking in recent years. After legislation of the mid-1900's culminating in crackdowns on organized crime in the industry, trucking had again returned to duplicity under the new leadership of corporate kingdoms allied with lobbyists and a near bankrupt government. To increase already massive profits and resulting taxes, companies were allowed to solicit drivers from developing nations. These mysterious men, bearded and dark-eyed, self-segregate from the mainstream, recognized often by their turbans, woolen Chitrali caps, Muslim skullcaps, or checkered scarves like those seen worn by terrorists in the post-9/11 media.

Others are smooth-faced, olive-colored Pacific Islanders, Hispanics, and Latinos from Mexico and Central and South American countries, and thin, undernourished-looking Blacks from several countries of Africa.

Throughout American history, any mass migration of foreigners into the United States from anywhere in the world meant that not all spoke intelligible English. Because this is true also of this new generation of drivers, many seasoned US-born truckers are suspicious of these immigrants and gossip about them, or hate them on sight, while at the same time having no real idea who they are, whether they are citizens, have families, are a new generation of hard workers, or outlaws.

These foreign-born drivers raise further suspicion by remaining separate from the majority of truckers, thereby causing mystery, racist responses, speculation over whether their licenses are legit, if they are here on green cards, sponsorships, fast-track naturalization because of driver shortages, or part of a recurring influx of foreign terrorists.

They bring their customs with them, some decorating their trucks with religious symbols that differ from traditional American faiths. This practice includes radical paintings on the sides of tractors or on the doors of trailers of bearded and turbaned warriors armed with scimitars.

To some old-school US truckers, this suggests the threat of clandestine terrorism, which further alienates this class of drivers, and regardless that this depiction seems to be proliferating on eighteen-wheelers, it goes unnoticed by run-of-the-mill automobile drivers on the highways—at least, nobody talks or tweets about it, except the opinionated truckers who are always quick to gossip on CB's or in truck stops, suggesting that all immigration in the US is slipshod.

What seasoned US truckers mostly agree on is that any new stream of low-cost immigrant drivers coming from impoverished or exploitive nations forces rates and wages lower, as then the big, successful American trucking companies and middlemen freight brokers can negotiate lower rates with more availability of drivers willing to accept low wages.

Many of these unsung male or female newcomers have been ushered into the industry by recruiters through federal tax incentive programs. Well-heeled carriers with large fleets or the big truck driving schools are quick to capitalize on this benefit. Drivers are then solicited by smart-mouthed, fast-talking, commissioned truck school operators and company salespeople who use the deceptive techniques and empty promises that military recruiters and car salesmen are known for.

Except for owner-operators, most new drivers in present-day trucking jobs are naïve and poor, either marginalized minorities or underprivileged whites. They are fair game for these peripheral industry speculators who promise them big money and freedom in open-road trucking.

Regardless of the racism that Sowles had personally experienced most of his life, he remained very reserved around most of the newly landed foreigners. He was not fond of these young men. It was well-known that a portion of them jockeyed the sealed container loads from the same ports and railyards along the nation's coasts and southern border where human trafficking or smuggling continues to be exposed.

Sowles actually steered clear of all over-the-road truckers, as most were eccentric, difficult, or cantankerous, and even more so with each other, and any conflict could result in a fistfight or wrestling bout. But it was the white drivers that really shook him, regardless that he was such a strong advocate of integration.

Some of the white guys are the "good old boys" and badasses that drive thirty-year-old, classic, long-nosed, restored Peterbilt tractors. They consider themselves to be the true American truckers. Aged, red-faced, divorced, and often mean, they have been trucking their entire working lives and are tough and condescending by nature. Sitting atop a six-hundred-horsepower diesel and eighteen monstrous tires adds to their self-importance.

A lot of these men are flatbedders. It is facing the rigors of hauling open flatbed freight under countless adverse conditions that gives some of them the image of being highway road warriors. They run hard and long in wicked weather, but they also seem to roll with impunity from certain established laws. Some drive fifteen miles per hour over speed limits, ignore rights-of-way on the highways, or bully their way around truck stops and rest area parking lots.

Not all are old-timers. There is also a new breed of weathered, lean, young, cowpoke types that appear to be right off cattle ranches.

They pull cattle or hay mostly, but some are also heavy haul flat-bedders. Many are ruddy from weather or alcohol abuse and pock-marked from having the chicken pox when they were kids. Summer or winter, many outfit themselves in gauche, urban cowboy gear—tight, too-long Wrangler jeans that rumple in numerous curly folds over the vamp of pointed-toe animal-skin boots. Their shirts are snap-button, plaid, and often sleeveless, designed to show off mus-cled red or tan arms that usually protrude from white chests, pale from not seeing the sun. They top their outfits off with ballcaps or intimidating wide-brimmed, western-style hats.

Maybe it is the stresses of trucking or simply living up to their images of being hard guys and aficionados of loud, twangy country music and its colorful lyrics, but many of these men are serious off-duty drinkers and chain-smokers, and they survive on truck stop hot dogs, pizza, peanut butter cups, and coffee. Short-fused, they can be smart-asses, loud talkers, and quick to mouth off or throw a punch.

Sowles had seen one lanky cowpoke pull his rig up to a red light, jump out, cross over to the car next to him, break the driver's window, punch the motorist out, and then return to his rig and drive off, while the dupe sat through three green light cycles trying to regain his dignity.

The exposed freight that flatbedders haul can offer an insider's glimpse of the state of the national economy or the severity of unre-ported threats from other nations. When times are good, and seem-ingly normal and peaceful, flatbeds carry heavy graders, backhoes, road scrapers, steel girders, pipe, lumber, stacks of wrapped sheetrock, roof trusses, and other industrial materials headed to highway recon-struction projects, housing tracts, and commercial building projects.

When times are lean or off-kilter, the flatbeds are either bare, their rumpled tarps bungeed to their decks, or they are loaded with heavy military assault vehicles painted in desert camouflage. This seems to offer a firsthand view of what might really be happening in the country and the world and also what's going unnoticed by the news outlets.

Flatbedders work harder than the drivers that haul enclosed box trailers with common or refrigerated freight. They are often seen on the roadside in the heat, snow, or rain, strapping, chaining, or tarping loads. Many are independent owner-operators who do not have support staff in the office, so they get behind in their taxes or basic bills which then feeds their frustration. In forty years, Sowles had never seen a flatbedder who wasn't a rough and tough guy.

There is another group of truckers in interstate commerce that live full-time in their rigs and drive long hauls only to eat and have shelter. Some are as thin as fenceposts and aged far beyond their actual years. They dress in the equivalent of rags or thrift-store clothing. There are also the big guys who weigh upward of four hundred pounds. Some overgrow their tractors the way a fish in a bowl does if you give it food and space. Year-round, they wear strap overalls or cut-off, 4X gym sweats tied with string, and giant tank tops exposing mottled flesh as pink as birthday cake. Most of these men are eternal nomads.

There is always the possibility of pissing some trucker off at a fuel island where everyone is in a hurry and also irritated over the high fuel prices. If a guy gets stuck waiting for a turn at the pump behind a big-headed slowpoke who has filled his rig and then let it sit in line blocking the access, there are generally words spoken.

Another good contest with some dude could ensue if a tired driver is cruising a truck stop lot at night, searching for a parking spot, and an egocentric nature boy, after having his shower, jumps out of the shadows in front of the moving rig with his bare chest puffed out, wearing black short shorts, parading around the parking lot in flip-flops as if he was at the gym for a photo shoot.

Some truckers disregard state gun laws and are reputed to carry small automatics or lightweight revolvers, and most are foolish enough to brag about their hardware at the breakfast counters. Sowles figured those guys were also arrogant or dumb enough to use their firearms.

If there was truly a group of deplorables in the United States, as Hillary Clinton had stated so clearly, it had to come in part from a cross section of the trucking industry. But, as with all stereotyping, there are many exceptions. Trucking has a large faction of good-hearted, generous, hardworking, and God-believing family men and women driving and living on the road, and much like carnies and wandering campers, many do share a common, yet unspoken bond, and as patriots of the road, they take the delivery of the nation's goods as seriously as being a civil servant or a member of the military.

Early in Sowles's career, when he was still a novice, he had met a white angel of a trucker. He asked the guy for help adjusting his trailer tandems. This is when the weight of the load is balanced throughout the trailer by locking the trailer's axels and wheels in place and moving the trailer forward or backward on a slide built under the floor. This adjusts the wheel position, so to optimally support the load weight to conform with federal highway laws.

Older trailers had a stiff lever at the rear that had to be pulled and then wedged or bungeed in place to release a set of thick, steel pins. This enabled the driver to slide the trailer over the axels. The lever had been stuck on Sowles's trailer so he could not get the axels moved into position without an expensive service call and a major loss of driving time.

It had been hot. The man whom Sowles asked for help was bronze from the sun and thin as a walking stick with taut sinews and tendons popping from both arms. He fought with the lever. After thirty minutes, he finally got the stubborn handle to move. Then he directed Sowles to move the trailer back and forth a few feet on the under-floor slide until they had the right axel setting. Sowles was grateful. He thanked him profusely, offering him sodas and water.

The man said sullenly, "Nah, no problem."

Then Sowles noticed the guy was bleeding severely from one arm. "You're bleedin'," Sowles said. "I'm sorry I put you through all that. I got a first aid kit. Lemme get you some bandages."

"Nah, I might look old but I can handle it, an' it don' matter none, no how." the man said, and he then walked away.

Sowles had been touched, and yet he had seen this devil-may-care attitude before with many white men, not just in trucking, but everywhere. It seemed that certain white men have a need to prove their prowess whenever a Black man is present, often under the guise of a favor.

Although Sowles had been very appreciative, he also knew this reserved approach did not always work well between white and Black men. White males' strong expressions of superior expertise often incite certain Black men to become more pugnacious. Sowles believed that it was an unspoken competition between men of both races that went beyond basic racial differences. Maybe it is jealousy or envy based, considering that so many white men believe that Black men are more powerful than white men, while Black men at the same time have been conditioned to feel and act inferior in the presence of white men.

The effort that Sowles went to in order to get along and succeed in the white-dominated industry was something that his father had discovered as a passenger train attendant, but it took Sowles numerous years of isolation to understand the syndrome.

He also learned over time that if a Black man laughed along with a white man's off-color jokes but stayed out of intimate or political conversations, he was cool with the good-ole boys, but push a white man in the wrong direction by trying to be an equal and a Black man would find out that Black people really were only tolerated by most of white male society.

This was a painful realization, but Sowles also recognized, just as his father had, that there are male drivers and workers of all stripes, and they are the breed of men that built the nation. These men had been the Black slaves, migrant Mexican farm laborers, poor white highway, tunnel, and skyscraper workers, miners, and those of many races and ethnicities that fought for the United States in wars defending the entire world.

Sowles also conceded to himself that many white drivers are just average, red-blooded guys from various walks of life in cities and impoverished rural areas. Most are honest, hardworking American taxpayers. But that didn't change Sowles's view, he knew it was smarter and safer to keep completely to himself, and yet when he did have to interact with these men, he maintained a big-smiled, jovial attitude, probably exactly what his father had learned to do while working with white men on the trains.

Some middle-aged truckers are on pensions from their second or third career after retiring from white-collar jobs, while others are blue-collar men who moved from other trades when the economy downturned as it had in the Bush and Obama administrations, and seemed to be doing again in the post-Trump era. There are also rigid military types. Sowles had never met anyone retired from the Navy or Air Force driving a truck, but there are plenty of ex-soldiers and former Marines from prior duty in the Middle East. Many have insignias from their branch of service on their rigs. Added to this new mix are ex-cops, Proud Boy equivalents, skinheads, and shaved-scalp white supremacists, many still loyal to confederate or right-wing values, with stars and bars painted on their rigs, regardless of where they are from.

Many African American drivers come from poor areas of the South and old, industrialized sections of eastern cities. These drivers are men or women. Both turn to long-haul trucking rather than struggle to compete with immigrants for diminishing farm or factory jobs.

Women truckers do make up an unusual and tough faction of drivers. Some have been married to truckers; others are mothers of grown kids, or they can be childless former waitresses or store clerks who were introduced to trucking as a way to earn a place of equality in the work force. Some of them are in partnership with other women or men and drive as teammates, sharing the truck's income and expenses. Most work as hard as men, although, as is true with some male drivers, there are those who use the truck as their primary place to live for as long as they can.

Except for owner-operators who are paid a percentage of the entire load rate, company driver income is computed by the mile. If the supervising load planner does not dispatch long runs, pay can be as low as minimum wage, regardless that drivers are in the tractor twenty-four hours a day for as long as the equipment is away from their home base, usually ten to twenty-one days.

The rigors of the job combined with these low wages disillusions most company paid drivers. They see companies growing their fleets, shops, locations, and buildings, but offering miniscule raises that are measured in pennies to their drivers while paying executive salaries to managers for supervising drivers who, by definition are self-sufficient.

These drivers become complainers and are fired or they quit the industry. They are all washout statistics and add to the turnover rate of over-the-road drivers which is estimated to be over 93 percent. This suggests that in a period of time, generally considered to be annual, for every one hundred drivers hired, ninety-three will leave within twelve months, and then commissions are paid to find drivers to replace the quitters who could have been retained by fair wages.

Resentful company drivers with no cash invested are known to abandon their assigned truck many miles from the home office, knowing that the cost of recovery is thousands of dollars. Should those same failed novices have a change of heart even in much later years, they are banned from reemployment in trucking by sophisticated computer tracking.

For those who survive the first years of hardship and avoid DOT recordable accidents or citations for equipment malfunctions or infractions, it is still an uphill climb for three to five more solid years of industry required accident-free or incident-free driving in order to be considered a professional. This seems appropriate, in view of the public safety factors involved in trucking, but it is not easily achieved; citations can be biased and routine and even small accidents are common.

An incident is a different matter. It can be an argument with a dispatcher, being late for a pickup or delivery, staying home longer than what a company determines a driver is entitled to, poor fuel mileage, or failing a DOT inspection with a company-owned truck or trailer when the company was the actual responsible party for maintaining the condition of the equipment.

All drivers whether owner-operators or employees are considered equal by several major factors: risking their lives from accidents and dangerous overnight parking, difficult communication with management, jeopardized health, foul weather, bad food, having no time for physical exercise or socialization, and being alienated from friends, loved ones, and society.

The long-haul life requires drivers to live on the road in sleeper cabs and search into the late night for parking spots in state-controlled rest areas only to discover the oasis blockaded by red cones and barriers during peak seasons. Or they will roam into the night, driving in circles inside a truck stop to discover all parking spaces are taken by early birds or abandoned vehicles.

A crazy marathon is the best description for the life of a long-hauler when each day and night consists of dangerous driving conditions, and then after enduring those risks, the driver has to rightly time finding a parking spot somewhere, and do so within federal limits of work shift and time allocations. These factors make the daily routine for even the most experienced trucker a matter of driving five-hundred to seven-hundred miles and then as safe haven parking is searched for sleeping, the possibility exists of exceeding their time allotment and violating federal law.

If an interstate driver exceeds eleven hours of drive time or fourteen total on duty hours in a twenty-four-hour shift, the driver is subject to expensive citations and threats of termination. These are obstruse DOT rules that companies monitor but many drivers try to

cheat. As a result, the federal government has mandated fully monitored electronic tracking.

Sporadic, poor rest and interrupted sleep is inevitable when a
driver is forced to park in unsafe and illegal spots on freeway ramps
or the shoulders of highways, abandoned lots, in the backyards of
industrial complexes, and on dark, bowery streets of major cities.
There is often the knock on the door from either law enforcement
or the addicted and mentally deranged homeless and criminal populations that are camped by the scores in filthy tents and dilapidated
lean-tos.

Unbeknownst to motorists—who resent truckers and do not
acknowledge the economic need for trucking, and see trucks and
rig drivers as road hogs, even daring trucks to highway challenges—
impaired sleep for a driver puts everyone at high risk for a fiery,
crushing accident.

Trucking is as close to being in the military as a man or woman
can get. There may be no visible enemy deliberately trying to kill
drivers, yet drivers are regularly killed in accidents and sometimes
murdered in their trucks by wrongdoers, making the business of long-
haul driving a stressful game of workers trying to earn a living while
wagering human lives and the safety of US highways against profits.

# *Seven*

## MR. SOULS

Sowles was able to get into a fuel island at the Shell without any waiting or conflicts with other drivers. He pumped one-hundred-eighty gallons of sweet-smelling, yellow-colored diesel fuel into the cylindrical side tanks, verbalizing aloud the same statement that he always made when filling the rig: "This shit go sky high if a man gets hit by some crazy foo' on the highway."

His statement came from memories of seeing too many sleeper-cab tractors melted into bubbling ash alongside a highway, their once-pretty plastic fenders, hood, and entire molded shell gone, and their frames only a thin, stick-like skeleton of smoking steel sitting on molten wheels.

When rigs would catch ablaze, it was often because of an unseen, small electrical failure or a fuel leak, but they were almost guaranteed to fully ignite in any high-speed collision. If the rig was hauling a flammable product in a steel-tank trailer, the contents would often explode into a conflagration of shrapnel and flames. The incident would make national news if enough people were killed. With a standard load of dry freight or even refrigerated foodstuffs, the box van would quickly burn its contents and itself to the ground, the same as any thin-walled barn.

Sowles had seen more than one incident where a burning trailer was full of Idaho potatoes, or onions or garlic from Oregon. The spuds or bulbs had burned excessively hot, popping like cherry bombs inside the flaming unit creating an acrid, noxious smoke resembling a plane crash.

These were daily, common sights along the interstate highway system—incidents that were nightmarish but would often go unreported to major news agencies unless a few people die or the event impacts the commutes of local citizens. Passing truck drivers or motorists never know what the outcome of these accidents are, and yet, when observing them, it seems impossible that anyone could escape alive.

When Sowles's two bomb-shaped tanks were full, he crept forward to let the guy behind him pull to the pumps. Sowles checked him out—white kid, overweight, wearing gym shorts, a tank top, and Nikes as if he was heading to Planet Fitness to try to lose the rolls of blubber that he accumulated from sitting in a seat eleven hours a day, seven days a week.

Sowles frowned, both at the kid's demeanor and the total on the pump: $1260.00, but thankfully the majority of the fuel would be there for the next trip, which Sowles hoped would be to Anywhere, USA, as long as it wasn't in California.

He pulled out of the fuel area and idled around the crowded asphalt lot, looking for temporary parking, while eyeing all of the dazed-looking white men as they ambled aimlessly around the lot on stiff legs. In some cases, their spines were permanently bent from sitting.

Sowles understood their exhaustion. It was from running repeated roundtrips from LA or Phoenix into the Northwest, doing round-the-clock shifts of eleven hours on to ten off, and fighting four days with the control knobs on the climate system, attempting to achieve a whisper of refrigerated air in LA, or enough defrost flow to clear a windshield in rainy, bumper-to-bumper Portland or Seattle traffic.

Trucking is tough but the opportunities for unskilled or semiskilled US workers are slim. This class of the labor force are regularly in competition with many undocumented immigrants working under-the-table for low-paying hourly jobs in the backrooms of franchised food service companies or for piecework labor rates in the trades. The lawful low-wage worker positions in retail services or manufacturing that require documentation are further impacted by other foreign laborers that actually have paperwork authorizing them to work in the US.

For unskilled Americans representing any nationality, poor alternatives to trucking exist if the candidate is aspiring and a well-spoken go-getter that can endure a lengthy application process for a job that requires wearing a shirt and tie or skirt and sweater in a big-box store, mall kiosk, or on the outside sales staff of any number of weak start-up companies. Then he or she can pitch smug consumers on signing up for various questionable services or products for minuscule commissions.

Long-haul trucking is an alternative for filling many US employment and income gaps, but both new, willing, or barely capable drivers and experienced truckers, sooner than later question why they choose to live like a hermit in a one-man land submarine twenty-four hours a day for weeks at a time, and risk health, mental wellness, orthopedic fitness, and the threat of loss of life. This is assuming their trips go well and aren't waylaid by lazy freight planners, greedy load brokers, breakdowns, bad highways, foul weather, and the recent aforementioned unprecedented high fuel prices.

Sowles's thoughts were interrupted as he continued to cruise the lot at the truck stop. He abruptly yanked the steering wheel a few degrees to the right to avoid running down a heavy, blonde, white chick waddling obliviously across the lot. Her nonchalance irritated him, but he knew that he was on edge from the prior night and just needed more sleep.

Spotting an open stall, he pulled through and parked, keeping the truck running. The classic sound of his well-warmed, beefy Cummins diesel engine was satisfying. The low rumble of a Cummins came from its bowels. It spoke power and strength, having the ability to pull over one-hundred-twenty-thousand pounds up long, steep mountain stretches for hundreds of thousands of miles without even a minor miss or falter. It reminded Sowles of an inboard motor on a properly powered small fishing trawler, a boat he had wanted after he spent two weeks one summer on a fifty-foot wooden trawler fishing in the Columbia River for salmon with an old, white seaman.

Settled now for a few minutes, he resumed watching his trucking colleagues wander the lot. It seemed that most of them forgot the danger associated with roaming around aimlessly among hundreds of rigs and their crazed or irritable drivers. He smiled, thinking that any pedestrian meandering in the parking lot of a truck rest area was at more risk than an acrobatic clown doing handstands on the taxiway of the Oakland Airport.

*Dumb crackers*, he thought. But then he corrected himself, speaking aloud, "Knock it off, Sowles. You're not a prejudiced man," as he remembered all the names he had been called throughout his lifetime: nigger, porch monkey, coon, spade, darkie, jigaboo.

"Take your pick," he said, knowing that he would always be viewed through the lens of racism. The stinging reminder of that labeling practice had punctured his soul, and yet he would correct himself when he used pejorative language to describe white men, as discrimination went against his grain. In his heart, men were men, fragile before whoever their maker was, and yet he wondered how the God his mother worshipped could allow such injustice and hurtfulness.

"It's not yours to take revenge," she had said. "Vengeance belongs to the Lawd."

Sowles tried to be a good guy, but he was very aware that because he was seen as colored, or Black, or Negro, or African American, as a darkie, porch monkey, spade, or nigger, he was assumed to be corrupt by almost everyone, including many members of his own race.

In his youth, he had endured razzing, even from other Black kids, because of having the Bible-based name, Noah. But by junior high school, his surname had trumped his birth name and given him some street status. The name Sowles offered neighborhood recognition and put him in the category of "cool," presuming that the name was pronounced correctly, and he made the pronunciation clear to all: "SOULS."

Becoming known as "Souls" or "Mr. Souls" had made him an unofficial legend on East 12th Street and International Boulevard, the former boulevard of pimps and pawn shops known as East 14th Street, also Foothill Boulevard, MacArthur Blvd., 23rd Avenue, and Fruitvale Avenue—some of the toughest streets in East Oakland, California.

As an adult, his last name became a subject of entertainment when white men discovered the irony. They all got a kick out of it, making him a novelty, and, much like his father had done, he would share in their mirth, acting the part of a monkey on a stick just to fit in, knowing that he was another Black man selling out. He hated himself for that behavior.

He stared out the window. There was the overweight blonde again. She was determinedly dragging her two hundred pounds across the truck parking area for some reason.

*Maybe a trucker's woman or wife*, he thought as he looked for her old man, expecting to see a rotund white man labor down the steps of a pristine new Freightliner Cascadia.

He was only half-right. A round trucker poured out of the driver's side of a rig and headed in her direction. The truck wasn't new. It was a battered, long-nose Freightliner similar to those he had seen earlier. Attached was a dented hazardous waste tank on wheels.

The guy wore a monster-sized tank top that hung down almost to his knees. It was so big that Sowles was not aware that such a size existed. His arms were enormous, soft ham hocks, red and pimply. For pants, he had the uniform: a pair of oversized, 4X sweatpants cut off at the knee.

"The only way he could get pants to fit his ass," Sowles said aloud but he regretted that he had even looked at the guy's short, roast-shaped thighs and how they merged with his shins and calves as though the man had lived a lifetime without knees.

The sight of the abuse made Sowles feel ill. The guy's limbs were streaked with swollen, purple-and-blue veins and red blotches as dying muscle struggled to keep him alive. Sowles wondered how this man had passed a DOT medical physical.

"Maybe he used the same lyin' chiropractor I did," he said under his breath.

He could see that the man was struggling to cover the short distance over the asphalt from point A, where his truck sat, to point B, where the woman was now sitting on a five-gallon plastic paint bucket that she had turned upside down. They both appeared to be panting and wheezing.

Sowles could feel the couple's pain. They were sad people, seemingly lost in the many whirlwinds of modern American society and the low end of trucking, with inflation, low wages, cheap, unhealthy fast food, failing health, waning physical strength, and very limited hopes.

"They're probably piss poor, having to live on the road in that junk Freightliner," he said, feeling grateful for who he was for the first time in days.

But then he saw the big woman get off her perch and saunter a few dozen feet to a new, shiny, white Ford F-150 4x4 Club Cab pickup. She took out a purse from the front seat, where two buff-colored Shih Tzus were yapping with their little pink tongues against the glass.

"Well, I guess folks need to have a few pleasures," he said, mumbling and chuckling to himself, knowing that for some poor, white truckers, all that it took for relative happiness was a new pickup and a Walmart flat screen, both on payments, a gift card at an Arby's or Wendy's, a dog or two, and a little smokable dope now and again.

That awareness reminded him of prejudicial slurs that had been said by whites about Blacks. "They live like animals, but if they get any money, the first thing they buy is a Cadillac."

"Maybe a Mercedes," Sowles said aloud, again half smiling, but with a deep feeling of sadness, remembering that his father had owned nice Buicks, and he traded them in every two to three years.

The guy smiled at the woman as she returned to the bucket and pulled a small brown lunch sack from her purse. She handed it to the guy.

"Maybe his lunch, but a dammed small bag for that fat boy," Sowles said.

The woman seemed fidgety as she spoke to the man, moving her hands around her big body like they were fluttering birds, but she relaxed when the guy counted out some cash from a wad that he pulled from the crotch of his sweats.

*That ain't his ole lady*, Sowles thought, as he began to realize how narrow his own life was becoming that he had to be entertained by the two eccentrics. But Sowles continued to observe them as the man pulled an even smaller plastic bag out of the woman's brown sack. It was filled with white capsules. The guy sniffed the contents of the bag.

"And that ain't no lunch," Sowles said under his breath. "No wonder she's waving her hands around like a foo'," he said. "Must be some good shit."

Sowles had been accustomed to drug dealings in the East Oakland neighborhood where he grew up. They had been as common as Bay Area overcast skies, but they had been small transactions—marijuana, Benzedrine, or downers like reds—not cartel-affiliated enterprises as they became in later years, but too many of his talented young friends were knifed to death in the streets in their early teens over those fifteen-dollar dope deals that had gone sour for untold and vague reasons.

Other Black boys were convicted of possession, mostly of weed. They were sent by juvenile courts to work camps, or if there was violence involved, they went to California Youth Authority institutions. Most advanced to state prison at age eighteen, where they were sentenced to long stretches of time and sometimes murdered by another inmate within a year. Sowles had avoided the cliques and gangs of his youth where those violators flourished, maybe because of basketball or his mother's religion, but he had been aware that he had been in dangerous opposition to the ghetto street code, "death before dishonor," making his earlier youth that much riskier.

"Where had that sayin' come from?" Sowles had asked his father, back at a time when they were still able to chat in the garage while the old man tinkered with his mower or cleaned and organized his many small garden tools.

"The ancient warriors of the Samurai," the old man had said. "It is the code for all them damn Black foo's who live by the sword."

"Is that same as livin' by the sword and dyin' by the sword?" Sowles asked. "You know, like what's in the Bible?"

"I 'magine it is," his father said. "Accordin' to yo' mama, it's the never-endin' battle between the Lawd an' devil. The war the white folks say we all needs to stay on the right side of."

"Yeah," young Sowles said, nodding as if he fully understood.

His father sat on a stool at his workbench. "I figgers that honor and pride are the same side of the coin, and so when a man gamble his honor and pride against danger, he must be ready to die for both by the forces of fate, as then there is little protection the Lawd can offer the man. Those friends a' y'all's who went to prison and died put theyselves into a war that destroyed them."

"What's on the other side of the coin, Pops?" he asked almost facetiously.

"God," the older man said. "At least, accordin' to your mama."

Sowles loved his father that day, even though he knew the old man had a pint of Ten High whiskey in the pocket of his pleated slacks.

His thoughts returned to the parking area of the truck stop. The two culprits were gone, as were both the Freightliner and the Ford F-150. It appeared that the woman also took the bucket.

Sowles realized that he had been so absorbed in watching their dope transaction and reminiscing about trucking and his family that he had failed to recognize that where he parked was forcing other rigs to maneuver around his rig.

"Not a good idea fo' them foos," he said, knowing that a contest or fight could ensue over even that minor of an inconvenience.

He spotted a good, open parking stall, one that offered a sweet back up, a "straight back," as it is called by professional drivers. He moved the rig, set up for the maneuver, and then backed the long trailer in effortlessly. But he was a little shaken, not because of the backing operation, but because to get into position for the backup, he came grill to grill with a parked, red Peterbilt with thin-haired, gaunt-faced white driver glaring at him from behind the wheel.

The guy had a flatbed piled with rebar behind the tractor. His rig had a big, toothy, chrome gargoyle on the nose of the hood and exaggerated vertical stacks that were high above his cab, as if they were two phalluses guarding an ancient temple. His thick tires were dressed, black, and oiled, partnered with perfectly shined chrome wheels that boasted pointed, lug nut covers resembling those on an emperor's chariot wheels in some 1960's film about ancient Rome.

What really caught Sowles's attention was a glance at the ominous artwork on the glossy paint. Brazenly painted behind the driver's door was a black Maltese cross, the number "13" inside a hexagram, and a crazed but colorful bald eagle. The bird had a beautiful, auburn-skinned very young woman in its talons, maybe a teen-ager. She was naked above the waist, her small, newly-formed breasts partially covered by long, raven-black hair.

The driver continued to stare at Sowles after he was backed in. He was emaciated, his face bone-white as if he was fresh out of chemotherapy.

"A flatbedder," Sowles said thinking that the guy was not exactly what Sowles would call a friendly down-home trucker who would stop to help a stranded motorist, unless it was a vulnerable-looking female. "An' he definitely don' look like no nigga lover," Sowles said, as he thought back to his many years of driving and the white roughnecks who had actually tried to run him off the road.

More than once, he had been on an interstate running at sixty-five to seventy in the right lane and come across some novice driving at fifty mph. When Sowles signaled to change lanes and checked his left mirror, a roaring Peterbilt pulling a flatbed full of industrial equipment deliberately tried to gain on him to prevent him from passing, the driver pushing his rig upward of eighty-five mph. Sowles aborted his lane change maneuver and hit his brakes to avoid impacting the slowpoke he had been trying to pass.

As the truck sped by, the upright six-inch or eight-inch exhaust pipes were clearly audible, loud, harsh, and insulting. Sowles had glanced over at the passing driver only to be facing a white, thick middle finger, pointing upright.

He glimpsed again at the ghostly figure in the truck facing him. There was the finger again.

# Eight
## BLUE AND RED

"I better get my Black ass outta here," Sowles mumbled. He pulled the rig out of the stall and headed toward the exit, but he was concerned that he might be followed. The guy was white and weird, a definite bad combination.

Sowles was disgusted. He knew numerous Black men who would have gone over to the guy's truck and pulled him out of the seat just for looking at them, but the man had forced him to leave through simple intimidation, again confirming his negative opinion of his manhood.

Back on US 101 and a few miles up the road, he was unable to relax into the comfort of the seat although the route was pleasant by day. A hedge of enormous trees surrounded the area; big, tall, and green, they overshadowed the road, appearing as gigantic beasts extending their emerald arms downward in an inviting gesture. The underbrush was also thick and lush.

He was only a half hour away from Eureka, but he aggressively pushed the pedal to the floor, ignoring the statewide truck speed limit of fifty-five mph. Soon he was moving at over sixty-five. He glanced in his mirror. The road behind was empty, but instead of relying on luck on the thirty-minute final leg of his journey, he calmed his anger and set the cruise control at sixty-two.

Focusing on the prior twenty-four hours, he admitted to himself that it had been unusual, starting with the Latino dude who loaded him in Milpitas.

"It's all cray-cray," he said aloud, this time chuckling nervously.

He was aware of a personality quirk he had developed over the years as a solo trucker. He talked to himself, but he was comfortable with the habit, deciding that it was common for a man who was consistently alone to talk aloud to himself as though he was with another individual.

Often, it would be some other person he spoke to. He wasn't certain who it was, but based on the insights of a former psychotherapist from years back, he assumed that it was his inner child. That would be the kid who he was in his youth, but who now as an adult cannot be differentiated from his own conscious self. The counselor's theory was that the little boy, Noah with all of his youthful characteristics, remained inside of him through his adolescence and continues to live inside him, while that same boy had become the man, Noah Sowles.

It was an amazing and yet strange concept that Sowles never fully grasped, but he had liked the idea in principle, except for the fact that he didn't really know the boy inside. Yet, he had gotten some relief from the theory, as it helped to explain why, as an older adult, he was still fearful of the unknown and of people, much as a young boy might be.

The therapist had explained that if there is chaos or lack of love in the childhood home, children get stuck at certain stages of their development and manifest immaturity throughout their lives. In other words, the inner child reveals itself in the adult's behaviors.

When considering his family, Sowles thought this was a credible theory. He was an only child. His mother was obsessed with religious beliefs that clouded her reason and kept her detached from him and his father, and his father was a closet alcoholic who was either absent from the home chasing women and gambling, or he was mostly invisible even when he was home, hiding in the garage or looking for excuses to drive to the market to save a few pennies on coffee or bread.

Even considering the inner child theory, Sowles was aware that he often spoke specifically to his deceased mother. Her death had not been anticipated or welcome. He missed her. He concluded also that he talked to ancestors he had never met, had never seen any photos of, and knew nothing about.

He felt that everyone heard him and even answered with advice, warnings, and simple reminders, and did so without excuses or commands. Theses dialogues had become very relaxed, but if they had been overheard, he would have been suspected of having a mental health problem.

Within the mental health or therapeutic community, the practice of talking to invisible friends or foes could be considered the makings of a borderline personality, one that slips in and out of fantasy thinking and reality or splits between healthy and aberrated behaviors.

Sowles was aware of this condition, so he was secretive about the habit and only indulged in it when he was alone in complete solitude, but at times, he had found himself having conversations with invisible people when he was in public. Then he was concerned. It was not a condition a commercial driver could present with and remain in the trucking industry.

His mother had regularly reminded him during his youth that there were angels who were available to communicate with him and help him, just as they had ministered to Jesus. That was comforting, but when he recently began to acknowledge the habit, he considered that he might simply be psychic, but he had no evidence of any telepathic effect on outcomes or people.

He reluctantly accepted that the practice was probably a form of communication with his inner being, but he had not wanted to fully accept that conclusion, as he had always felt, even as a child, that he had some type of special unity and unspoken communication with some unseen connection. As a kid, it had made him feel special. As an adult, he wasn't sure what he felt, except that it was a quality that he believed went hand in hand with his fear and obsessions.

He was a few miles north of the Shell fuel stop when the forest began to separate and the highway coursed into a beautiful valley of amber grass. In the near distance, the endless Pacific Ocean sparkled like crystal.

He lowered his window and inhaled the sea air while slowing down a few miles an hour to enjoy the moment. Glancing in his side mirror, he noticed a white SUV with a heavy black grill guard following close behind. It was a late model Ford Explorer.

"CHP? What now?" he asked aloud.

The Ford SUV was the preferred choice for the California Highway Patrol on Northern California rural roads and interstates. This particular model was fast and could handle snow and mud. The grill guard was for pushing stalled cars off the traffic lanes.

He slowed further, adjusting his speed to an exact fifty-five mph. Continuing up the road, he hoped it was just a routine trailer license check. After the tough, sleepless night in the lot and the discomfort at the Shell truck stop with the ghastly looking driver, the last thing he needed that morning was an official stop for a level-three registration and driver's license check, or worse, a lengthy level-one, tractor-trailer, equipment, and permit book inspection.

The car followed for another thousand feet or so, but finally swung out into the left lane and roared past the rig. Sowles saw that there were two very casually dressed plainclothes cops in the front seat. The standard issue Remington 12 gauge separated the men. The Ford disappeared in the distance as Sowles entered the general port area.

"Adios, motherfuckers," Sowles said, as he spotted the entry into the recycling area of the port. "We gonna stop anyway and get this shitload outta this box."

He slowed, turned left, and rolled about a mile to a small, wooden, shed-like building with one door and a big window. He had stopped at thousands of these guard shacks over the years, but this one felt different the instant he rolled up to the limit line.

A very dark Negro man with a face that actually shined jumped to his feet and rapidly exited the shack. He was dressed in a black paramilitary-styled uniform with bloused boots and had a large handled .45-caliber handgun holstered on his hip. He flagged Sowles to a stop and then gave him very specific unloading instructions, speaking with a deliberate and intimidating African accent. The guy's attitude was overly threatening and far out of character for a straightforward transaction at a junk cardboard dumpsite.

Sowles felt as if he had crossed a border into an unknown foreign land but knew that it was the .45 automatic and the uniform that gave the guy the extreme attitude. Sowles quietly listened and nodded obediently while glancing inside the little wooden office to see if the guy was alone. He smirked. The self-important, official-acting guard had a blazing electric heater inside, a broken swivel chair, and a surplus US Army desk that was soda stained and cluttered with bent soda cans and empty Doritos bags.

*This badass from Africa*, Sowles thought. *Brothah think he a corn-chip ninja.*

He briefly considered that they might chew the fat, given that they shared some form of common ancestry. *Bad idea*, he quickly reasoned. He was disturbed by the man's overbearing control and authority just to drop a load of junk cardboard. The trip had been gloomy enough.

Sowles finally just nodded with a few uh-huhs, and when the man was done lecturing, Sowles idled slowly forward and then shifted up and headed deeper into the facility. Much like the yard in Milpitas, it was acres of junk cardboard and other recyclables.

He drove to a staging area in the mud, where three other truck-and-trailer combinations sat. It was obvious that he was number four in line, so he parked directly behind the rigs, shut off his engine, and fell into the bunk. He was soon asleep.

After a series of garbled, convoluted stories and events running wild in his mind as if he was watching a broken film reel, he was awakened with a jolt by repeated loud knocks on his driver's side door. His heart pounding, he sat upright and reached for his pepper spray. The trucks that had been in front of him were gone and the sun's position suggested early afternoon. He quickly regained his senses, realizing that a few hours had passed. A Mexican guy stood outside of the truck.

Sowles opened the door. "I was sleepin', man, I'm sorry," Sowles said.

"I am Juan. I be knocking for one hour, maybe two, senor. You no answer. I think maybe, you be dead."

"I'm sorry, man," Sowles said. "I was asleep. I need to get unloaded."

"I know, senor, but my wife, she is waiting. Es time for me to go to her por me comer."

"What's that?"

"Lunche," senor."

"I'll give you an extra twenty bucks," Sowles said.

The guy thought about his offer and then shook his head. "Es okay, amigo, I unload you, for no extra, thees time." He signed the paperwork and motioned him toward a portable ramp sitting among bundled piles of paper and cardboard.

Sowles climbed down from the truck and fought his way back through the wind to open the trailer doors. He was greeted by hundreds of pieces of newspaper trash blowing in every direction as the Pacific gusts battered the area.

After he wrestled the doors open against the gale, he backed in with his trailer until he touched the ramp. Juan chained the trailer to the ramp to prevent a mishap, and unlike the Americanized Latino in Milpitas, Juan was efficient and fast. In fifteen minutes, he had completed the unload and had cross-docked it into the ocean container. He then unchained the rig and disappeared, leaving Sowles alone in the windy sea of junk paper products.

Sowles was done. Eureka had not been an insurmountable problem, but it was getting to be later in the afternoon. He shut the doors and rolled to the gate, showed the paperwork to the ridiculous African man, and headed out to the main highway. He parked on the shoulder.

Grabbing his phone, he made a call. A Latino voice answered. "Mr. Sowles, my main man. What it is, Holmes?"

"I'm done up in Eureka, empty, Rudy. How about getting my Black ass outta here? I gotta bad feelin' up here with these people, man. This place ain't normal."

"You all good, Mr. Sowles. I'm gonna get you goin', man, but probably not till tomorrow, brother."

"Tomorrow, Rudy? Come on, man. These foo's up here fixin' to lynch my ass."

"You got life insurance, bro. On the company. Ten grand for accidental death, bro. Not to worry, my man. You'll do good."

"Not if they kill my ass."

"Wait a minute, Holmes, I think I got you somethin' on the computer. It's goin' to Phoenix, man…yeah, Phoenix with one extra paid stop in Tucson," Rudy said.

"Yeah? Good!" Sowles said. "When?"

"Tonight. So do good and stay alive for a few hours, at leas' till you get the load."

"Right," Sowles said, half smiling at Rudy's attempt to keep things funny.

"So, you can roll south to this shipper in Ukiah," Rudy said. "You know, about one-hundred-fifty miles, man, three hours tops, eh? Then pick up later in the evening. See how I take care of you, my man? You be good, and you get to deadhead south, what'd I say, one-hundred-fifty miles? Then you go to sunny Arizona. You golden, bro."

"What's the product?" Sowles asked.

"Beer and IPA," Rudy said. "Chilled. 36 degrees."

"Okay, all good, but what's IPA?" Sowles asked.

"India Pale Ale…where you from, my man?"

"You know where I'm from. Oakland, man," Sowles said. "Them folks drink Martell."

Rudy chuckled. "Don't Mr. Sowles wanna know what the beer load pay?"

"As long as you booked it Rudy, I know you got the good bread, man," Sowles said.

"That's my soul man…I tell you what, bro, get goin'," he said. "Go to Ukiah now and take a break at one a them Indian casinos. They gots one or two right near town, man. An' they gots lotsa parkin', man, and you know…buffets, lobster, all you can eat, man. I'll text you the dispatch."

"Yeah, I've seen those places, man. Maybe I will check one out. Thanks," Sowles said.

"Yeah, you bet, Mr. Sowles. Jus' make sure you don't fall in love and miss the load."

"Sho, Rudy."

"Hey, I gotsa question for you, man," Rudy said.

"What's that?"

"You ever see that show about the white sheriff, you know, the big, tall blonde-headed dude in Montana or some shit?"

"What show?"

"It's a white dude, sheriff show."

"Nah, man. I don' think so," Sowles said.

"It's modern. Maybe in Montana or Wyoming. He's gotta fine, blonde chica for a deputy. It don' matter, man, I'm jus sayin'."

"Whachu sayin', Rudy? What, man?"

"Jus don't fuck around with no Indian chicks at them casinos. They got connections. I seen it on the show."

Sowles smiled, wishing he could fuck around with a beautiful, dark-haired Indian woman. "Okay," he said. "Sho' 'nuff," Sowles laughed and ended the call. He slapped the stick into gear and pulled away from the shoulder.

Immediately after the call ended, the little i Phone chimed again. Sowles saw that it was Rudy and quickly answered. "Mr. Sowles, my friend," Rudy said, his voice then sounding gloomy. "I didn't want to tell you, man, but the state is fucking with owner operators. They outlawing it, man. We gots to put our heads together, Holmes."

Sowles felt his stomach roll. "Outlawin' it?" He asked. "Whachu mean? How can I be an outlaw?"

"I don't wanna mess up your trip to Arizona. We be talking later," Rudy said. "I'm froggy, bro, I gotta jump." He abruptly hung up.

Sowles felt alone and faraway, that empty, deserted sensation that truckers have after completing a run and having any cryptic conversation with their office. "Shit! I made it up here," he said. "But what crazy booshit I gotta deal with now with the damn state?"

Getting his wheels rolling and back in rhythm on US 101 South, gave Sowles a slight feeling of relief. At least he was getting out of the region that did him the injustice of a lousy night's sleep the night before and a phony arrest over forty years earlier. *But what the hell was Rudy referring to?*

He cranked on his satellite radio and ran through a few stations, finally tuning into a Dan Bongino podcast.

"The Democrat Party has highjacked the press, but we see the game," Bongino said. The popular Fox News commentator and self-acclaimed replacement for Rush Limbaugh was into some rap about dishonest reporting.

Sowles liked Bongino and considered him an intelligent and insightful man's man who was more often than not on the correct side of the conservative argument, but at the same time, Sowles was tired of the Bongino rhetoric. It seemed to be nothing more than sensationalist talk and veiled, empty threats to destroy the Democratic Party.

Bongino spoke as if only he had inside information on the conservative movement that was supposedly taking back the Trump loss. Then Bongino went into his typical, New York tough guy tirade about punishing the DNC and impeaching the current president.

Sowles was fundamentally a middle of the road thinker. He had liked the former president, Trump because, like Bongino, Trump was a man's man, a leader, a businessman, and he took no shit, but Sowles also thought he was a loose cannon on a ship during a storm at sea. Sowles wasn't surprised that the former president lost. On the other hand, he disliked the current president for being the polar opposite, soft and ambiguous, possibly even a pathological liar, and he seemed to have a weak grip on the realities that the American people face.

"Wha' the hell I know?" he asked himself aloud. "Maybe Kamala can save the world. All the folks loved Obama. They might like Kamala even mo' if she shake that big booty enough."

He laughed aloud. He was eleven years older than Kamala Harris, but they had almost been neighbors in Oakland. He thought she was intelligent and attractive, but also silly and immature, a lot like Sheylinn. He wanted to like her but believed that she had gotten her shoo-in as VP only because of racial and feminist politics.

Bongino wrapped up a short segment with his New York accented tough guy talk about the struggle the Republicans had trying to take both houses of Congress. Sowles turned the radio off and glanced in his left mirror.

"What these dudes want?" he asked aloud.

It was the same SUV from earlier. Again, it was gaining rapidly on his tail. Quickly it was right up on his ass, disappearing behind the back of his trailer.

Sowles envisioned the tailgating cop running his trailer license and eyeballing his tires and brake lights at each curve that the rig maneuvered through.

"Shut me down, mofo! Maybe I can catch up on my sleep," he said, knowing he hadn't been speeding.

Hoping the cops would pass him and move on to whatever they were supposed to be doing, he slowed down to forty-five, an exact ten miles under the limit.

It worked. The car roared past him at about seventy-five. Sowles glanced down at the vehicle. It was the same unmarked Ford Explorer, definitely the CHP's SUV model of choice.

*Undercover, definitely*, Sowles thought. "Fuck 'em," he said aloud.

The car disappeared around the next bend. Sowles inhaled deeply and exhaled, momentarily fogging the windshield. He navigated around several more curves. Traveling about two more miles, he realized that he was nearing the property where he had spent the night. As he came around the bend where the turnout was, he saw the backside of the sign. It was damaged but painted with the same company name as he remembered the front side: Scully Brother's Fuel. It had three similar bent pieces of conduit with dead-looking lightbulbs dangling out of the tubes.

The CHP SUV was parked behind the sign.

"Shit! Who are these assholes?"

He passed the car at about fifty and immediately it pulled in behind him. He didn't have time to think before he saw the telltale small emergency lights flashing in the Ford's grill.

BLUE, RED, BLUE, RED, BLUE, RED, BLUE, RED.

"What do the white boys want?" he asked himself aloud, but immediately braked, signaled, and pulled to the right just beyond the Scully Brother's property line.

Shutting the engine down, he turned his emergency four-ways on and sat there with both hands on the steering wheel, listening to the flashers for what felt like an eternity.

CLICK-CLACK, CLICK-CLACK, CLICK-CLACK, CLICK-CLACK.

In short seconds, there were two armed white men looking up at him. One held the Remington 12 gauge pointed up at the driver's window. The other guy had a sawed-off that didn't fit with any police standard issue weapon. Neither presented a badge nor wore a side holster.

The first man was tall, overweight, and clean-shaven, with almost shoulder-length, sandy-blonde hair. Sowles figured him for about forty-five and thought that he resembled a former popular TV wrestler. His partner was younger, thirtyish, medium height, athletic-looking, with dark, medium-length wavy hair and a full face of handsome beard stubble.

Sowles figured they were deep undercover, especially with the non-regulation sawed-off. "Gotta be drug enforcement," he mumbled. He showed them his hands. *"But why the Highway Patrol involved in that shit?"*

# Nine

## THE SHINY COBRA

"Keep those hands where I can see them," the older man said, as he cautiously opened Sowles's door, pointing the big Remington directly at Sowles's face. He motioned upward with the barrel. "I want you to then turnaround, back out of the truck, and then step down."

"That's right! Do what the man says, pappy," the younger man said. He seemed nervous.

With his palms upward and over his head, Sowles was unable to brace himself. So as if he was a man without arms, he carefully turned around and backed into the door frame, leaning his chest on the seat to prevent himself from falling backward over four feet to the pavement. When his feet were finally on the ground, his face and shirt were covered with perspiration.

"Turn around and face me," the older man said.

Sowles obeyed. He stared into both men's faces. He could see from their reactions that they were aware of him memorizing their features. Both men kept their weapons at waist level, but pointing them directly at Sowles's large, upper body.

"What's your business here, old Tom?" the first man asked.

Sowles resented the racial slur, but he responded politely with a question. "What'd I do wrong, officer?" Sowles asked.

The younger man snapped back. "You ain't the one askin' the questions, boy. Ain't that right, coon? Ain't we askin' the questions?" he asked Sowles, nudging his weapon closer.

Sowles could see that the younger man was unstable. "Yes," Sowles said.

"Good," the young guy said.

Then the young kid put the barrel of his weapon within short inches of Sowles's sternum. "Don't make him ask you again, old Tom."

"I guess you ain't cops, are ya?" Sowles said, almost spitting the words. "I'm drivin' to Ukiah. I gotta get a load of beer tonight," Sowles said.

"You empty then?" the older man asked.

Sowles nodded but didn't answer the question. He figured they were backwoods hippies, dopers off the grid as far as he could surmise, probably looking to steal a load.

"Empty or loaded, man?" the young guy asked.

"I ain't got nothin'," Sowles said. "I said, I'm pickin' up. Take a look."

"This coon's a smart-ass. Let me have him," the younger man said.

"Chill, Aaron. I got it handled," the older man said.

Sowles scowled. "Aaron, ahh, yes, Aaron, a Jewish priest and the brother of Moses, fits the hair and beard," he mumbled, as he felt the cold steel of Aaron's barrel on his chest.

"You're a smart-ass coon, ain't ya?" Aaron asked.

"I ain't done nothin'. I'm comin' back from a cardboard delivery in Eureka," Sowles said, figuring that he might die whether he spoke to the men or not. "What d' y'all want?"

"Well, that's real nice, old Tom, but I didn't ask you where you came from." The big guy then looked at Aaron. "Didn't you just tell this dumb sumbitch that we ask the questions here?"

"Yep, I sure as fuck did, Winnie," Aaron said.

Sowles had both their names now, Aaron and Winnie.

"I ain't here to cause no trouble," Sowles said.

Winnie inched closer. "There he goes talkin' again when he wasn't addressed. I don' know what we're gonna do with you, old Tom." He looked at Aaron again. "What d' ya think, Aaron? What should we do with this big mouth, Black sumbitch?"

"Take his truck and fuck him up," Aaron said. He began laughing. "Good rhyme, huh?" he asked Sowles.

Sowles looked away. He was starting to consider the possibility that they might kill him.

Winnie glared at Sowles. "What were you doing on the Scully property last night?"

"Scully property?" Sowles asked.

"Yes, the Scully property. Don't play stupid with me, old Tom."

Aaron interrupted, stepping closer to Sowles with his shotgun pointed in his face. "Boy, I will fuck you up. I mean I will kill your Black ass right now. Answer the man's question!"

"I'll ask it again," Winnie said. "What were you doin' on the Scully property last night? This place right here, Scully Brother's, right here, Scully's place, ya dumb fuck, you're damned near standin' on it."

Sowles thought fast. "Scully Brother's? Oh, here on the lot, ya mean. I was sleepin'. I was tired, man, you know what I mean? I was 'bout to run outta diesel."

Both men stepped back a few inches, keeping their weapons leveled at Sowles chest. He could see that they were contemplating something, maybe what they could steal. "I swear, I didn't do nothin' or take nothin'!" Sowles said. "Look inside."

"Shut up," Winnie said. "I don't know what you did or didn't do, but you ain't goin' to Ukiah." He nodded to Aaron. "Zip ties on this buck."

Aaron nodded. "My pleasure."

"You own the rig, old Tom?" Winnie asked, returning his attention to Sowles.

Sowles nodded. Aaron giggled stupidly. "I can drive that piss-poor Kenworth," he said.

"You ain't drivin' the rig," Winnie said. He pointed to Sowles. "He is."

Sowles shook his head. "My company know 'zactly where I'm at and what I'm doin'. They ain't gonna be happy if y'all take me off my route."

"Like we give a shit," Aaron said, as he moved behind Sowles and began searching him. Sowles tried to pull away. Without hesitating, Aaron coldcocked Sowles in the back of his head with the butt of his weapon. Sowles went facedown. He squirmed and then became motionless. Aaron smashed him again in the back of the head. He zip-tied his wrists.

"I guess I am drivin'," Aaron said.

"What the fuck, Aaron! You better not a killed him, ya dumbass," Winnie said.

"He ain't dead. Look, he's breathin', and there ain't hardly no blood. Take more than that to waste that big fucker."

Winnie spit. "Now we gotta wait till he comes to, cuz we sure ain't liftin' that big bastard back into the rig. You better pray to your Buddha statue that the cops don't roll up while we're waitin' for the old boy to wake up."

"I couldn't help it, Win," he said, whining. "The black sumbitch wasn't gonna let me put them zip ties on him. I can tell those kinda things, Win. He pissed me off."

Winnie tossed his shotgun in the back of the Ford and got in the driver's seat. He shut off the strobe lights and backed the car into a position that blocked Sowles from the view of any passing motorist.

"Put the scattergun in the car," Winnie said. "Some city boys see us holdin' shotguns out here and we'll be on the fuckin' ground with the CHP up our asses. And wake that fucker up!"

Aaron tossed the shotgun in the Explorer and then went back to Sowles and stood over his near lifeless body. "Maybe I'll piss on him to wake him up," Aaron said as he poured a Mountain Dew over Sowles head and face.

"You're a fuckin' sadist!" Winnie said, laughing, as Sowles slowly rolled to the side and opened his eyes. "There ya go. Stand his ass up and get him back up in the rig," Winnie said.

Aaron pulled a black automatic from inside his belt. He told Sowles to stand.

With his hands still bound, Sowles struggled to his feet. "How the hell do I gets in without fallin'?" he asked.

"Ain't my problem…just hurry it up, bitch-ass," Aaron said, as he walked him up to the steps of the tractor. Sowles squirmed his way up into the driver's seat of the tractor. Aaron glanced at Winnie. "The sonofabitch is zip-tied, now how's he s'posed t' drive?"

"Is that a Glock in your fuckin' hand?" Winnie asked. "Well, dip-shit, you're gonna hold it on him and cut the frigging ties with your knife, and then he's gonna drive. It's that simple."

"What if he gets the jump on me?" Aaron asked.

"Shoot him."

"Will ya at least come over here and hold your pistol on the fucker while I mosey over to the other door?" Aaron asked.

Winnie got out of the Ford, holding a sharp-looking, shiny, snub-nose Colt Cobra revolver on Sowles. Aaron went around to the passenger seat and climbed in. He shoved the barrel of the Glock against Sowles's lower jaw and, trying to avoid the blood that had run from Sowles's wounds, he cut the plastic zip ties with a large hunting knife that had been hanging from his belt.

Sowles started the rig. He could see that Aaron was not completely sure of himself. Sowles also concluded that if Winnie really wanted him dead, he would have already killed him.

Winnie jumped back into the Ford and pulled onto the highway. Aaron pushed the Glock tighter against Sowles's cheek. "Get movin'," he said.

Sowles idled up behind Winnie, slowly shifting the gears. "Where we goin'?" he asked.

"Are you fuckin' stupid, boy? Follow Winnie up there," Aaron said.

Sowles nodded, briefly considering that he could push Winnie's Ford into a tree. Instead, he passively followed the Ford.

The two vehicles slowly rolled about five hundred feet to a dirt road across from the Scully property. Winnie made a turn, and Sowles followed.

The blood on the back of Sowles's head and neck had dried, forming a hard crust. The humiliation of being assaulted, wounded and insulted disturbed him more than the pain. Keeping one eye on Aaron, he hoped for an opportunity to either grab the gun or slam a backfist or elbow strike in his throat, knowing that either blow could kill Aaron, but Aaron would invariably fire the gun, probably more than once. Sowles knew he would probably get hit, somewhere fatal.

Aaron fidgeted in the seat. "I know what you're thinkin', boy, but you make one jigaboo move, and I will fuck you up," Aaron said. "I don't give a shit, man. I've done plenty a killin', motherfucker. Afghanistan, Iraq. I do not give one fuck about your Black ass. Just make a move."

Sowles cringed with silent anger, while Aaron toyed with the gun as if each move was an unspoken threat. "Radio work?" Aaron asked.

Sowles nodded. "Satellite, yeah. Over a hundred channels. Knock yourself out."

"That's what I'm talkin' 'bout, boy, now you're gettin' it," Aaron said, as he spun through a few stations, finally landing on some punk metal. He jolted his head back and forth to a tribal rhythm of incessant and repetitive, one-note bass guitar chords that to Sowles sounded like the inside of an MRI machine. The vocalist attempted his best version of a growl as he recited anarchist poetry that he must have believed would change modern civilization.

"You do know that's demonic shit?" Sowles asked.

Aaron cackled like a hyena. "Demonic? Good! I fuckin' hope so!" Aaron said, almost choking with laughter. "Shut the fuck up!" Aaron said as he turned the radio off. "Drive the rig."

They sat in silence for several minutes as Sowles continued to drive. "I understand where you're comin' from," he said to Aaron.

"What's that you're chirpin'?" Aaron said. "You don' know nothin' about me, 'boo."

"I'm jus' sayin', I just remember what it was like," Sowles said.

"What what's like?" Aaron asked. "What the fuck are you talkin' about, boy?"

"Tryin' to be a badass all the time. I'm jus' sayin', I can see y'all ain't really a killer."

"Winnie wants you alive, so let's keep it that way, and quit the philosophical bullshit," Aaron said. He again pointed the gun directly at Sowles. "I told you, I'm ex combat. I kill shit."

"I don't think y'all want to shoot some ole Black truck driver trying to make a livin'."

Aaron ignored the comment. "Winnie will be turnin' left up yonder onto another gravel road. Make sure you follow him, and take that turn wide, fuckwad. Don't even get this rig stuck in the mud or some damned drainage ditch."

# Ten

## YA GOTTA LOVE IT

The unpaved road stretched over numerous miles of rough, meandering, wooded terrain northeast of Eureka where sporadic groves of tall redwoods turned daylight into dark shade. As they rolled farther east, green timberlands of Douglas fir carpeted the mountainsides. Rapid creeks ran alongside the road in some areas. Sowles could see where they had washed out in the winter months, probably making the road impassable. At higher elevations, he could see the Pacific Ocean on the western horizon. It twinkled silver, orange, and blue in the late day sun. At those moments, he almost forgot that he had been abducted.

About thirty miles into the wilderness, the rugged landscape shed its trees and opened into an amber valley where grazing cattle filled the open range. Here, the road was straight for a several miles before it began climbing again into an area that had suffered from an ancient fire. Many nude and blackened trees had toppled into odd piles. Others still upright were dead and stripped, making the mountainside look as if it was a cushion of charred needles.

Wet weather seemed to have only recently cleared, but it left only a chilly late afternoon sun in its wake and bottomless mud that resembled lava. The winding travel required avoiding the thick mire, as it could easily bury the tractor's wheels. Aaron was quick to warn Sowles that if the rig got stuck in the mud, he would kill him on the spot.

According to the truck's odometer, they had wound over thirty-five miles through the remote region when the two-vehicle caravan dropped into another gigantic valley that had been cultivated into good farmland. The crop was beautifully green. It appeared to be alfalfa or some other species of flowering grain. The area opened into a center of activity, where they were greeted with waves from men and women riding muddy-looking ATVs.

Sowles immediately realized that these people were not outdoor enthusiasts. They all wore full camouflage combat fatigues and had shotguns or scoped assault rifles strapped on their backs. They appeared to be overseeing other men and women who were doing farming chores.

Both the men and women were young, tan, and attractive. There were quite a few pregnant women, some in their teens, but several appeared to be even younger. Most were dark-skinned and many looked Hispanic, although some were possibly Asian; others could be Middle Eastern or local Native Americans, probably from remaining nearby small reservations.

Tents and a few well-built lean-tos dotted the landscape only a few hundred yards from the road. They were surrounded by small groups of people; many were children and women. Some were also armed with high-tech rifles. Sowles was reminded of scenes from a film about the Khmer Rouge takeover of Cambodia and old newsclips of Jim Jones's Peoples Temple.

He began to grasp the truth: he was a prisoner on his way into an armed encampment. He realized then that it was a fortified farming commune, but not a peace-loving collective like those seen in magazine articles in the sixties and seventies. It appeared to be a guerrilla camp, maybe for training of domestic terrorists or a back country militia except there were no insignias or flags.

He was surprised to discover that he was no longer frightened. The irrational fear that had been plaguing him the night before was gone. After having stared down the barrels of two shotguns and two pistols and surviving the harsh blows of Aaron's rifle butt, he felt he was emotionally prepared to accept whatever was ahead. It was a new feeling, not so much of courage but the absence of paranoia. For the first time in his life, he realized that he might be facing death and that sensation made him feel vibrant as if he was actually living his life.

Winnie's Explorer passed by a large, Native American man, who seemed to be taking his job of directing traffic very seriously. The guy waved Sowles down and questioned him looking up into the opened door of the truck. Aaron abruptly interrupted, explaining that they had an appointment with Doctor Scully, the owner of the property.

The man nodded respectfully to Aaron and waved them forward. They continued to follow Winnie as he pulled the Explorer onto a nicely paved drive that was lavishly landscaped with numerous well-tailored small fruit trees, hedges, and beautifully groomed flowerbeds. It led toward a large multistory home, best described as an estate mansion, similar to those Sowles had seen while driving the truck among the vineyards in the Napa or Sonoma wine regions of the state.

In the distance, at about the length of a football field, there were large warehouse structures that seemed to have been styled and painted red to resemble traditional, Pennsylvania styled barns. Nearby was a cluster of single-storied, condominium-like buildings. Possibly living quarters, they resembled the old-fashioned highway motels of the 1950's. Several young men, and women with children appeared to be loitering in the area, but some were unloading black or gray pick-up trucks with what appeared to be boxes or luggage. Many were half-clad, and a few were conspicuously armed with weapons similar to those that the ATV riders carried.

"Stop on the road behind Winnie," Aaron said, barking as if he was the straw boss at the old Angola prison. "Keep it about two-hundred feet from the house, and then shut the noise off."

The respect the guard had shown Aaron, combined with Aaron's unfeeling and commanding style indicated that he had likely been in some level of authority over soldiers when he was in the Middle East, making his prior statement that he had killed men become more real.

Sowles stopped and set the brakes, and then he shut the engine down. He watched Winnie carefully as the lumbering man jumped out of the Ford and double-timed it back to the truck. He was carrying his Colt handgun. He pointed it up at Sowles.

Aaron climbed down and walked around the front of the truck. "Get outta the truck," he said. He also pointed his automatic hand-gun directly at Sowles's face.

Sowles climbed down, again backwards and struggling to maintain his balance.

Winnie chuckled like an idiot. "Well, old Tom, you're about to become the guest of honor."

"Yeah, hoss?" Sowles asked. "You gonna roast a nigga?"

Winnie didn't answer. Both men continued to point their handguns at Sowles's big torso.

Aaron's eyes were cold and dark. "Consider your day a lucky one, boy," he said in what Sowles had come to recognize was his unhinged tone of voice, a tenor that suggested that the young man could fly off the handle without any provocation.

"Listen up, boy," Aaron added. "Number one: you're gonna meet with the owner of the land, but you get this straight—people here don' exactly take to smart-ass niggers, so you best stand down with your big mouth and pay close attention. You dig?"

Sowles nodded.

"Very good," Aaron said. "Number two: we're both gonna walk you up to the house, but you even think about tryin' to run, an' I will pop a cap on ya, sure as shit. Ya got that, boy?"

Again, Sowles only nodded.

"Use your words, asshole," Aaron said.

"Yeah, I got it," Sowles said.

"Good," Aaron said. "Number three. There's a number three. Can you count that high?"

"What d' y'all think, white boy?" Sowles asked. He was losing his composure.

"Listen up, blackie," Aaron said.

Sowles eyes met Aaron's. For a moment Aaron flinched but he quickly regained his power.

"If I just happen to get a fleck a dust in one eye," he said. "And I have to shoot at your ass and just happen to miss ya, then someone else will shoot and hit ya…lots folks here on this land been trained on our range, and you can't count how many are armed…you got that, too?"

"I got it," Sowles said.

"That's real good," Aaron said. "Real good."

Aaron snapped out a brown-papered, store-bought cigarette from a cardboard box. He lit it with a camo-colored, plastic Bic lighter, took a drag, and blew the smoke in Sowles's direction.

"So then, you understand I ain't playin', right?" Aaron said.

Sowles face had hardened like black marble. "I heard your words, kid, but I done had 'bout 'nuff a both of your white asses," he said. "Either one of you call me 'boy' or 'bitch' or 'coon' 'gain and you're gonna have to kill this crazy nigga, but 'for y'all do, I'm gonna snap y'all's skinny white neck," he said. He was surprised to hear himself make such a threat.

"Is that a fact?" Aaron asked. He pushed up against Sowles and put the gun barrel in the middle of Sowles's forehead. "And how you gonna do that? How the fuck you gonna snap my skinny Jew boy neck? You bad ass now?" He slammed Sowles up against the truck. "I will put your brains inna fuckin' jelly jar, motherfucker."

"*Stop*, goddamnit, Aaron!" Winnie said, yelling. "We need him in one piece."

Still glaring at Sowles, Aaron backed away. "One piece, eh? One piece a shit."

"You don't have to get into a pissing contest with him every few minutes. Just zip-tie him, and let's get this shit over with," Winnie said.

"Yeah, yeah," Aaron said. He glared at Winnie as he put new plastic restraints on Sowles's wrists. "I'll let his nigger threat slide... for now," he said. "I was jus' givin' him a heads-up, Win."

"Okay," Winnie said. "It isn't necessary, Aaron. You're not making anyone's life easier."

"Oh, you getting soft, Winnie?'

"No, I'm not, but you proved your point. Showin' off ain't cuttin' it, man."

Aaron stuffed the Glock into Sowles's lower back. Sowles felt the barrel push against his spine. He squirmed. Aaron chuckled. "Like I said—a jelly jar."

Winnie ignored Aaron. Instead, he looked somewhat earnestly at Sowles.

"Listen," he said calmly. "There's at least forty miles of rough land, mountain cats, and black bears before you'll reach anything more than a shithole Hoopa reservation or a bunch of crazy meth cooks that are shacked up in an abandoned post office liquor store. You understand?"

Sowles nodded. Winnie continued. "Even if you made it that far, the wild dogs those dopers got runnin' around their place and their booby traps will get ya... you copy?"

"I got it," Sowles said with a sour scowl, deciding then that neither man would kill him in front of the people that were watching, including whoever the owner might be. But he knew that Winnie was correct about the remote area. Trying to make a break, wouldn't work, not with meth cooks out there...and there was still the reminder of the many missing people in the redwoods.

Aaron began pushing Sowles toward the walkway leading to the house. "I'll shoot his ass if he tries anything," Aaron said, laughing. "But then again, I guess the boss can't talk with ya if I kill ya," he said, chuckling. "He might can me, and then I'd have to get a real job, like you, wouldn't I, Mister Black truck driver?"

Sowles ignored the comment and with a man on each arm, he finally reached the front of the house. He was surprised when two athletic-looking, thirtyish women met them on the walkway. Both women were naturally beautiful. One was a long-maned Irish- or Scottish-looking redhead with sharp eyebrows, green eyes, and a few innocent freckles. The other was stunning, black-haired and Native American-looking. She appeared to also have some Negro or Middle Eastern ancestry that immediately intrigued Sowles.

Both women were dressed in tight blue jeans and wore hefty automatic pistols in fast-draw holsters high on their trim hips. Neither woman seemed to wear any makeup or adornment, but when Sowles noticed their feet, he saw that they both wore stylish matching sandals and had perfectly painted toenails, as if they had spent the afternoon in a San Francisco nail salon.

All four spoke in whispers. It appeared the women gave Winnie instructions. When they had finished, the two men double-timed it back to the Explorer and the truck. Aaron drove the rig, and both men headed in the direction of the barns.

Sowles realized then that they had officially stolen his rig... and him.

The Native American-looking woman seemed disturbed by the bloody wound on his head. She quickly examined it and told him that she would treat him within a few minutes. When he tried to make eye contact with her, she looked away.

Both women escorted him into a palatial great room tastefully furnished with rich leather and hardwoods. He waited, standing motionless in one spot as if he had been mustered on the deck of a merchant ship for a formal fire and lifeboat drill. Alone for the first time since he had been abducted, he was able to assess the throbbing in his head and neck. It felt serious, but trying to ignore the pain, he studied the room.

In one corner, there was a large, natural stone fireplace. A raging fire danced inside the hearth. There were several oil paintings hanging on all four of the elegantly plastered white walls. They were of various Northern California landscapes, rocky ocean scenes, and a few stunning big city day and night skylines. Even with his untrained eye, he could see they were collectible quality.

The quiet few moments were soon interrupted by a blonde-haired, fortyish white man quietly entering the room. He had feminine-looking, yellow dreadlocks sprouting from his head.

"Good afternoon," the man whispered almost inaudibly, showing his white teeth in a big, Hollywood-style smile. "I understand that your visit has been unpleasant thus far," he said.

Sowles was surprised. The young man resembled a well-known and internationally famous blonde haired movie actor. "Was them yo' white crackers that kidnapped me?" he asked.

"I'm aware that you were assaulted…but kidnapped? Such a harsh and felonious word. Might we call it something else? How about assembling for a long-anticipated meeting?"

"What do that mean?" Sowles could feel his face flushing with anger.

"It's semantics, my friend, but nonetheless, our meeting is overdue. Relax, please. Won't you sit down?" He graciously motioned to a nicely upholstered chair.

"No, man. I ain't sittin'! Listen, man, this is America, the USA. Y'all can't do this shit."

"Do what?"

"Kidnap a nigga, that's what. We in California. It's the twenty-first century. White men can't just steal a black motherfucker off the street."

"Relax, my friend—tell me about yourself, Mr. Sowles?"

"How the hell you know my name? And don't call me your friend, white boy!

"I enjoy your name," the young man said calmly, ignoring Sowles's anger.

"How you know it? From my driver's license?"

CALIFORNIA ROLL

The man laughed. "No. I've known it for a while. Sowles! Right? As in, soul, s-o-u-l."

"Yes, that's it, Sowles! Noah Sowles! S-O-W-L-E-S!"

"Well, Mr. Souls, Mr. Noah S-o-w-l-e-s. You are a gifted man."

"Gifted? You outta yo' ragged-ass mind, man. Whachu mean, *gifted*?"

"You have gifted names; first, Noah, a biblical name. And Souls. Very fitting. Yes! Noah commanded a wooden ship. He saved the world and seven souls. You can save many souls too."

"I don' need to save no souls other than mine."

"We all need to save humankind, Mr. Noah Sowles. You don't agree?"

"What in the fuck is you talkin' 'bout, man?" Sowles said. "Let me the fuck outta here!"

"Please, Mr. Noah Sowles. No worries. It is propitious, timely that we should finally meet face to face, albeit under rather, shall we say, difficult circumstances?"

"Difficult? Booshit," Sowles said. "Yo' racist white boys kidnapped my ass."

"As I said, I'm sorry for the barbaric treatment you were subjected to." The young man smiled. "We will make that up to you, I promise." He smiled again. "This is Anna," he said, motioning to the dark-haired Native woman as she reentered the room. "She will direct you to our infirmary...please try to relax." He then walked away without another word, disappearing into a long hallway.

"Wait," Sowles said, yelling after the man. "Where she takin' me? What about my truck? My wallet? My cell phone an' shit?"

There was no response.

Anna led Sowles down the same hallway and then into what was a well-lit, fully equipped doctor's examination room. The odor of unrecognizable chemicals hung in the air.

"Wait!" Sowles said. "I don't want y'all touchin' my head."

"Please be calm, Mr. Sowles. I will help you."

87

"Are you a doctor?" Sowles asked, squirming from the pain.

"I'm a nurse," she said, as she directed him onto a modern cushioned table. She cut off his shirt with a pair of shears and then cleaned the crusted head wound and the dried blood from his neck and torso, carefully dabbing him with a cloth and some organic brand of antiseptic soap and then rinsing him with warm water.

"This will help the stiffness," she said. She wrapped a compress around his neck.

"Thank you," Sowles said as he began to relax. "Will you cut the zip ties?" he asked.

"No. I'm sorry. I can't. But I will stitch your wound if you remain calm."

"Why you people doin' this?" Sowles said, trying to control himself. "Why am I here?"

"I cannot answer your questions," she said. "Now, please, relax. This head wound is deep. I need to join it with a few stitches," she said. "I'll have to shave a small spot where you still have trace amounts of hair" she said.

"I thought I was all bald," Sowles said, half-jokingly as he attempted to schmooze the very attractive woman.

"Please, be calm, and I'll give you some anesthetic," she said.

Sowles relaxed. Her hands were like warm silk as she gently touched and shaved a part of his scalp. "You mean, you gonna give me Novocain?" he asked.

He felt a pinprick at the base of his skull.

# Eleven

## CHOCOLATE CHIP COOKIES

Sowles awoke to an afternoon sun drearily shining through a lightly tinted, draped window. The long hangings had been partially shut, but he could see that the opening offered a view into the redwood forest. It appeared misty. The tree limbs outside the window were wet, heavy, and sluggish looking.

He was lying in a comfortable, hotel-sized bed and was clad in lightweight, blue pajamas that resembled scrubs. The zip ties were gone. He examined his hands. Both wrists were bandaged with several small, clear Band-Aids where the restraints had abraded his skin.

Struggling with what felt like a violent migraine, he forced his head and aching torso upright and let his back rest on several plush pillows. His neck was wrapped in a support compress and the back and side of his head were bandaged with gauze with some type of a waterproof covering. His head felt enormous, the size of a basketball. It pulsated in rhythm with his heartbeat, each thump causing his teeth to ache.

"Where am I?" he said, mumbling as he scanned the room realizing that it could have been the master bedroom of any chic suburban home or hotel suite, or even an exclusive room on a cruise ship. It was furnished with modern hardwood furniture and smelled of burning firewood.

Noticing two bottles of ginger ale sitting in a bucket of melting ice on the nightstand alongside an unopened bottle of Tylenol, he greedily grabbed the medicine and fought with the protective wrapping and cap. Once he had access to the caplets, he popped several into his mouth and then wrestled the beverage out of the ice. Then, while chugging a full bottle of the soda, he struggled to get out of the bed and stumbled toward what he assumed was the bathroom.

"I guess I am the guest of honor," he said aloud as he found the toilet and relieved himself in the clear water. Examining the elegantly granite-tiled suite, he saw that it consisted of two chambers. One housed a stunning glass shower big enough for two adults.

Staring dumbly in the mirror at his own muddled eyes for at least thirty seconds, he finally decided to remove the bandages, discovering that his face was swollen and drawn as if he had been sparring in his old karate dojo. He then retraced his memory: getting the truck unloaded alongside the Eureka port jetty, Rudy and his silly jokes, the planned trip to Phoenix, and whatever it was that Rudy was talking about with the State of California. "More booshit," he said, but his thoughts shifted quickly to Winnie and Aaron, the smack behind his head, the feeling that he had been swimming in a dark pool, followed by a threatening ride through the forest.

"Damned white punk-asses! Where's my shit? My phone?" he yelled, as he staggered back into the bedroom and stumbled in circles opening the drawers and the closets. "Where's my clothes? My shoes? My wallet?"

He turned the knob on the door that led out of the suite. It didn't budge. The deadlock had a key slot on the inside. He banged on it with the back of both fists. "Y'all got this bitch locked good!" he yelled. He rattled the knob. "Open the door!"

There was no response. Hurrying to the window, he discovered that it had no jamb or tracks. It was a single sheet of glass without any type of latch. He hit it hard with the back of his fist. It felt like impenetrable steel.

"Thick," he said. "Bulletproof."

His vision blurred from the aching in his head. He found his way back onto the bed. Reclining seemed to offer the only relief from the throbbing in his temples. His mind foggy and disconnected, he buried his head in the pillows and tried to assemble some plan for escape.

His feeble thoughts were interrupted when he noticed a wooden armoire across the room. Jumping to his feet, dizziness forced him to lose balance and he fell back on the bed. He tried again.

"Easy, Mr. Sowles," he said aloud, as he carefully slipped one foot in front of the other. He opened the doors of the armoire. Inside sat a typical flat-screen TV monitor.

"A television? A goddamned TV? Where's my stuff?" he asked, again yelling.

There was no response. It was deadly silent in the room.

"Answer me!" he yelled at the walls and ceiling. "What do you want from me?"

Grabbing the TV remote from its charger, he pressed the power button. The screen instantly came to life, lighting the now darkening room in diffused shades of various colors. Again, he stumbled back onto the bed. Sitting on the edge of the mattress, he raced through several blacked-out channels, finally stopping at what appeared to be a recording of a live conference event.

A well-groomed, blonde man casually dressed in an open-collared shirt was sitting at a table, flanked by a man in a business suit and a well-dressed woman, both with water bottles in front of them on the table.

"That's him! That's the smart-ass white boy! Where the dreads?" Sowles asked loudly.

After a few moments of dead silence, the young man stood.

"Good morning, ladies and gentlemen. Thank you all for being with us today. For those of you here whom I've not yet had the pleasure of meeting, my name is Finn Scully," he said. "I'm known as Doctor Scully, but pay no mind to formalities. Just call me your friend." He then waited for the applause and laughter to ebb. "I hope you all have enjoyed your visit," he said.

The camera panned to the sizable audience. Sowles noticed that it was all white men and women. The camera then returned to Scully. He smiled widely and resumed speaking.

"Our little slice of Shangri-la, the Emerald Triangle consists of the Humboldt, Trinity, and Mendocino counties. Within our fertile paradise, previous generations of our families and friends successfully grew hybrid varieties of exceptional quality cannabis since the 1960s."

The audience clapped, some whistling. Sowles watched intently. Scully continued.

"Today we can proudly make a claim similar to the past statements made by the grape growers of Sonoma and Napa counties. As they have proclaimed themselves the 'Wine Country,' we can say with confidence, 'We are the Weed Country!'"

The audience hooted. Sowles scowled. "So that's it! A goddamned weed farm," he said.

Scully continued after the audience became silent.

"Until the relaxation of California laws resulting from the passing of two very significant propositions, many of our predecessors, both twentieth century and early twenty-first century cannabis users and professional growers, suffered persecution, injuries, and even death from armed trespassers."

The crowd hissed. He waited for them to quiet and then resumed his speech.

"These vigilantes were local residents of the region, making their night raids and other acts of violence comparable to former illegal efforts of the KKK and other citizen hate groups in various parts of the US that have taken various laws or interpretations of laws into their own hands."

Sowles nodded. "KKK, eh?"

Scully worked the crowd into obvious physical reactions. Some scratched nervously. Others fidgeted in their seats. Some stood and walked toward the aisle. To Sowles, it seemed that Scully's remarks comparing some of the past reactionary local citizenry to the KKK had likely landed on a few former culprits or maybe their living relatives.

Scully continued talking.

"Just as past Southern KKK attackers had been given the unwritten support of corrupt officials and government, the oppressors of our former community were eventually given the assets and equipment of entire state and federal law enforcement bureaus and agencies to effectively destroy our predecessors and their farms."

Sowles paused the video. He was both surprised and impressed that Scully had openly criticized and challenged government and law enforcement in this taped program, and also made a bold comparison between the oppression of Black Americans by the KKK and the past subjugation of marijuana users and growers in his region of the state.

As much as Sowles tried to remain outside of the radical racism in the US, it had been becoming obvious to him that the current BLM movement was not unfounded, any more than the civil rights leaders, activists, and Black Panthers of the 1960s had not had a justifiable cause. Sowles had never experienced the racist tactics of the KKK, regardless that KKK violence was practiced in various regions of California and the western US and went ignored by local or state law enforcement, but he had experienced other racism and oppression not limited to but including the illegal arrest in Humboldt County which he realized later had been early racial profiling.

Sowles resumed the program. Scully had stopped to drink from a large ceramic mug, while also soaking up the crowd's reaction. He then continued.

"I witnessed this mayhem and resulting family catastrophes." Scully said. He seemed saddened but he continued speaking. "It began with the literal destruction of acreage by foliage poisoning or crop burnings. Grandparents, fathers, and mothers were sentenced to lengthy prison terms, given massive out-of-jurisdictional fines, and had their land and assets seized and forfeited. Some people simply disappeared never to be heard from again."

The camera again panned the dead silent audience. They appeared hypnotized.

Sully continued speaking.

"These people had been a generation of peace-loving students and flower children who, in some cases, lived with family elders in communal settings much like our farm has established. These people enjoyed the relaxing benefits of cannabis. Yet, they became punished untouchables and criminals, their children sent to foster homes. Lives were destroyed, ruined, ended."

Scully took another drink from the mug and surveyed the crowd. He seemed to be smirking at his last statement, as if he had made a private joke. He then continued.

"Regardless of their educations, university degrees, published articles, and technological advancements or scientific knowledge of the agribusiness of cannabis farming, these growers were also ultimately treated as a foreign enemy by state and federal politicians."

Scully paused again, carefully watching the crowd for reactions. He then continued, but with an odd twinkle in both eyes and another almost taunting half-smile.

"Paramilitary-style law enforcement and the agencies they represented both developed a profitable joint venture of sanctioned prosecution utilizing state funds for investigations, raids, seizures, exorbitant bail, court costs, fines, and sentences."

Now almost panting with passion, Scully drained whatever was in the cup. The crowd waited and watched in silent admiration as he continued.

"This, in addition to government grants or allocations, provided for growth and expansion of local, state, and federal courts and state and federal correctional facilities, as well as the further development of privatized prisons. Prosecuting weed smokers and growers became a top revenue producing endeavor for the US and state governments with California in the lead. No less than three State of California and federal administrations oversaw this oppression.

The crowd roared. Many stood. Scully mesmerized the group.

"At that time, arguments were presented citing government's attempts at eradicating marijuana and its growers while also citing prior generations special considerations to tobacco, spirits, wine, and Big Pharma industries; all whose products that were by the time of this oppression competing with cannabis. It then seemed that having the munchies for chocolate chip cookies became a cause célèbre but also one more probable cause for persecution, arrest and prosecution."

People laughed and clapped for at least three minutes while Scully remained standing. When the noise ceased, he introduced the two people seated alongside. Both were Democratic US Congressional representatives from different districts in the region. They gave boring, canned tributes to Scully, referring to him as Doctor Scully an ally of freedom.

Scully soaked up the compliments and then sat, smiling at the audience. Finally, he raised both palms and made a final statement. "I am here for all of you!"

The crowd screamed with passion for the young man. When the cheering subsided, the two politicians spoke about conjoined marijuana industry and government alliances that were creating social welfare programs in the impoverished Triangle region, followed by promises of job growth from the cannabis commerce.

Sowles shut the TV off. "A damned dope farm! And the usual white-ass politicians reassure the folks that they'll all live happily-ever-after," he said. "But why me? What do these white-ass foo's want from me?" he asked himself, half-mumbling.

Reflecting on what Scully had said, he remembered that before the California propositions were passed, making weed lawful for medical purposes and then making it legal to grow, the various government authorities that had jurisdiction over the region and over marijuana had treated the growers with the same violence as southern Blacks had been treated for centuries.

"Untouchables! Criminals, Scully had said," Sowles muttered.

Those words hit home for Sowles, as did Scully's statements about law enforcement against the growers being its own profitable industry in the Triangle. He remembered again his firsthand experience with the travesty forty years earlier with the California Highway Patrol.

"No wonder all them foo's outside got guns!" Sowles said.

He shut the armoire and reclined on the bed, letting the pillow sooth his aching head and overtaxed mind. "But why they grab my Black ass off the highway?" he asked himself, as he started to drift off to sleep.

In what felt like at least an hour, the lock tumbler rattled and clicked. He heard the door open, and he jumped onto his bare feet, nearly falling on his face on the night table.

It was the two women. They both still wore their automatic pistols at their midriffs, and both had changed into military camos.

Again, his eyes went straight to Anna. She ignored him.

The redheaded woman frowned. "Me name is Mary," she said with an Irish accent. "We'll be gettin' yar clothin'," she said. "Lemme see yar hands."

"My hands? What for?" Sowles asked.

"Open them wide, naw."

Sowles opened his palms. Mary glanced at both sides and inspected between his fingers.

"What are you looking for, a nuclear weapon?" Sowles asked.

She ignored his comment. "Sit."

Sowles sat on the bed. "Where's my phone?" Sowles asked.

"Ya cannot 'ave yar phone," Mary said.

Mary stepped into a parade rest stance as Anna approached him holding a large pair of blue slacks, with a big matching sports jacket draped over a wire clothes hanger. She had a starched white shirt on another hanger and a pair of black oxfords under her arm.

She set everything on the bed. "Mr. Sowles, this is your clothing. Doctor Scully will see you soon," she said, as she tucked the hangers under her arm.

"What am I gettin' dressed up in these fancy clothes for, my funeral?"

"Doctor Scully will explain," Anna said.

"Doctor Scully? Doctor Scully the crazy little white boy?"

"He is the owner of the land. You met him on Tuesday. I recommend you mind your manners, sir."

"What do you mean, Tuesday? Isn't today Tuesday? How long I been in this room?"

"Today is Friday. You've been here three days."

"That ain't possible, unless y'all drugged me!" he said to Anna.

"It was for your own good. Your head wound was severe," she said. "It needed the time to begin healing."

"I remember now. You gave me a needle to take away the pain in the back of my head...you gave me some bad shit!"

"You needed a sedative."

"A three-day sedative?" he asked, his voice becoming more aggressive. "And no food?"

"You were in no condition to eat," she said. "We have been monitoring your health."

"You call two white boys beatin' my ass with a shotgun butt *monitorin' my health*?"

"You'll find a toothbrush and toothpaste in one of the shoes," Anna said. "I will collect the toothbrush when we return. You will hand it over or you will be sedated again." She looked at Mary who seemed to be nodding eagerly at the thought of exacting punishment.

Sowles was irritated with the Native American woman, but her beauty had him wishing that he was forty years younger. "What d' you people want from me?" he asked her.

"Doctor Scully will explain."

"You keep sayin' that the dude'll explain! I'm jus' a damned truck driver. I ain't no cop or narc, I'm a dumbass Black brother drivin' a big rig, tryin' to stash 'nuff money to bury my ass someplace 'sides a damn nigga cemetery. Why'd that whiteboy kidnap me?"

"You will be dining with Doctor Scully," Anna said, ignoring his rant and motioning Mary toward the door. "One of us will come for you…take a shower and get dressed."

"Do he want me to wear underwear?" Sowles asked, as he examined the clothing.

"The underwear is inside the breast pocket of the coat," Anna said.

Watching Sowles cautiously, they backed toward the door. Sowles pulled out a pair of large, black, silk boxers from the jacket pocket. He held them up to the light.

"Now that's what I'm talkin' about," he said, smiling at Anna.

"The socks are in one shoe." Her voice was flat and unemotional.

As they were leaving, Sowles noticed that she had taken all the clothes hangers. He knew that the women were aware that he could fashion them into weapons. That simple gesture combined with the order about the toothbrush made it very clear to him that he was formally now an official prisoner.

The two women exited the room, securing the lock from the outside.

# Twelve

## LANGOUSTES

Sowles removed his neck compress and labored his sore body into the shower, brushing his teeth under the warm water. He washed and rinsed. While drying, he again examined his face in mirror. The water pressure must have reconfigured and calmed his bumps and wounds as he looked better, but he needed a shave, and it was clear that there was no razor to be found anywhere in the upscale bathroom. Again, he realized the implication of being held captive by the obvious group of fanatics. They wouldn't allow him anything that could be used as a weapon.

As he dressed in the fashionable clothing, he remembered his one truly significant date with Sheylinn, the junior and senior prom when he wore a blue suit. He also reflected on the two funerals he had attended, his father's first and then his mother's. At both events, he wore a black suit.

As he viewed himself in a full-length mirror, he had to admit that he admired the fit of the clothing the women had provided. It was as if they had tailored it specifically for him, and the black shoes were sharp, a high-quality leather wing tip. "Allen Edmonds," he said. "Never heard of 'em, but cool…nice."

He looked sharp, even with his week's growth of beard. An old memory of the deceased singer, Marvin Gaye came to mind from decades earlier when the singer had grown a beard. "Sheylinn had such a crush on that brother," he said, mumbling into the mirror.

It took several more minutes before the two women came through the door. Both had changed into casual but colorful, loose-fitting, Oaxacan-style white cotton dresses, as if they were twins. They were both still strapped heavy. *At least 9mm*, Sowles thought.

He handed Anna the toothbrush. She smiled ever so slightly.

The women were quiet, each of them taking him by an arm, almost as if they were escorts. They had strong grips reminiscent of the guards at his trial back in the seventies. As they guided him down the hallway, he felt like he was walking the green mile, but, in a quirky manner, he was entertained by the attention of the two attractive women.

"I gotta tell y'all, it's sho' nice being escorted by you two fine baby girls," he said to both of their emotionless faces as they led him into a large dining room, where another fireplace roared in the corner. The hearth and chimney were meticulously made from well-placed river stones. Again, the smell of woodsmoke hung over the room suggesting an almost festive sensation.

A long, uncovered, hardwood dining table with seating for twelve was set with two place settings. A modern-looking, intricate, glass-and-pewter chandelier hung over the center. Sowles had seen something similar in a Union Square store during the holidays in San Francisco.

The room itself was large and pleasant, with a soft white finish, a hardwood floor with a few ruby-colored woolen rugs, and a matching hardwood baseboard. Several well-done oil paintings of landscapes, European castles, and colorful sections of old-world cities hung prominently on each wall. Each was framed with fine gilded wood, just like the paintings he had seen in the entryway.

Sowles didn't grasp the true magnitude of the wealth, but he did recognize that Scully appeared to have become very affluent as a dope grower, but there seemed to be more to the equation. Scully had to be connected on a much higher level than just to only some old, dead hippies who had left behind several acres of pot. There was a lot of competition growing weed on the West Coast. Everyone with access to seeds was in the business.

Remembering a few odd movies, Sowles expected a goon valet or maybe a dwarf steward to attend to them, but Mary and Anna seated him and then stood by. He could smell the faint odors of each of the women's noticeably expensive perfumed soap. He smiled. *It's not Irish Spring*, he thought.

He waited alone at the table, feeling uncomfortable, insulted, and ridiculous. After a few minutes of silence, Scully softly padded into the room as if his feet had not touched the floor. He sat at the head of the table, folded his hands in some gesture that resembled praying or meditating, and bowed silently. The women followed his gesture.

Sowles felt ridiculous, but tipped his head forward out of respect for whatever ritual they were indulging in. He glanced at Scully. He was chanting or praying in an undertone, but then he suddenly looked up directly at Sowles as if he knew he was being watched. He smiled, closed his eyes, and continued with the ritual.

After a few minutes more of meditation, Scully nodded to the women. They left the room. Sowles and Scully were alone in silence except for the loud crackling of the fire, which had gotten quite bigger as if someone had added wood. Sowles remained quiet, wondering with curiosity and doubt where the evening was headed. Finally, Scully spoke.

"Mr. Sowles, you look quite dignified this evening. Might we start our evening by me calling you Noah?" he asked.

Sowles looked into his blue eyes. They were youthfully anxious at moments, but would change and appear to be very experienced and aged. Then he would appear much older than suggested by his otherwise boyish facial features, skin, blonde hair, stylish dreadlocks, and athletic, trim frame.

"I don' care what you call me, man!" Sowles said. "Call me outta this damned place. What's your thing, man? You set up some gas station down there and kidnap Black men?"

"Noah, I have no doubt that you are baffled and angered by your experience."

Sowles glared at him but Scully just smiled. "As I'd said, I'm deeply sorry for the physical wounds that you've suffered. I do hope that you understand that was not in any way at my direction."

"Your direction? Then who's behind this booshit, if it ain't y'all?"

Scully again only smiled. That in itself disarmed Sowles. For starters his smile was overly sweet and charming. In addition, he was wishy-washy, ambiguous and deceptive, and to Sowles he seemed soft, almost effeminate at times. He had perfectly manicured fingernails that were polished to a clear luster. He reminded Sowles of the white men on East 14th Street in Oakland who had tried to pick him up when he was a kid. Scully may have been a refined, handsome young man, but he didn't have a strong male edge like any of the men Sowles knew in the Black community or in the trucking business.

"You gay, man? You like old Black men?" Sowles asked, his voice deadpan and serious.

"Please, Noah. You have to understand that the universe outside of Noah Sowles's mind is not black or white, right or wrong, gay or straight. It simply is what it is. We must be cautious of our interpretations and I must warn you about thinking in terms of stereotypes. Humans should only have opinions that are highly flexible, or they will be broken as if brittle steel."

Sowles looked hard at Scully, fully aware that he could break his neck.

"That includes you, man."

"Please elaborate, Noah," Scully said.

Sowles felt the chill. "Y'all's got me locked in a goddamned bedroom, and that ain't no opinion, man, it's a fact," he said, "a natural fuckin' fact. That's what I'm sayin'."

"Noah, I'm aware that you have been confined in much worse environments. Is that not so? Have you not been in jail and the Merchant Marines? And certainly, trucking is confining."

"How in the hell you know all this booshit?" Sowles asked.

"It's my business to know things, Noah."

Sowles nodded. "I guess," he said, aware that Scully was probably a compulsive liar and had gotten the information from his driver's license.

We live in the age of information. You're aware of that reality?"

"Yes, I'm aware a more than yo' ass is aware of."

"You are confirming something else that I know."

"What's that?"

"That you must stop displaying outbursts of your temper."

"You got the white man's silver tongue, ain't you? But you ain't answering my questions! Tell me why two dumbass crackers abducted a Black truck driver off a damned US highway, stole his damned truck, and then locked the nigga in a room."

"You're inquisitive. I like that, Noah," Scully said. "Answers add to knowledge, and knowledge truly is power, just as the wise men say."

"Fuck the wise men," Sowles said.

They were both distracted as Mary entered the dining room. Her hair was long and vibrantly orangish red. She also wore bright red lipstick. Scully smiled at her and then nodded to Sowles.

"Do you like, lobster, Noah? I do hope so."

"Never had it, an' why the hell you bring an' old nigga driver to yo' fancy dinner?"

"Please refrain from using the N-word, Noah."

Sowles laughed heartily. "The N-word!" he said. "Y'all surprise my ass with yo' false morals." Sowles laughed. "You worried about the word 'nigger,' eh? When you kidnapped my Black ass and had y'all's white boys beat me down?"

Scully didn't respond to Sowles observation. He just smiled. Sowles had to admit to himself that the young man's charm was appealing but in an almost repulsive manner.

"So, what's next, Mr. Scully?" Sowles asked.

"Doctor Scully," the young man said. "Well, dinner first. You are in for a treat. Lobster tails thermidor will be the bill of fare this evening. We've flown in several cold-water species—live, of course." Again, he smiled, his white teeth sparkling under the light of the chandelier. "How about that, Noah? It will be served with a wild and brown rice mix grown in the San Joaquin region of the state. What do you say?"

Before Sowles could answer, Scully nodded to Mary. "White, of course, nothing coastal, please," he said softly. He looked back at Sowles. "Delta rice, yes? Sound tasty?"

Sowles nodded, as he cautiously watched Mary exit the room. "Rice," he said sullenly.

"So then, Noah, we shall dine like neighboring kings," Scully said. Sowles could only frown and look away.

Scully became silent as Mary reentered the room and poured him a small sample of the wine. He glanced at the label and motioned to her to pour Sowles a glass. When she had finished, she filled the remainder of Scully's glass and waited for him. Scully then read the label aloud.

"Kathleen's Vineyard. An excellent Chardonnay! My old friend, Jess. May his crooked soul live in eternal unrest...I guess the stock-holders sold to investors in Santa Barbara," he said, wincing at his statement. "Please, Mary, continue to chill it for us while we chat."

Mary left the room with the bottle. Scully stared at his glass. Sowles scrutinized the young man. Regardless of the circumstances, he was somewhat amazed at Scully's manners and gift of gab. And. irrespective of his reference to past dope growing associates in the redwood region, Scully himself had never been a dirt farmer; that was very obvious.

"Noah. The two men who brought you here did not do it with my authority. It was not a deliberate action on my part."

"Deliberate?" Sowles asked. "Now you sound like Nixon or Bill Clinton."

"I'll take the Clinton compliment. Nixon disappointed me," he said. "Never give up."

Scully again pondered the amber wine in his glass for a moment. "Pretty, isn't it?" he asked, chuckling. "I'm saying that I did not devise a plan to bring you to our sanctuary. The two men, Winnie and Aaron, who brought you here, decided you could be useful."

"Useful? Now ain't that a bitch," Sowles said. "Y'all are some crazy white folks."

"No, Winnie and Aaron are simply opportunists. One could call them criminals or sociopaths, I guess, but really, they are entrepreneurs and would-be businessmen. They brought you to me because they saw a significant opportunity."

"Why me? I'm a worn-out, old Black trucker...what, man? Y'all need a house nigger?"

"Please, Noah, I've asked you to not speak like that. I am not a racist."

"Y'all say this wasn't yo' idea, but then you said you were waitin' fo' me. You a damn lie."

Scully chuckled. "A liar? Well, a little, perhaps, at least, so it's been said, but I've warned you about stereotypes. Regardless, I believe in equal opportunity or failure for all, and now it's your turn, my friend."

He cleared his throat and then sipped from the wine goblet again.

"It was assumed that you could be useful to my organization," he said. "It's that simple. And now that you are here, I am giving great thought to their observations. I believe that they were correct. You are the type of man I can use, and so I have something that will offer you long term financial reward as well as the kind of status that should be of great interest to you."

"What I am interested in is gettin' my Black ass outta here."

"Be patient. There is more to be revealed," Scully said.

"I'm sho' you woulda been a success down in Mississippi or Louisiana over the past coupla hunnert years."

"Yes, I'm sure I should have…or could have been, or maybe I was." He laughed.

What's that mean?" Sowles asked.

Scully laughed again. "I sympathize with your confusion, given the current unusual circumstances, but suffice it to say, I can simply make you very rich, fat, and happy…I will assume that you watched the video during your stay in our suite?" he asked, examining his fingernails.

Sowles nodded.

Scully lifted his wine glass. "Excellent!"

Sowles didn't lift his glass but instead just stared at the pretentious young man.

Scully ignored Sowles's lack of etiquette. "Then, for the moment, let's just eat, drink, and be merry," Scully said. "Perhaps we will talk further over brunch tomorrow."

Scully glanced over his shoulder at both Mary and Anna as they entered the room followed by two preteen children. The boy was wearing a handsome black tuxedo. He carried covered casserole dishes on a tray. A cute, but very young blonde child resembling an overly made-up JonBenet Ramsey and wearing a bright-red, long dress followed. She smiled knowledgably at both Scully and Sowles as if she was years older. She then spread soft linen napkins on both men's laps.

"My children, give Mr. Sowles two langoustes in his casserole. I'm sure he's quite famished after his ordeal," Scully said. "Then give me a big hug."

The boy served both of them while the girl stood by adjusting the tableware, and then they ran to Scully, hugged him, kissed his cheek and then left the room. Mary followed and quickly returned with the wine. She refilled the glasses and again left.

Sowles nervously nibbled at the elegant meal while he suspiciously eyed Scully, who in turn only sipped his wine and did not touch the food. Sowles was unfamiliar with the entire dining protocol. His face was hot. He was thirsty. He needed water.

Scully saw Sowles's discomfort. He looked over his shoulder. Mary appeared in the room within seconds.

Scully lustfully eyed Mary. "Pellegrino, bottled. Absolutely no cans." He then smiled at Sowles, again showing his perfect teeth. "Did I get that right, Noah…cold water? Everybody always wants ice water!" He laughed. "You've heard that, eh?"

Sowles nodded dumbly. He was feeling unbalanced after a few sips of the Chardonnay. He fidgeted in his chair.

Scully commented. "Not used to dining with the rich and famous, I see."

Sowles seemed to have trouble breathing. Never having spent much time around any whites and having no exposure to any upper-middle or upper classes, he was threatened by Scully's dominant personality and how he stared at him. His blue eyes seemed as though they could penetrate his thoughts and feelings. He wanted to run from the room, but not before getting his fair share of the aromatic and attractive lobster casserole.

Mary had slipped out of the room. She quickly returned with glasses and a sealed bottle.

Scully nodded with approval as she let both men view the label. She poured the water and again left the room. Scully then raised his glass. "Excellent, water, Noah, just excellent…now, enjoy your meal, and we shall talk again," he said as he splashed his water in his casserole dish.

Sowles was taken off balance by Scully's aggressive performance with the water glass but equally intimidated by the sophistication of Scully and his children and wives, or whoever everybody was. He carefully watched Scully as he finished his wine and stood, but then Scully left the room without a word, leaving the entire watered-down casserole of delicately prepared lobster and cream sauce untouched, as if it was a spoiled piece of artwork.

Sowles was alone. He decided not to wait any further. He devoured his meal and drained his water and wine. At the exact moment he finished, the two women returned.

"Come, Mr. Sowles," Anna said, as she helped him from his chair. Sowles stood.

Both women escorted him. He stumbled half-drunk, feeling as if he had been among royalty, but he had a dark sense of dread not unlike the feeling he'd had while parked on Scully's property.

"So, what was that whole dinner s'posed to be 'bout?" he asked.

"I will only tell you that Doctor Scully does not like debate," Anna said.

Sowles was surprised that Anna was not threatening him but seemed to be giving advice.

The women unlocked and opened the door to his room. As he entered, he turned around to take one last look at Anna. He noticed that both the women's automatic handguns were gone. His mind raced with thoughts of overpowering both of them, but he froze and instead watched the door shut, remembering Aaron's threats and Winnie's advice about escaping.

He hadn't heard the lock slam into position and considered the possibility that one of the women had made a mistake and not locked him in. He checked the door. He was not pleasantly surprised. The handle was immovable, the door as solid as concrete.

He glanced at the bed and saw that it had been made and turned down. The sheets were fresh, and his pajamas were folded nicely under his pillow as if his mother had visited. He undressed and draped the custom clothing over the door of the armoire. Curious about the bathroom, he entered the granite enclave and saw that it had been cleaned thoroughly. It was immaculate, the mirror glistened, and all the towels were brand new and neatly hung.

He wondered if Anna did the work. Or was it one of the young Hispanic-looking women he saw on the road? It didn't matter. He was a captive in a bedroom suite.

The entire situation was intimidating and yet also fascinating. He was being held against his will, in fact, he was a prisoner, but he was being treated literally as if he was a guest of honor, just as Winnie had said.

*Why?* he silently asked himself.

All of it was too much to comprehend. He intuitively knew that Scully must have a dangerous and deceptive purpose behind the charade.

He crawled into bed and lay staring at the ceiling.

# *Thirteen*

## ROOM SERVICE

"Wake up!"

Sowles opened his eyes in the darkness of mid-night. Winnie was standing over him, with Aaron nearby. "Get outta that bed, asshole," Winnie said, as he and Aaron pulled Sowles onto his feet. "Get his wrists, Aaron," Winnie said.

Before Sowles could grasp what was happening, Aaron had yanked both of his arms behind his back. Sowles attempted to pull away, but Aaron quickly cinched the sharp plastic ties around his wrists.

"If you don't want that Black head beaten to mush, you better pay attention," Aaron said.

Aaron then cinched a set of leg irons around Sowles's ankles, and both men quickly dragged him out of the room and into the same hallway that the two women had escorted him down just hours before. His bare feet stung from the friction of the carpet. In the dim light of night, he saw that they both wore their handguns in holsters.

"What y'all doin'? What'd I do wrong?"

"Shut up," Aaron said, as he opened a heavy, solid steel door that led to a descending metal staircase lit by a single red bulb. With Aaron leading the way and Winnie above him, they led him down one difficult step at a time, to another identical door at the foot of the stairs. Aaron pulled on two opposing levers that simultaneously unlocked a hefty double-latch system.

They both pushed him into a pitch-black room. Winnie forced him to his knees and stood over him with a high-intensity flashlight pointed directly in his eyes as he shoved the cold barrel of his Colt revolver snug against his forehead.

Sowles felt his shins sink into about three inches of musty-smelling cold water. "Please!" he said, reminded instantly that it wasn't the first time he had begged in his life. Many years earlier, he had pleaded on his knees to Sheylinn, begging her to stay married.

"We told you to shut up!" Winnie said, as he cocked the revolver.

"Please!" Sowles said. "I'll do whatever Doctor Scully wants. Please! Please!"

"It's too late," Winnie said.

"Wait a minute, Win," Aaron said. He brushed Winnie aside. "We got money tied up in this boy!" He slapped Sowles across his face. The blow snapped Sowles's head to the side.

"Why? Please! What do y'all want me to do?"

Aaron then circled around behind him and pushed him hard with the flat sole of his boot. Unable to protect himself with both of his hands restrained, Sowles fell face-first into the filthy water, smashing his forehead on the concrete floor. In the next seconds, he waited for the bullet that would end his life, but instead, there was silence. Then he heard the door slam and the familiar sound of a lock snapping into place, the same sound as the lockup in the Eureka jail.

He lay in the slime, waiting, but the room remained quiet. They had gone. He was in total darkness. He struggled against a concrete wall to stand on his feet, his toes numb from the water.

"Why you doin' this to me?" he asked, sobbing. Why you lyin' to me, Scully?

The room had the icy dampness of the bilges on an old freighter he had shipped out on in his youth. The odor reminded him of the filthy laundry room stink of the Eureka jail. Attempting to hobble through the icy water, he slipped and fell again.

With the wrist and leg restraints, he had the coordination of a giant, wounded turtle but after a few minutes of shuffling in the water, he found another wall to support himself against, and he was able to stand. He then slid along the rough concrete, using his forehead as a guide.

When he reached a corner, he rested and then repeated the maneuver until he had mapped out three walls. As he continued down the fourth wall, he smacked into a steel folding chair, knocking it over with a loud clatter.

His heart pounded as if he had been jolted with electricity. He waited, expecting the door to open, but the room remained morbidly quiet except for the raspy noise of his breathing and the very faint sound of water rippling against the walls.

Making another attempt, using the same maneuver, he finally made his way around the room. In only a few minutes, he had marked off the entire perimeter, determining that the dimensions were about forty-two feet square and there was nothing else in the room besides the metal chair.

He found the chair again and sitting in the water and using his toes, he manipulated it upright and then labored to his feet again and sat, folding his thick, muscular legs under the steel seat and resting his frozen feet on the little crossbar that held the frame intact.

His thoughts returned to the comfortable bedroom he had been in only moments earlier and the dinner and wine he had been served. He realized that something had gone very wrong. He had offended Scully, and the man must have ordered that he be punished. His life was obviously at extreme risk, but why hadn't Winnie just shot him? What more did they have in mind?

He needed to urinate but could not open the fly on the pajamas. He let go and felt the warm liquid soak his legs. The odor of ammonia mixed with the smell of Cajun sauce wafted up from the floor as his expended liquid mixed with the filthy water. Then his guts rumbled from the heavy meal. "No!" he said, as he tensed the muscles in his abdomen.

He then stood, leaning against the wall, and by sliding his torso up and down several times, he manipulated the heavy, water-soaked pants below his hips. He then braced himself against the wall. Crouching low, inches above the water, he let his bowels go, reflecting on the fragility of his life. When he was finished, he could not maneuver the soaked pants back up above his hips. They dropped around his ankles and rested on the chains.

Soaked, shivering, and inhaling the odors of his own waste, he rested his burning eyes. After a few minutes, he noticed that there was a thin sliver of light coming from what looked like the top of the foundation. It appeared to be at the ceiling level of the basement room. He at least then was able to determine that it was daylight outside. The night was over.

His lungs were hungry for fresh air. By maneuvering the chair with his feet, he was able to get it under the slit. Then, kneeling onto the smooth metal seat of the chair, he attempted to snake his hips into a position that would enable him to stand on the chair.

"Sonofabitch!" he yelled, as he fell into the water, painfully slamming his hip on the concrete floor. Immediately aware that he was lying in his own urine and feces, he rolled onto his stomach and crawled to the wall, where he was able to stand, again using the wall as support. Back on his feet, dripping with the stench of sewage, he blubbered in the darkness.

"They gonna kill you, Sowles. You a dead man."

His mind raced with images of what death would be.

Hobbling and shuffling, he found the chair again and sat, breathing the rancid odor of his own feces. "You a buck naked nigga in yo' own shit, 'zactly where they wants you, an' they gonna kill you, brother. They gonna kill you same as they killed all the people's Black asses."

Visions of Oscar Grant's murder on the BART platform four miles from his mother's house in Oakland flashed through his mind, and then he remembered the twisted, agonized face of George Floyd in Minnesota as he begged to be allowed to breathe, and finally, the TV images, stills, and internet photos of other beaten or murdered African Americans over the past two centuries.

"What is this world you made? Is this what a Black man was made fo'?" he asked aloud.

His heart pounded as he remembered the black-and-white 1960s television faces of Medgar Evers, Sam Cooke, Malcolm X, Martin Luther King Jr.—all men of meaning and purpose, deceased, murdered. But he was a man of no meaning, no real dedication. There would be no celebrations, no photographs or documentaries about Noah Sowles.

His chin resting on his upper torso, he drifted in and out of what felt like a wide-awake attempt at sleep. After what seemed to be only minutes, he heard the lock rattle on the steel door. His spine stiffened as the door opened revealing a wedge of dim red light from the stairwell. Uncomfortable by his nakedness and filth, he stood, expecting to be confronted by the two men, but was humiliated to discover Mary and another woman. Mary referred to her as Erika, and she too was young and attractive, a stout, curvy blonde who looked Scandinavian with two thickly braided, childlike pigtails. Immediately Sowles was further cowed when he realized that both women wore black rubber industrial aprons and elbow-length gloves, and Mary had an automatic pistol pointed at his chest.

Sowles then recognized that Erika was likely the mother of the young girl who had been in the dining room. The boy might belong to Anna. Sowles then knew fully that Scully was far removed from normal civilization and its mores. Sowles further understood that realization alone confirmed the abnormal peril he was facing.

With his pants wrapped around the leg chains, still bound at his wrists, soaking wet, smelling like a barnyard hog, and half-clad with his genitals exposed, the two women wrestled him up the stairs and then pulled him down the hallway through a door that led outside to a concrete pad where it was cool and shady. Immediately he began shivering and quaking as if he was dying of pneumonia

Threatening him with her pistol, Mary forced him to his knees, while Erika ripped off his pajama top. They then circled him, keenly examining his naked body as if he was on display. Mary then hosed him down with high-pressure, cold water. It beat against his shivering body and splashed onto the pavement, draining into a scupper that seemed made for just that purpose.

"Why are you people doin' this to me?" he asked. "I ain't done nothin' wrong!"

"Quit actin' the maggot, ya Black fool!" Mary yelled.

"Stop!" he yelled. "Please!"

"We're cleanin' the filth offa ya!" Mary said. "Naw, open your arse cheeks and let's get that mess outta there!" she said, cackling with laughter as she increased the pressure and aimed the heavy stream of water directly at his exposed backside and genitals.

"Do you think he's had enough?" Erika asked, as he screamed in pain.

"What are ya, a nigga lover naw, are ya?" Mary said. "Feck naw, 'e ain't hed 'nuff!'"

Erika turned away and walked toward the door that led to the house.

"Come back 'ere an' do yar duty,' Mary said. "Or I'll have yar pretty little arse under the hose with 'im!" Erika ignored her. Mary yelled again. "You'll be primpin' in a labor camp by tomorrow, ya Swedish cunt!"

Mary then continued to hose Sowles for several more minutes before she was interrupted by a strong arm around her neck that pulled her to the pavement. It was Anna. "You're not supposed to kill him!" she said. She spun the circular handle that shut the gate valve and stopped the water. "In the house, woman!" she said to Mary.

Mary glared at her as she labored to stand up and headed toward the large home. Anna helped Sowles to his feet and threw a heavy blanket around his quaking body. She then guided him back inside. He stumbled down the hallway into the same examination room where she had first attended to his wound. She grabbed a handful of large towels and began drying him.

"Sit, Mr. Sowles," Anna said. "Can I trust you?" she asked.

"I never did cause no trouble fo' y'all," he said as he tried in vain to control his shaking body.

She reached into a cabinet and poured him a small glass of whiskey.

"I don't drink whiskey...my father...," Sowles said.

"It's good stuff," she said, as she cut the zip ties and removed the leg irons.

Sowles drank the brown liquid and began to calm down. "Why are they doin' this to me?"

"I told you, he doesn't want any opposition. This is Doctor Scully's world. You are his captive, and either you conform to his demands, or he will torment you until it destroys you. While he's doing it, he'll have you believing that he is helping you."

"I seen that. But why me? Why? Tell me, please, tell me," he said, trying to prevent himself from sobbing.

"He has his agenda. It's who he is. I can't explain it all, but let me try to make this simple. Just agree with him, and it will get easier."

"He's like a slaveholder! I can't!"

"We all said we couldn't," Anna said. "But be advised, Doctor Scully does not allow the word *can't*. He will punish you for saying *can't*."

Sowles asked for another shot of whiskey. Anna poured.

"Mr. Sowles, I'm telling you, make it easy on yourself," she said. "Agree with him." She then gathered him together under a fresh blanket and walked him back down the hallway. When they reached the room, she told him to shower and rest.

"When Doctor Scully is ready to see you again, someone will bring your clothing," she said. "Be cautious with him, please. He is capable of anything."

"Why are you helpin' me now?" he asked.

She ignored the question and without showing any emotion or facial response, she pulled the door shut from the outside and locked it.

# Fourteen

## PINCHES PUERCOS

"No way! You gots the whole story wrong."

Rudy Mendoza shook his head. He was a fortyish, prematurely graying and weary-looking Latino, but with a sharp, touched-up, black Fu Manchu. He sat at a cramped desk inside a shabby office trailer. Standing across from him were two uniformed Oakland PD officers—a young blonde man, Patrolman LeFebvre, and a young Latina woman, Sergeant Reyes.

"Sowles is my main boy. That's his rig. He didn't stole no truck," Rudy said to Reyes.

"What do you mean, 'your main boy'?" Reyes asked. "According to DMV records, Sowles is about seventy years of age, isn't he?"

Rudy saw that Reyes was all business. *Cold as a witch's tit*, he thought. "Sowles be my main man, I mean, that's what I'm talkin' 'bout," Rudy said. "I mean like, Sowles been here for a lotta years, man. He's good peoples."

"Then why are we here, Mr. Mendoza?"

"The dude was s'posed t' get a load but he ain't been in touch; that's all," Rudy said. "That ain't like Sowles."

"And you called in and suggested criminal activity?" Reyes asked.

"What criminal activity? No, man. I ain't said that."

"Our call records indicate grand theft auto."

"What 'grand theft auto'? I didn't say my Subaru WRX was missin'," Rudy said.

He leaned forward and put his head on his desk. "I tole you, that's his rig...his rig, I said. I mean, his truck an' trailer. I mean, the dude's straight up."

"Then it could be conversion of bank owned property, fraud, maybe," she said looking at Lefebvre. "There are lenders involved and insurance companies.

"And the load contents," Lefebvre said, nodding.

Reyes didn't respond to Lefebvre. Instead, she focused her dark eyes on Rudy. "I think maybe you know something, Mr. Mendoza."

"Why you cappin' on me, *hermana*? I ain't done nothin'. I'm just tryin to find Sowles, I'm saying, we real shorthanded," he said.

"Relax, Mr. Mendoza." LeFebvre said. "You ever been arrested, sir?" he asked.

"Oh, so now I'm 'sir,' and here we go round the rosies with some arrested boolshit," Rudy said, but then he hesitated before he continued speaking. "Once or twice, nothing big. I done county time for weed back in the day, but it wasn't nothing, just some homegrown."

"Sales and distribution," LeFebvre said looking at Reyes.

"Uh, huh," she said. "We are here to find Mr. Sowles," she said to both men.

"Yeah?" Rudy asked. "So why you tryin' to bag me then?" He scanned both their faces.

"You're not under arrest, Mr. Mendoza," Reyes said.

"We need information," Le Febvre said.

"Yeah, right...I tol' you, Sowles is cool. He's number one, okay?"

Rudy stared off in the distance at a photo on the wall of Sowles and him leaning against Sowles' truck. "I can give him my wallet. He give you the shirt offa his back."

"Let's talk further about the vehicles in question, Mr. Mendoza," Reyes said.

"Vehicles? You mean the truck or the reefer trailer?" Rudy asked. "I mean the truck is a vehicle, right? An' the trailer is a trailer, eh? Why you call that a vehicle?"

"Both are vehicles, Mr. Mendoza. Do you have any financial interest in those units, Mr. Mendoza?" Reyes asked.

"Me? Hell no. I mean, I ain't got no money for that stuff. I'm just the dispatcher."

"How long you been with the company, Rudy?" LeFebvre asked.

"Me? Ten years."

"And Sowles?"

"Longer than me. I dunno. I don' read no personnel files. Ain't my job. Maybe he's here for fifteen years or more. The dude used t' live down the street, man. I mean East 23$^{rd}$, maybe a few miles from the yard. He's ol' school, bro."

Reyes stared at Rudy. "Are you invested in this company, Mr. Mendoza?"

Rudy chuckled. "I tole you already, I ain't got no cash. The owners are from India. Mannie Patel, he's the boss. He's over there now, somewhere, doin' his thing." Rudy looked outside his tiny office window. "You see them two rigs there?"

LeFebvre looked. In the distance was a gravel lot with two older big rigs and trailers.

"We haul a lotta stuff," Rudy said. "That's all we got to work with now, them two. Nobody gettin' rich. We need Sowles and his truck and trailer."

"That's why we're here, Mr. Mendoza," Reyes said.

"Don't sound like that to me. Sound more like you tryin' to pop me and Sowles for some game," Rudy said. "I mean, ain't that what you cops do, bustin' black and brown peoples?"

"I'm Mexican-American, Mr. Mendoza," Reyes said. Her face flushed.

Rudy looked into her eyes. "What about him?" he asked, motioning to LeFebvre.

"We just do our jobs, pal," LeFebvre said.

"Then jus' fin' the dude!" Rudy said "I don't wanna hear no cop talk. Sowles wouldn't pull no prank, man. The dude's for real. You got the license number, so go about your biz. Do whatever it is you do, put out an APB, call the CHP, get the FBI. Jus' fin' Sowles! He ain't stole his own rig, an' he ain't doin' none a what you tryin' to be sayin', man."

"Please calm down, Mr. Mendoza," Reyes said.

"The dude's gone," Rudy said. "He might be crashed down some damn mountain while you here givin' me a hard time with some grand theft auto boolshit and some insurance companies, and fraud, like we was onto something, some kinda caper or some shit."

"So, you're certain that the GPS systems on the two vehicles are disabled. Did Sowles disable them?" LeFebvre asked.

"Sowles an' me ain't rocket scientists, Holmes. We don' under-stand that shit," Rudy said.

"What do you mean, 'me,' Mr. Mendoza?" Reyes asked. "You said, 'me,' when referring to dismantling the GPS systems."

"There you go again s'pectin' me a some boolshit. I jus' mean, we ain't got trained in electronics. We're drivers…truckers, we slow at that shit. Sowles can't hardly use an iPhone."

"I'm glad you brought that up," LeFebvre said. "You stated earlier that the last cell phone conversation with Sowles was when he was in the Eureka area." LeFebvre looked at Reyes. "The provider stated that the mobile device pinged two towers near the Eureka coast and then one in the Fortuna area before it went down," he said to Reyes.

Reyes's face was blank. "I'm aware of that, Officer LeFebvre," she said.

Rudy and LeFebvre exchanged quick glances.

Reyes cinched up her big belt and turned toward the door. "We'll be moving this upstairs, Mr. Mendoza. Someone from our investiga-tive division will want to ask you further questions."

"Do I need a lawyer?" Rudy asked, straight-faced.

"You tell me, Mr. Mendoza. Do you?" She walked down the rickety wooden steps of the trailer into a yard full of paper, cardboard, and junk metal engine parts. LeFebvre followed.

Rudy stood and ran out the door. "Wait! There's somethin' else," he said.

Both officers turned around. LeFebvre took out a notepad and a pencil. Reyes tapped her service weapon. Rudy shuffled on his feet like an embarrassed boxer who had been caught with a light jab. "Sowles was s'posed t' get a beer load, you know, custom beer, or some craft beer they call it, and some ale...heavy load, big weight, chilled, high-dollar load, good coin, you know?"

Reyes cinched up her belt a second time. "All the more reason he might take the trailer, eh, Rudy? That beer was worth what, a hundred thousand dollars? Good score, I'd say. Did you plan the load for him, Rudy?"

"No! I mean yes, but you ain't gettin' what I'm sayin'! He didn't picked it up."

LeFebvre looked at Reyes. She nodded very slightly.

Rudy seemed more relaxed. "The shipper called me," he said. "He was pissed off 'cuz Sowles ain't picked it up in Ukiah. So, check it out, if he was gonna pull some shit, he'd a taken the beer load, right? I mean anyone would, right?"

"Not anyone," she said. "Thank you, Mr. Mendoza."

The two cops opened the doors of the black-and-white. Removing their batons, they prepared to get inside. Rudy approached them again.

"Sowles be writin' a book about trucking," he said.

"How is that relevant, Mr. Mendoza?" Reyes asked.

"I'm just trying to say, you know, maybe some people got to him, you know, like 'cuz the book, it says some stuff, 'bout trucking, you know, like not cool stuff? People don' like that shit."

"We'll be in touch," Reyes said, as she and LeFebvre got in the car, slamming the doors.

Rudy watched them as they pulled out of the lot onto Howard Street.

"*Pinches puercos*," he said, as he turned and walked up the steps.

Back at his desk, he punched a number on his mobile phone.

A robotic female voice came out of the little device: "You have reached 510-339-4145. Please leave a message at the tone."

"Holmes, man, I don' know where you at, but I called you bro, a hundred times…the cops, they out and about. We all lookin' for you, bro…call me if you get this message. No worries. We just want you back, you know, safe an' sound." He slammed the phone on his desk.

Disoriented and unbalanced, as if he had been drinking heavily, Sowles had to lean against the wall of the granite shower enclosure to avoid collapsing. After ten minutes of the steaming shower, he climbed into the relative safety of the king-sized bed. He felt like a child huddled under the blankets, remembering that when he was a boy, he would pretend that his bed was a warm boat and the entire bedroom and world surrounding it was a frigid ocean.

He was not fully able to process whether the horror he had experienced the night before, and whether the shame of being naked and hosed down by the two women was real and had actually happened, or if it had been a dream or illusion that was slowly leading him into madness.

He had seen his share of documentaries on concentration camps, and his father had spoken of other atrocities committed by the nation's enemies, and, as was true with most Americans, he was aware of US torture tactics in the Middle East and at Guantanamo, but to think that he was the prisoner of unhinged white people was beyond his reason and had him doubting his own reality.

He fell asleep quickly in the security of the afternoon daylight and slept soundly, but as the night ensued, he tossed and turned until a few hours before dawn in anticipation of another horrifying middle-of-the-night battering. Finally, he gave up the idea of sleeping and paced the room until the sun rose. Only when morning broke was he able to catch an hour of sleep before he heard the sound of the door unlocking.

Mary and Erika entered the room. They both looked refreshed in clean, pressed, forest camos, with their boots shined and bloused as if they were planned for a conference with the commanding general of a US Army facility. Mary had a wrapped package under one arm. "Put these on yer arse," she said. "Doctor Scully is waitin' far ya."

Sowles silently nodded, as he took the package and waited for the women to leave the room as they had done the previous time that they had brought him clothing.

"You'll be dressin' yer Black hind end in front of us, now, boyo," Mary said, her voice cold. "And, be sure, any a yer foolhardy harseshite will get you down the steps ag'in," she said.

He nodded and whispered, "Yes, ma'am," as he opened the package and saw a standard issue blue denim prison outfit consisting of baggy pants, a matching, thin, loose-fitting jacket, and a pair of flat, rubber sole, slip-on sneakers; there was no underwear or socks.

"It's prison gear," he said.

"Ya betcha! Naw, get crackin'," Mary said.

Sowles dressed quickly. The women did not restrain his wrists. They took him out of the room, locking the door behind. They quickly escorted him down the hallway, where an old song from his youth was penetrating the corridor and walls. He couldn't place who it was—some famous white boy group from the sixties when he had been in high school with Sheylinn. The lead singer's voice was melancholy but determined. He was singing about riding on a storm and something about being born. Immediately Sowles thought about Reverend Persons' admonitions about becoming born again.

A fireplace roared inside the dining room. Scully was already waiting at the head of the table. His eyes closed, he was intently listening and rhythmically nodding and tapping the table.

"Do you remember The Doors, Noah?"

"I heard a 'em," Sowles said.

Scully laughed. "I find that song applicable to your circumstance," he said.

Sowles didn't respond. He could see that his silence irritated Scully.

"Yes, you're in a bit of a storm," Scully said.

"Your storm, Scully," Sowles said.

Scully ignored him, smiling to himself. "Yes, maybe, but circling back to Jim Morrison. I knew him well. He was such a volatile fellow, strong-willed, yet such a gifted poet. A lot like you."

Sowles remained quiet, observing Scully intently, anticipating his moves.

"I just can't say enough about Jim. I worked with him…a pleasure, really, even his death—and the flowers!"

As Sowles watched Scully, his youthful appearance and sparkling blue eyes seemed to have been replaced by a sharp jaw, a bulky-looking forehead, and an emotionless, blue stare. With the exception of his outlandish hairstyle, his face resembled the typical, angry white men seen in so many old news reports of the 1960s Southern states' racial crises.

"Sit, Noah," Scully said. He waved Erika out of the room. Mary stood by.

Sowles obeyed, sitting at the center of the table, to the left side of Scully. Scully folded his hands and stared into Noah's eyes. "You have an eye allergy."

"How you know?" Sowles asked.

"I know," Scully said, brushing off the question. "As you are undoubtedly now aware, we are not pleased at present, and I am not certain how we are going to resolve our dissatisfaction."

Sowles was puzzled by Scully's statements. "Y'all not pleased? What I done?" he asked.

Scully chuckled and looked at Mary. She smiled. Sowles avoided her stare and turned his attention back to Scully. "Y'all white people beat my head, kick my ass, threaten to kill me, y'all holdin' me prisoner, and torturin' me, and y'all ain't pleased? That's some booshit, there, fo' real!"

"Noah, please put your displeasure in the past for the moment. I must say, I had hoped you would find your suite and our cuisine enjoyable and discern from our dinner conversation that I have a purpose for you, and therein you would indicate a willingness and motivation to discuss this purpose. I might add, again, a purpose that will make you rich in your near future."

"My near future? I ain't on a damned job interview."

"Please, Noah."

"How you gonna discuss a plan fo' my future? How you talkin' 'bout my future when you got me in yo' prison?"

"Your future can be anything you choose, but first you must accept that you are here."

"Damn right, I'm here! Why?" Sowles said. "Why am here in yo' prison?"

"Why, you ask, Noah?" Scully laughed. "There is no 'why' anymore, there is only 'now' and 'is,' Noah."

"What's that booshit you talkin', Scully? 'Now' and 'is' what?"

"Time and space, Noah. You are not in your truck. Not in your mother's little wooden house in Oakland. It's not 1975 and you're not driving to K-Mart in your classic red Volvo. No, my friend you are here, now. You are here, with me, now. That is all that matters, Noah...not 'why,' but here and now. It's the 'what is,' my friend."

"You talkin' shit, Scully, pure-ass, foolish, booshit, white-boy talk."

Scully's laughter echoed in the large dining room. "I love how you American Negroes converse," he said. "Your slang, your vernacular. Yes. It is so much fun! But I suggest that you eliminate those Ebonics, get rid of them, they racially stereotype you as much less of a man than you really are."

"How do you know so much about my life?" Sowles asked.

"You should know the answer to that question, Noah." Scully said, still chuckling. "By the way, the book?"

"What book?" Sowles asked.

"Your novel. The one you are writing."

"I ain't got no novel. Y'all got me confused with some other nigga. I ain't wrote no story."

Scully smiled. "Did I not remind you that knowledge begets power?"

"Yeah, man, so what?"

"It is my business to know things. You can know things, too, Noah, lots of things—I can teach you everything, in fact, including how to write a bestseller."

"I don' know what you're talkin' 'bout, some novel shit. All's I wants t' know is why inna hell you keepin' me inna prison like a Black-ass slave you got off some damned auction block?"

"This is not prison." Scully frowned. "You are free to go."

"How man? How do I go? You got my ass locked up!"

"You die, Noah. Then you will be free."

"You crazy, Scully. You a sick, wicked, twisted man."

"Noah, I am not. I am your friend, if you come with me, join me."

"Come where?"

"Come with me. Join me. Embrace the *now* with me," he said, but then shook his head. "I see you are confused. I am so sorry for your inability to see truth."

"What truth, man? The truth that you callin' the plays, Scully. You causin' me torment!"

Scully again laughed. It was a booming laughter that made his chest heave.

Sowles noticed that Scully seemed to have aged. His face seemed thinner, paler, almost a translucent, milky white, similar to the strange guy in the Peterbilt at the truck stop.

Scully noticed his discomfort. "You just remembered something just now, didn't you?"

"No, I ain't remembered nothin'," Sowles said. He felt a shudder of fear in his back and shoulders.

"As you wish, my friend." Scully smiled. His face again became warm and inviting.

"Certainly, you remember that just recently we had our excellent lobster, yes?" Scully asked. "I told you then that Winston and Aaron brought you to me because they are opportunists, and they thought you'd be useful." He stopped talking and looked penetratingly at Sowles.

"So what?" Sowles said, raising his voice. He stood.

"Back in the seat, blackie," Mary said. She nudged Sowles back into the chair.

Scully continued to sit calmly at the head of the table. He remained silent until Sowles spoke again. "Those two dudes is pure-ass white racists," Sowles said. "What side you on, Scully?"

"I am on your side. Racial discussions do not figure into my plans. All men in my realm of influence have equal opportunity to live or find their release."

"Yo' two punk-ass crackers Winnie an' Aaron see that shit different," Sowles said.

"Winston and Aaron saw opportunity," Scully said. "They know I like opportunity," he said, smiling. "Now, Noah, I understand that you are upset again, but please be aware, I do not wish ill upon you, not even when you are disobedient or disloyal. I want to offer you opportunity first and then a long future of prosperity and love."

"Y'all are tryin' to mess my mind up. Why you doin' this shit tryin' to confuse a man?"

"I want to help you, Noah, and in doing so, together, we will help others. Is that not an equitable cause?"

"You ain't helpin' me. And fo' sho' y'all ain't equitable in yo' cause to enslave a man."

"You are correct. I have no actual rights. I do everything I do, Noah, because I can, and I can because I am."

"Booshit, Scully!" Sowles said. Then he glared at the young man. "Y'all is as crazy as a motherfucker," he said. "What makes you think you can take a man's freedom away?"

"I really am trying to help you, Noah. If only you could see what rewards there can be."

"You can't help me or no man with y'all's prison," Sowles said. He felt the urge to dive across the table and overpower Scully, pound him into pulp.

Mary sensed his impulse and touched her 9mm. Sowles calmed his anger, knowing he would be killed instantly. "You can't hurt people while you say y'all's helpin' 'em!" he said. "You ain't a virtuous man. This some sinful booshit, you doin', Scully.

"Ah, sin, yes…now we talk of man being sinful," Scully said. "Noah, my friend, it does indeed surprise me that you see yourself a victim of sin when you have caused so much pain."

"What I done? I ain't done shit…an' how you know shit 'bout me anyhow?"

Scully laughed. "Let's start with the pain you caused your father and mother."

"Don't you bring my father or my mama into this booshit!"

"Ah, the righteous man speaks. Then let's examine the two abortions with Sheylinn."

"I didn't do that. She did that! I didn't take them babies' lives," Sowles said.

"It's okay if you did. I'm sure it was an operational necessity."

"A what?" Sowles asked. His face was wrinkled with confusion. "What's that mean?"

Scully ignored the question. "How many other women?" Scully asked.

"What? None!"

Scully laughed. "Do the names Ko and Robbie mean anything to you?"

"I don' know what you trippin' 'bout."

"Ko, the Korean prostitute in Inchon Bay. She had a few scars on her face, but she was still quite attractive. Do you remember your liberty in Korea? She did write you several times after you sailed to tell you she was pregnant. Do you still have her little black-and-white Polaroid photos?"

Sowles felt his face become heated. Scully laughed again. "And Robbie, she was where? Rohnert Park, just down the street from the college where Sheylinn attended. Adorable, young, white girl... aborted twice."

Sowles glared. "You ain't got shit fo' proof a that! That was forty or fifty years ago, an' I loved them women."

"Ahh! Love! Another fool for the human concept of love, failed love at that! If you want the love of a woman, you can choose from my many female beauties, but we must first address your cowardice! There's also a lifetime of failure in that record!"

"My cowardice?"

How do you explain that weakness, that inability to respond to the glory of battle and the shedding of the blood of fools? And how did you respond when your father told you that you were a coward?"

"How can you know my father or me, man? Who are you? What gives you the right to make them moral judgments on me? You ain't got shit on me! That war was wrong and illegal, an' they sent Black brothers who had no civil rights except to die fo' the white man's war."

"Ah, Noah, perhaps, yes, so you see, I should gather your people and teach all of you the truth!"

"My people? The truth? What you talkin' 'bout?"

"Your people are all enslaved, but I can free them all." Scully smiled again, his white teeth lighting the room. He rested both of his hands on the arms of the chair in the manner of a king on a throne. "You have been enslaved for centuries and yet, even with your emancipation, you have allowed yourselves to be enslaved to negative memories, your own self-persecution, harassment, and the murders of each other. Where has it all taken you, Noah Sowles?"

Sowles covered his ears. "No more. I don't wanna hear it!"

"Then I shall tell you where: hiding in the galley of a merchant ship with a bunch of lost pirates and then into total isolation inside the cab of a commercial truck for almost fifty years. And you argue with me when I offer you true freedom?"

Sowles looked away. He felt his stomach turn. Scully chuckled like schoolboy. "This is now, Noah, your moment. I can free you from your burdens, your real chains."

"You're a white man who tells black lies. You are a damned livin' lie, Scully, fo' sho'."

Scully laughed. "Perhaps, but what is a lie? Is it not just another truth?"

Sowles didn't answer. He was examining his big hands and the abrasions and cuts on his wrists from the restraints.

"Do you see answers in those two big Black hands?" Scully asked.

Sowles showed Scully his wounded wrists. "It's what your zip ties done."

Scully then lifted his own hands from the chair's arms. He held his palms up toward the ceiling, enabling Sowles to examine his wrists. They both had the identical pattern of scars.

Scully smiled again. "Nothing is as it seems, Noah."

Sowles was flabbergasted. "Y'all got a pile a magic tricks, Scully, but how am I s'posed to accept the pain an' shit y'all puttin' me through?"

"Do you want to use your two big Black hands on me, Noah? Destroy me?"

"Maybe. Y'all torturin' me like I'm in some Gitmo or Afghanistan prison."

"You are not at Abu Ghraib or Guantanamo. I feed you lobster, Noah. I give you a suite to relax in. But be aware, those scars on your hands could be on your back," Scully said. "We have at least one cat-o'-nine-tails in our armory." He looked at Mary. She nodded.

"I don't know 'bout no cats, man. Why you talkin' to me like you's my father?"

Scully stood. "I can be that and much more to you. Now, please stop testing my patience," he said, as he sniffed the air. "Do you smell that scent?" he asked.

"Marijuana," Sowles said. "That's y'all's thing, ain't it?"

"You did understand the video of my town hall meeting! I'm so glad! Yes!"

"I said, I saw it," Sowles said.

"Yes! Excellent, wasn't it?"

"I got the message, Scully. You a dope grower. So what?"

"Yes, and isn't it wonderful that I am!" He sniffed the air again.

"Ain't no big deal, nowadays," Sowles said. "Everybody a player in the game these days, man."

"I love the smell of dope. It's cotton candy to me," Scully said. "I only laugh now at those miserable pink-faced bureaucrats that tried to stop the growth, stop the spirit for so many years."

"Y'all head trippin'!" Sowles said.

"It's no head trip, my friend. Cannabis is the catalyst for taking humankind into a new era of universal, collective consciousness."

"I'm done with this booshit talk, Scully. Jus' lemme go back t' my room!"

"My room," Scully said. "You do like smoke, don't you?" he asked. "Of course, you do! It's the elixir for the rebirth of human-kind. It is the turning point for civilization's new awareness."

"What do you want me to say?" Sowles asked. "That I'm gonna start smokin' yo' weed? I left that life in a doughnut shop in Rohnert Park, California forty years ago. I'm just an old nigga now, a nothin'. I'm barely a damn human bein'."

"You are wrong, Noah. You are useful, valuable. And we have much work to do."

Sowles thought about Anna's advice. "What you really want me to do?" he asked.

"I have all the smoke any man could want. Hundreds of acres. Tens of thousands of pounds. And it never stops growing! With smoke, I want you to help me enlighten the ignorant and foolish."

"So, yo' dudes kidnapped me an' brought me to you so's I can be in yo' weed game?"

"Just agree, Noah. Just say it! Say, 'I agree, Doctor Scully'."

"It ain't feasible" Sowles said. "I ain't yo' best choice. I ain't no good t' y'all, Scully. I got no fight left in me, man! Tell yo' two white boys to kidnap some young dude."

"Aaron and Winston did exactly as I would have done. They saw the vision."

"Vison? There ain't no vision in this fucked up white man's world," Sowles said.

"You are wrong again, Noah, my friend," Scully said. "You choose to see everyone and everything as your enemy. I am here as your best friend."

"That's just pure-ass, booshit, white-boy nonsense talk," Sowles said.

"It is reality. I am reality."

"Look, man, then let's get real then. I ain't no Denzel. Why don't you go snatch him up, at least he could pay you some ransom an' he got some real influence with people."

Scully frowned. "I know Denzel very well. A good actor, but—"

"—you a damned liar," Sowles said. "If you know him, go get his ass fo' yo' plans."

"I can have him here anytime; I'll ask him to autograph a few movie posters, just for you."

"You crazy, man," Sowles said.

"Maybe from the film where he takes the young rookie cop on a romp. That was a wicked hit," Scully said. "I was there for his award." He smiled warmly. "Or would you prefer Samuel L. Jackson's signed headshots?" he asked. "He and I golf in Napa. I can get a hold of him right now."

"Fuck you, Scully! You is ragged-ass crazy! Yo' ass gonna be grass someday. God gonna punish yo' ass. God an' Jesus gonna bring justice, man."

"Enough!" Scully said, banging the tightly clenched knuckles of his right fist on the table. "God?" Scully screamed. "Jesus!" he yelled. "Enough! Get him out of here, Mary. I've had enough of his insolence!"

Mary lunged for Sowles as Scully continued to bang the table. She grabbed her cell phone.

"Code Three," Mary said. "Now boyos."

"Get him out of here, I said! Now!" Scully screamed again as if he was a frightened woman. "God? There is no God!"

Mary yelled into her phone. "You an' yer boyo get yer little white arses in 'ere naw!" she said, and then she put her handgun against Sowles's temple.

"No! Please! No!" Sowles said. "I'm sorry."

Within seconds, Winnie came into the room, with Aaron trailing. "Ya just wouldn't listen, would ya, ya dumb boo?" Winnie said.

Aaron tightened zip ties on his wrists. Sowles shrieked in pain.

Both men then forcibly pulled him out of the room. They struggled down the hallway to the first big door leading to the stairwell. Winnie wrestled it open while Aaron kept his pistol barrel glued to Sowles's ear. One clumsy step at a time, they tried to descend to the second steel entry door, but as Sowles resisted, they finally pushed him down the stairs. He tumbled into a heap at the bottom, moaning as if he was a wounded animal.

Winnie forced the heavy door open and the two men pushed and kicked him until he crawled into the dark cell. Aaron cut his clothes off with the large hunting knife and stripped him naked, and then, surprisingly he cut the wrist restraints.

"Clean your own ass next time!" he said, and the two men exited and shut the door.

Sowles heard the lock slam securely into its resting place, and instantly he felt the menacing, odious atmosphere of the room. It was just a few degrees above freezing, barely enough to keep the three inches of water puddled on the floor from solidifying.

Again, in total darkness, he felt his way around all four walls as the water soaked through his canvas shoes. The air had the same musty smell as before, with the added odor of his own stale urine and shit from the previous night.

"No chair! They took the chair!" he yelled, loud enough that anyone listening could hear as he sloshed across the room, stumbling over a large metal object. Nearly falling in the sewage, he reached down and blindly felt for it in the dark. It was a large, janitor's double bucket on wheels. A heavy, stringy, wooden-handled wet mop was protruding out of the pail.

He grabbed the mop handle and threw it across the room in the direction of the slit of light. It hit the panel with a dull, wet sound. He then picked up the pail, and with the full force of his two-hundred pounds, he threw it at the wall. It bounced off with an earsplitting clatter. He picked it up and threw it a second time. Again, it clanked loudly against the concrete wall.

# *Sixteen*

## A LEAF IN A STORM

Sowles waited, his body shivering both from fear and the freezing water. Staring in the pitch dark at the general area of the door, he expected Aaron and Winnie to come crashing back into the cell. Each second that passed felt like an eternity as he crouched in the fouled water in eerie silence anticipating his death.

It was clear to him that he had pushed Scully as far as he could and that his suspicions were correct. Scully was deranged. Sowles knew that his own life was more at risk at that juncture than at any previous time since he was abducted. He also knew that he had to find a way to escape, regardless of Aaron's warning that he would be shot on sight as a runaway.

The rotten stench inside the room was dissipating and replaced with the recognizable, powerful, sweet fragrance of burning marijuana. Within seconds, he felt the familiar and comfortable lightheadedness associated with the drug. As his senses became more acute from the high, he could hear the very faint sound of rushing air. The fumes were being blown in through a small overhead vent that he quickly realized was part of the building's HVAC system.

Even in the darkness of the room, Sowles was aware that thick smoke was quickly filling the small space. As if the building had been set afire, the temperature in the room rapidly increased and the small space transformed from near frigid into a steam room of dense haze combined with the choking odor of burning marijuana.

Sowles knew that suffocating from breathing clouds of burning cannabis may not be the most sophisticated way of killing him, but any burning material expelled carbon monoxide, and it seemed clear that he was being gassed and asphyxiated with marijuana smoke. His blood cells would soon be deprived of oxygen.

As his breathing became more difficult, he felt as if he was being smothered. Staying alive became all that mattered, and that was strictly a matter of timing—five minutes to an hour.

Flipping the bucket on its mouth, he stood on it, hoping he could find cleaner air closer to the ceiling, but the hot air had blended with the smoke and risen to the highest point in the room. Then, remembering what is taught about escaping burning buildings by crawling on the floor, he realized that his only chance for survival was to get down on his knees and lower his face just inches above the sewage. The air was foul with the stench of his own waste, but at least he was able to breathe.

The few moments of relief were interrupted by a brilliant white light that illuminated the small room as if it was daylight. It came from several tiny, recessed, overhead, high-intensity lamps. It was the first time he had seen the room in any light. All four walls, about four feet above the water level were spattered and filthy with brown stains that he assumed were blood. It was likely that someone before him had been severely beaten or murdered in the room.

In the intensely bright light, he was stunned to see a small, brown-faced man leaning against the wall in the far corner. He was dressed in a white smock and wore pants that appeared to be made with a pattern of very tiny black and white checkers. Greasy, blackish-gray hair fell over his eyes. He smoked a short, unfiltered cigarette butt, spitting tobacco every few seconds.

"Who you?" Sowles asked.

The man cackled as he pointed a small, nicotine-stained hand at Sowles. "You know me. I'm Chief Cook."

"You can't be Chief Cook.

"I Chief Cook and you Third Cook."

"I'm Second Cook and Baker now," Sowles said.

"Second Cook, Third Cook, no matter, you still no good naked nigga," he said. You get off Black, naked ass and mop deck, now! Now! You mop deck, or I tell Captain you no good, crooked nigga, and he put you over side! You go over side of ship!"

The guy was his Filipino chief cook in the early 1970's on the SS Pierce, a barely seaworthy US freighter. The old man had been a horrible, mean racist. He had hated Sowles and had threatened him with the punishment of being thrown overboard. Only Sowles's union delegate had been able to save him from the ongoing harassment by threatening the Chief Cook with a fine.

Sowles stared at the old man for several seconds. "You ain't real!"

The man hooted. "I too real. I very real. Now, you clean deck, or you go inna drink!"

Sowles moved toward him and reached out. "You only in my mind," he said unable to touch the man.

The little man laughed like a drunken jester. "Mop deck, nigga! Now!"

Sowles grabbed the mop. His breath came in short gasps, as he struggled to take in oxygen while mopping in the suffocating air of the room. He swabbed the concrete floor, pushing and smearing the feculence and muck.

"You mop deck mo' bettah!" the little man said. "Deck dirty, you clean good!"

The light snapped off. Simultaneously there was the loud and repeated ringing of a tinny sounding bell similar to the thumb operated bell on Sowles's tricycle when he was a child. The man vanished in the darkness like a roadside shadow.

"Where'd you go, ya Filipino-ass foo'?" Sowles yelled, but his voice was weak.

There were no responses.

"Come back you little bitch!" His lungs felt heavy, as if they had been filled with mud.

After another several dizzying minutes of struggling to fill his lungs with breathable oxygen, the smoke in the room had begun to clear and the air was cooling. He could feel a cold breeze drifting down from the vent. Relieved he turned the bucket over and sat down.

The overhead light flashed on again, but then it immediately went dark again. The bell rang again. The cycle repeated several times: ON. OFF. ON. OFF. ON. OFF. ON. OFF. ON. OFF. Each time the bell rang in unison with the light flashing as if it was part of a carnival scare house. Sowles held his ears and paced the room as though he had become a crazed mental patient.

Then the light stayed on. The Filipino cook was again standing in the corner of the room, smoking and laughing. The voice of Jim Morrison began to flow from somewhere in the ceiling, "Turn out the light, turn out the light." An organ player hammered the keys in the background, while Morrison's voice echoed against the walls. The light went out again.

Sowles froze in the dark as he heard the sound of the door banging open. He backed up into the far corner of the room as Winnie and Aaron stomped into the room. In the available red light from the staircase, he could see that both men were dressed in black rainsuits.

"No!" Sowles yelled as he held his testicles in place with his left hand. Then surprising himself, he pivoted slightly and snapped a clean outside right crescent kick in the air. It caught Winnie solidly on the side of his head near his temple. He went down on his knees in the shitty water. Sowles then kicked him in the face with full frontal kick. Winnie collapsed in the sewage.

"Motherfucker!" Aaron yelled. He pulled his Glock and cold-cocked Sowles in the temple.

Sowles shook the blow off and squared off with Aaron.

The bell then rang again and Aaron pointed the gun at Sowles chest.

"That's it, boy! Freeze! Or you're DOA!" Aaron said.

Winnie had gotten up off the floor and had his Colt drawn. His mouth was bleeding. "Zip-tie the shit-eater," he said, glaring at Sowles. "I'm gonna let Mary have ya now, old Tom."

"And she is pissy and horny!" Aaron said. He grabbed Sowles. "Let's go, Sambo. Time for some Irish dance," he said as he zip-tied Sowles's wrists behind his back. Both men then took a shoulder and elbow and pulled him through the door. On the journey up the stairs, they each had to struggle to pull his dead weight.

"Get the lead out," Aaron said. "Or I'm gonna beat your brains out!"

Stumbling like a spent MMA cage fighter, Sowles coughed and wheezed.

When they finally reached the upper landing, they dragged him through the hallway and out the same door as Mary and the young blonde woman Erika had done the day before. Again, he was outside the building, heading toward the concrete wash pad.

With one swift leg, Winnie swept him to the pavement. He fell on his back, his head smacking hard against the concrete. For just a moment, everything went black, but within seconds he became aware that Aaron was circling him and viciously spraying him with the high-pressure industrial hose. Winnie stood by, watching as if he was a sadistic wrestling referee waiting for a beaten loser to get up from the mat so that his opponent could beat him down again.

Staying committed to the nozzle, Aaron dug his boots into a solid stance. He looked like a fireman dedicated to a blaze as he directed a steady, powerful stream of water, battering Sowles's head and body while spinning him on the concrete.

Gasping for breath and trying to protect his genitals and his face at the same time, Sowles rolled onto his side. In the distance, he could see Mary coming toward them.

"Get his black arse softened up for me!" she said cackling. "I'm gonna shew him the how to and what far."

Aaron continued hosing Sowles. He was diligent, focusing the heavy stream of water directly at his backside and as the pressure spun him like a log, he forced the blast on his chest and face until Sowles rolled again. Then Aaron aimed the full pressure directly at his genitals.

Sowles screamed and tried to protect himself but Aaron followed him with the jet of water continuing for another minute or so while Mary seemed to grow impatient. Sowles was only semiconscious when Mary finally cut the water pressure.

Aaron glared at her. "What the fuck?" he asked.

Winnie interrupted what appeared to be a quarrel in the making. He motioned to Sowles crumpled body. "He's had enough of that game."

"I was just getting started," Aaron said, chuckling to both Winnie and Mary.

"Mary's gonna show him something new," Winnie said.

"Like what, straight-up waterboarding?" Aaron asked.

"Nah," Mary said, laughing. "Gimme me the Black savage. I'm gonna wire brush thet shiny arse real goot." She showed them an antique wooden-handled wire brush used for scraping paint from a ship's hull.

The three of them tried to get Sowles's attention but he appeared unconscious. "Think he's dead?" Aaron asked.

"Naw, 'e ain't done yet, 'e's fakin' et," Mary said. "Lemme 'ave a go at 'im."

Winnie nodded. He and Aaron walked away, leaving Sowles folded on the cement with Mary standing over him holding the brush. Sowles could hear their chuckling in the distance as Mary kicked him a few times. "Time t' get yar black ass inna mood far a cleanin' boyo," she said.

"Please! Tell Doctor Scully that I'll do whatever he wants," Sowles said, as he watched the water drain into the grated opening in the concrete. Then, shivering like a leaf in a storm, he tucked his body into a fetal position and whimpered, but then screamed as Mary began scrubbing his backside grating the thick wire bristles back and forth on his bloody skin. He instinctively protected his genitals as she tried to force the brush between his legs.

"Let me do my work, ya black bastard," she said as Sowles screamed. She scrubbed harder until he became silent. She then stepped back. "I think the lad went out on me," she said. "How's he gonna appreciate the effort I'm offerin'?" she cackled.

Sowles was breathing in short gasps when he finally opened his eyes and saw Anna standing above him, holding two soft fingers against his neck. "You did this?" she asked Mary who was then circling around Sowles splashing in his watery blood like a hungry predator that had just attacked its next meal.

"Aye, an' what's it to ya?" Mary asked. "It's 'bout time we got serious with the black menace," she said to Anna. "Winnie says the boyo goes straight to the shower. I'll do the 'onors."

"You sick bitch," Anna said. "He needs help," she added, as she covered him with a blanket that quickly became blood soaked. "If nothing else, he needs bandages and ointment, water and a sedative for pain."

"Feck 'im," Mary said. "Lemme 'ave 'im some more."

Then ignoring Mary, Anna patted Sowles's face. "Come on, Mister Sowles," Anna said. "Look alive. You're gonna be alright." She cut the wrist restraints. "You have to get on your feet."

Sowles struggled to his knees. "No, more please," he mumbled. "They're gonna kill me," he said.

"You're not gonna die today, Mr. Sowles," Anna said, turning to Mary. "You're not taking him, either. You will help me get him back into the room, or I promise you, I will beat your Irish ass into next Tuesday."

Mary laughed defiantly but didn't argue any further. She grabbed a shoulder, while Anna secured the blanket around him and got him to stand. They both walked him into the house and down the hallway into the bedroom suite and maneuvered him into the large granite shower.

He was bleeding from several eight-inch abrasions on his buttocks. Anna turned on the water very softly and adjusted the temperature.

"Make it steamin', lass! Don't waste a good feckin' moment a crisis," Mary said.

"I know you heard me, woman. I won't repeat myself," Anna said.

"No more, please!" Sowles said, flailing. He collapsed onto the granite floor nearly breaking the glass doors.

"I can't lift him," Anna said. He was unable to stand, even with Anna holding his arms.

"I'm gettin' the lads," Mary said. She stomped toward the door.

"No!" Anna was on her feet. Grabbing her own wrist with her opposite hand, she formed an arm bar and pushed against Mary's neck, driving her into a wall.

"I will dance on your grave," Anna said as she mashed her arm against Mary's throat, forcing the trapped woman to struggle for breath. "There, there my little freckled missy," Anna said softly. "How does suffocation feel, darling?"

Then Anna yanked Mary's handgun from her holster and stuffed it in her own belt. She then dropped Mary to the floor. "I warned you, bitch," she said, putting the pistol to the weakened woman's forehead. "Now, you have one choice; when the men come back, you tell them you were having hot flashes and needed rest."

"You're a damned nigger lover far shar," Mary said. "En a half-breed cunt."

"Maybe so, but I am also the nigger loving, half-breed cunt who will cut your heart out and eat it," Anna said. "If you don't follow my requests, I'm gonna hurt you badly and then I'm gonna kill you."

"Doctor Scully is prob'ly gonna kill this bugger anyway," Mary said. "So, what's the big feckin' difference if he goes to hes maker now or later? Why d' ya care?"

"He will not be abused any further!" Anna said. "Not in front of me. He's had enough. I will not bear the moral accountability of him being murdered as I stand by. So, you're gonna shut your Coleen face and get him bandages, ointment and clothes. You have five seconds to move!"

"So, the game has changed, I'm seein'," Mary said as she scuttled out of the room.

Sowles had opened his eyes but was on his side on the shower floor in a heap of his own legs and arms watching his own blood wash down the drain.

"Can you hear me, Mr. Sowles?" Anna asked.

"Uh-huh," he said, whispering almost inaudibly.

"Okay. We have to get you cleaned up."

"No, please. I can't. No."

"I told you, we are not allowed to say 'no' or 'can't'!" She helped him grab the safety bar in the shower, assisted him onto his feet, and then gently rinsed his abrasions. She winced at the damage that the brush had caused to his back and the soft flesh of his gluts. "I'm so sorry, Mr. Sowles, but you have to hurry now," she said and handed him fresh white towels. "Put them up against the wounds you can reach," she said as she turned away to allow him privacy.

"Okay," Sowles said. "I'm so much in pain."

"I know," Anna said.

After a few more minutes, Mary entered the room with a few small pads of gauze, a spent tube of ointment and a roll of adhesive tape no larger than a twenty-five-cent piece. She tossed the items onto the floor of the bathroom. "Get yerself crackin' on that there, you two sweethearts! Knock yerselves out!" she said, laughing.

Sowles carefully patted the ointment on the areas he was able to reach. Anna helped him with his back while Mary stared at them both in disbelief. She chuckled nervously as she glanced behind at the door of the bedroom suite.

Aaron and Winnie surprised all three of them as they unexpectedly entered the room. "Get a towel around that bloody sonofabitch," Winnie said. "Then get him dressed in this!" He tossed a rumpled, beige-colored garment in Anna's direction.

Anna glared at Mary. "You heard him, get a towel."

Mary angrily tossed a towel in Sowles's direction.

"What's been takin' so long?" Winnie asked Anna.

"He's a big man," Anna said. A lot of blood from the wounds…
he's suffering, and Mary's been feeling a little ill, but I believe all has
been secured." She glared at Mary.

"Ya sick, Mary?" Winnie asked. "Too bad. Look alive. Where's
your weapon?" he asked.

"It was having some problem with the slide. Jammed, I guess,"
Anna said before Mary could respond.

Winnie nodded. "Lemme see it." He motioned to Anna.

"I fixed it for her," Anna said, and she handed the gun to Winnie.
"It's good to go now."

"I'll have a look at it," Winnie said, stuffing the pistol in his belt.

Aaron noticed that Anna and Mary made angry eye contact. "You
two girls fightin' over the big Black man?" he asked and then laughed.

"Don't start, Aaron," Winnie said. "We gotta get movin'. Doctor
Scully wants him fully bandaged and then dressed in that official
tunic and prepared for a formal hearing in the big room!"

Aaron laughed. "Yeah, yeah," he said as he glared at Sowles. "Get
your Black ass in gear and put your nighty on!"

Everyone except Anna was entertained as they watched both
Sowles and Anna dry his big frame and struggle to bandage his
wounds without causing him further pain. With Anna's help, he then
cautiously slipped into the long, earth-colored sackcloth gown.

When Winnie saw that Sowles was covered, he told Mary and
Anna to zip-tie his wrists. They hurriedly followed his directions, but
Winnie's face was wrinkled with anger. "All of you, heads up. Get
him in the Big Room immediately," he said. "Doctor Scully is having
a meltdown!"

"Sowles needs a real doctor and proper bandaging, and food and
water," Anna said.

"Too bad! That black bastard is lucky he got this far," Winnie said.

# Seventeen

## DETERMINATION

While Winnie raced ahead, Aaron and the women directed the half conscious, stumbling Sowles down the familiar, carpeted hallway, first into an unusual dark section of the massive home, and then inside a poorly lighted wide concrete stairwell. The passage took them down, deep under the building and into an unpainted, cement corridor big enough for vehicles to drive through. Sowles thought it resembled photos he'd seen of a Nazi military bunker or maybe an underground railway in some big city airport.

A long passageway finally led to a convention room about the size of a decent sized dance hall, except it was fully carpeted in an elegant red wool. Sowles thought that it could have been the same room that Scully had filmed his town meeting in, except instead of being set up with auditorium seating there was a group of tall stage lights that sat in the exact center, illuminating a single spot on the floor as if it had been prepared for a night club act.

In the spotlight was a single metal folding chair like the one in the dungeon. Scully sat directly opposite about ten feet away in a stylish, large, cushioned, black leather armchair. He was wearing an antiquated-looking red robe that matched the carpet color. It was open at the neck. Underneath, Sowles could see black, stylish business suit with a starched white shirt and a nicely knotted, black cravat.

Surrounding this central point of the room was a circle of twelve very comfortable-looking armchairs that appeared to be about thirty feet from the lighting and placed as if they were in the hour positions of a clock.

As the group brought Sowles stumbling toward Scully, the young man stood up and seemed to back away as if he was intimidated by the big man.

"Seat him in the chair across from me," he said to Aaron.

Aaron pushed Sowles into the chair. Scully smugly observed him from his safe distance as Sowles winced from the pain of his fresh wounds. Only when Sowles was securely seated did Scully then sit and relax. He crossed one leg over the other as if he was the host of a talk-show. Elegantly raising his chin, he smiled casually and motioned to the group with an open hand, palm upward.

"You will find your robes folded in your seats. Each one of you will sit at the ninety-degree points of the circle. I want Winnie in the twelve o'clock position," Scully said.

Everyone tossed black robes around their shoulders. All four sat, appearing rigid and emotionless.

Still unshaven and now very unkempt, Sowles was also clearly depleted from the previous horrors and the abrasions that Mary had inflicted. Dressed in the baggy, partially bloodstained gown, barefooted, with his wrists zip-tied behind his back, he looked pathetic and near death, barely capable of lowering his head and mumbling to himself.

From his chair, Scully examined the four robe-clad adjudicators, nodding as he confirmed that Winnie was at the head of the circle and everyone else had settled in the other three designated spots, with Aaron at the next position on Winnie's left, Anna to his left, and then Mary.

"We shall now proceed," Scully then said.

Sowles glanced up and tried to make eye contact with Anna, but because of the glare of the lighting, he could not see anyone other than Scully.

Scully finally stood and walked around the circle with the cadence and demeanor of a British prosecutor. He offered smiles and made charming eye contact with his four colleagues. Everyone smiled in response but avoided one another's glances. There was an uncomfortable silence in the room for over two minutes until Scully finally spoke.

"I'm aware that we have had some confusion this morning," he said. "But I am pleased to now see that we are all gathered harmoniously. Before we begin the proceedings, I must ask if there is any dissension still remaining among any of you?"

Starting with Winnie, each member responded with a firm "Nay" or "No."

"Excellent," Scully said. He took a fresh breath.

"We are here today to determine a ruling for Noah Calvin Sowles," he said. Then, looking at Sowles, he smiled in his usual fashion.

Sowles didn't look up. "A ruling? For what?" he asked quietly, almost whispering.

"We are ready to reveal that to you, my friend," Scully said, again smiling cordially and bowing as if he was a maître d' inviting Sowles to a table for a luncheon. "I must say, I am disappointed. I had such bigger hopes, but it is now the moment for your determination."

"My determination? What do that mean?" Sowles asked, speaking into the blinding glare of the great lights. "You got some kinda court here, an' now you gonna punish me more?"

"This is not a court. The panel is not a jury to determine a verdict. Neither will a verdict be issued. A judgment has already been decided. We are here to determine how to proceed."

"Then what y'all call it if it ain't a court?" Sowles asked squirming from the physical pain.

"Because you are here in the room, it has already been determined that you are accountable for a breach. In essence, a guilty verdict already exists. It will be the comments or testimony of the four witnesses that will determine your sentence."

"Whachu mean, guilty an' a sentence?" Sowles asked. "I ain't done nothin'."

"Silence. You will soon understand," Scully said.

"I ain't been charged with nothin', no crime, nothin'. I'm here because y'all kidnapped me and I questioned y'all 'bout it...but you already locked me in yo' prison cell, beat my ass, an' tried to kill me. Ain't that enough? Why you gonna sentence me when I ain't done nothin'? It's 'cuz I'm Black! That's it! Ain't it?"

"No, this is not a race-based matter. As I've said, I had a plan for the future that included you, regardless that you are Black. I requested that you join me in my vision," Scully said. "Instead, you have rejected and reviled that vision and insulted me with your arrogance and ignorance."

"So, I disagreed with you, an' that's a crime in y'all's way of thinkin'?"

"As a matter of fact, Noah, yes, it is. You have not honored me. That is your offense."

"Y'all is too much! Don't I get no representation, like a lawyer or somethin'?"

"I am your counsel, Noah."

"I ain't that smart of a man, but leas' I know is y'all can't be my lawyer and be the judge and the prosecutor!"

"It is what it is, Noah, but you are welcome to speak on your own behalf."

"So, leas' tell me how's can I's s'posed t' see yo' vision if I ain't you? Tell me that!"

"I have done all I can for you." Scully shook his head, as if he was a disappointed father.

"What?" Sowles said. "You snatch me offa the highway an' put me inna prison cell, inna damn dirty cellar, beat my ass, and try to suffocate me, an' then have a nasty white woman try to scrub away my Black skin? That's how you done all you can fo' me?"

"I've told you that we have a mission to accomplish. If you were willing and perceptive, you would have already volunteered to join me in my work and saved us these time-consuming efforts, but you missed the point, my purposes, and you resisted my vision with your challenges and defensiveness. It has all become so clear," Scully said, looking at the four observers.

"Now you're gonna kill me?" Sowles asked. "Murder me, when I ain't done nothin'?"

"Now, I must admit that you are not as useful as Winnie and Aaron assumed."

"But I'm a good person. I don' deserve to die fo' nothin'."

"Perhaps, Noah, but 'good' is relative, open to interpretation."

"I don' know what that mean!" Sowles said.

"No human soul is indispensable!" Scully said forcefully. "Even the best, the brightest, and the most talented are replaceable," he said, continuing to walk around the circle.

I jus' know y'all can't kill a man 'cuz he disagrees."

"I'm a man of vision and reason, Noah. I do not kill people. I let them decide when and how they want to release themselves."

"I can't. I ain't choosin' my own death!"

"Noah. I have not used the word 'death.' This is your word choice. You fear the eternal loss of your being."

"Well, if you ain't plannin' on killin' me what is you plannin' on?"

"I did not say that you will not come to an end. I said that I will not kill you."

"Well, I sho' as hell ain't committin' no suicide!"

"Who else would give you that type of freedom of choice? Not your mother's god. He gives life and then takes it back on his schedule, but then in his audacity he will punish you if you do take your own life."

"I don' wanna talk 'bout my mother or her church, or God—none a that!" Sowles said.

"Then we will not discuss that subject further. I am not unreasonable, Noah."

"Unreasonable? You talkin' bout unreasonable! This whole booshit is unreasonable. There ain't no reason fo' yo' whole game, fo' lyin' t' me an' fo' puttin' me in yo' dungeon."

"You make me out to be very unfair, Noah."

"Y'all is sayin' you ain't unfair, jus' 'cuz, you's the great Doctor Scully, you's the man, you's the man everyone believes in, but y'all is very unfair and unreasonable."

"Your statement does not feel to me that you're trying to flatter me," Scully said.

"Them ain't meant to be kind words to flatter y'all. They's truthful words, Scully. Y'all got the power, man, to be fair, to be kind, or to be wicked, but y'all choosin' t' be wicked!"

Aaron stood. "Do you want me to remove him, Doctor Scully?"

"No, Aaron, thank you. We will let Noah have his freedom of speech that you Americans so love to boast of," Scully said. "You may continue speaking on your own behalf, Noah."

"I said most a my piece, but maybe I gots more t' say—'cept for some lobster and a nice room, all's I seen is wickedness come outta you, man."

"Perhaps, Noah. Many do consider me to be a very flawed being, but that is irrelevant. We must now make decisions and a determination about you, Noah, not about me."

"What decisions and determination are y'all talkin' 'bout?" Sowles said, as he slumped further in the chair like a sack of potatoes. "Y'all oughta know you can't just take a Black man fo' no reason an' then beat his ass, an' kill him 'cuz he don' like bein' snatched!"

"I will allow you a few minutes to calm yourself and regain your strength, but we do not have eternity to finalize your determination."

"I don' need no rest," Sowles said. "You gonna kill me? Right? Ain't that the plan?"

Scully didn't answer. The four observers fidgeted. Finally, Sowles spoke forcefully.

"I sees what you got here, all folks who be oppressed or forgotten; an Irish woman who's fulla jealousy an' ancient evil, a lost soldier who can't get over the wars he fought, an Indian woman from some tribe that was destroyed, and some old movie actor wrestler who done lost too many fights. I sees all of it, an' I sees now, you want an ole, lost nigga."

"Ah, Noah. I chose you for your insight. You are perceptive," Scully said. "But look again. How do you know the people you mention are even real? Maybe they are part of your story, your imagination. That novel you hide from the world."

"I tole you, man, that novel ain't mine. It ain't me."

"I think you're confused, Noah," Scully said.

"No. I ain't confused."

"Yes, Noah. You are. I ask you again, what makes you think this is even real?"

"It's real, Scully. Your people here, on the road, all of it. It's all real. I heard their racist words. I feel the pain. I wallowed in my own shit. I seen my blood on the concrete. I felt the brush that woman took t' me. I saw how the folks loved you at that meetin' you had onna TV," Sowles said. "Hundreds a them. They were real. This shit is real.

"I'm going to ask you a serious question, then Noah," Scully said.

"What?" Sowles responded.

"So what?" Scully said and he began laughing hysterically until he coughed.

"What you mean, 'so what'?" Sowles asked.

"I mean, so what if you think this is real or unreal? Your fantasy mind matters not. You are here, now, and it is what it is, my friend, real, unreal, none of those concepts now matter. I've said before you are not somewhere else. You are here, now, with me and it is what it is, or so it seems."

"You talk in circles, man," Sowles said. "So gimme another chance," Sowles said. "That can be another 'it is what it is', right?"

"Chance!" Scully said. "Oh, how we love 'chance'. The game of chance, the chance for romance. 'Chance,' such a strange word," Scully said. "What you mean, Noah, is take a further risk with you. You don't want me to give you a chance. You want me to take a chance."

"Fuck that circle talk. I know you can gimme another chance or take another chance, 'cuz you is you, I mean, you is the great leader a people, an' the man a great 'telligence, an' that makes you capable a givin' or takin' chances."

"But you've had so many chances, several, Noah."

"Yes. But what was them chances? Damn crawfish an' some white wine fo' a dumb nigga? Y'all know a nigga don' really get no real chances, no real big choices, Scully. I am a nigga, a coon, a jiga-boo. I am the foo' of y'all's white culture. I am a nothin'. I needs a real chance."

"I've tried to tell you that very thing…yet you continue to demean your skin color. I do not see color, Noah. There is no color in my life, no rainbows, no purple hearts, no red blood, and no black and white flesh. Everything is what it is.

"Well, that's who I am, man. I mean, it's wha' I am. I'm a Black-skinned man."

"That's no longer an excuse, Noah!"

"I can't change my skin, or how everyone includin' me sees it. I'm a Black man!"

"Noah, please, be calm…did you on several occasions tell Anna and Mary, or Winnie and Aaron that you would do what I asked?"

"Yes," Sowles said. "I did. I damned sure did."

"Then why have you forced my patience and brought us to this determination inquiry?"

"'Cuz, I'm a dumb nigga. I tol' you. Ask Aaron an' Winnie. They'll tell y'all. I'm a dumb coon, a Black bastard, a nigga."

"How can you claim that is why you have not willingly given me your total commitment?"

"I dunno nothin'. I'm a dumb, Black foo'. I always jus' gettin' by bein' the foo', that's all."

"Noah. I chose you! Do not degrade yourself further. It reflects upon me!"

"That's all I knows how to do," Sowles said. "I ain't nothin', I'm jus' a Black foo'.

"I don't accept that as a defense, Noah Sowles."

"Well, accept this, I needs you, Doctor Scully t' make me a better man fo' yo' purpose."

"This is what I've tried to offer you in our lengthy time together."

"What lengthy time? A coupla days?" Sowles asked.

"Oh no, Noah. We have been together longer than a few days… much, much longer."

"I don't understand what you sayin'."

"I'm sorry, Noah. I wish you did."

"I need yo' help!" Sowles said, pleading to the hot lights. "I need you to show me what you want. Teach me, Doctor Scully. Show me all what you want me to learn."

"Noah. I do appreciate your newfound awareness and attempt at humility."

"Then, gimme 'nother chance, Doctor Scully. Please! One more chance!"

"Noah! As long as you have continued to denigrate your own character and project your self-loathing onto me, I've been forced to subject you to discipline that I never wanted. Trust me, Noah. I never wanted to cause you discomfort, but now we are here."

"I'm lost inside my own mind, Doctor Scully," Sowles said. "I never got no education. I don't know nothin'. My mind ain't as good as y'all's. My mind is Black too, remember that."

"Perhaps that's very truthful. But, again, now we must proceed, Noah."

"Proceed to what?" Sowles asked, pleading.

"The now is now. Let me remind you, this is a determination inquiry to decide your fate."

"I reckon y'all have to murder me, 'cuz I ain't gonna commit suicide," Sowles said.

"There will be no murder," Doctor Scully said.

"Suicide is against my beliefs. Killin' me will be yo' crime, not mine."

"The sinful man of self-righteous wisdom speaks a truth!" Scully said. "Your logic is a twisted human response, but insightful, creative," he said, as he walked around the circle and embellished his position with his many gesticulations as if he was a classic stage actor. Sowles was reminded of Reverend Persons's antics and how similar they were.

Sowles stared into the void of the bright lights. "You the man in charge, Doctor Scully. Like the Black brothahs say, 'you's de boss.' You can be fair, Boss man, or you can be unfair, 'cuz you is you. You's the main man."

Scully stared intently at Sowles. "Well, Noah, yes, I am considered a leader," he said softly. "Thank you for finally acknowledging my position."

"It's cool, Doctor Scully," Sowles said.

"It has taken a while for you to do so," Scully said as he paced and the panel of four watched him in anticipation.

Finally, he spoke again. "In an act of objectivity, I will defer to the wisdom of the adjudicatory panel," he said, as he stepped to the outer rim of the circle and looked at each of the four onlookers. "I will welcome any opinions each of you wish to express regarding Noah's determination."

Mary was quick to raise her hand. "I say we jos' get rid a 'is arse, burn 'im up straightaway. It's 'ficient, so it is, an' et ain't no real work far any a' us, en' not but a wee bit a disposal effort."

Scully nodded. "Well, yes, a good hot fire, you're saying."

"Aye," Mary said. "Aye, hot as the fire a' Dublin." She nodded her head in satisfaction.

"Yes," Scully said. "But we would be burning his remains in any case…but point taken. Mary advocates for burning…on wood, for the intense heat, I assume"

"Aye, Doctor Scully. Indeed. A foine ash from stout hardwood'll satisfy the accords of the ancients that matter, en' they'll be good shine upon us then," Mary said.

"Yes," Scully said. He turned toward the others. "Winston? Anna? Aaron?"

Winnie said that he wanted to give Sowles another opportunity, as he had seen potential in him since they first exchanged words on the highway. "He's a strong man, a determined man, but as we see, he is an old man and a self-admitted, ignorant Negro. However, he has discretion. I believe he can be valuable. Reeducation is very likely in order, training, of course, and the like."

"Excellent, Winston," Scully said. "I thank you for that insight."

"You're welcome, sir," Winnie said.

Scully raised a finger as an afterthought. "But, Winston, Noah assaulted you as you oversaw his reconditioning, did he not? And yet, you still would elect to give him further quarter?"

"Yes, because he's a fighter and a survivor, a good man to have on hand," Winnie said.

"Yes, okay, point taken," Scully said.

"Thank you, sir," Winnie said.

"But also, Winston, Aaron and you have a capital interest in Noah," Scully said.

"Yes," Winnie said softly. "Yes, sir. That is correct. I have a financial interest in him, as does Aaron."

"And that influences you, does it not, Winston?" Scully asked. "I wouldn't want to think that would, shall we say, *color your opinion*," he said with a wicked smile as his flickering blue eyes bored scornfully into Noah's now ashen face.

"No, sir. I am speaking for the man and how he might benefit himself and our goals."

"Are you quite positive?" Scully asked.

"I am not swayed by my financial interests," Winnie said. "I only see your purpose."

"Thank you, Winston," Scully said. "Thank you."

"I do firmly believe he can be useful to you and the vision," Winnie said.

"I'll not be casting a vote," Scully said. "But I believe Noah is past the reprieve you suggest."

Scully then looked adoringly at Anna. "However, we shall know more as we hear from our lovely Anna."

Everyone watched Anna. She was quiet for several moments before she spoke.

"Mr. Sowles has long been lost between the spirits of white men and the spirits of all peoples of color. He needs the direction that a properly led tribe will provide," she said.

"Interesting, Anna. A 'properly led tribe', you say? Will you elaborate?"

"Yes, Doctor Scully. He will prove himself under the free direction of a great leader. That leadership is yours, Doctor Scully. He should be given an opportunity, but one unhindered by captivity or incarceration. Then he can demonstrate himself and his skills to you," she said.

Scully beamed with pride. "Very nice! Very nice insight!" he said. "Thank you, Anna."

Scully looked at Mary. She was violently shaking her head. "Please, Mary," he said. "Anna brings so much Native-American wisdom to all matters."

Mary glared at Anna as she continued to address Scully and the other three panelists.

"Doctor Scully," Anna said. "Mr. Sowles has a very strong totem spirit."

"Continue," Scully said.

"He has been lost," she said. "He is a bear who has wandered beyond the trees into the valley. I believe much as Winnie does. Mr. Sowles can be reeducated and trained."

"Maybe in a zoo," Mary said interrupting.

"Please, Mary," Scully said. His eyes were thoughtful. "I thank you for that vision, Anna. Please be seated," Scully said.

"Thank you, sir, but no zoo," Anna said. Her tone was graceful and conciliatory. "He needs to be returned to the wild." She looked hard at Mary.

Sowles was grateful for Anna's support and surprised at her humility, but Mary's statement about a zoo as if he was an animal went deep. And yet on another level, he was flattered at the idea of being compared to a bear. *A black bear, eh?* he thought as he waited and watched to see what Scully's next response was, but Scully had disappeared in the glare as he intently focused on Aaron.

"You have had the opportunity to spend time with Noah. What say you, Aaron?"

"Gimme a minute, Doctor Scully?" Aaron asked. "I gotta think some more."

"Yes, Aaron. Take some time," Scully said. He returned to face Sowles. "You see, Noah," he said. "I have made some good choices in my people. They are practical, intelligent, and fair in their own right. I have tutored them properly."

"Then tutor me now, too," Sowles said.

"How would you propose I do that now, after your past rejection of me, Noah?"

"I'll be one of your people, like Winnie and Aaron. I'll check out yo' vision. Winnie is right, I'm an ol' fool, but I can do right by y'all."

"*Sacrebleu!*" Scully said. "Listen to this man's testimony. I'm feeling excited!"

Scully then examined Aaron. "Are you prepared to give Mr. Sowles a fresh page on which he can write a new chapter?"

Aaron stood, as if he was Lincoln addressing the US Senate. He cleared his throat. "I don't know anything about him writing any new chapters," he said and then paused.

"Speak freely, man!" Scully said, almost impatiently.

"My first thoughts were to hang him," Aaron said. "But after all that's been said…"

"So, you now have second thoughts in that regard? Speak up, man!" Scully said.

"In all respect, I'm not in agreement with Mary. Hanging always was the solution for the jigaboos, not burning.

"Yes, Aaron, continue," Scully said.

"As far as Winnie and Anna's positions, it's hard to retrain and reeducate coons after all the bullshit laws that have been passed in Congress over the past generations."

"Ah, yes, perhaps," Scully said. "Of course, maybe, yes, but let's refrain from stereotyping his race." He paused and examined his fingernails. "Granted, Negro's have achieved freedom and success in the last hundred or so years. But let us be clear, Noah was not brought to us initially and now again to this counsel room because he is Black."

Aaron spoke again. "Well, I'm whatcha call a 'full-blown racist', so I ain't sure what to do with the boy," he said as he sneered at Sowles.

"Then, I have to ask you the same question I asked Winnie. Is your confusion because you wish to protect your investment?"

"No! I mean, yes, I care about having my time and money invested in the dude, but make no mistake, all said and done, I don' give a rat's ass about his life or his death." Aaron cleared his throat. "You gotta understand, I've already seen a lot a dumbshit guys like him in combat. Sooner or later, they fuck up and either blow their own asses to shit, or someone else ends up a pile of mush because of the other dumbass. When we saw a new boy first strap his gear on, we knew then if he would cave in when we went out on patrol in some shithole and get us all killed."

Scully stared at Aaron. "Interesting observation. I appreciate that you've had some grand combat experiences, but do you have a statement to make about Noah in that regard?"

"I ain't fond a' the sumbitch at all, everybody knows that," Aaron said. "And truth is, I ain't never been a nigger lover, but if he can demonstrate that he can buck up and cut the mustard in the field, then I'm willin' to forego execution to let the dude show us his shit"

"Interesting," Scully said. "You're suggesting we put him in a field position?"

"I thought that was our initial intention, but I'll tell you, I can respect any man if he's got some real testicles," Aaron said. "Because then I can work with that man, but if he screws up, I ain't one to be messin' around a'tall."

Aaron sat back down with a satisfied look on his face. Scully was expressionless.

"It seems you have ambivalence about Noah, and that's understandable," Scully said. "As for his testicles, I'm not sure after Mary's little bathhouse punishment."

"Yeah," Aaron said. "I guess."

Mary stood. "I never touched his black balls."

"Please, Mary," Scully said and then returned his attention to Aaron. "You've had some unique experiences with Noah, as Winston has, but are you also now saying that you're willing to work with him? Do I have that correct?"

"Uhm," Aaron said. "I guess...yeah. I'll help him get his feet on the ground."

"This is quite a change of direction from where we began," Scully said. "Why?"

"I admit, I guess I'm not too proud to say that I want to protect my investment."

The room was silent for several minutes while Scully examined his fingernails. "Don't guess, Aaron—yes or no to Noah Calvin Sowles?"

"Fuck it, give the sumbitch a chance," Aaron finally said after glancing quickly at both Winnie and Anna and then noticing that Mary was glaring.

Scully interrupted. "All of you now, please stand. Noah may also stand."

Sowles glanced at the panelists while avoiding Scully's intense stare. After the four stood, Sowles feebly rose from his hard chair. Vulnerable to everyone's thoughts or decisions, he hoped only to protect himself from further injury and somehow be returned to the life he had known.

Scully smiled. "The opinion of your peers has proven to be in your favor," he said. He paused and studied his fingernails, rubbing them against his robe and reexamining the shine. "And, because I do not interfere with a panel majority, you are given a temporary Stay of Determination, but there will be a probationary period. If the panel is not unanimously in your favor at the time of review, you will not be given a determination hearing again but will instead go directly to a repercussion hearing."

Sowles was bent over and deflated, as if the air had been drained out of his body.

"What do it mean, 'zactly? Do it mean I'm a free man?" he asked looking up at Scully.

Scully ignored him. "Aaron. Cut his restraints," he said as he walked regally toward the door, but then he suddenly stopped in the entryway and turned around. He pointed one steady finger directly at Aaron. "You're up, player."

# Eighteen

## PRAIRIE DOGS

Aaron yanked the same combat knife out of the sheath that was strapped to his belt. He cut Sowles's zip ties. Anna then quickly escorted Sowles out of the auditorium, through a steel door that led to an immediate grassy field.

"The grass will sooth your feet," Anna said. "In turn, your other pain will dissipate from your foot reflexes." She then led him toward the motel-like living quarters to a single, small cottage separated from the other buildings. Almost mindless from the trauma of the hearing, he was vaguely aware that the entire area was no longer teeming with activity and appeared abandoned.

Inside the small abode a light was burning overhead, coming from a single globe that resembled the bulbs on the sign alongside the state highway. Hanging below the lamp was a very old-fashioned bead chain.

Sowles noticed a folded stack of dark gray work clothes and a pair of black boots sitting prominently on the bare floor.

"Look like some damn plumber's clothes to me," Sowles said mumbling to himself while still wincing from the pain of Mary's scourging.

"Doctor Scully is sending you on a mission."

""A mission? What, the man want me to fix the pipes in his dungeon?"

"You will be leaving the farm with Aaron," she said.

"Yeah, but I mean, the whole thing with Aaron, the beatdowns an' racism, an' insults. I don' know if I'll be able to do alls I gotta do with the dude, you know, I mean, they messed my ass up."

"Get dressed." She turned away. "You'll figure that out. You're the bear, and don't you forget that, Mr. Sowles!"

He dropped the robe and pulled the pants and shirt on. "No boxer shorts?" he asked.

"Everything with Doctor Scully is *now*," she said.

"I just was hopin' fo' some shorts, you know, maybe to protect my shit down there?"

"You must understand the concept that the *now* changes, moment to moment."

"What that got to do with some damn underwear?"

"Nothing," she said. "No underwear is his way of showing you that he is still in control."

"He a mean-ass little white boy," Sowles said.

"Yes, but he did grant you a Stay of Determination.

"Okay, yeah, a 'stay of determination', whatever that means," Sowles said.

"There is always more to be revealed."

"Whachu mean, mo' to be revealed?" Sowles asked. "What's to be revealed?"

"More. Always more. Everything is temporary," she said. "There is always more to be discovered in every moment."

"Do that mean I gets underwear when it get revealed?"

"You will have many answers soon," she said.

"I need some answers now," he said, as he began surveying the room. It was nothing like the suite in the manor house. It was small and appeared clean but was plain and outdated, resembling a dingy, Depression-era, southwest highway cabana.

He was disgusted. "Don't look like the Claremont Hotel. It's some damn modern-day slave quarters!" he said looking at the white-washed, thick, adobe-styled walls with a few hangings of faded prints of drab desert scenes and a water closet that dominated the space. It consisted of a narrow metal shower, a small porcelain basin and toilet, and a scratched metal mirror that distorted his face, making it appear colorless.

"It's temporary," Anna said.

"Whatever," Sowles said, frowning at the door with its paper-thin pane of glass and antiquated green-checkered curtains.

"It is better than confinement in the basement," Anna said. "Just be strong and stay in the moment."

"What 'bout you? You's guardin' me, right? So, I ain't 'zactly free."

She ignored the question. He frowned. "Where's the bed?" he asked.

"There is no bed. You won't be sleeping. You will be leaving soon. Your journey is long. I will first see that you have food, and then we will talk further." She went out the door.

He began to take in the entire area. Across the room, there were three pieces of furniture, a child's size chest of drawers that sat prominently against one wall with a small, wooden table and a sin-gle, old-fashioned chair sitting alongside. On the table sat a small, plain-looking box. Opening it, he discovered hundreds of tiny card-board puzzle pieces, but spreading them out, he realized that the photo of the puzzle on the box top was missing. There was no way of knowing how to assemble the pieces.

He cautiously pulled open one drawer of the dresser. Inside, there was a nicely folded pair of brown tightly creased, men's pleated slacks that were the exact style his father had worn when he mowed the lawn. Unfolding them, he discovered that they were fouled with an overpowering stench of grease and stale urine. Recoiling in fear and disgust, he stuffed them back inside, slammed the drawer shut, and then raced to the basin to wash his hands. The water didn't flow. Looking under the sink, he saw that there were no pipes and no drain.

"More tricks!" he said. "Ain't that right, Scully? You still fulla booshit tricks."

He sat in the chair, rubbing his hands on his fresh pants. It had become early evening by the time Anna returned. She set a covered tray on the small table.

"Please, now eat. It will strengthen you in case you must fast for a length of time."

He was surprised to see a pile of scrambled eggs, corned beef hash, three pieces of toast, coffee, a few fresh bananas, a segmented green apple, and a quart of coffee.

"Where is Scully gonna send me?" Sowles asked.

She didn't answer.

Sowles frowned and began eating. Soon, he was devouring the meal and chugging the coffee as if he had never seen food.

"We have little time together now," she said. "So, you must listen carefully to me. You have already discovered that there are many wicked forces surrounding you. These are seen and unseen. They enter your mind and grow like roots inside of your body, choking you."

"I don't know what to do," he said.

"Start by listening," she said.

"Everythin' I been feelin' an' goin' through since I drove my rig onto Scully Brother's lot is like a dream I can't wake up from," Sowles said. "It's like none a it's real, but then it becomes real, real with pain an' always death right there in my face…it don' make no sense…I mean, is you even real? Who are you?"

"Just try to understand the next few things I tell you. More will be revealed later."

"There y'all go again with the 'mo' t' be revealed' booshit."

"Listen! You must learn how to survive. To do so, you must begin by overcoming Aaron."

"Y'all got that right," Sowles said. "I smacked down Winnie in the basement, but I didn't get my chance with Aaron, not yet, but I will. I'm gonna kick his white ass 'specially good."

"No," she said. "You cannot conquer him with force. He has the soul of a confused jackal that has been separated from his den. He is vicious, reckless, and rabid. You can only conquer him and overcome his violence with camaraderie, as you would with any dog."

"Y'all mean, like, friendship? That's crazy. I can't be that crazy foo's friend."

"He is an immature boy at the core. Friendship is the way of reaching his inner being."

"What the hell that mean?"

"For you to survive the journey ahead, you must discover the child inside of Aaron. Then you can tame that child and overcome his violence with your friendship, maturity, and strength. Only then will you be able to truly overpower Aaron."

Sowles felt a chill travel up his spine, remembering the therapist from his past.

"Where'd you hear that 'bout that child inside stuff?" he asked.

"Never mind that now," she said. "Aaron is your current challenge. When you are able to find the heart of the tolerant bear inside yourself, you will then have patience with the child inside of Aaron and will defeat the wicked jackal that has taken over Aaron's soul."

"I ain't gonna kiss the dude's ass. He beat me down more than once."

"Yes, but he also stood up for you today."

"I dunno," Sowles said. "He first said I was a nigga needin' to be lynched."

"Yes, I just told you that he is confused, but, as you saw, he also enabled your freedom to be here. Aaron made the majority rule," she said. "You must fully befriend the jackal."

"What 'bout Winnie and Mary?"

"Winnie and Mary are not your challenge. All you need to know about them is that they are prairie dogs. They cater to Doctor Scully's entertainment needs. Simple jesters or entertainers of lower intelligence, they pop up and down in their burrows as needed to entertain him."

"Y'all mean, like, clowns?" Sowles asked. "Maybe like jack-in-the boxes?"

"They are sycophants. He controls them, but you can ignore them and overpower them with your invisible bear power. With them, your bear power should take the form of indifference."

"What is my 'bear power an' the form a indifference'? What you mean to ignore 'em?"

"You must understand, the bear is mighty and ferocious," she said.

"I hear y'all but I'm hearin that y'all wan' me to be nice to the chumps."

"When the bear is content, it is either bored, sleepy, or indifferent, and it will ignore humans and other animals," she said.

"Say some more," Sowles said.

"If you ignore the prairie dogs and their stupidity, they will stay in their holes. Overall, you can compel Winnie and Mary to shrink in your presence by being neutral and indifferent with them."

"Girl, that's some heavy talk," Sowles said.

"You must be emotionally detached from Winnie and Mary, and they will be easy to overcome. They will either just shrink away or do what you want."

"Maybe I understan' a little a what y'all sayin', but hip me on Scully, he got all the damn power. How do I deal with him?"

"Doctor Scully cannot be conquered. First, he is a pathological liar beyond human psychological understanding. Secondly, he is a trickster, so for you to achieve success he must be tricked."

"How?"

"This must be start with a form of flattery. Did you understand how or why he relinquished his authority to the panel? It was when you began telling him that he was intelligent and in charge, and that he was the boss. You flattered him and he became too distracted and self-centered to continue his prosecution, so he let the panel take control."

"You's right! He did. He went from gettin' ready to kill my ass to lettin' y'all get involved in the discussion an' then his whole damned attitude changed!"

"Yes! He believed that you are loyal to him and that you admire him. You tricked him!"

"Damn, girl! You got the knowledge!" Sowles said.

"Just remember," she said. "Doctor Scully has a need for flattery, a form of worship. By making him think you are loyal to him above everything else, above all people, even above your own pride or beliefs, you can weaken him and trick him into relenting on his own convictions."

"Man, that's some serious booshit."

I'm not finished," she said. "Once you have catered to his pride with flattery and he is weakened, you must then overpower his evil with your spirit of goodness."

"That's a lot fo' me t' fit inta my bald head," he said. "What spirit of goodness."

"The Great Spirit inside of you that lives only to love."

"This some heavy talk, woman. I dunno, but thank you fo' helpin' me."

"I have something I must confess to you," she said.

"Me? No, girl. Y'all don' need t' tell me none a yo' secrets," he said.

"I do, Mr. Sowles. You must know now. You have a chip in your neck!"

"A what? A chip? Like a trackin' device?" He instinctively reached behind his head and rubbed the base of his skull. "No, don' say that! That's some crazy booshit."

"It's true. The day they brought you in and I had you in the infirmary. I gave you an injection for pain, but I also installed the chip."

"You?" He stood and began pacing. "Y'all did that t' me? So, you wicked and crazy, too! I thought you was helpin' me! I thought I could trust you," he said.

"I'm sorry. Please, listen. Let me explain."

"They ain't no explainin', girl. You bad as Scully."

Anna saw the visible sadness in his face. "I'm sorry. I was forced to install the chip," she said. "If I hadn't, I'd have been severely punished, probably tortured, destroyed."

He slowly began to calm. "Why's you tellin' me now?"

"Because, you are worth saving," she said. "I want to help you to be free."

"Take the chip out then," he said.

"It is embedded in your fatty tissues. I can't remove it. But it is organic and it does have a shelf life, although that is years, however, I can give you an injection that will dissolve it sooner.

"Ain't that some convenient booshit," Sowles said.

"It's for tracking and mood monitoring and control. I can modify the programming, so it only monitors your moods but does not control them further. I can also disable the GPS function."

"A fuckin' mood and GPS chip," Sowles said. "That's some pure-ass booshit."

"It fluctuates between location tracking and observing or stimulating moods," Anna said. "I'll adjust it to monitor moods only. No tracking or triggering emotions."

"Y'all been trackin' and controllin' my moods? That's why I been crazy as a mofo!"

"Doctor Scully has. Let me help you now."

"Won't Scully know 'bout whachu did? He'll punish you fo' sho'."

"I'll take the risk. I have the software. I report the data. If he becomes suspicious, I will explain that it is malfunctioning because of your dark flesh," she said. "Now, sit, and be calm."

He followed her directions. She then placed both palms on his temples. His breathing slowed. She circled behind his chair. Using a small needle, she gave him an injection.

"Stay seated." She then opened a mobile device and made some quick modifications. She smiled warmly. "You will regain your normal senses in one minute. You can expect Aaron to come soon. Be prepared. Stay aware." She then dashed out the door, disappearing in the dusk of evening.

Sowles was dazed but relaxed. He could feel less pressure in his head and a renewed strength. For the first time in many days, he was without an ominous feeling of fear or a pending emotional or physical threat. The fact that he had been almost killed numerous times seemed to be fading in his memory. But his thoughts were quickly interrupted by two black vehicles pulling up in front of the cottage, a Land Rover and a Grand Cherokee.

Winnie bent his big frame out of the Land Rover and Aaron jumped out of the Jeep. He was wearing the same gray work clothes as Sowles was, making him appear docile and tamed. Sowles discovered it was only a facade when Aaron snapped a volley of insulting orders.

"Sowles. Grab your Black ball sack," Aaron said, as they stomped through the front door. "We're goin' truckin', and you're the designated driver." Aaron carried his small shotgun and had his automatic pistol stuck in his belt.

Sowles felt a panicky need to hide, but there was no escape in the tiny room. He despised Aaron's ongoing disrespect and racism, but he was reminded of his father's patience with white men's racial inferences and Anna's counsel about Aaron. He cautiously observed Aaron. "I'm ready," he said to Aaron.

"Get your Black ass in gear then," Aaron said.

Sowles remembered how he had wanted to kill Aaron when they were in the truck the first day. He knew that if he had killed him and survived, his life would be very different.

His thoughts returned to Anna's statements about befriending Aaron and working with Winnie's weakness. He turned toward Winnie who then seemed to be less in control.

"If we are rollin' and I'm drivin'," he said, "then, I needs my license and my DOT medical card."

Winnie seemed dumbfounded. He looked at Aaron. "What's he talkin' about?"

Aaron started laughing uncontrollably, as though he had breathed nitrous oxide.

"Screw the driver's license," he said. "If we get nailed, it's gonna be a shootout! Licenses and shit ain't gonna matter."

"What d' y'all mean, a shootout?" Sowles asked. "What we haulin'?"

"What do you think we're carryin'?" Aaron said. "What the hell business we in?"

"I thought the weed business was legal," Sowles said.

"Legal to grow, man," Aaron said. "At least here in Cali it is, but the feds ain't legalized it, and transportin' over state lines is a federal rap no matter how you pack the pipe," he said, still laughing. "Now, I already told you, get your Black ass in gear!"

"It's in gear, so where we goin'?" Sowles asked.

"El Paso. Then the shit's goin' into Juarez."

"We can't take no weed into Mexico," Sowles said. "Them federales ain't goin' fo' that."

"We ain't taking it in," Aaron said. "The Mexicoons will."

Sowles knew then that even without the chip tracking him, any escape was unlikely. He was officially in the mix. His choices appeared to be death or luck.

"Now, chill your ass and get your shit straight," Aaron said.

Sowles was also beginning to consider that maybe the whole purpose of the abduction or hijack, or whatever Scully and the rest of the crew chose to call it, was to get a commercial truck, trailer, and driver to haul their product. *But, with all of Scully's money and influence, why hadn't he just bought a rig?*

Sowles turned back to Winnie. "We don' need no shootouts, Winnie. We need to protect the weed, right? Ain't that the goal?" Sowles asked. "Protect it an' get it to the receiver?"

"Sometimes men gotta be ready to get it on with law enforcement," Winnie said coolly.

"But if I got my commercial license in my pocket an' my medical certificate, an' we gets pulled over, it's all good, man," Sowles said. "Ain't no conflict with the man."

"How's it all good?" Winnie asked. He seemed completely nonchalant.

"Then we won't have no argument. To them pigs, I'm just another dumb nigga truck driver makin' his damned livin', an' so they'll mess 'roun' an' check the lights or brakes, or some other booshit with the rig, but we ain't gonna get inta no gunfight an' lose Doctor Scully's product an' the truck an' all, an' maybe our damned lives too!"

Winnie nodded dumbly. "Okay," he said.

"Whachu mean, 'okay'? I thought you was the boss!"

Winnie was deadpan. He no longer seemed to be in charge. He remained quiet.

"I 'cept that you the boss, Winnie, but I knows the game with the DOT," Sowles said. "If they stop us, I'll talk my shit and get us outta all a that booshit, and we be cool if I gots my license an' medical card. Then we ain't gonna be in no shootout."

"Yeah? I guess," Winnie said.

"You guess? So, now you guessin' too? You ain't feelin' me, Winnie, my man!" Sowles said. "Check this shit out, man. If I ain't got my license and medical papers, an' we gets stopped, they shut down the rig, an' that means the rig don't move, an' even if they ain't found the dope yet, they gonna be talkin' shit 'bout the load an' wantin' to see the load an' shit. Then, when Aaron get all foolish, we be dead an' the weed gone."

Winnie nodded. "He does make a good point," he said to Aaron.

"I does," Sowles said. "If the cops be poppin' me fo' no license an' shit, they also be lookin' at all our shit, an' maybe lookin' at y'all's weed inside the damn trailer."

Winnie seemed convinced. He turned to Aaron. "Listen to this dude, man."

"Fuck it," Aaron said. He sat down at Sowles's small dining table.

"Doctor Scully wanted an old, experienced driver," Winnie said. "This dude knows the business."

"Whatever!" Aaron said. "I don't have the time or energy for this philosophizing. I'll just put together this jigsaw puzzle while you and your new friend there talk monkey business."

Aaron began incredulously examining the pieces and the unlabeled box. Frustrated with the lack of a photograph, he swiped the entire pile onto the floor and sat there glaring at Sowles.

Sowles focused on Winnie. "If Aaron start some a his foo' ass shootin' over some stupid booshit, we gonna be dead mofos when SWAT come anyway, an' there go the weed fo' sho'."

"He is already thinking like one of the team, Aaron," Winnie said. "Go get his license and the other paperwork from my office, Aaron."

Sowles saw the hatred in Aaron's face. "Yeah, Win, sure. Whatever you say there, bud."

"Just get it!" Winnie said. "Can't I be your uncle just once without a ration of shit?"

"His uncle?" Sowles whispered as Aaron pounded out of the room. "I missed that part," he said as he thought about an old song by Sly Stone. *A damn family affair.*

Hearing Sowles comment, Winnie seemed embarrassed. He and Sowles sat silently as Aaron peeled out in the Jeep, spinning rocks in his wake. When Aaron returned five minutes later, he had the license and a little white card. He snarled at Winnie and flung the paperwork at Sowles. Sowles then appealed to Winnie again.

"What 'bout a gun?" Sowles said. If you talkin' shootouts and shit, I need a piece."

"Whoa!" Aaron said. "His Black ass ain't getting no gun! That's the craziest shit I heard yet." Aaron approached Sowles. "You ain't getting no gun, dipshit." Aaron turned to Winnie. "Winnie, look, man," he said. "A few hours ago, he was a prisoner in the basement."

"Cool it, Aaron, please," Winnie said. "I can't hear myself think."

"Think, Win, use your brain!" Aaron said. "We were plannin' on takin' him out in the bushes and tuning him up, and now we're gonna arm him? And then I gotta ride with the dude?"

Sowles turned to Winnie. "If I'm on the squad now, man, I need a piece," he said. "That's a natural fact. I mean, Doctor Scully was gonna cancel my ass today, now he wan' me to step inna ring and run my game, an' y'all, I mean, we all made commitments to the man. So, I need a piece."

"Ain't happening," Aaron said. That's as dumb as giving the Taliban a buncha our military hardware and then eatin' lamb shanks together in their fuckin' caves," Aaron said and then stomped outside. On the porch he tapped a black cigarillo out of a box, lit it, and came back into the room, blowing smoke like an angry bull and glaring at Sowles.

The odor was perfumed, maybe pipe tobacco mixed with marijuana. It was the same sweet scent as the smoke in the basement. Sowles eyed Aaron suspiciously. The look in Aaron's eyes told him that Aaron had been involved in the drug-induced horror of the previous night, and probably with Mary as his assistant.

"Fuck me raw, Winnie," Aaron said. "He ain't getting a gun," he said. He grabbed Sowles and spun him around, facing him. "You're on some kinda probation, right? A Stay of Determination? So shut the fuck up about what you want, asshole!"

"All's I'm sayin' is I need a cornerman. Y'all been wantin' to kill my ass since y'all beat me down. Now Smith & Wesson will do me jus' right," Sowles said.

"You ain't got a vote," Aaron said. "We don't give a coon anything made by Smith & Wesson."

"Relax, Aaron, with the mouth, man," Winnie said. "I thought you might be getting Doctor Scully's drift. This is not his appointed time for a Minneapolis type race riot up here in the woods."

"No, Win! If he has a gun, we'll be lucky he doesn't use it on us," he said, snapping back at Winnie." I shit you not! I gotta ride with the dipshit! No gun!"

"Okay, Aaron. Point taken," Winnie said. "You're right. You're ridin' with him."

"There ya go, Sowles, no gun!" Aaron said. "Now shut your pie-hole, head for that truck, and get this shit in gear." He glared at Sowles. "You heard me asshole. Move, before I put a foot in your ass!"

Sowles moseyed out of the cabin and leaned up against the porch railing, while Aaron lingered behind with Winnie, both talking in hushed tones. Within a few moments Sowles was startled by something moving behind him in the underbrush.

It was Anna.

"I just wanted to tell you again to be safe, Mr. Sowles," she said, whispering, as she came up on the porch. "Also, I wanted to smudge you before you left."

"Damn, girl," Sowles said. He stepped back. "I'm not sure I'm up for that, baby girl. I mean, why didn't you bring that up when we's back in the room?" he asked, his eyes devouring her beauty.

"No!" she said. "Smudge! Smudging is not what you're thinking, Mr. Sowles! I'm young enough to be your granddaughter."

"Daughter, maybe," Sowles said. "I ain't that damned old!"

"Yes, maybe a daughter, Mr. Sowles," she said.

"So, what's 'smudge' then? It sounds damned sexy to me, girl," Sowles said, chuckling.

"Smudging is an ancient Native American custom," Anna said. "Just wait." She pulled out a small bundle of straw that was tied with a string. "This is sage," she said. "It comes from sagebrush, you know?"

"Look like it come from an old broom," Sowles said. "I seen that stuff befo'."

"It's not 'stuff,' Mr. Sowles. It has magical properties of healing and strength building," she said. "I've wrapped it with some juniper and lavender from my herb garden."

"No weed, right?" Sowles asked. "I can't have no weed smoke on me," he said, remembering when he was arrested with Katy.

"No weed, and it's one-hundred-percent organic. It will protect you on your journey."

"A'ight!" he said. "I'm down fo' yo' smudge."

She lit the stalks and walked around Sowles, waving the burning clump, surrounding him with smoke, chanting and singing softly in a Native language while he stood there, admiring her beautiful face and sniffing the air. "I like it," he said. "It smell good, like Whole Foods, like, y'all know, where the white folks go fo' them 'spensive lotions an' vitamins an' candles an' booshit."

"I never went to that place," she said, blushing. "But forget that now! It's time! Time to go. Vaya con Dios, Mr. Sowles."

"What do that mean?"

"You will find out," she said.

"I hope it's good," he said. "I won't forget you. I'll see you again," he said. "Maybe I can help you someday, like, we can go to Whole Foods fo' some some candles an' things."

"Maybe. If we can both stay alive. Only then, if we shall meet again, it must be in this life. If so, I will then show and tell you the secrets of families and of the ancient bears in the Great Lands. But you must survive this life to know these things."

"I'll be back, Anna."

She didn't respond. She had disappeared into the woods.

# Nineteen

## THE SIXTY-FOUR-MILLION-DOLLAR QUESTION

Sowles was alone, staring at the remains of the herb bundle as it smoldered in the gravel. "Someone gotta watch over that girl," he said, whispering to himself. He felt the familiar, empty, alone feeling again, similar to when Sheylinn had left him for the professor.

Despite all that he had experienced, including sadness over just saying goodbye to Anna, he was beginning to feel strangely positive with the idea of being part of Scully's crew. Regardless of how criminal or deviant they were, he was at least discovering a purpose greater than mindless driving around the country, delivering sundries, destroying his spine in a hard truck seat.

Dropping a load of weed in Texas seemed harmless enough. He remembered teenage friends he had in Oakland who had gotten big as dope dealers and stayed out of prison long enough to get wealthy. Although he had run from that danger, he had been intrigued by the life. Then, for years, he had regretted not going into the infantry when he realized that the Vietnam War had offered men a rite of passage. But now he was in the shit for sure, and it was energizing.

During the several days—or whatever time it had been while he endured the ordeals that Scully put him through—he assumed he was a dead man. But with the inquiry decided, and soon getting back in the truck with a purpose, he had positive feelings, almost a sexual energy, like he had felt when he went down between Sheylinn's legs for the first time over forty years earlier.

His reveling was interrupted by the rattle of the rig rolling up pulling a trailer. He stared. The truck, trailer and wheels had been repainted a matching, lustrous translucent silver gray. It was obvious that Scully and company had thought the color scheme through. Similar to painting warships in "battleship gray," or stealth bombers with non-reflective paint, the entire semi would be almost invisible on the highway at high speeds, and possibly radar resistant.

Aaron was behind the wheel, revving the engine.

"Stop that shit! That's a Cummins!" Sowles said.

Aaron didn't hear Sowles. He was deafened by the loud throatiness and clatter of the powerful motor. He pulled the eighteen-wheel monster alongside the cottage, raced the odometer up to two-thousand rpms, and held it there for a while before he shut it down. It wound to a stop.

"We're outta here in thirty," he said, as he climbed down. He was beaming with pride, as if he was eight years old. He then disappeared. Sowles figured he was getting down with Mary or maybe even with Winnie or Scully. He hoped it was not Anna.

While Aaron was away, Sowles became a professional trucker again. He did an official, by the book, one-hundred-fifty-two-point pre-trip inspection, checking every system on the entire rig that could possibly fail and leave them stranded or trigger some bored cop to pull them over.

While walking around the tractor and trailer, he saw that the license plates on both tractor and trailer had been changed to Texas and that the GPS systems on both units had been removed.

"No wonder Rudy never got the cops after the equipment," he muttered.

The numbers on the tractor's doors were also different, as was the company name. Instead of reading, "Leased to Patel's Transport, Oakland, CA," the name had been changed to "Scully's Feeds & Seeds, Eureka, CA." The number and name were decaled in a barely readable slate color.

While Sowles inspected the unit, Aaron rolled up in the Jeep. He yelled out the window to Sowles. "I'm ready. Get in the rig and put a fire in the hole, Sowles. We're rollin'."

"I had that sucker full of fuel, over twelve hundred bucks! Do I get my money back?" Sowles asked.

"Don't ask stupid questions!"

"I spent my bread on it the day you guys kidnapped my ass."

"Too bad! I topped it off at Scully's with my money!"

"I thought that place was closed and didn't have no diesel," Sowles said.

"I'll be a doorman in a Juarez whorehouse," Aaron said. "Scully's got more underground fuel reserved than OPEC. Just get in the seat and start the bitch!"

Sowles frowned at Aaron's bullshit as they climbed into the truck. Aaron threw his bag and shotgun behind the seats and settled in on the passenger side. Sowles cranked the engine. Again, the old, sweet, thumping beat of his Cummins motor filled the evening.

"Now let's roll, Sowles. We gotta get! We got a big job to do. Let's go!"

Sowles found his leather baseball cap in the door pocket and pulled it over his head.

"Check this computer out, man," Sowles said to Aaron, as he pointed to a small lighted screen protruding from the dashboard. "This be the Department of Transportation electronic logs, man. That shit there's gonna track our time, that plastic box gonna tell me when I have to stop."

"Stop? We ain't stoppin', Sowles," Aaron said.

"I gotta complies with they laws."

Aaron started laughing. "Fuck the laws, man. We're hauling dope, dude."

"It's the law," Sowles said.

"You think I give a shit about some half-ass laws, especially some electronic monitoring?"

"You don' understan', man, it's like that computer gimme eleven hours an' that's it."

"Screw the computer," Aaron said.

"That eleven hours sure as hell ain't gettin' us nowhere's near no El Paso…we'll still be in California. You ain't feelin' me," Sowles said.

"I said, screw that computer. That's exactly what I'm feelin'."

Sowles was frustrated. "It's jus' like I was sayin' 'bout my license and medical papers. If I mess up with the logs an' we gets pulled in, we in the same shit, we gonna get shut down an' they might be lookin' inside the mofo."

"What d' you mean, shut down?" Ain't nobody turnin' off the truck!"

"Nah, man, 'shut down' mean the DOT violate the truck and driver and stop your ass right where you is, an' maybe even tow the motherfucker."

"Fuck those pigs," Aaron said. He pulled his Glock.

Sowles raised his arms, protecting his face. "Wait! I'm jus' tryin' to do the right thing!"

"Shut your yap, Sowles," Aaron said, and he smashed the computer screen with the butt of the weapon. "There, that's the right thing. I fixed it. Solved. Case closed. End of story."

"Now we gonna be in trouble fo' sho' if we gets stopped."

"Drive the truck, Sowles. I ain't Winnie or Doctor Scully. I ain't playing with your ass. This shit needs to get to El Paso ASAP…no fuckin' around, no bullshit logs or laws or federal headaches. To hell with all that shit, man! We are in the game, man…forget the damned law."

"Wait, dude," Sowles said. He reached up into a storage area.

"Hold it, Sowles," Aaron said. He leveled the Glock at Sowles's chest.

"No, man, I ain't doin' nothin'. I'm jus' gettin' my paper logbook."

"Your what?"

"My paper logs. I can fill these out and tear 'em up and make new ones, an' change the times an' dates an' shit t' get us where we's goin! Jus' let me figure the shit out. Damn, man!"

"You best figure the shit out, Sowles," Aaron said. "I'm losin' my serenity, dude."

"Put the gun away, bro," Sowles said. "You know you ain't gonna kill my ass before we get this shit to the Mexican border."

Aaron smiled. "I ain't your bro, and I wasn't really plannin' on killin' your ass, Sowles, unless you drive me crazy. You're the designated driver. I told ya. You're in it to win it with us now. Seems you went from bein' on Doctor Scully's shit list to bein' his new BFF."

"What's that supposed to mean, foo'? I ain't gay, man!"

"It just means 'Best Friend Forever,' dipshit."

"If you ain't plannin' on killin' me, what's all yo' badass booshit with yo' gun 'bout?"

"It's my nature. I'm a Scorpio, man. I sting sometimes, just 'cause I have to."

"Well, I'm a Cancer, so keep that shit under control now, man, and we'll get the shit done," Sowles said, as he scribbled in the logbook.

Aaron chuckled and sat back. "Sure, Sowles."

Sowles turned all the lights on, checked both mirrors, looked right and left.

"Hurry it up, Sowles," Aaron said.

Sowles then laughed and repeated the action to be certain he was clear to roll. He slipped it into gear. The mechanical monster purred. He smiled and settled in.

They rolled out of the parking area and were soon on the same gravel road they had driven in on when he was brought to Scully. He smoothly shifted into the gears, while observing the curves and soft spots in the dark as they bumped along the backwoods road into the midevening.

After an hour of silence, with the exception of one warning from Aaron about the deep mud on the backroad, Sowles turned left onto US 101 and headed south toward the North Bay Area. Both of them were quiet and serious. They seemed to be very different men than they had been over the prior time they'd been around each other. After another two hours of silence, except for the sound of the motor and the wheels on the asphalt, Sowles broke the stillness.

"Hey, man. You know somethin'? I believe that you and Winnie and Scully had this shit all figured out from Jump Street. You guys grabbed me fo' the rig but then decided a big nigga was a good man to have aroun'. Ain't I right?"

"Don't fool your ass, Sowles. Winnie an' me sold you to Doctor Scully."

"Sold me? Like a fuckin' country nigga slave? What kinda evil shit is that?"

"We snatched you off the highway and sold your ass to Scully like you were Frederick Douglass's great granddaddy," Aaron said. He laughed like a hyena in an animated jungle movie.

"Yeah, sold my black ass, an' had yo' Irish ho try to rub the skin off it with a wire brush. Damn good thing Anna done her smoke healin' or I wouldn't be drivin' this dope truck fo' yo' own sad asses!" Sowles said, squirming in the seat and remembering the intense pain that seemed to have mysteriously disappeared. "An get yo' history straight foo,' Frederick Douglass 'scaped and showed them racist crackers what a Black man be capable of!" he said. "But lemme as' you a mo' significant question, did yo' Doctor Scully send you out lookin' fo' a slave nigga with a big rig?'

"Ask Doctor Scully."

"Or did y'all jus' happen to snatch my ass an' make yo' deal with Scully, you know, after the fact, I'm sayin'?"

"You heard me. I dare your ass to ask Doctor Scully."

"Come on, man, we done had our differences, but we in a partnership now, bro…talk to me, my man. See what I'm sayin'?"

"Sowles, I can take you or leave you. Like I told you the day I busted your head, I'm a combat soldier—special forces assault tactics, hand to hand, mind control. I'd a just as soon wasted your ass that day, except you were worth big bucks to Scully… see what I'm sayin'?"

"Yeah, man. I got you," Sowles said. "You fulla shit, you an' Scully, the whole thing."

"We gave you your life back. You better be cool with your flappin' lips."

"Fuck you dudes," Sowles said. "My life? It was never y'all's t' take! Scully buys my Black ass, has me beat up, and talks his shit, and now I'm supposed to worship all yo' asses?"

"Dude, you do not know who Scully is. You do not know what he is capable of."

"Maybe not, but I'm plain sick a his damn ass."

After another hour, they drove through the North Bay Area wine region and the affluent, celebrated estates of Geyserville and Healdsburg, the home of Francis Ford Coppola's winery and the retreats of various other celebrities. Soon they were in Santa Rosa, and then Cotati, where Sowles had lived with Sheylinn.

Sowles noticed that Aaron began to doze as they crossed the mudlands and bird preserves that led to Vallejo and the northern section of the San Francisco Bay. He briefly considered smashing his face, but decided Scully would quickly figure that out and the shit would fly.

By 11:00 PM they were on Interstate 5, heading through the dusty San Joaquin Valley toward LA.

"I know all these roads and towns," he said. "You got the right nigga," he said.

"I dunno about 'right,' but I got me a nigga," Aaron said. "We'll see what you got."

"We sho' will, mofo," Sowles said.

Both of them knew there were plenty of places where Sowles could make a move. They had over two-hundred miles of dark highway, then the desolate Tehachapi Mountains, over the winding grapevine down into Santa Clarita, and then the greater LA basin.

Sowles glanced over at Aaron. "Y'all know, in 'bout five hours we comin' inta the Santa Clarita area. It's the meth capitol of Cali. Lotsa badass doper bikers down there lookin' fo' t' fuck up some dope dealers an' steal their shit."

Aaron gritted his teeth. "That's why I'm packin' heavy with a coupla good pieces. Not to worry. I'll shoot bikers, too, I don't give a shit."

Sowles was quiet. He knew that beyond Santa Clarita, they would be okay as long as they kept moving. Soon they would run Interstate 210 through the San Fernando Valley area into the hills of La Canada and Flintridge, through the well-heeled town of Pasadena, and drop down to the I-10 at San Dimas. Then they would be heading into the desert, Palm Springs, on the direct route to Phoenix and Tucson, and finally into the badlands of Arizona and southern New Mexico.

It would be in those southwestern states and then El Paso where Sowles was worried about getting jacked up by the police or US Border Patrol and getting into a combat situation over Aaron's attitude, or maybe worse, having a mob of thousands of illegal migrants and members of the cartels blocking the roads.

Although he had never confirmed his suspicions, Sowles also feared that the DOT in New Mexico was using random X-ray technology on trucks and trailers without warning the carriers, the drivers, or the general public. Nobody he had ever talked with about this theory was able to shed any light on it.

If they were X-rayed, Aaron would absolutely create a shootout. But if they did make it out of New Mexico, the Texas border and El Paso would only be a few miles from New Mexico's state line. Texas was known to be strict with criminals but not nosy with truckers, so that was a plus, but the desperate and hungry migrant hordes could be a different story.

Sowles knew that there was potential trouble ahead. For decades Ciudad Juarez, Mexico had only been separated from El Paso by a thin, corrugated tin fence. The Trump wall had failed, and the border had been left open to hordes of displaced incoming migrants, leaving the entire area an uncontrollable entry point for armed Mexican cartel activity, sex and slave trafficking, and hard drug importations from Central America and Asia. The entire region was big trouble.

Sowles glanced again at Aaron. "You know, man, we on I-5 now and soon 'nuff we be goin' by some weigh stations, fo' sho' on the grapevine, and definitely when we get to Arizona and New Mexico… I'm good with my paper logs, I mean, I'll fix those mofos, but I'm jus' sayin', man."

"Sayin' what? What are you sayin', Sowles? The weight is right. We know our shit! Now, I told you before, just drive the fucking thing! I do not give one shit about your logs or any bullshit regulations."

"I'm sayin' a man can get stopped or pulled in fo' inspection or some other booshit."

"Don' stop."

"Whachu mean, don' stop? I don' stop, they send a Black Hawk helicopter after our asses…I gotta stop if they pulls us in, an' them's the places where it can happen…that's all, man, jus' a heads-up fo' y'all."

"Fuck 'em," Aaron said.

"I ain't sayin' they gonna find the shit. I'm jus' sayin' we gotta be coo'. You chill an' let me do the talkin', man. I'll tell them you my fren' an' you wanna learn 'bout truck drivin' from a pro…it's the way we plays it, but you gotta be chill, man. That's what I'm sayin'."

"Fine, just drive the truck, Sowles. I'm tired of your Black ass…if we get into some shit, I told you, I'll draw down on the motherfuckers."

"We ain't gonna get in no shit as long as you don' start playin' some Clint Eastwood booshit…let me as' you a question, man.

Is that weed wrapped so it don' smell? These foo's has got sniffin' dogs, man."

"It's triple bagged and wrapped. Ain't no smell," Aaron said.

"It got a padlock, right?"

"No, man. We don't want anyone thinking there's anything valuable in there, and if we lock it, then that means a key or a combination, and keys get lost, so do combinations."

"How's that? How do a fuckin' combination get lost?"

"Men get killed, that's how," Aaron said.

"Shit man, you motherfuckers is too much. I 'sume y'all got a seal on the trailer?"

"What's that?" Aaron asked.

"See, I told your ass, man, you guys don't know shit," Sowles said. "All loads get sealed by the shipper. It don' mean shit, 'cuz you can cut 'em with a pocketknife, but when the seal's on the door a the trailer, it looks official. You feel me?"

"Nah, I don' feel your bullshit."

"Okay, man, fuck you then," Sowles said. He was finally getting tired of Aaron's mouth.

"Fuck me?" Aaron asked. "I'll bust your head again, Sowles. Just drive the truck!"

"You got a bill of lading?" Sowles asked. His voice was calm.

"What the fuck's that?"

"Paperwork on the load…the fact that you don' know what the fuck that is tells my ass you ain't got shit for paperwork…ain't this a bitch? You motherfuckers is backwoods, cracker-ass amateurs."

"Shut the fuck up, Sowles," Aaron said.

Sowles continued to drive. The two of them were quiet for several minutes, until Aaron unexpectedly broke the ice. "You got any of those seals?"

"Wha' you think? Look in the damn glove box an' find that shit, man," Sowles said. "Damn! We gotta write up a bill of lading too," he said. "An' what 'bout the ID number?"

"Will you chill on this legal shit?" Aaron said. "All the ID numbers were changed."

Sowles laughed. "Then all's I know is we gonna stop at one 'em big truck stops and buy a book a BOLs, an' you payin', bitch, 'cuz I ain't got no money 'cuz you foo's ain't gave me my wallet."

Aaron only seemed to be paying half attention as he fumbled through the glove box. "Is this a seal?" he asked, pulling out a short piece of flexible red plastic.

"Bingo! We got a motherfuckin' winner!" Sowles said. "When we stop fo' a BOL book, we need t' put that seal on the door of the trailer. Hang on to the bitch."

"When's that supposed to happen? There ain't nothin' out here on this interstate," Aaron said, as he motioned out the window.

"Soon, goddamnit, Santa Nella….wha', you gettin' scared now?"

Aaron pulled his Glock from his pants. "This look scared, nigga?"

"Sho' do, white-ass, cracker foo," Sowles said.

"Just drive, Sowles."

"We drivin', bro," Sowles said.

"Don't piss me off," Aaron said.

"I ain't, man, but we gotta have our minds straight on this shit."

After about another ninety minutes, Sowles pointed to some lights in the near distance. "That's Santa Nella, man. We stoppin' an' getting a BOL book an' puttin' the damned seal on."

"Who made you the boss, fuckwad?" Aaron asked.

"I'm the driver. The driver always the boss a' the truck an' the fuckin' trip!"

"Is that a fact?" Aaron asked.

"It sho' is. I don' care if you're Mister UPS or J.B. Hunt hisself. If you's ridin' in the second seat, I'm the boss a the truck," Sowles said.

"Who's J.B. Hunt?" Aaron asked.

"Never mind. You a fuckin' dumb saltine cracker fo' sho'," Sowles said, as he pulled into a colorful and well-lit truck stop. He backed the rig into a long stall, with two semis flanking him.

"Oh, now I get it," Aaron said. "You're planning on the great escape, some kinda runaway slave thing." He pulled his Glock. "I'm on your elbow. Just give me a reason."

"I'm gonna say this one more time, Aaron, whatever the fuck yo' Jewish white boy name is," Sowles said. "Me an' you gonna have some serious shit real soon. I'm talkin' duelin' at ten fuckin' paces if you don' stop the 'bitch' booshit and 'nigga' name callin'."

"Sure, Sowles, you betcha, 'cuz you don' have a gun to duel at ten paces. You better just prove your Black ass on this trip, or Scully's gonna let me either bust your balls doing hard labor on the farm or lynch you inna goddamned tree."

"I'll prove my Black ass, but you ever thought 'bout bein' frens an' workin' together?"

"Just shut up before I seriously lose my temper," Aaron said. "Friends, my ass."

"You a white boy bluff," Sowles said. "But let's just chill both our asses and get this business handled and done."

"Make no mistake, we will get it done. But now you answer a question for me."

"Now you askin' fo' advice? What the fuck you want?"

"Just tell me one thing, Mr. Badass Sowles. I gotta know."

"What is this shit? The sixty-four-million-dollar question?" Sowles asked.

"Just tell me, Sowles, why is it if a white man calls a Black dude a 'nigga,' the Black dude gets all crazy and shit, but you Blacks are always calling each other niggas every other freakin' word that comes outta your mouths?"

"Shit, man. That easy, foo'," Sowles said. "We the niggas."

# Twenty

## JOB ONE

"Check out the sushi," Aaron said, as he surveyed the chilled food section of the convenience store inside the truck stop. "Niggas like fish, right?"

"Why you askin' me that stupid shit? We ain't on no picnic together, motherfucker."

"I was just bein' friendly after what we were talking about in the truck, you know about the N-word and all."

"Now you callin' it the N-word?" Sowles asked. "Y'all white people is too much. One damn minute, y'all is callin us niggas an' puttin' us in prison, an' the next minute, you 'pologizin' fo' yo' bad booshit an' talkin' 'bout the N-word an' how racist an' wrong it is. White people is fulla booshit, man! Lotsa big-ass talk, always."

"Screw you, old man," Aaron said. "You're gonna drive the truck and shut up, and I'm gonna get some of this California roll and eat it in front of your ass." Aaron grabbed a transparent plastic box filled with the colorful contents.

"Foo', that Chinese raw fish," Sowles said.

"It's Japanese, and this is cooked, crab, shrimp, and some, maybe, uh, looks like avocado."

"I don' give a fuck what that shit is. That shit you droolin' over look stale as a motherfucker. Suit yo'self," Sowles said.

"Don' worry about it, Sowles. Go see if they got some chitlins and greens. And I saw some watermelon slices over there, too. They're wrapped up in plastic."

"Fuck you, white boy. I'm gettin' me a coupla Oscar Meyers an' a Rockstar."

"What? No Louisiana hot links?"

"No, man, that's a honky myth 'bout niggas and hot links. By the way, my brother, I tole you, I ain't got no bread, so's you buyin' my shit fo' me, or we parked here in Santa Nella fo' the rest a yo' life and Scully's weed sittin' fo'ever."

"I'll take care of it," Aaron said, as he grabbed a bottle of milk from a cooler.

"Better check the date on that shit, too," Sowles said. "These truck stops got no morals when it come to servin' truck drivers high-priced, old, stale booshit they calls food," he said, as he handed Aaron the book of bill of lading forms. "Y'all payin' fo' this, too."

"Relax, Sowles," Aaron said, as he paid the clerk. She was a tired, Native American woman, too old to remind Sowles of Anna, but she made him think of the Northern California Indian legends and how they had shaken him up the night before he was hijacked.

He balanced the two hot dogs and a sixteen-ounce watermelon-mango energy drink in one big hand and carried the BOL book in the other. "Thanks, man," he said to Aaron.

"Yeah," Aaron said. "Here." He handed Sowles fifty dollars. "I don' wanna babysit your ass every time you need to stuff that over-weight gut of yours."

"Damn, man, you's learnin'!" Sowles said, smiling widely. "You alla sudden gettin' human with yo' N-word and now a US Grant. Y'all becomin' a rare white boy, ain't ya?"

"Sowles, just chill. Like I said, I don't wanna have to be payin' for your shit every time we stop. Someone might think I'm friends with your Black ass."

"I thought you was my fren', even though I owe your ass a serious beat down."

"Be careful, old man," Aaron said. "I ain't some old, forgivin' burn-out like Winnie. I'd've definitely beat your ass for those two kicks you gave him. I shit you not!"

"Well, ain't we friends, white boy?" Sowles said, laughing heartily. He wolfed both hot dogs and drained the drink. Belching loudly, he opened the trailer doors and stood there, staring at the perfectly bundled load of weed.

"What the fuck you doin', man?" Aaron asked.

"Checkin' the product, makin' sure it be loaded properly. I'm a trucker, 'member?" he asked. He then shut the doors, secured the lock levers in place, and then showed Aaron the procedure with the door seal.

They returned to the cab and sat in the dark while Aaron ate from the plastic box dipping the little pieces in soy-sauce and humming with satisfaction with each bite. When Aaron was done, Sowles grabbed a pen from his storage pocket. He began writing in the BOL book. "What's Doctor Scully call his weed farm?" he asked.

"Scully Family Farms."

"Ain't that sweet. Do he sell jams and jellies too?"

"Fuck off, Sowles."

"Believe yo' ass, be nice or I'm gonna fuck off an' leave your ass out here in the dark."

"I don't think so, Sowles," Aaron said, as he toyed with his handgun.

"What the fuck do I write on this motherfucker for the product? And where the shit goin'? An' we needs a receiver on the paperwork…yo' ass know what a consignee is?"

"Gimme a minute," Aaron said. He seemed deep in thought.

"Think, motherfucker, 'cuz we gotta get this shit straight."

"I said, lemme think!"

"This is America, man," Sowles said. "You ain't in Iraq or Afghanistan or Pakistan, or wherever it is you white boys fight yo' white people wars an' shit. We gotta have our shit together here with this paperwork if you don' wanna be lookin' at Corcoran."

"Corcoran?" Aaron said.

"Prison down here in the valley. Charles Manson's old home before the motherfucker died a some kinda colon cancer or some shit."

"Fuck Corcoran," Aaron said.

"Cool. Whatever y'all say. Now, y'all wanna tell me who the fuck gonna be receiver and what the fuck the product gonna be called?"

"Uh, shit, uh...put, uh, birdseed on there."

"Birdseed goin' to Texas and into Mexico?" Sowles said. "Don' fit, foo'. Mexicans don't feed they birds. They can't feed they own damn selves."

"You're right," Aaron said. "What do the Mexicans buy, ya think?"

"You askin' me? What the fuck do I know 'bout what the Mexicans buy, man! The cartels buy guns. Go ahead, foo', put that shit down on the paper! Put guns! Y'all crazy, like I said, you's amateurs at this smugglin' shit. I thought y'all's some big-ass, international playahs."

"Quiet, motherfucker, I'm thinkin'...it's goin' to the border," Aaron said.

"Yeah, so? We already know that shit!" Sowles said.

"But the Mexicans take it across into Juarez," Aaron said.

"Yeah? So?" Sowles asked.

"And the Chinks take it from there," Aaron said. "Put rice on that paperwork...yeah, that's it, man, rice from Sacramento...damn, I'm good! Ain't I?"

Sowles kept writing. "Yeah. Rice. You good on that one. You a bitch with yo' shit, Aaron. But you ain't said nothin' befo' 'bout no Chinese, man," he said. "Chinese is ruthless, man."

"Hon Ying Traders. We work with those dudes all the time. For Chinks, they're stand-up gangster dudes. Uh...address, uh. Lemme look." He opened his mobile phone.

"So's who the fuck it goin' to?" Sowles could see that Aaron's face had gotten pale.

"Just write in there, uh, Barrazza Forwarders. They're right on the border."

"How inna fuck you spell that shit?"

"Gimme that sumbitch." He snatched the book and pen from Sowles, scribbled on the page, and tossed it back.

Sowles looked at it. "What street?"

"Ah, shit…Roja Street…111. R O J A. Write that shit down and get the fuck outta here."

Sowles finished the task, signed the paperwork, folded a copy, and put it in the door pocket. "Let me as' you another question," he said.

"Not this shit again," Aaron said. "Drive the motherfucker."

"Fo' real now. I thought Scully was some organized crime playah. Why we doin' this amateur shit?" Sowles asked, as he started the truck and rolled out onto the access road. "And by the way, how much do this shit weigh?" He asked.

"I told you, we're cool…under 35,000 pounds," Aaron said. "And, Scully has his shit together. He's got it goin' on in business, politics, money, international investments, trade, and growing good dope. I'd say that makes him a player."

"I ain't feelin' that with none a this booshit, stupid stuff, man," Sowles said. "An' now y'all talkin' 'bout Chinese gangsters! Shit, man. Them foo's don't play…an' wha' the hell they want with a buncha damn homegrown weed anyway?"

"The Chinks oversee the edible THC manufacturing business in Mexico, gummy bears and worms, gum drops, and other high potency candy; and make no mistake, man, the Chinks are cool, but they stopped coming to the Triangle to buy our weed because they didn't want to transport it to El Paso, so Winnie and I put this deal together."

"This deal? You mean grabbin' my ass and goin' in the stolen truck business?"

"Yeah, something like that. Me and Winnie figured out snatching your ass and having you be our transporter was the fast track to keeping the Chinks in our game…you dig?"

"I don' wanna 'dig.' If the shit goes bad, I take the heat," Sowles said.

"I'm here, too, ain't I? And nobody's takin' any heat if we get caught."

"Yeah, you here, but I'm the foo' nigga drivin'. They gonna bust my ass fo' sho'!"

"Like I said, I'll shoot it out before I get in the back of any cop car," Aaron said.

"Damn," Sowles said. "I was right. Y'all is some crazy motherfuckers."

"Hey, man, it beats bein' in Special Forces in fucked-up wars a man can't win."

"I guess I ain't gonna argue on that topic," Sowles said. "I didn't do no foo'-ass wars."

"Just drive the rig and impress this upon your brain: this mission is better than being burned at the stake by Mary-had-a-little-lamb."

"Mary-had-a-little-lamb?" Sowles asked, chuckling.

"Yeah, Mary. She wants to roast your ass."

"She a fine little redhaired nasty baby, but a cold bitch. She yo' squeeze, bro?"

"Nah. I mean, I fuck her now and then, but she's a little Scotch-Irish ballbuster."

"Damn straight. Pretty little ho wanna burn my ass onna fuckin' woodpile!"

"That's what I said, didn't I?"

"Yeah, man, you did. Don't remind me again."

"I think Mary fucks Scully too," Aaron said.

"Well people gotta get it where they get it," Sowles said. "Sound like a Motown song, don' it?" he said, laughing heartily, trying to change the subject. "Gotta get it where ya get it."

"You're an old man, Sowles…Motown? Man, fuck that dumbass shit."

"It's a damned good thing I'm old, 'cuz I'm smart with wisdom, and if I die or end up in some Corcoran or Quentin, it won't be like I had a long life ahead a me."

"You ain't gonna die, unless I kill your Black ass."

"As my memory tells me, motherfucker, you was gonna hang my ass yesterday."

"Just drive, Sowles! I'm done talkin' shit."

Sowles continued on I-5 for less than ten miles before he rousted Aaron again.

"So, why y'all didn't just buy a big rig with all the man's bread?"

"Use your head. If Doctor Scully just bought a rig, where was he gonna get a driver?"

"You wanted to drive the motherfucker," Sowles said. "Aaron-the-trucker-man."

"I only like to play around with trucks. I'm not into being a truck driver."

Y'all's damn right, 'cuz y'all don' know shit 'bout commercial drivin'."

"I can drive this prick, but I don't wanna know shit about all the laws and infractions and hassles the government puts on you morons."

"Damn straight, you don't," Sowles said. "But y'all didn't need to kidnap my ass. Y'all coulda got some punk-ass offa Craigslist."

"Yeah? Run an ad for someone to haul dope? No way, dude. We needed to bring a guy into the game. Someone we could get a good handle on. We had to grab your ass, man."

"Yeah, well, y'all did yo' shit, an' I ain't 'zactly joyful," Sowles said.

"Yeah? I guess," Aaron said, laughing. "But who was better than some broke-dick, under-the-radar, old Black man? And, as far as the truck and trailer goes, that was a bonus! You had some good equipment and made it all that much more of a score."

"Yeah, it's a good rig, but my dick ain't broke, so don' even get that shit spread around, man," Sowles said. "I ain't playin' wichu on that subject."

"You sure about that?" Aaron asked.

"'Bout what?"

"Your dick not bein' broke?"

"Fo'get my dick, and hold the thought, man. Lemme get this shit straight."

"Get what straight?" Aaron asked.

"Listen. So y'all snatch a Black dude, beat his ass, feed him lobster, and put him in the hole, jus' so he'll drive yo' shit?"

"You're driving it, ain't ya?" Aaron snickered.

"I am, yassuh, mistuh boss man. I am. I'm a drivin' this truck."

"Okay, then. Drive the sonofabitch! The Chinks are punctual motherfuckers. They don't fuck around. They want this load, and they want their shit shipped back up into Cali."

"What shit? What you talkin' 'bout? 'Their shit'?" Sowles asked.

"What the fuck you think, man? You think the Chinks ain't got game? You think this is just about sellin' some stink weed? It's gelcaps, man, lotsa Chink pills comin' back, fentanyl mix."

"Pills? Fentanyl?" Sowles thought for a moment and then yelled at Aaron. "Motherfucker! That's some murder shit there! That ain't jus' some booshit homegrown weed and damn candy edibles, man. Fentanyl's some fucked-up bad-ass dope."

"Don't let Doctor Scully hear that smack talk, Sowles," Aaron said. "That's his payment. It's his game. He distributes it into the four quadrants of the US and then up into Canada and Alaska, across the strait into Russia, Scandinavia, and then all of Europe. His profit is fifty times more than the weed brings.

"So, y'all kidnapped my ass and fucked me up until I was ready to join your shit, an' now you got me goin' on with some yo' booshit fentanyl?"

"You're in now, man...Stockholm syndrome," Aaron said.

"What? What's that mean?"

"It's a hostage conversion process."

"What you talkin' 'bout?"

"Take a prisoner and convert the fucker to your side. It's done in warfare, international hostage taking, black ops, various crimes… happens all the time, dude."

"That some Patty Hearst shit y'all got goin' on!"

"Patty Hearst was before I was born, but yeah, she did join her kidnappers."

"Symbionese Liberation Army—some badass, Black mother-fuckers," Sowles said.

"Yeah, the SLA." Aaron frowned. "They were fuckin' niggas for sure."

"An' they was all dead niggas, in a minute, in one fuckin' white-ass, honky, SWAT raid."

"We don't die, Sowles," Aaron said. His face had become as cold as white marble.

"You is one funny motherfucker," Sowles said. "Mister badass white boy…we all die, man! We gonna be next," he said. "Police gonna lay us out an' take our dead-ass pictures like we was international cartel gangsters."

He downshifted and then passed a slow-moving freight hauler. "Slow, bitch ass Swift trucks!" he said, snarling at the road hog. "You know what SWIFT mean?"

"Nah…don't know and don't care."

"Sho' Wish I had a Faster Truck," he said, and cracked up. "Hey, man, so you sayin' Scully is a playah in these businesses an' shit… then who is the man? And where the hell these brothers a his?"

"You ask too many questions, Sowles."

"It's just conversation, man," Sowles said.

"Maybe you forgot," Aaron said.

"I ain't forgot shit," Sowles said.

"No?" Aaron asked. "You forgot that this morning, you were a Black chump begging Scully for your life," Aaron said. "You ain't exactly, Danny Glover playin' the bashful hero."

"Be nice, white boy," Sowles said.

"You're stretching my shit thin, Sowles," Aaron said.

"It's just you an' me talkin' now, man. Be cool," Sowles said.

"I guaran-fucking-tee you, I will gun your Black ass down if you fuck around," Aaron said, pointing his Glock at Sowles.

"I'm gonna tell yo' ass somethin', Aaron, your shit be gettin' old. You know damned well you ain't gonna shoot my ass an' wreck the rig, an' fuck up Scully's dope an' shit."

Aaron didn't answer. Sowles got quiet. He focused on the road. Aaron seemed bored. He fidgeted with his gun until he finally spoke. "You know, man, I had a lot to do with saving your ass from pruning buds in leg irons on the farm for the rest of your life."

"That was then, foo'. Now is now, an' I'm tired a you pullin' that Glock every time y'all gits an insect up yo' anus. Y'all know you ain't gonna shoot my ass!" Sowles said. "I'm tired a yo' shit. Jus' gimme a smoke an' be cool now, an' make sure it don't have dope in it. Okay, brother?"

"We aren't brothers, Sowles." Aaron held out the pack.

"No? Why?" Sowles asked, as he snapped a dark cigarillo into his mouth.

Aaron reached across with his flaring Bic. Sowles inhaled deeply and blew the smoke at the windshield.

"If we ain't brothers in this weed delivery, you best get it into yo' honky mind, I ain't 'zactly happy 'bout you beatin' my ass down with yo' shotgun out on the highway," Sowles said. "Like I was some goddamned Rodney King mofo."

"That was an operational necessity," Aaron said.

"What the fuck does that mean?"

"The mission is always Job One." Aaron said.

"Job One?" Sowles said, half yelling. "This shit ain't no TV commercial, man!"

"Priority," Aaron said.

"Well, I definitely ain't coo' with none a y'all's puttin' my ass in yo' fuckin' Gitmo prison down them stairs an' fuckin' me up with a buncha weed smoke an' a damn water hose."

"You done now?" Aaron asked.

"No, I ain't done, goddamnit!"

You need to be done, Sowles. I need some rest from your chatter."

"No, man I gotta says my piece. I mean, I'm doin' this thang for y'all, an' y'all know I'm in this deal with yo' asses. We together inna big picture, now, but I got my options. I can wreck this motherfucker an' deal with the consequences. So, you wanna chill, or we gonna be at war sooner or later?"

"I like war," Aaron said.

Sowles became quiet and drove a few more miles. "Damn, all I did was ask about Scully. Fuck, he my boss, too, man!" Sowles said.

"Look, man. Nobody knows all there is to know about Doctor Scully," Aaron said. "He says that's his family's land, but Winnie says that's all bullshit. I think he's from Europe, maybe, like Norway or some other cold-ass place, maybe Sweden or Russia. He's cold all the time, shivering and putting on heavy coats."

"How can he be from those places?" Sowles asked. "He talk like he from Disneyland."

"The dude speaks over fifteen languages besides that poony way he talks English."

"Where you white boys get y'all words? 'Poony,' man? You too much with y'all white boy booshit."

"Don't push it, Sowles."

"We cool, man. He speak Chinese, too?"

"He speaks several dialects of Chinese."

"Nah, he don't," Sowles said.

"He does, and all the European languages. Polish and Russian."

"No he don't," Sowles said.

"Yup, and some shit from India and Pakistan. I even heard him speaking classic Latin."

"No, man, he don' speak no Latin," Sowles said. "Now you booshittin' me fo' sho'."

"I'm tellin' ya, he speaks ancient Latin."

"Nobody speaks that shit. How you hear this shit? Him talkin' on the phone? Wha'?"

"No, man, Doctor Scully never talks on the phone. He never texts or emails either."

"Damn, that's some crazy shit! How y'all hear it?"

"Foreign businessmen that come to the property. I even heard him singing in different languages."

"Singin' too, eh? That's strange shit. So, wha' y'all mean, he cold all the time? The cat got pneumonia or some disease…what, AIDS, maybe? The cat got HIV, man? He look kinda weak and gayish to me, I mean a blonde white boy with dreads and the polished fingernails and all."

"Nah, he's not gay, maybe a little bisexual, but all I know is the dude's cold all the time."

"What's that shit mean, 'cold alla time'?" Sowles asked.

"I mean, he's shivering and complaining about it," Aaron said. "He hates the cold weather and pisses and moans about it. I dunno, dude gets all pissed off when it's cold. He's always got a fireplace going in some room, even in summer."

"Weird, white boy shit!" Sowles said.

"The dude's what they call, 'eccentric', I guess," Aaron said.

"Say what? What the fuck's up with his name Finn or Scully? What that shit, some Swedish or German or somethin'?" Sowles asked. "I think the man is a Nazi, maybe. Whachu think?"

"Scully ain't his real name," Aaron said.

"How you know? So, then wha' the man's name be?" Sowles asked.

"He goes by a bunch of names," Aaron said.

"No shit? The man use aliases? Like what?"

"I can't pronounce them. But that's enough Q-and-A, you're gettin' on my last nerve."

"Come on, man. We only talkin', man, you know, we *chattin'*, like white folks say."

Aaron didn't answer. Sowles pushed him a little further. "Jus' tell me what the deal is on this motherfucker an' his brothers, the Scully Brother's gas station, an' all that booshit."

"There ain't no Scully brothers," Aaron said. "That's his front for the game. That gas station keeps him cool with the locals in the Triangle—just another good old, homegrown boy."

"Yeah, he homegrown, alright. The man got his game, fo' sho'," Sowles said. "Who's all the people 'roun' the farm?"

"Trimmers, cutters, irrigation workers, botanist technicians, and laborers mostly," Aaron said. "And the groupies and weed worshippers—old hippies and burnouts from all over. Most of the younger freaks been off the grid since their grandparents left Haight-Ashbury in the sixties."

"How do they eat, man? He feed lobster to all them motherfuckers?" Sowles asked.

"You writin' a book, Sowles?"

"Maybe," Sowles said.

"Well, you know what they say, leave that chapter out."

"Come on, man, I'll put you in the story, man."

"Whatever, Sowles. I'll tell you this, most of the burnouts just stay loaded, but he lets them grow their own food."

"The boy Scully do got it goin' on. He got himself his own world," Sowles said.

"That's what I told you, Sowles. And I suggest you call him 'Doctor Scully.'"

"Doctor a what, man? Dude be into some Jim Jones Number Two shit…he ain't no MD, he got the people dependin' on his booshit an' eatin' outta his little white hand."

"Except for being cold all the time, he is one adaptable dude, like a chameleon. I'll tell you that," Aaron said. "He can fit in anywhere. He's got connections with big money people all over the world. The dude's like a king, man. No one can get in the middle of his game," he said.

"Except maybe the feds," Sowles said.

"No, he's got his people there, too. And his shit is bigger than some weed and pills, man, and you're in it now, Sowles, so chill your ass so you don't end up fertilizer for the farm."

"I tol' y'all, man, don' keep givin' me them booshit threats, man," Sowles said.

"Ain't my threat, dude. Doctor Scully is in the dude in charge."

"I sho' ain't seein' his ass right now! So, he trackin' the truck or what?" Sowles asked.

"I thought these shit-boxes had built in tracking systems in the engine computer."

"I removed that shit, man, long time ago," Sowles said. "Deleted that booshit."

"Well, you can be sure he's tracking us with something. His brain probably."

"Whachu mean, man? You mean the computer chips?"

"That too, but I told you, man, the dude has connections, eyes, man, everywhere."

"Man, that's shit's crazy!" Sowles said. "But whachu mean, his shit is bigger than dope? Ain't that enough criminal enterprise fo' the dude?"

"It's bigger than dope. Russia, China, Middle East, man...big deals, man."

What? Guns? None a them damn foo's need guns, man. They already got lotsa guns."

"No, man, it ain't guns. It's bigger than guns," Aaron said. "It's bigger than all that."

"Whachu mean?" Sowles asked.

"How'd you get here?" Aaron asked.

"Whachu mean?" Sowles asked again.

"What I mean is, how did you end up on Scully's list of things to do?"

"Whachu think, foo'? Y'all hijacked and kidnapped my ass—"
Sowles stopped talking midsentence.

"That's all I'm sayin', Sowles. Now just chill your ass an' drive the
damned truck."

# *Twenty-one*

## TURNOVER

Heading toward the dark outline of the Tehachapi Mountain range, Sowles drove in silence, while Aaron stared wide-eyed out the windshield. After an hour, Sowles tapped the radio power button. The calm was interrupted by a zealous, late-night evangelist.

"In recent years, there have been far too many discussions throughout the ecumenical community on the topic of deception in churches by men of the ministry who give hollow blessings to their congregational members in exchange for allegiance to the church, tithes, labor, professional skills, and so forth."

"There ya go, Sowles," Aaron said. "Religion is truly for the ignorant."

The radio signal faded out and was replaced by the fuzzy twang of a country-western crooner. It hissed in and out between the two stations. Sowles retuned it. The reception improved. The same commentator continued.

"The blessings I was referring to are in the form of so-called hands-on healings and specific prayer requests prior to surgery, job interviews, marriages, or other similar events."

Aaron reached over and pushed the button to off. "I had enough."

"Chill, man, I'll find some music, then," Sowles said. He turned the radio back on and tried to adjust the reception between overlapping stations.

"La, la, la, la, la, la, la, la—"

The radio faded in and out again, back to the first station.

"When the careworn parishioner realizes…sssssssss…sssssssss… that whatever…"

"Turn that fucker off," Aaron said.

Ignoring Aaron, Sowles tuned the radio in again.

"Whatever was prayed for does not materialize, faith is weak… sssssssss…sssssssss…the lost and the demoralized soul departs the church…sssssssss…sssssssss…we must remember that the Lord is the lighthouse and the beacon for the illumination of mankind—"

Aaron turned the radio off again. "Done. No more," he said. "What are you, some Jesus freak, born-again, fool-ass Christian?"

"A little Jesus ain't gonna hurt our asses, 'specially in the dope smugglin' business. We need all the help we can get." He turned the radio on again.

"Thank you, Pastor Greene. Brothers and sisters that was Pastor Paul Greene of the Faithful Cross Church in Phoenix. Please stay with us while we take—"

Aaron turned the radio off again. "That's it, Sowles. We're done with Jesus."

"Good thing my mama ain't here," Sowles said. "She'd straighten out your shit with Jesus."

"Good for your mama," Aaron said, as he toyed with his Glock. "Lotta good that Jesus talk did you. Look at your ass, a dumb, Black-ass truck driver about to get shot."

"Go ahead, kill my Black ass! You ain't gonna get far in this rig without me."

"Don't force me, asshole! I don't wanna hear no more Jesus rap! That's it. You got it? There ain't no Jesus. It's all made-up fairy tales!"

"I'm drivin' this motherfucker. It's my choice," Sowles said. He turned the radio on again.

The pastor rambled. "If given the opportunity, who among the righteous would not raise one hand and solve the glaring issues of the world?"

A crazed grin came across Aaron's face. He turned the radio off again. "I need you to drive this truck, but we ain't listening to the Hour of Power. He stuck the gun barrel up against the radio.

"No, foo'! You shoot that radio, an' that bullet goin' right into the engine an' wires, an' shit, and we be walkin' Scully's dope to El Paso."

"Then get your head outta your ass," Aaron said. He pointed the gun again at Sowles.

"Chill with that damn gun, Aaron," Sowles said. "I tol' y'all the day you beat my ass down on the highway and took me out to that dope farm, y'all ain't no murderer. I'm tellin' your ass again, man, you ain't a killer. Y'all ain't got the balls t' kill this nigga."

"Don't be so sure. I told you, I killed a buncha camel jockeys in the Middle East."

"Well, this ain't Baghdad, an' we gotta get through this shit together, man. We got dope, and we got the Chinese an' fentanyl an' shit t' deal with."

"Then drive and stop with the Jesus propaganda."

"Man, you know this dope shit is wicked, man. We gonna bring evil upon ourselves. Maybe we need Jesus!"

"Stop, Sowles!"

"We can walk away from this right now. We can park this truck an' jam!" Sowles said.

"No!" Aaron said. His back slumped against the door.

"It's a corrupt business," Sowles said.

The gun was resting on Aaron's chest as he leaned back in the seat. He relaxed his finger on the trigger, but still pointed the barrel directly at Sowles. "We ain't quittin'," he said, his speech slurring as his eyes began closing.

"You sleepy, man?" Sowles headed for the shoulder with the rig. "Hang on!" he said.

"What are you doin', man?" Aaron asked. He was struggling to keep his eyes open.

"I think we got a bad steer tire, man. Hang on!"

"What?" Aaron asked. He hung onto the safety bar.

The tractor and trailer ground into the gravel. Sowles slammed on the brakes, and the heavy rig came to a shuddering stop. In the flash of less than a second, Sowles snapped a powerful outward hand-sword strike that landed hard, directly across the bridge of Aaron's nose. Blood immediately spattered on the windshield and passenger glass. Aaron groaned and instinctively moved both hands to his face to protect himself from another strike. The Glock dropped in his lap.

Sowles swept the gun into his big palm and quickly stuffed it into his belt. He then rammed the shift lever back into gear and stomped the pedal. Swerving back into the empty lane, he swiftly accelerated. Within brief seconds, the truck was under control.

"I tol' your ass to chill, white boy," Sowles said. He threw him a dirty rag that he kept balled up in the door pocket. "Now get yo' shit straight and get that blood cleaned up off the glass an' yo' damned face."

"You fucker! You broke my nose! It hurts bad, man!" Aaron said. He pinched his nose shut in an attempt to stop the blood from pouring out.

"Damned straight, I broke yo' nose," Sowles said. "That was some overdue business I had with yo' ass. I been tellin' ya t' chill, or we was gonna get down sooner or later, man. Well, the sooner happened befo' the later."

"Gimme back the gun," Aaron said, his teeth bared and snarling. The smeared blood on his nose, mouth and beard combined with his fury made him look like the violent jackal that Anna had described.

"It my gun now," Sowles said. "An' definitely don' yo' ass think you goin' in the back t' get yo' shotgun."

"I won't be needin' the scattergun, Sowles. You ain't met SIG Sauer yet."

"What do that shit mean?" Sowles asked. "Who the fuck is Sig Sour?"

Aaron pulled a black, 4.5-inch barrel, 9mm automatic out of his jacket. He pointed it directly at Sowles's big chest. "Say hello to Mister SIG of the Swiss Industrial Group."

"What you doin', man?" Sowles asked. "I thought we was gettin' to be frens, now, bro."

"You're outta your Black-ass mind. You busted my nose, man."

"It was nothin' but a tap, bro. "I'll fix it fo' ya," Sowles said.

"Gimme the Glock!" Aaron said. "Before I kill your Black ass."

"I ain't," Sowles said. While forcibly trying to manage the rig and keep it in the lane, he pulled the Glock out of his pants and pointed it at Aaron. "I don' wanna shoot your ass, Aaron, but we damn sho' in showdown fo' sho' if the shit don't chill, an' then this rig an' both our asses an' Scully an' the Chink load goin' straight over a damn cliff!"

"You don' have the testicles to wreck this truck."

"Watch me, man!" He headed for the shoulder at sixty miles per hour. "Them Chinese foo's ain't gettin' they weed, an' Scully ain't getting his fentanyl, an' if yo' skinny ass live through the crash, it sho' as shit be fucked good by Scully."

"Okay, alright, alright, alright, Sowles. I got it. Be cool, man. Just put the gun back in your pants and drive this thing straight," Aaron said. Beads of sweat had formed on his forehead.

"Okay," Sowles said. He brought the rig back under control, but still held the pistol near his lap. "So, we bein' coo' now, right? No more booshit? We got equality now?"

"I'm sick, man, my guts are spinning, and now a busted nose," Aaron said. "I ain't got the stomach for this equality bullshit with you, so just chill. We gotta get this shit to Texas or we're both gonna be dead," Aaron said. "Fuck it, you got the piece you were sniveling to Winnie about. Now we're gonna do this shit together, and get it done."

"Job One, right?" Sowles smiled as he cocked his head, pointed the pistol at the windshield and bent his wrist inward so the gun was horizontal in the ghetto gangster fashion. "It's gettin' hectic now, y'all. Mr. Sowles be cruisin' heavy!"

"I see you don't know how to use a handgun," Aaron said. He seemed calmer.

Sowles laughed. "Yeah, I do, man." He made several tough faces as he aimed the gun.

"You ain't the Notorious B.I.G., so don't try to play some badass!" Aaron said, pulling off his bloody jacket.

"Biggy dead," Sowles said.

"We're both gonna be dead if you play around with that handgun. Now watch this," Aaron said. He held up the SIG and demonstrated the clip release, the slide, and emptying a round from the chamber. Then he showed Sowles the empty weapon and let him glance at the loaded clip. "Pretty, aren't they," Aaron said, smiling at rows of copper-colored rounds.

"Yeah, I guess," Sowles said.

Aaron quickly popped the clip back in, chambered a round, and set the safety lever. "You see that shit?"

"Yeah, man. I seen it, but why you showin' me that shit? I knock that chip in yo' head straight?"

"Fuck the chip, just want you to be prepared to use that Glock if we get into the shit with meth dealers in Santa Clarita or Albuquerque or with any cops." Aaron said as he wiped away blood with the back of his hand.

"I'm coo', man," Sowles said. "Y'all wan' me t' straighten yo' nose?"

"Sowles, you busted my fucking Jewish nose, an' I am not exactly pleased. You read me? But we ain't nowhere near outta this shit yet," Aaron said. "So, fuck my nose and just pay attention while I give you some basic handgun combat theory." He held the SIG up and pointed it toward the windshield.

"Wha' y'all talkin' 'bout?"

"I'm gonna teach you some basic shit in case we get fucked-up by anyone."

Sowles smiled. He was amazed. Anna had been correct about Aaron's inner child."

"Okay," Sowles said, but he was flabbergasted. Aaron and he been through a death match since their first encounter, but it was as if they were two kids who had a fight in the schoolyard, and after the fracas, they were becoming closer. Aaron was befriending him just as Anna had said. The inner child theory was real just as Sowles's therapist had said in years past.

Aaron seemed completely relaxed. "At short distances, you won't have much trouble," he said.

"I'm damn sho' glad you keepin' my ass informed and bein' my BFF. I swear yo' computer chip is malfunctionin'."

"Don't be a dickhead, Sowles. I'm teaching you how to survive… what I'm saying is, you only need two, maybe three, rapid shots to the largest part of the body to end most attack situations, so go for the chest first. I know that's easy to say, but it's your best bet when it's up close and personal. The head is very hard to hit in a frenetic situation."

"Okay, so we pals, now?" Sowles said. "Funny how a Glock make a Black man equal."

"Just listen up, dude. This is business."

"I hear ya, pal," Sowles said.

"If we get into a firefight," Aaron said. "Where there's distance between us and some bad boys or a gung-ho tactical squad, we're in deep shit anyway, even with handguns. You then have to repel the enemy with repeated fire. It's wasteful, but its effective."

"Yeah, makes sense," Sowles said.

"If you lay down a blanket of rounds, it makes it harder for them to shoot at you while you try to make your escape…you got it?"

Sowles smiled warmly and nodded. "Yo' chip definitely ain't workin' right. You too nice."

"You'll need these," Aaron said. He pulled three loaded clips from his jacket pocket. "Fifteen rounds each. If you need more than that, it's already over, because either you sucked at shooting or you were seriously fucking outnumbered."

"What d' ya mean?" Sowles asked.

"I mean, you got over sixty rounds right now with those three and what's in the gun. You gotta get whatever job that you're on over and done with using those rounds."

"Alright," Sowles said.

"What I said this morning in the hearing about hanging your ass was because a lotta Black people ain't exactly cool. But you got a lotta guts, Sowles, a lotta heart."

"Yeah?" Sowles asked. "Thanks, man."

"We're even now," Aaron said. "I admit, I been crazy toward you, man. Scully keeps us that way, you know? The chip."

"Yeah, the chip, man—the mood thing an' the mind control," Sowles said. "Even when they been deactivated, they got residuals in yo' fat cells, like weed. It cray-cray, man, no matter how y'all look at it."

"We gotta make this trip happen," Aaron said. "No matter what."

"We doin' it, bro," Sowles said.

"We fuck this up, and Doctor Scully will hunt us down and stuff us like we're wild elk."

"I heard that," Sowles said.

"I mean, you know the truck and the whole routine with the DOT assholes."

"I got it under control," Sowles said. He started waving the handgun and singing a hip-hop song from the 1990's. "Thanks, man, I like the feel of this bad boy. It's getting hectic."

"Stop playin' around, Sowles. You're a grown man," he said. "Now, listen, it should go smooth with the Chinks in El Paso, but you never know," he said. "Mexicans, cops, gangbangers."

"All them foo's is fo' real! Specially the Chinese!"

"Everyone's for real, Sowles," Aaron said. "Make no mistake, it is all for real."

"Yeah, well, them Chinks definitely do not like niggas," Sowles said.

"Yeah, but the Chinks are Doctor Scully's pals," Aaron said. "Basically, we're all on the same team."

"You hope, dawg," Sowles said.

"Just understand, Sowles, this is a bigger deal than meets the eye, and it needs to happen." He stopped talking. His breathing was shallow and labored. He was sucking air in short gulps. "There's a lot you don't know yet."

"What up, man?" Sowles asked. "You chokin' on yo' blood?"

"I feel real sick," Aaron said.

"Damn sushi," Sowles said.

"Just forget it. I'm no stranger to injuries," Aaron said. "But I'm feeling real sick, man. I'm gonna try to get some rest. Don't kill me while I sleep."

"Hell no, bro. We together, now…we in it to win it now, man."

"Are you cool?" Aaron asked.

"Yeah, man. I'm coo', we coo', man. We all good," Sowles said smiling.

# Twenty-two

## PARKING AREA B

Aaron quietly cleaned up most of his blood and then dozed. Sowles thought back to his youth. With the exception of the Black Panthers, the kids in his neighborhood in the 1960s had no access to guns. The street kids had relied on knives, or choke chains, or whatever club, tire iron, or antique sword turned up from some father's garage or war trunk. With the Glock in his belt, he was newly empowered. The weight of the gun and the three heavy clips in the bag gave him a feeling of security like nothing he had ever before experienced in his life.

He was aware that each state had its own gun laws, and many of them restricted any open carry in a vehicle. Because it was almost impossible to route any over-the-road rig through only the states that did allow a driver to carry a weapon, most drivers, except the few crazy crackers, were unarmed and vulnerable out on the open highway. The Glock 9mm with the backup three clips felt as good as it gets.

Aaron and he were silent for over a half hour. Sowles drove on into the night ribbon of Interstate 5 and headed for the mountains that would lead them into Southern California. At one point, he changed lanes from the curb lane into the passing lane and then quickly cut back into the curb lane. He repeated the maneuver.

Aaron stirred. He coughed. "What're you doin' weavin', man?" Aaron asked. "You're trashin' my stomach."

Sowles stared into his left mirror. "Someone followin' us."

"What do you mean? Is it the cops?"

"It could be. It look like a SUV. I been watchin' the same damn headlights an' yellow fog lamps fo' a while," Sowles said.

"Can you let 'em get alongside and squeeze 'em off the road?"

"Not if they cops, man, and 'sides, man, I ain't at the point of killin' folks yet. But whoever they is, they definitely been followin' us fo' a long time. But cops mighta pulled us over by now. Who'd be followin' us, man?"

"I dunno, man, but I'm tellin' you, I feel real sick," Aaron said. He seemed disoriented.

"Must be some a Scully's people behin' us, eh?" Sowles asked. "Y'all must know. Y'all's on to yo' Doctor Scully's crazy shit."

"I'm sick, man."

"That's what I'm talkin' 'bout, bro. I'm coo' and easy does it an' all, but what 'bout yo' ass? Y'all sick, man, maybe from them demons an' dope an' crazy shit y'all bring into yo' life."

"No, I'm sick, real sick," Aaron said. "It's my stomach. I feel like I got a knife inside of my guts."

"It's all that nose blood mixin' with that booshit milk an' sushi fish shit," Sowles said.

Aaron slumped forward. "I'm real sick. Maybe it is that sushi or the milk, mixed with the blood," he said. "I'm real sick." He slid against the window.

"My mama always said the demons tryin' to take us to our grave. Maybe they makin' you sick. Them demons put you on to that sushi shit. White boys can't hold their mud against that kinda evil, bro."

"Stop that bullshit talk, Sowles. It's food poisoning," he said, as his stomach retched.

"You don' think the demons don' use the tools 'vailable to their asses?" Sowles asked. "They used that sushi roll shit to get yo' ass, man. Maybe we oughta stop this truck, Aaron. Maybe we gotta get outta this motherfucker."

"Don't stop this truck, Sowles, I'm telling you! We won't live through this shit if you stop this truck. Scully and the Chinks will kill us both! You got that?"

"Okay, Aaron. Okay. Yeah. Okay. I got it, man...I'm drivin', we coo', man." Sowles could see that Aaron was becoming crazed.

Sowles continued to drive, humming the love song that had been interrupted earlier. Aaron stared straight ahead. Both men were silent for several minutes, until Sowles finally spoke again.

"We got a weigh station comin' up in three minutes," Sowles said. "Make sure that blood be all cleaned up." He looked at Aaron's face. It had changed from pale white to red and feverish looking. "You ain't lookin' good, man. I'm stoppin' at the weigh station. You can puke that sushi up outside on the pavement."

"Don't stop! I'm tellin' you, Sowles! Don't stop!" Aaron said while he wiped up the last visible traces of his blood.

"I gotta, man. If I don' stop, the cops will send a chase car out fo' us fo' sho', an' 'sides, man, I gotta lose this foo' followin' behin' us. The motherfucker is tailin' us fo' sho'."

"Are you trippin'? You makin' that shit up?" Aaron asked. He began retching.

"No, man!" Sowles said. "I ain't makin' shit up."

Aaron continued to retch.

"I'll be a motherfucker," Sowles said.

He took off his ballcap and tossed it into Aaron's lap. "Puke in this, Einstein," he said. "And listen yo' ass up, man, I ain't makin' shit up...somebody's on our ass inna SUV an' been there fo' a while."

"Don't stop! Drive this fucker," Aaron said, but then he began vomiting in the hat. "I can't hardly move. My bones and my joints are aching," he said. He struggled to raise his arm and push the button on the switch to drop the window.

"I definitely ain't feelin' yo' pain, right now. You fuckin' up my ballcap," Sowles said as Aaron moaned.

"You gave it to me, BFF," Aaron said while gagging.

"Listen, man, we either got some DEA on our ass or Scully got a tail on us, or mo' people than you an' me an' his crew know that we gotta big load a dope," Sowles said. "I'm gonna be rollin' up on the scale an' losin' whoever this motherfucker is behind our asses."

Aaron was quiet except for the sound of puking in Sowles's ballcap.

"Chill now! We gonna be in front of a buncha DOT pigs in a few minutes!"

"I'm real sick, man."

"Get yo' baby-ass shit together now, foo'!" Sowles said. "Be coo' now!"

Out of the corner of one eye, he watched Aaron vomit again into his ballcap, while the rig crawled into the scale area at about three miles per hour. First the tractor and then the trailer bumped onto the metal plates of the platform, making a loud, clattering metal sound. He stopped at a red light while the truck was weighed. At the same time, a dark Jeep passed them on the left.

"There that car go," Sowles said. "That gotta be Scully's Jeep!" Sowles said.

"I saw it," Aaron said. "Different wheels." He vomited again.

"Who then? They weren't no ghost, man," Sowles said. He watched the signal at the scale, waiting for it to turn green. "Them cops watchin' us, too, man," he said. "Everybody got an eye on our damn asses."

Inside the big-windowed, well-lit adjacent building, a half dozen California Highway Patrol officers were standing around, either looking stupidly at each other and playing grab-ass or staring out the window at the rig on the scale.

Sowles read his gross weight: seventy-three-thousand pounds. It was well within the law, but he was greeted by an ill-fated voice over the outside loudspeaker:

"PLEASE PULL INTO PARKING AREA B."

"That's it, bro. They pullin' us in fo' a damned inspection!"

The light switched to green.

"You got that blood cleaned up?"

"Yeah, but don't pull in! Keep going," Aaron said between dry heaves. "We can't take the chance. Run the fuckers!"

"No, man, just chill. Hide your gun now! Toss it inna back. I'll do the talkin'."

Sowles slowly guided the rig into the long parking stall and stopped. He tossed his handgun and ammo behind his seat. A young, white uniformed officer came over to the driver's window.

"Sir, I will need you to wait here until we have an open bay for a level-one inspection."

"Yes, officer," Sowles said. "But, sir, I have a big problem."

"What's that, driver?"

"My passenger be sick. I think he has some serious food poisonin'."

The cop walked around to the other side. "You alright, sir?" he asked Aaron through the open window.

Aaron nodded but didn't answer. He held his hands over his nose and mouth.

"One minute," the officer said. He walked back around to Sowles. "Wait here."

Sowles nodded.

The cop covered his nose and mouth trying to control his gagging as he walked toward the office. Within short minutes, he returned wearing a pair of gloves, a mask and a face shield. He was followed by a ranking senior officer, a thick African American woman who was popping out of her uniform. She labored toward Sowles's window. When she reached him, she adjusted her face mask. The other officer went back to Aaron's window but kept his distance.

Sowles knew the outcome could go in one of two directions. The Black officer would either create some camaraderie with him or be a self-obsessed narcist and fuck with him.

"I'm Sergeant James," the woman said, her voice flat. "Your passenger ill?"

"Yes, ma'am," Sowles said.

"Food poisoning, you think?"

"Yes, ma'am, sushi fish, California roll. He real sick."

"Do you think he can make the hour into Valencia, or should we call an ambulance?"

Sowles looked at Aaron. "Can ya make it, partner?" he asked. Aaron mumbled and groaned while nodding and pointing forward.

"He says, yes, officer. Says he can make it."

"Okay, wait," she said, and she walked over to Aaron's window. The young white cop turned away from the odor. The sergeant glanced at Aaron and then returned to the driver's door.

Sowles waited anxiously, his heart racing, as she mumbled unintelligibly into a shoulder microphone. She then returned her attention to Sowles.

"Very well, then. Give it about thirty seconds, and when you see a cruiser pull up in front of you, go ahead and pull out slowly and follow the car to the exit."

"Yes, ma'am. Thank you, ma'am."

"Be safe, driver."

"Thank you, Sergeant. You too," Sowles said.

Both cops walked back to the scale office. A few seconds later, a black-and-white sedan pulled into position, with its red-and-blue lights flashing. Short bursts of the cruiser's siren bleated in the night air.

WHOOP! WHOOP!

The next thought that came into Sowles's mind was whether he should have folded up the entire escapade at the weigh station and told the cops and then suffered through the legal fallout.

WHOOP! WHOOP!

Sowles followed the cop out of the state property and then headed south, back onto I-5; although they were free from the CHP, he was very aware that he was eight-hundred-forty miles from the Texas state line and still had Arizona and New Mexico to pass through before they would enter the border town of El Paso. He realized that Aaron and he were not likely to survive a DOT inspection in Arizona or New Mexico, regardless of how much talking or soft-shoeing either of them did. He also knew that both southwestern states had far less socially conscious DOT officers than California's CHP and were rumored to use even minor trucking violations as a source of funding for state deficits.

He glanced at Aaron who had become semiconscious. Sowles was able to think more clearly without their ongoing banter. As he observed the young man, it seemed he was far sicker than a simple case of food poisoning. His breathing was shallow, his face had become bluish-white, and there were traces of foam around his mouth. It was possible that either the fish or the milk had actual life-threatening toxins or Aaron had some other problem, very possibly drug related, considering the fentanyl discussion and Aaron's ongoing, inconsistent state of mind and behavior.

Sowles glanced in the back bunk area. Aaron, in his delirium, had actually followed Sowles's directions and tossed his pistol in the back where the shotgun was hidden when they were pulled in for the inspection. Sowles realized then that he was finally in a position to take full control of the situation. He considered pulling over, opening the passenger door, and literally pushing Aaron out on the pavement. But, as he watched the young man writhe in pain, Sowles felt pity for the kid. He kept driving, while trying to formulate a plan that would make sense.

# Twenty-three

## FREE AT LAST

Having run the I-5 in California many times, Sowles knew there would be no worthwhile health clinic before Valencia, about fifty miles south, but getting involved with any emergency medical team anywhere would involve reports and maybe even the local police. Stopping with load of dope was not in anyone's best interests.

Aaron groaned again. More foam had gathered around his mouth.

"I hope your ass don' die, my man," Sowles said. "But we takes our chances in this world a crime an' rebellion, don't we, bro?"

Aaron was unresponsive except for an occasional moan. Sowles knew there was no telling how Aaron might react at an acute care clinic once he was on a gurney or even revived. Sowles decided that the young man was a dangerous criminal, regardless of his occasional good intentions. Sowles also was well aware that Aaron had wanted him dead more than once. He decided that he would not gamble his own life or risk going to prison over some discussion at a hospital emergency room about Aaron or their trip that would bring the police to the scene.

He was forty-three miles from Castaic. He decided he would stop there, at a well-known truck stop, and determine then what he would do with Aaron. Despite the fifty-five mile per hour speed limit, he hammered the throttle and pushed the rig as fast as he was willing to risk, hoping that other speeding trucks and his stealth paint increased his odds of not getting pulled over.

Forty minutes later, he approached the crest of the last mountain, before beginning the long descent into Castaic. The speed limit on the downhill stretch was thirty-five for big rigs.

"Shit!" he said, as he foot-braked and then hit the engine brake switch.

The truck slowed down to about thirty miles per hour, with a shudder and rapping sound in the exhaust.

"Okay, baby, float on down into Castaic, now," he said. "Six miles, sweetie."

It was only another eight minutes, and he was pulling into the truck stop. It felt like his lucky day. For the first time in the many years that he had run the I-5, he found a spot on the fuel island of the usually cramped facility without waiting.

He kept the Cummins at an idle, jumped out, and ran around to the passenger door.

"Come on, foo'. I'm gonna get you some help," he said.

Aaron was like an oversized rag doll, only partially responsive. "Get my bag and my guns," he said, his voice barely audible.

"Fuck that, man. You can't take that shit in there. Yo' ass jus' need a doctor, bro!"

Sowles helped him down the steps of the cab and then locked the doors using the passenger side power button. He got underneath him and easily lifted him onto his back, as if he was a wounded soldier. He hobbled into the men's restroom. Several drivers were flabbergasted at the spectacle of the bearlike Black man carrying a long-haired, skinny, white, hippie kid. Immediately, the chatter started, led by a young man in a turban who was interrupted as he washed his feet in the sink. Other men laughed at the spectacle and bantered in at least three non-English languages.

Aaron had become unconscious. Sowles put him in a stall and shut the door. He then ran to the fuel desk inside the convenience store.

"Hey! Help! Help! There's a dude havin' some kinda fit in the men's room. He's foamin' at the mouth. I think he be poisoned or dyin'—maybe he OD'd on some bad dope."

Two young counter people, a man and a woman, ran toward the men's room, both with their cell phones in hand.

"Wait here, sir, please!" the woman said.

Sowles glanced around at a few dumbfounded, half-asleep, white drivers milling around the candy aisle in the convenience store. When he confirmed they were not a threat, he headed for the back door leading out to the fuel islands. Within seconds, he was in the truck. With luck still on his side, he was able to pull forward and maneuver the rig out of the parking lot.

"Later, foo'. I wish yo' ass the best," he said, as he tossed the filthy ballcap out the window. He then examined the two mirrors to see if he was followed. A minute later, he was on I-5 South, heading down the long path toward the Los Angeles area.

"Now, do I turn this bitch 'roun' and head fo' Oakland, or do I takes the shit to El Paso?"

As he spoke the words, the frightening reminder of Scully's court of inquiry flashed through his mind, along with the torture in the dungeon, being battered with the water hose, and the threat of being forced into a labor program and working in the confines of Scully's acreage.

Also remembering the inferences that Aaron had made about Scully not letting them escape and coming after both of them, he realized that he had been dealing with something larger than just a dope grower in Humboldt County. The man was an enigma of sorts, with influences that spread across the region and very possibly the world.

The more he wrestled with his thoughts, it became clearer to him that to return to Oakland with a trailer full of dope and attempt to tell the story to the Oakland Police and the DEA would also be risking his freedom. They wouldn't protect him, but instead would consider him a collaborative suspect. Who would believe that he was imprisoned in the Emerald Triangle?

There was no escape. Becoming a fugitive from Scully and whoever else was involved with his enterprise, including the Chinese or the Mexicans, and being subject to all of their twisted ideas of retribution, or being held by government agencies did not add up to a solution.

He cranked both windows down to vacate the stale odor of Aaron's vomitus and made the decision that he would drive the dope to El Paso and then deal with whatever was next. But in the back of his mind, he had no intention of bringing the rig or any fentanyl back to Humboldt.

His forehead wrinkled. "But if I don' bring the pills back, then Scully ain't gettin' his big payoff fo' the weed when the pills move," he said. "Then my ass is fucked fo' sho'."

Again, he glanced in the mirrors. "El Paso or bust," he said, chuckling nervously, while remembering that Aaron's bag was still onboard, partially covering his two weapons. Sowles knew that he needed to dispose of any personal effects that belonged to the kid.

There was an exit a mile or so ahead that was for an abandoned, outdoor paintball obstacle course. As he approached the off-ramp, he eased the rig up to the stop sign and then made a left turn, parking under the highway in total blackness where he was completely invisible to anyone.

He then jumped back into the sleeper section and put Aaron's shotgun and the 9mm ammo sack under the lower bunk. Grabbing the Glock and the SIG Sauer, he buried them in a storage drawer. He then grabbed Aaron's bag. It was heavy. Rummaging through a few T-shirts, pairs of socks, gloves, and a woolen cap, he found three boxes of 12-gauge 00 buckshot shells, one-hundred rounds of boxed 9mm ammo, and an envelope with forty crisp fifties.

"Damned straight!" he said. "That's what I'm talkin' 'bout! Thanks, mofo." He laughed and stuffed the money in his pocket. "I hope y'all find whatever yo' Aaron ass be lookin' fo'!"

He hid all the munitions under the bunk and climbed out of the tractor with the bag. He smelled the woolen cap and decided to keep it, but he dumped the rest of the clothing onto the highway. After foraging for a few good-sized rocks, he put them in the bag and zipped it shut. He felt relieved. The long ordeal with Aaron was almost over.

Grabbing the two plastic handles and using a strong sidearm, as if he was throwing a powerful basketball pass, he flung the sack several dozen feet into the nearby underbrush and bushes. "There we go," he said. "History, motherfucker. That's what we do," he said.

Bounding up the truck's steps, he climbed into the driver's seat, slipped the transmission into gear, and jumped on the fuel pedal. Quickly pulling away from the gravel shoulder, he cut a tight U-turn and got in position for fast access to the southbound entry ramp.

As he merged into the traffic lane, he gradually became aware that his circumstances had changed significantly. He was alone and on his own. "Free at last!" he said, cackling.

The mirth was short-lived. Deep inside his gut, he felt the old "what's next?" fear of the future. "Be cool, Mr. Sowles," he said aloud. "You knows the route. Just drive the motherfucker," he said, thinking of Aaron's constant rebukes.

He was aware that when he reached the major truck exit for I-210 East, just north of Valencia, he would begin the official eastbound journey that would lead almost directly to El Paso, Texas. Soon enough he would have to face the Chinese.

He attempted to relax into the seat and sing a few bars from the famous old Marty Robbins ballad about old El Paso, but within only a few minutes, the excitement of traveling to Texas to follow in the paths of great cowboys and fatalistic lovers had begun to wear off.

The familiar sleepiness that came from driving the rig solo settled over him, as if it was a warm mist. He flipped on the radio. Adjusting the stations while trying to drive in a straight line and not wipe out a Japanese sedan and a stainless bulk food tanker, he attempted to find the podcast that he had been listening to when Aaron had begun having his tantrum. After skimming through several fuzzy stations, he found another evangelist.

"We are in training for the power and the kingdom to be bestowed upon us. Our great God wants to give each of His children something special, something beyond the understanding of the eyes...this is the supernatural and holy spiritual mystery not yet revealed, but it will be shown soon, as we near the end of the reign of the nations and the return of Jesus."

Sowles chuckled. "Yeah, man, whatever y'all say."

"A man cannot fully know the glory and peace of Christ and his gifts to us through his sacrifice for our sins, unless that same man has experienced and witnessed his own sins and the sins of the actions of others."

"My daddy always tol' me I'd fuck my life up 'cuz a white folks."

Renewed with some form of twisted faith, he felt alert enough to stay focused. He shut the radio off and continued to power the rig in a southeasterly direction, into the barren wasteland known as the Southern California Colorado Desert Region.

# Twenty-four

## STOP ON BY

Within the next two hours, he exceeded the DOT-allotted legal driving time. In good conscience, with the intention of trying to comply with at least that one law, he pulled off the interstate into a threadbare section of a desert town in the Coachella Valley area of California to track down a truck stop that he remembered from past trips.

The exit led onto a strip of frontage road near the interstate highway. It was beat up from daily desert heat and Southern California seismic activity. The asphalt surface appeared as if it hadn't had any grading or a new topcoat since it was first laid down in the 1930s.

In the pinkish light from the lamp poles that separated the freeway from the adjacent county road, Sowles drove past houses that had been built long before the interstate was constructed. They were all single story, unpainted, wooden, shack-like structures, some with amateur looking, rickety add-ons attached to wobbly walls. Others had travel trailers parked alongside, with makeshift porticos and exposed plywood roofs connecting the structures. Many were missing glass windows, which appeared to have been replaced with thick, translucent, weather-beaten plastic, as if someone had a big roll of the material and had peddled it door to door. Barely readable hand-painted signs similar to Scully's fuel stop offered homemade tamales, bargain rates for auto and truck repairs, and puppies for sale. These were tacked to fences or walls. Sowles was cautious to avoid grazing any number of junky cars that lined the roadway only inches from a wide drainage ditch.

Sowles's heart sunk. The abject poverty seemed worse than in the Black communities of either East or West Oakland, both areas long known for ghetto scarcity on all levels. The desert town made him far more aware of the decimation of US Native American cultures. His prior traveling had revealed that the rural desert communities were populated by many impoverished indigenous peoples that had mixed with generations of migrant Hispanics. Neither population had done well in the United States, and they seemed far worse off than his ancestors or lost relatives and Black friends, in spite of all their past plights with slavery, segregation, and abuse.

The short journey through the town's outskirts returned his thoughts to two significant reminders: the Indian myths that surrounded the Emerald Triangle that had kept him immobilized on Scully's property on the fateful evening that then led to his current predicament, and then Anna's sweet face and kindheartedness. He realized then that returning to rescue her from all of what Finn Scully seemed to represent might be the only significant responsibility left in his life.

He needed to stop. The lights of the large truck stop twinkled half a minute ahead.

As with many other truck stops in the deserts of the southwestern areas, the facility was part of a large, lively-looking, Native American casino. A tickling thrill went through his stomach when he saw the jolly invitations of the brightly colored, artistically created neon tubes that were wound into bright Ferris wheels and multicolored caricatures of cowboys saddled on big-toothed horses. These were combined with billboard pictures of beautiful young women with pursed lips, beckoning drivers to "STOP ON BY."

"Not tonight, Mr. Sowles. No lovin'," he said to himself as he envisioned a beautiful mixed-race whore and a multicourse buffet dinner.

Despite the prolific signage and exciting billboards, the casino's expansive parking lot was mostly vacant, giving him very private parking choices. He could covertly reassess his situation, check the guns and ammo, and get the paper logs in order.

After he was parked in a 90-foot spot specifically designed for a tractor and trailer, Aaron came to mind. The image of him smashing the computer flashed through Sowles's memory. Aaron had known long before Sowles knew that the load was crucial to the Chinese and the return load was worth untold millions of dollars. Aaron had more on the line than he revealed.

Sowles got the paper logs in order by tearing up a few pages and recreating the trip, showing a different, much later, and farther south starting point. This deception then allowed him to have driven farther than what he could have gone if he had been running legally. It wasn't a perfect solution, but it was better than running as a total renegade.

When he was finished with the paperwork, he flopped on the bottom bunk, recognizing that for the first time in his long life, he felt relatively secure with himself. Whether it was from having access to the three guns inside the truck, the radio preachers and their sermons, or everything he had endured since first beginning the trip to Eureka, for the first time he was okay—at least for now—but he was well aware that the Mexicans and Chinese were still waiting.

He swallowed the remaining slight taste of fear and drifted off to sleep with a relative sense of calm. He was surprised the next morning when he awoke after 9:00. He couldn't remember the last time he'd had a full night's sleep.

He was still his clothes. The ugly, crustiness of the gray work uniform was enough motivation for him to leave the security of the truck and investigate the truck stop for some fresh clothing, but once inside, he refused to spend money on sand-colored walking shorts and a chartreuse tank top advertising Indio, California. Feeling flush with the money he'd found in Aaron's bag, he took a fourteen-dollar trucker's shower, but crawled back into the same stale clothes, and then sat down to a nineteen-dollar, all-you-can-eat buffet breakfast that consisted of every foodstuff that any long-haul trucker could want.

It was the first day of comparative freedom he had enjoyed since leaving Oakland the day of his cardboard pickup, but he was still uncertain how many days had passed.

While the waitress splashed coffee in his cup, he asked her the day and the month.

"November 16," she said, showing little interest in Sowles, other than making some inaudible comment about it being the election month.

Sowles's brow furrowed with deep creases. He placed both palms on his forehead and held them there. "I know y'all might think I'm tryin' t' mess with y'all," he said, talking to the tabletop. "But I needs t' ask you what year it is."

"What's the matter? You been humpin' the road too long?"

"Yeah, somethin' like that. I got smacked in my head." He leaned forward and rubbed the spot on the back of his head, hoping she'd give him a little sympathy.

"It's 2022," she said, and then walked away with a blank look on her face.

The year made sense, but he seemed to remember leaving Oakland early in the first week of October. If so, well over a month had passed, but he was only aware of about three or four days. *Somethin' is fo' sho' fucked-up*—he thought.

But what had Scully really been referring to with the inauspicious comment about him having been there a long time? Had he lost time the way people who have been abducted on extraterrestrial spacecraft claim to have? Or had he been drugged beyond his mind's ability to comprehend time? Had he simply been unconscious—or maybe worse, was it the computer chip? Had he imagined some of what he thought he had experienced?

These were confusing concepts and questions. They also brought Rudy Mendoza to mind, and maybe even the Patel family, the owners of the transport company. Were they involved in the larger plot of weed transportation? Rudy was Latino, and he had sent him on the unusual run from Milpitas to Eureka, and Rudy had some affiliates in Oakland who were street-level thugs.

"It really don' matter, I got the power now," he said quietly as he thought about the weapons and the control that he had over the load. But he knew that he had experienced something inexplicable, and he also was very aware that Scully's conspiracies were the cause, and Scully was still very much in charge.

Sowles's heart raced. He wanted to contact Rudy. *Maybe I should get homeboy up to speed an' tell him I'm alive*—he thought. But he really wanted to pick Rudy's brain for info, to drill down into the Latino dispatcher's mind to determine if he knew anything, or if he had a secret connection to Humboldt. "But Rudy's my fren' fo' years," Sowles said to himself, whispering. "An' I don' have a good story to tell Rudy." Sowles knew he would have to stay incognito. Rudy and everyone else would have to wait.

He cashed out the waitress and walked back to the truck. It was time to roll. He had Arizona and a whole different set of state laws to deal with in two hours.

Inside the rig, he carefully picked the broken shards and pieces out of the computer screen that Aaron had smashed. If he was pulled in for another inspection, he could explain that it was broken by some foolhardy panic stop and a can of menudo or beans hit the screen.

To alter temporary log paperwork was an infraction. It was not something that he or most contemporary, conscientious drivers did, but the mission he was on, his own life, and maybe Anna's life, was far more important to him than a regulatory hours-of-service violation.

He had made it clear to Aaron that keeping the trailer doors sealed was vital. The cops rarely inspected standard truck freight without specific criminal suspicion, so even if he was violated on some minor DOT issue related to an ordinary paperwork, logs, or equipment inspection, the load would probably be a nonissue. The police would accept that it was rice.

Worrying about getting violations seemed stupid under the odd circumstances. He was packing three illegal firearms and at least two-hundred rounds of ammo across what would be four state lines, and he was also driving a rig with phony license plates, and with the truck and trailer weighing seventy-three thousand total pounds—half the weight was nineteen tons of weed.

"You got it goin' on, now," he said aloud. "Just be cool, Mr. Sowles."

It was almost noon when he finally slipped back into his former long-haul driving comfort zone. He was rolling on I-10 Eastbound but was still six-hundred-seventy-five miles out of El Paso. He knew he could probably make it legally by the following day once he got into the open desert states where the speed limit for truckers was leg-islated at seventy-five mph. Until then, he would be slugging along at California's fifty-five mph limit.

Although he had gotten some sleep during the night, he had not been back on the straight desert highway for more than fifteen min-utes when he felt the empty, mindless boredom known as white-line fever sweep over him and start to lull him asleep. It was the plague of long-haul drivers. When combined with loneliness and stress, this completed the recipe for disaster.

The advent of energy drinks and the flood of their availability throughout the marketplace laid to waste the theory that a thermos of coffee was the cure for mental depletion or exhaustion. Sowles had discovered that the only thing that saved him from having to sleep for several hours multiple times a day was a sixteen-ounce, highly caffeinated drink filled with B vitamins and other chemicals. As simple as the solution seemed, discovering the syndrome was not a new finding. He recognized this chronic sleepiness as a condition similar to motion sickness or drunkenness.

When he had been a young merchant seaman in the Pacific, and when he'd also worked briefly on the salmon boat, he had experienced firsthand or witnessed other men suffering from the same disorder. It would lay merchant sailors up in their bunks in constant, deep sleep around the clock. They would only emerge from their drug-like sleep for brief meals or to suffer through their work shifts, and when finished, they returned directly to their bunks.

Sailors had laughed about it and attributed the condition to the gentle rocking and warmth of the ship, even suggesting that living on a ship in peacetime was like being in a warm womb, but it occurred even during violent storms, when the ship was ice cold and he had been told by old salts, even in the aftermath of a battle.

The cure was not coffee, doing jumping jacks or other physical activity. Having induced anxiety, fear, danger, or challenging human contact seemed to remedy the condition, making violence a form of treatment. On the ships, men picked arguments and fights just to stay alert. In their trucks, they created problems on the road with other truckers and motorists, argued with other truckers on CB's or mobile phones for hours at a stretch on meaningless subjects, and they texted incessantly, compelling state legislatures to pass stringent laws against both practices.

While racing down I-10, Sowles realized that he consciously missed the dysfunctional companionship of Aaron and the stimulation of their ongoing arguments and contests, even more so because any one of their interactions could have been life-threatening. For the short time they were in the truck together, arguing with Aaron had kept him alert and strangely motivated.

Sowles realized that Aaron and he might have experienced some camaraderie and positive communication under different circumstances. Sowles would have enjoyed Aaron in a constructive environment. He would have been happy to discuss life and its meanings for Black and Caucasian Americans and the significance of melding the two cultures together for a future free from all forms of prejudice and segregation.

Being alone was familiar to Sowles, but having encountered Scully, his crew, Anna, and then Aaron, he realized that, in his truck, he had been isolated from people for far too many years. Something better had to be on the horizon.

# Twenty-five

## FLINT AND STONE

In one of their rare compatible conversations, before Sowles had wrested the gun from Aaron, Sowles had told Aaron a simple fable. It was a story he'd fashioned himself about two ancient spear hunters, a very dark Negro and a white man reddened by the sun, both from tribes and cultures completely unknown to each other. They encountered each other by surprise while stalking prey in the forest.

Each man had been hungry for days, so each suffered from failing vision, throbbing pains in their heads, and debilitating fatigue. Accordingly, when they encountered each other, they both knew that their lives were at risk at the hand of the other man. Each man raised his spear to attack, but then hesitated. Then, accepting their fatigue, both slowly lowered their weapons, and they stared at each other for several minutes before they both just dropped their spears and sat down.

Using grunts and hand gestures, over the next hours, they were able to communicate their individual plights. Then, by painstaking dances and chants, they directed each other's attention to the sun and stars and to an awareness of something greater than themselves at work. Soon, they were nodding and laughing and realized that together they could stalk and take down a boar more efficiently that one man could run after the animal and chase his own spear if he missed. With much acknowledgement and hilarity over the discovery, they proceeded to explain, again with only their hand gestures, another discovery—that while one man gutted and skinned, the other man could find fuel for fire and haggle with small stones to create a cookfire.

Sowles ended the story by explaining that the men hunted and ate together and slept under the same tree for two days, and on the morning of the third day, they built a small monument of fronds and twigs to commemorate their hunting success and friendship.

"When the two dudes finally split up," Sowles said. "They weren't 'fraid a each other an' ready to fuck each other up."

Aaron had been silent for a few moments. Then all he said was, "Sowles, you are too fucking much." But then he smiled warmly for the first time since they had crossed paths.

In that moment, Sowles felt the same kind of kinship with the tempestuous man as he had with his disaffected father years prior in their garage discussions of men's right and wrong decisions. Sowles knew then that Aaron and he could have taken a different path, but he concluded that it happened the way it had for a reason.

Sowles was sorrowed for abandoning Aaron but equally disturbed over his ambivalent feelings. Aaron had caused him a lot of fear, pain, and difficulty, and yet Sowles pitied him and hoped he had survived whatever illness he had been suffering from. Sowles actually felt that there was unfinished business between both of them and considered that a return to Humboldt would set that straight. Scully would have learned of Aaron's fate and assuming Aaron hadn't already blamed Sowles for the current situation, there could possibly be some reconciliation.

At this stage of his trip, running the last miles of California, Sowles did not know what lay ahead or how he would manage himself when he got to where he was going, if he actually even got there. He only knew that he was determined to do the right thing, even though he wasn't convinced of what that really was. There was more to discover down the road, and part of that had to do with Sowles himself, as he was as attracted and excited by the mission as he was frightened and repulsed. He knew his decision did not have to be the criminal choice of trafficking illegal and dangerous drugs.

Sowles was also aware that with Aaron gone, he could walk away, as he had suggested to his misguided captor that they both do. But Scully had left his indelible mark. It was only a day earlier that Scully was prepared to severely punish him, and he may still intend on following through at some point. Yet there was another possible outcome that Sowles considered; under the changed circumstances, getting back to Humboldt County could easily create a good future for him in the lucrative business that Scully oversaw, but that was a difficult choice, especially given that Sowles had prided himself in being a law-abiding man prior to being taken captive.

As he drove through the barren desert regions of Southeastern California, rapidly approaching his destination, he pondered these thoughts and reflected on Aaron's statement about Stockholm syndrome. Sowles knew that he had become committed to his captors' goals and felt compelled to complete the risky assignment. He also wanted to bathe in what might be Scully's positive response when he discovered that he had succeeded without Aaron.

And then, of course, there was Anna's face and sweet soul lingering prominently in his mind. Sowles knew that Anna was far too beautiful and wise for any average man such as he was, and she was far too young for him in any case, but he felt compelled to see her again.

For what reason he longed for Anna, he wasn't sure. Maybe to rescue her, maybe just to know her, to experience her heart and mind. She had a strong yet also maternal quality. She represented the Earth and the souls of many lost Native-American tribes both of Northern California and the region he was driving in. She was also close in age to any one of the daughters he might have had if there had never been any of the secretive abortions that Scully had remined him of.

Sowles thoughts returned to the present as he crossed the border at Blythe. Once in Arizona, his stomach jumped until he saw that the AZDOT weigh station at Ehrenburg was closed. "Slam Dunk-Two Points!" he said, laughing as he pushed the accelerator pedal to the floor and ramped the speed up to the legal limit of 75 MPH. "Adios, mofos!"

For much of the afternoon, he drove across Arizona, passing through the outskirts of Phoenix, Tucson, and numerous small, nasty desert hangouts that could scarcely be called towns. At Bowie, near New Mexico's border, a lone scale operator weighed him without incident.

Crossing into New Mexico, he pulled into the station at Lordsburg. When he saw what he believed were the X-ray machines, he held his breath, but the signs directed him to a twenty-mph weigh-in-motion ramp. At seventy-three thousand pounds, he was given a green light without having to stop.

His confidence was high at that point, until he realized that he had another weigh station in eastern New Mexico just before the Texas border. He suspected it also to be X-raying loads. It would be the last serious DOT threat before entering the Lone Star State which was known for not harassing truckers with repeated, troublesome weigh stops or overly fussy inspections.

His luck stayed true. The New Mexico station was under serious construction that made it look as if it had been hit by a wayward spacecraft headed for Area 51. He blew by it at seventy-five, just as he blew by a renowned, country-western store, wishing he could stop in and buy some duds and two leather holsters to impress the Mexicans and Chinese.

He was almost home free as far as DOT was concerned, but soon he would be in the city of El Paso, and common sense told him that would be where the rubber really hit the road. He was well aware that the Mexicans hated and feared Negroes and therefore were dangerous, and the Chinese considered even highly educated Black Americans to be far below the intellectual and social levels of their culture. They would not take well to him.

In El Paso, he would have to be on his best game.

# Twenty-six
## A MAN'S GOTTA EAT

BEEP. BEEP. BEEP. BEEP.

The noise seemed to be coming from the dashboard, an incessant, penetrating, high-pitched beeping sound similar to a fire alarm embedded in the ceiling of a home. It hooted in both of his eardrums, making his temples throb and his jaw hurt. Memories of a dentist drilling on a bad molar with a high-speed air drill flashed through his mind.

He examined the tractor's instrument panel trying to find a computerized warning lamp. Nothing. Then pulling the truck over, he shut the engine down. The beeping continued and without the engine noise muting the sound, it was louder. It seemed to be coming from the floor.

His next thought was that something had been installed while Scully had the rig. The vision of a planted device somehow monitoring everything up to that point made his brain swirl.

Grabbing the one flashlight that Scully's crew hadn't found and stripped from the cab, he bolted from the seat and crawled underneath the tractor, examining the cables, wires, drive line parts, axels, wheels, and the frame. The noise seemed to have faded, suggesting that it had to be coming from the interior of the truck. He scrambled back inside, dropped to his knees, and surveyed every inch of the floor and under the bunk.

BEEP. BEEP. BEEP. BEEP.

The sound was coming from under the passenger seat. He cautiously lifted the floor mat.

BEEP. BEEP. BEEP. BEEP.

It was Aaron's android phone.

Aaron must have dropped it during their commotion or when Sowles lifted him out of the truck. There was no incoming call, but instead, it had a text message with only a sad, frowning emoji face and a heart with an arrow running through it.

*Mary? Those wheels weren't different on the Jeep as Aaron in his delirium had suggested. It must have been Mary in the SUV. Or Winnie. Why?*

The sender wanted to be undercover. Whoever the person was used a five-digit phishing number. Someone was looking for Aaron, which meant someone was also looking for Sowles.

"Well, y'all on a need-to-know basis now, whoever yo' ass is," Sowles said.

He was undecided whether to disable it, toss it, or keep it to see if another message might come through. The decision was made when he climbed down from the seat and put the device on the pavement. With his boot heel, he ground the plastic face until it was shards of junk.

"Nah," he said. Then he put it under a drive tire, knowing it would be crushed to granules when he pulled out, but he remained concerned. These were devious people, and everyone's behavior after the determination hearing had been dangerous and unusually ambiguous. Maybe Aaron and Mary had something going on, or maybe Mary and Winnie were monitoring Aaron and Sowles for some reason. And as for Scully, he was the master of all deception. *Who knew what anyone was orchestrating?*

Sowles fired up the truck and returned to the highway. Again, rolling east toward Texas, he reviewed his options, but he knew they hadn't really changed. He was less than an hour from El Paso. There was no turning around and heading back to Oakland. It was too late. *He would do this!* The awareness became official when he saw a big, green, overhead sign: EL PASO–40. He punched the throttle and ran the rig up to eighty mph.

Thirty minutes later, he was exiting I-10 into a dark, old section of the freight depot district in El Paso. Without a GPS, he would have to stop and ask some night watchman or shady transient for directions. Instead, not wanting to risk himself or the load, he relied on his instincts and followed his trucker's nose. Both were correct. He drove a few blocks directly to Roja Street. The next step was even easier. Number 111 was three addresses from the corner.

It was a typical warehouse facility common to the border and freight towns of Texas, New Mexico or Arizona—bad outdoor lighting, piles of junk, and a good-sized, old building with a few beat-up docks. Sowles could see from the poor signage that it was shared by several different struggling tenants, each of them probably competing with one another for freight forwarding in and out of Mexico.

Many Mexican nationals had anchored relatives in the US in trucking who had visas and tiny offices that were nothing more than fly-by-night outfits with an address and desk, but they enabled the Mexican carriers to license and operate both in the States and Mexico. They could then pick up and deliver in both countries, even though American truckers with passports could not do the same in Mexico. US truckers considered this just one more relatively unknown inequity orchestrated by the DOT, and more than likely in concert with the US State Department. Most blamed former presidents Clinton and Obama.

Sowles carefully navigated through the front lot, avoiding stacks of spent pallets, a stripped-to-the-bone, old BMW 2002, and a few old Japanese sedans and motorcycles that were in some stage of repair. Finding a spot, he stopped and knocked on an unmarked steel door. There was no answer. He knocked again, harder.

The door opened slowly. Sowles backed away. A frizzy-haired, fried-looking African American woman stuck her head out. She eye-balled Sowles. "Whachu wan', brother?"

"I gotta load fo'…" He stopped talking. There was a heavy smell of marijuana smoke coming from inside the room, with the faint sound of some Mexican music and hushed laughter.

"What load, motherfuckah?" the woman asked. "You ain't got mah freight, nigga! That ain't mah freight!"

"Where's Barrazza Forwarders?" he asked.

"We don' take no freight fo' no Mexican freight peoples. Y'all bettah get yo' Black ass t' steppin', man."

As she shut the door, Sowles heard a gravelly voiced Mexican man in the room. He quickly sprinted back to the truck, deciding to find a path through the junk to the rear of the building. As he began to move the rig, a late-model Mercedes sedan pulled up on him. It was accompanied by a spanking new, gaudy, bright metallic-blue Ford F-250 Crew Cab.

Five men jumped out of the two vehicles. In the scant light, Sowles could see the three men from the Mercedes were Asians. All were well-dressed, and one was much older than the others. A second man was muscular, maybe a bodyguard. The other man was young, slight, and very proper looking.

The two men from the Ford were Hispanic and tough looking, but both were well attired in designer jeans and shiny leather jackets. There was no conversation between any of the men. The driver of the pickup called out to Sowles in English.

"Bring the trailer around back. Put it in dock two."

Sowles nodded. "Yes, sir."

"Ahora, chango loco!" the guy said.

Sowles knew the Mexican slang term for crazy monkey. He felt his jaw tighten to the point of pain. "Mexicoons," he snarled.

The men returned to their vehicles. Sowles let the Mercedes go ahead of his rig. The pickup followed Sowles. When he was behind the building, he discovered that the rear lot was also a truckyard nightmare with abandoned trailers, partially dismantled forklifts, numerous stacks of pallets, and rows of forty-foot steel shipping containers. This made Sowles's backup maneuver nearly impossible. After making three embarrassing and unsuccessful attempts, he climbed down and surveyed the situation, shaking his head and muttering to himself.

The Chinese men had been watching him curiously. The tough-looking one got out of the Mercedes and spoke with the passenger in the pickup. Both Mexican men jumped out and moved the pallets, cursing in Spanish the entire time.

When Sowles had better access, he quickly popped the seal and opened the back doors. He confirmed that the product was intact, well stacked, floor to ceiling, and secured at the rear. He then jumped back in the cab, smoothly maneuvered the trailer up against the dock, and then sat and waited for the familiar bumping sound and rocking of a forklift unloading the box. It didn't happen. Instead, he was interrupted at his driver's window by the tough-looking Chinese guy and the other young, well-dressed man.

"We know who you are Mr. Sowles. We have been waiting for you. Please come into the warehouse," the young man said in perfect English.

Knowing that he needed to play the "dumb nigga" role until he was out of the facility, Sowles nodded but didn't move. He waited stupidly, continuing to smile and nod.

As the two men turned momentarily aside to converse, Sowles quickly grabbed the Glock from the storage drawer and stuffed it inside his pants. He then climbed down.

"Please put your hands on your head," the young man said.

"Wha's up with this booshit?" Sowles asked.

"Do it!" the big guy said. He quickly patted Sowles down, immediately finding the handgun. He grabbed it and showed it to the young man. "We have a bad nigga," he said. Then he grabbed Sowles from behind jamming the Glock into the small of his back and walked him toward the warehouse door. "You a tough nigga, ain't you, old man?" He laughed and pushed the gun barrel even tighter against his spine.

They escorted him into the warehouse, where the two Mexican men had begun unloading the cargo and taking inventory. Sowles could then see there were many thousand opaquely wrapped packages sitting on about twenty expertly shrink-wrapped pallets.

Everyone in the supply chain was obviously skilled. The Mexican workers counted and transferred the packages onto different pallets and rewrapped each stack. A third Hispanic man, who had been waiting inside, forklifted each pallet into an unmarked fifty-three-foot steel intermodal container that Sowles had noticed while backing into his dock. It had been previously docked next to his spot to enable the cross-dock reloading for re-shipment across the Mexican border.

"Sit, please, Mr. Sowles," the young Chinese man said. "May we get you a soda or some tea perhaps?" he asked, as he graciously pulled out three chairs that sat around a card table.

Sowles shook his head. "No, man, I'm coo'," he said. "Y'all takes my gun an' calls me a nigga an' then offers me a soda! Whassup with that booshit? An' how the hell y'all know my name?"

The bodyguard snarled. "It's our business to know things, pal," he said as the old Chinese man nodded in agreement and dragged his aging body to the table.

"We take gun so no accident happening, Missa Sowes," the old man said. "Now, please, we awe awawe that anotha man a name a Aaaon was to come whish you. Whewe is thes man?"

"He got sick...uh, I took him to get some help. I dropped him off."

"I see. You dlopped hin off? Whewe yo dlop hin off?"

"Uh, in Castaic."

"Wha' is this place, Castake?"

"Southern California." Sowles proceeded to explain. At first, the two other men nodded, but then the young man spoke. "So where is the money, Mr. Sowles?"

"You mean the two grand the dude had in his bag?"

"No, Mr. Sowles," the young man said. "This Aaron man had two-hundred-and-fifty-thousand dollars cash he was delivering to us for a prior transaction."

"I dunno nothin' 'bout any a' that shit," Sowles said, his brow wrinkling.

"You know nothing of the chips Doctor Scully purchased from us?" he asked.

"Chips? I don' know 'bout no chips. What kinda chips, Frito-Lay?"

The bodyguard leaned in on Sowles, but the old man motioned him back. "Spesho computah chips we send to the Docta Scully, microchips, fo da people," the old man said.

"They put a chip in my neck, man. Y'all talkin' 'bout that kinda chip?"

The older man's face became red. He feebly slapped the table with his palm. "Yes! That is chip. We send sampow ordah a the chips by a Fedex to a Docta Scully. Aaron hab money fo' us. Whewe is thish Aaaon and whewe is ouw money?"

"The fuck if I know. Maybe you shoulda used PayPal," Sowles said.

The bodyguard smacked Sowles in the back of his head. "You do not speak to Father Ying in that manner again!"

Sowles smiled. "Okay, man, don't fuck up my chip in my damn head!" He turned to the young man. "I'm coo', man. I'm just a driver. I don' know 'bout no Aaron and Scully deals. I mean, they some underworld gangsters, but I ain't involved with none a' they shit."

Sowles saw that all three men were insulted by his statement about gangsters.

"I ain't judgin' y'all as crooks or nothin', I mean, I know y'all's gotta eat, right?" Sowles said. "But look, man, this cat Aaron be pullin' some booshit with yo' cash, man, maybe, an' that be one pile a nonsense I ain't figgered on. Y'all see wha' I'm sayin'?"

"How do I know this Aaron became ill and you then dropped him in Castaic, California? Maybe you killed him and you have our money," the young man said.

"No, man. He was sick offa some California Roll, I mean throwin' up bad, man, an' I brought the load to y'all because I knew it was up to me to do the job."

"You say, you took full responsibility?" the young man asked. "Interesting," he said "Why?

"I felt an obligation to this Aaron cat because I thought he was gonna die," Sowles said. "And I was responsible to Doctor Scully because he had made me a deal—"

"A deal? So, Doctor Scully is not your employer?"

"It's hard to explain, man."

"Do explain, Mr. Sowles," the young man said.

"Okay, man," Sowles said. "I mean, it's fucked-up, but I had to bring the load here. If I took the load back to Scully, I figgered he'd fuck me up, an' if I didn't take it to you here in El Paso, both y'all'd be after my ass fo' the resta my damn life."

"Yes, Mr. Sowles, we would be after your ass for many generations, Mr. Sowles."

"Well, I ain't had no kids, but I get y'all's point. I knew I had to bring the load or I'd be in some nasty shit...but check it out, man, if I was a thief, I coulda heisted the damned weed, but instead y'all's weed is right here in front a y'all's asses, so you gotta know, I ain't yo' thief, an' I did not take y'all's 250K. That's wha' I'm sayin'."

"Yes? Then where is the money, Mr. Sowles?" the young man asked. He then motioned to the bodyguard. "Go search the tractor!"

# Twenty-seven

## AIN'T BUT A PEANUT

"You're a Negro, Mr. Sowles. Why should we believe you?" the young man asked.

"I'm here with the weed, ain't I, man? I never knew Aaron had no big money with him…I didn't hang with the cat. He was tryin' to kill my ass since jump."

"Jump? What is 'jump?'"

"Jump street, you know."

"Where is jump street?"

"Man, it's ghetto slang, man. It means from the beginnin'."

"Oh," the young man said. He looked at his father and began speaking rapidly in Mandarin. The father nodded several times. Then the father spoke directly to Sowles.

"So, Missah Sowles, you say you a no criminal, okay, but you a Negro, so maybe you awe criminal. How do we know?" the father asked, his false teeth starting to chatter.

Sowles glared at the old man. "Damn, I guess I can't argue 'gainst that shit, old man. You're right, I'm a nigga, but I ain't stol' y'all's money," he said. "I mean, that dude Aaron probably wasn't sick. He was just fakin' that shit to get away with y'all's quarter mil."

The younger Chinese man nodded. "Yes. And I want that money back. That is my family's money. We sent an order of microchips to Doctor Scully and payment of two-hundred-and-fifty-thousand dollars US was supposed to accompany the load you brought."

Sowles nodded. "Yeah, man, I know, that's wha' y'all's been tellin' me fo' ten minutes'"

"We are very wealthy people, Mr. Sowles, but our honor is most valuable."

"I hear that," Sowles said. "I s'pose honor an' respect, is all's a man's got nowadays."

"Yes, Mr. Sowles. You are correct. We must now decide whether we believe you."

"Believe me, man. I'm gettin' good at this international crime shit. If y'all wanna work together on this shit, I can makes a plan to get y'all yo' honor back, an' maybe y'all's bread."

"Our bread? I'm sorry. I don't understand."

Sowles laughed. "Man, let me go back up to Scully's an' handle all this shit."

The debate was interrupted by the three Mexican men. They were motioning to the young Chinese man that the load had been fully transferred into the shipping container. While the young man shared a hushed conversation with the three men, the father sat across from Sowles, examining his face.

"You vely dark," the old man said. "Vely black." He pointed a bony finger at Sowles.

Sowles wanted to snatch the gnarly appendage and break it but he became distracted watching the young Chinese man hand the lead Mexican lumper about three-quarters of an inch of crisp, green American hundreds. The three Mexican men nodded, sat down together, and popped several bottles of orange soda. The young

Chinese man returned to the table. He and the father conversed in Mandarin, both nodding and grunting.

They were interrupted by the bodyguard. "There's no money in that truck, but these will interest you," he said. He set Aaron's SIG, the sawed-off, and all of the ammo on the table.

"Operational necessity," Sowles said.

"What you say?" The bodyguard said. He appeared ready to pistol whip Sowles.

"Never mind. Do me a favor, man," he said to the young man. "Call Scully or text the dude," Sowles said as he anticipated the bodyguard's hammer fist on the back of his head.

"Doctor Scully does not speak on the phone or use text messages," the young man said.

Sowles nodded. He remembered that Aaron had made that same comment. "Then email his ass then," he said.

"No, Mr. Sowles. We do not email, and neither does Doctor Scully."

All three men stared at Sowles. The young man spoke again. "What are your suggestions or proposals, Mr. Sowles? Please tell us before we decide your fate," he said.

"My fate?" Sowles asked. "Whachu talkin' 'bout, my fate?"

"Answer Mr. Ying, nigga!" the bodyguard said.

"Yeah, okay, chill, man!" Sowles said, snapping at the bodyguard. He then returned his attention to the young man.

"Check it out, Mr. Ying, my fate an' yo' honor, an' yo' money is fo' real, so check it out, you say you got fucked outta yo' two-hundred-fitty grand, an' it's yo' honor at stake. I can feel y'all honor an' shit, but 250K ain't nothin' but a peanut when y'all gots twenty-seven-million dollars a Scully's weed in yo' house right now. I mean, that 250K is a tip."

"A tip? What is a tip, Mr. Sowles?"

"You know, a, uh, uh, a gratuity, you know, a tip, like a write-off, maybe. Like when ya go into a restaurant and ya give the waitress a few dollars."

"We do not enjoy this tradition."

"Y'all s'posed t' tip the restaurant ho 'cuz she be nice and put yo' food in front of y'ass."

"Chinese do not honor this European tradition," the young man said.

"Y'all write that tip stuff off, right? I mean, y'all know that shit, man."

"Yes, maybe a tip is tax deductible, but we do not concern ourselves with US federal tax law, Mr. Sowles, and we do not want to give any tip," the young man said, as he and his father shook their heads in disagreement. "Why are you wasting our time with this nonsense?"

"I feel y'all, man. Your time is important, but I'm jus' sayin', the two-hundred-fitty grand is a small amount of bread to get yo' honor all fucked-up over…an' shit, man, fuckin' me up ain't gonna help y'all, but I can dig it, y'all want yo' money and yo' pride."

"Ah, yes, Mr. Sowles. This is the word, 'pride,' yes," the young man said.

Sowles smiled widely. "What is yo' name, my brother?" he asked.

The young man seemed perplexed. "Uh, my name is Ronald," he said.

"Ronald? Damn. That's a strange name for a Chinese dude, ain't it? I mean shouldn't it be, like Ho, or Lee, or Kong, or Yan, or something?"

"Actually, my name is Rong."

"Wrong, like w r o n g?" Sowles asked.

"No, dude. Rong, like R o n g. My father studied in US and married my mother here, but then they had to run from FBI back to our home in China, where I was born. I am Rong Ying, the first son of Hon Ying, my father here you see. I am called Ronald here in the US."

"Rong Ying," Sowles said. "That's cool, man, like yin an' yang, and Cheech an' Chong, eh?" Sowles said. "But that FBI shit, man, I dunno, man, that's some hard shit to deal with. I'm jus' sayin'."

"Pay attention, please, Mr. Sowles! My father is getting very impatient with you," he said, as he motioned to the older man, who was tapping his yellowed nails on the table. "He says you are being a 'crazy lying nigga' and he wants to 'fuck you up.'"

"Let's jus' chill. Y'all don' have t' get irrational or nothin', pullin' a damn race card and threatenin' my ass. I'm workin' us up a plan." Sowles said. "See wha' I'm sayin'?"

"Okay, Mr. Sowles, but please get to the point of your proposal."

"You alright, Rong…Ron," Sowles said. "You alright."

"Ron, Mr. Sowles, Ron."

"Yeah, Ron," Sowles said. He then stated the facts as he saw them, explaining again that the Ying's had twenty-seven-million dollars' worth of Scully's hybrid marijuana at US street price, which, as he reminded them, was undeniably worth more in Scandinavia or Western Europe or Australia, and wherever else they sold it.

"Not to mention them damn expensive THC gum drops and gummy worms y'all's makin'," Sowles said. "So, tell yo' pops, yo' honor an' yo' financial future is a sweet ass guarantee," Sowles said.

"My father does not accept any chicanery in business," Ron said.

"I dunno what that shit means, Ron, but I ain't here to fuck up y'all's plans, man," Sowles said. He then explained that they had not discussed the second leg of the operation with the fentanyl cut pills.

"Now, Ron, my man, I figure y'all is probably puttin' another fitty-million dollahs or so in yo' britches with them pills," Sowles said. "I mean, cuz I can see y'all ain't no foo's, and ya probably make that shit yo' ownselves in China. I mean, y'all's some manufacturers an' traders."

Ron and his father were now listening intently. Sowles leaned toward Ron.

"So, I say we get them pills an' get our shit finalized," Sowles said. "An' then I roll back to Scully all good and friendly, y'all know, with the pills an' whatever fentanyl shit y'all exchangin' fo' his weed, an' that way, we keep everything cool. That'd be Job One. Feel me?"

"I feel you, Mr. Sowles, but you have not said how we will get our 250K back!" Ron said. "I think you are avoiding this issue. You feel me?"

"Well, uh, I'm workin' up a Plan B an' C fo' y'all," Sowles said. "Be cool, my brother."

The bodyguard examined the three guns. Sowles watched him carefully, while Ron's father continued to eyeball him. Sowles scratched his head and smiled warily again at the three Mexican men who had emptied their soda bottles and seemed to be getting irritable.

"Can y'all get some more Fanta for those cats?" Sowles asked.

The bodyguard nodded to Ron and lumbered over to an old refrigerator that sat in the corner of the room. Sowles returned his attention to Ron and his father.

"Check it out, man," Sowles said. "Aaron stole y'all's money an' he booshitted my ass. He's probably back up in the Triangle right now, tryin' to get next to some fine, redheaded, Irish ho named Mary." He remembered the frowning emoji and heart on the phone and then the SUV at the weigh station. It was all starting to fit together— Aaron, Mary, the Chinese debt, the cash.

Ron and his father began chattering in Mandarin again, and, after several minutes, they turned to Sowles. "My father says maybe you're too smart of a cookie for a Negro."

"Yeah? So, nows I'm an uppity nigga, eh?" Sowles said. "Fuck that shit, Ron. I'll find Aaron's ass and deal with the dude," he said. "But I need them guns, bro."

Ron smiled widely. "You will have them when you leave with our fentanyl load, but only if my father agrees that you are not a co-conspirator with this Aaron shit ball."

"Man, how many times I gotta tell y'all? This Aaron dude was sick to his stomach, either that, or like I said, the foo' booshitted my ass."

"Yes, Mr. Sowles. But my father says you are skilled in the art of bullshit and deception also. How do you plan to convince my father otherwise?"

"Ron, listen man, I dropped Aaron's ass in Castaic, and I came here. If I was involved with any crooked booshit with y'all's money an' shit, I'd a sold y'all's weed to some hooked-up nigga bangers down at the Crenshaw Walmart in LA. See wha' I'm sayin'?"

# *Twenty-eight*
## THE SILK ROAD

"Mr. Sowles," Ron said. "My father is giving some consideration to allowing you to live, but only if you can enhance our position. This piece of excrement, Aaron, offended our family. Hon Ying Trading must have its recompense."

"Well, Ron, tell yo' pops, first, man, it ain't smart t' kill my ass, 'cuz if he do, how we gonna get this load up to Scully an' handle all this Aaron booshit fo' yo' pop's recomp…uh mess?"

"A good observation, Mr. Sowles, however, the insult incurred by the loss of 250K has my father very unhappy. He says that our family honor must now be set in a high tree like a glass bird, to be enjoyed only at a distance from the decks of his garden, but after the pills are delivered to Doctor Scully, and we determine the status of the Aaron cockroach, my father will set the bird free to peck out all of his enemies' eyes."

"That's crazy shit, Ron!" Sowles said. "Y'all gots some wicked juju traditions!"

"Thank you, sir. But you do not want to also become an enemy of my father or his bird."

"No shit! But I ain't done nothin' t' get that motherfucker after my eyeballs!"

"Be aware, Mr. Sowles, there is another issue," Ron said. "My father is elderly, just as you are. He says that at your advanced age, you are much too old to track this Aaron robber and exact a reprimand that will satisfy the Ying honor. My father wishes to have assistance from our colleagues, and then we will also be traveling to the Emerald Triangle to oversee the operation."

"Aw, Ron, tell yo' pops that's real kind a him, but y'all don' have t' go outta y'all's way. I'm one-hundred-percent coo' with handlin' this shit."

"Thank you for your consideration, Mr. Sowles, but my father worries that you are too old for this task, and, to be honest with you, he worries that maybe you are just too Black."

"Damn, Ron, that pigment shit be gettin' too technical, bro. An' lemme say, man, at my age, I'm still a badass nigga. I got me a George Foreman punch, an' I gots some good-ass kicks from my Tang Soo Do trainin'."

"Tang Soo Do is Korean. We are Chinese. We totally disagree with this style," Ron said.

"Well, Ron, y'all know, if y'all gimme back them guns, I be coo' as Chilly Willy, man."

"Mr. Sowles. These points you make do not appease my father. He insists that we take a domestic flight to San Francisco. We will visit with our many friends in Chinatown and dine in the restaurants where we have some investments. Then we will drive to the Emerald Triangle."

"Y'all don' need to do that, Ron," Sowles said. "I mean, flyin' is fuckin' dangerous these days," he said, frowning. "You know, people hittin' an' slappin' each other an' shit, and the masks, an' the Emerald Triangle ain't 'zactly safe fo' either a y'all neither, with all them crazy Indian legends, white boys on dope, an' them big-ass redwood trees an' shit."

"Do not worry, I will bring some of our friends from CSP."

"What's that?" Sowles asked. "CSP?"

"Chinese Secret Police," Ron said. "Very capable men."

"Damn, Ron! Now that shit's definitely goin' too far, man. This is America, man! We don' need no Chinaman police runnin' 'roun' our shit here in the US. I don' care how damn coo' they are....that ain't the solution, Ron."

"Our friends are retired from the agency. They all own beach property on the West Coast. They are, 'cool,' as you say. We will have them come for the reunion with my father, then go to the Emerald Triangle to view the redwood trees and the souvenirs, and then we will all search for the scumbag Aaron."

"Uh, yeah. I hear y'all on that fo' sho'," Sowles said. "Specially the souvenirs an' shit, but why have them get they shit all up into the booshit, man?"

"Why are you trying to talk me out of my professional involvement, Mr. Sowles?"

"I'm jus' tryin' to save y'all some stress, my brother, I mean, with this Aaron booshit," Sowles said. He then whispered, "But lemme be truthful, Ron, there be a young girl up there I gotta catch up with, man. I need, whacha call, my alone time free from hassles."

"Mr. Sowles, a young girl is the nemesis of a man's success, especially an old man."

"Nah, it ain't whachu thinkin', Ron. She an' me just gotta talk, man. See wha' I'm sayin'?"

"You surprise me, Mr. Sowles."

"All's I'm sayin', man, is y'all don' need no Chinese army up there."

"It will only be a few undercover agents. The team will augment this plan B of yours."

"Yeah, that's right, my damn plan B," Sowles said. His face sunk. "I near forgot."

"Then we shall proceed with our immediate matters and effect plan B."

"I hear ya, Ron, but lemme ask y'all a question. Y'all's gonna have the Mexicoons load them pills, or do the nigga gotta do it?"

"No, Mr. Sowles, the Mexican men will load your trailer with the pharmaceuticals," Ron said, as he motioned to the three men and clapped his hands. They stood.

"*Muy bueno*," Sowles said, smirking at the Mexicans. They nodded and then frowned.

"May I interest you now in that soda or tea, Mr. Sowles?" Ron asked.

"Yeah, Ron, please, man. This talkin' and figurin' out shit got me dry as a mofo."

"Mofo?"

"Fanta orange, if the esse's ain't drained it all," Sowles said.

Ron's father and the bodyguard appeared to have lost interest in the discussion and had taken out a small Chinese checkers game and set the marbles in place. Ron walked away. When he returned, he was carrying two six packs of bottled orange sodas. He cordially handed a bottle to everyone, while Sowles watched the trailer-loading process.

The pills had been locked in the warehouse, so the cargo had to be prepped for shipping. Sowles saw again that the Chinese and the Mexicans took the shipping business seriously. The Mexican men were sharp. They stacked four pallets four feet high with paper-wrapped, interlocking cartons the size of shoeboxes, then they neatly wrapped each of the four-foot pallets in shiny paper, labeled "Ivanhoe's Doggie Treats," and then they shrink-wrapped each pallet with clear plastic. Then the pallets were forklifted into the nose of the trailer and covered with an insulated blanket.

"You see, Mr. Sowles," Ron said. "We Chinese are ancient traders. We prepare all shipments for rough travel, foreign invaders, and the prying eyes of spies or officials."

"Yeah, man, y'all is good with that shit," Sowles said, as he strapped the load with thick trucker's belts.

When the Mexicans were finished, they stood around drinking their sodas.

"*Gracias*, man," Sowles said to the lead man as he rechecked the load strap.

"*Si, cabron*," the man said under his breath as he walked away.

Sowles was pleased that it was a very light load. It made for good fuel efficiency and speed, and, even better, it reduced his chances of being weighed at every border station.

Most western states can read a rig's gross weight from scales built into the highway, and the computer will bypass a very light unit. It saves industry time, and for irritable drivers, it reduces the risk of a full-blown level-one inspection. For Sowles, it likely meant a bypass at every weigh station.

Sowles asked about the actual quantity of pills, and Ron told him that, assuming the Chinese manufacturers had not cheated him, the total was approximately 7.7 million pills with a street value of $153 million dollars.

"Whooooeee! Damn!" Sowles said. "I was way off on them numbers, eh, Ron? I said, 'fitty million.' Y'all givin' Scully six times the street price fo' that weed. What is up with that shit? Y'all's confusin' me with these numbers. Yo' pops must really like that Scully dude."

"Mr. Sowles. We do not allow ourselves to like or dislike people or things."

"Yeah, man, I can dig that, but six times the value, man! Whassup with that?"

"We are generous in our business dealings, but we also expect thoroughness, loyalty, and complete efficiency. Doctor Scully has proven himself with a quality weed product and service."

Sowles nodded. "It's a damned shame that foo' Aaron fucked that shit up."

"I will share more with you, Mr. Sowles, because I am coming to enjoy your amusing personality," Ron said. "It is not so 'fucked up,' as you suggest. We have sustainable mortgages on Doctor Scully's many acres and crops, and our pills are processed in one of our rural provinces for about four US cents each. We trade peanuts for gold, Mr. Sowles. Our returns are unfathomable when our commissions and royalties are computed."

"No booshit?" Sowles said.

"Yes, and bear in mind, Doctor Scully must move the pills to realize his true profit. So, you see, we have less exposure in secondary markets, in the overall US supply chain, and in the final retail transactions."

"Y'all is blisterin' with yo' game, man! But you still gotta move the weed."

"A good observation, but Mexicans have many decades of experience in marijuana trafficking, Mr. Sowles. Their dope management skills have been highly perfected over generations. And as mentioned, the next many loads of weed will be the raw material for processing candy for the lucrative market that you have indicated an awareness of."

"Yeah, candy, that's a trip, man," Sowles said. "Mexicans always been famous fo' gettin' folks fucked up on weed, fo' sho'," he added.

"Caution with stereotypes, Mr. Sowles. Yes, it is a lucrative arrangement, however, I regret one issue…how do you say this word…uh, uh, 'botch.' I am concerned over this botch with this amoeba, Aaron. His defection has caused doubt and now also might create a botch in the other highly specialized international markets we are currently working in and those we are testing."

"I hear ya," Sowles said. "Y'all is concerned 'bout yo' territorial expansion and product or service development. So, what if Scully just pays the two-hunnert-fitty grand, an' y'all be done with the shit? I means, hell, y'all can jus' settle yo' shit and let the honor booshit go. See wha' I'm sayin'?"

"No. That is how you Americans think, restitution…yes, restitution is in order, but offenses cannot be settled only with repayment when any honor has been breached."

"I guess," Sowles said. He seemed confused.

"Never guess, Mr. Sowles," Ron said. He handed Sowles a bill of lading.

Sowles read it. The shipper was Hon Ying Traders. The forwarding agent who had brought it into the US only days earlier was listed as Barrazza Forwarders. It was described as 'pet food,' and consigned to Scully Family Farms.

"That is in order. No guessing, you see," Ron said. "Now, about finding this Aaron rabbit turd. It seems he has absconded with money but also with information that must never be disclosed. Our CSP friends will be providing big support and will guarantee that he will not talk about our larger plans."

"Ah, yeah, Ron, uh, that's real cool a y'all, but like I said, man, I prefer to work alone, you know without support, more like a secret agent. Y'all see wha' I'm sayin'?"

"That is unacceptable, sir. Our CSP friends, my bodyguard, that is my dear younger brother whom you've just met, my father, and I will be there as a safety net. You need to understand, Mr. Sowles. My father is still not fully convinced that you and Aaron are not co-conspirators. Regardless of the developing communication between you and me, I'll have to regularly reassure his doubts."

"I got that part, man, yo' pops ain't fond a niggas, but I will find that dude, Aaron."

"I hope we can trust you, Mr. Sowles. If so, you have a profitable future. If not, you could befall the wrath of my father's glass bird."

Ron, please, no damn birds. I'm bringin' y'alls dope back to Scully 'cuz it was part of my deal with him, an' now I'm all wrapped up in yo' chips an' this Aaron $250K booshit, when all that was bitch-ass Aaron's fault. I mean, I be doin' y'all right, man, an' 'cuz I'm goin' out my way an' all, instead a y'all's warnin's an' shit, how about some love fo' my efforts?"

"Love, Mr. Sowles?"

"A gratuity instead of some evil threat, man. I mean, y'all makin' serious bank here."

"As I've said, Chinese are not known for giving gratuities."

"Well shit, then, forget a goddamned tip, just pay me to track down Aaron."

"Your compensation on this return load is the same as it was on the load you brought to us. All transportation costs are paid by Doctor Scully. These are all his products," Ron said.

Sowles reflected on the fact that his payment was his freedom from Scully's wrath.

The bodyguard pulled away from the Chinese checkers game and whispered to Ron.

Ron motioned to Sowles. "My assistant, my, how do you say? My short-fused brother has asked me if I need him to intervene.

"Tell that bigheaded foo', 'we jus' talkin', Ron. Damn, man!"

"Mr. Sowles, let's proceed now. I want to fully emphasize to you that Doctor Scully cannot be alienated by these efforts to find this derelict, Aaron. Our purpose is to protect the honor of the Ying family, but we also must not damage any business relationships in the Emerald Triangle. If we can collect the stolen two-hundred-fifty-thousand dollars, then so much the better, but we will accept the financial loss if necessary."

"Sure, Ron," Sowles said. "But if the dude fucked us all, I'll kick his white-ass."

"You must not kill him. If he is found, we must interrogate him before he is processed."

"Processed?" Sowles asked. "Damn, what is processed?"

"Like making soy sauce, Mr. Sowles. We liquify the soybean, and in a sense, similar to extracting THC under pressure," he said. "Aaron, the cockroach will be processed." He handed Sowles a colorful, Chinese cloth bag. "Your munitions."

"Thanks, but I didn't understand. Y'all gonna waste Aaron?" he asked.

"No 'waste,' Mr. Sowles. The Chinese do not waste anything," Ron said. "But what you must understand is the Aaron ass-wipe is our business now. Your business is delivering this load to Doctor Scully in the Triangle. It is his legitimate payment and is vitally important, as we all have other international business with him that must continue. He motioned to the double-stacked line of steel boxes in the yard. "Do you see those oceangoing containers? Those are also an opportunity for you, Mr. Sowles."

Sowles nodded dumbly. Playing the nigger routine was just about over. He had his guns and ammo, and he was almost back on the road, but Ron seemed to be studying his face.

"I have come to enjoy you, Mr. Sowles. I will say, people are our greatest asset," he said as he bowed and then walked away toward the Chinese Checkers game.

Sowles felt his pulse increase. At first, he didn't understand the reason, but quickly he was reminded and then troubled by all of the past statements made by Anna, by Aaron, and now Ron.

A quarter-million dollars' worth of computer chips was not the industry Aaron referred to, or that Ron had been alluding to, and marijuana was small potatoes in the international world of drug smuggling. Neither did chips nor fentanyl require forty-foot oceangoing containers. Family honor was not the whole picture either, not in the twenty-first century, so what else could Scully and the Ying cartel be involved with?

Sowles gulped another bottle of Fanta in an attempt to calm his thoughts. His mind raced—

*Aaron's rap 'bout people on the farm bein' 'freaks off the grid' and then Scully kidnappin' me might be pieces of another puzzle with no picture on the box. Was Scully snatchin' folks for temporary labor and his pleasures and then forwardin' them to the Chinese in exchange for somethin'? That could explain buyin' microchips for trackin' people. Were homeless or marginalized po' folks providin' a supply of prospects which were converted into other merchandise?*

Sowles knew that California is known for its mild weather, making it the ideal landing spot for many displaced down-and-outers from all over the United States. It was no secret that the East Bay, Stockton,

Sacramento, East LA, and the Inland Empire were some of the most prolific areas in the country for homelessness, addicted street people, youth gangs, displaced casualties from the mental health system, and early released, unemployable felons from the prisons. Added to this burgeoning population is the new influx of undocumented and wandering migrants crossing the entire US-Mexican border from Texas to California that are estimated to be in the millions.

Ron had boasted a statement about the Chinese being ancient traders. Sowles thought back to his junior college history classes and church Bible studies of the Old Testament. What had been the most significant merchandise in the ancient world?

*Slaves!*

Was it possible that Scully and the Ying family in collusion with the Mexican cartels had found a feedstock of human beings and were beginning to trade the dopers and burnouts on the farm, and the incoming migrants to the Chinese? Then had the Chinese moved them into labor camps and organ harvesting mills, or was it a combination of both? What commodity were the Chinese giving Scully in return?

*What commodity?* Sowles thought. *And are they only in the early stages of launchin' that business as a start-up or is it up an' runnin'?*

Sowles remembered hearing rumors about the Chinese being suspected of having work camps. The rumor was that they were also harvesting human organs. Was Scully planning on using lost and disregarded fuckups for labor until he could trade them through the Ying cartel to China, and maybe even beyond?

If Scully was sending human riffraff to the other side of the world via the Ying cartel, then it was hugely profitable, but Scully likely wasn't forwarding any humans in exchange only for pills, or computer chips, or even wholly for cash. He had his drug network intact, and he was established financially enough to know that there is a point that all paper cash becomes an impossible commodity to manage, if nothing else but for storage and concealment. So, what could

Scully either be planning on getting or already receiving in exchange for people?

Sowles and Aaron had talked about Scully possibly coming from one of the Scandinavian countries or maybe an Eastern nation. Europe and Asia represented the largest landmass in the world and the most populated countries on Earth. Their consumer demand for prostitution, drugs, pornography, snuff films, was vast, as was true throughout the world, but a major difference with Europe and the East was also the untold millions of beautiful young women trying to negotiate their way into the West, where they believed that they could upgrade to futures in corporate America, government, film, and with well-heeled men.

Sowles remembered the disproportionate number of women over men as Aaron and he drove onto the Scully property on the first day.

*Was Scully receivin' attractive women from 'round the world in exchange for both large quantities of fentanyl, walkin' wounded labor-ers, an' the new migrants that were bein' disseminated an' considered to be unaccountable inside the U.S., and if so, were some of the incomin' women an' girls headed into US prostitution an' slave markets an' others redistributed back into European an' Eastern sex markets as supply an' demand necessitated?*

Sowles recollected that on the farm, there were multitudes of beau-tiful women or all nationalities, but many of them were olive skinned and resembled Anna. He assumed they were Native American, but could some be Hispanic, Portuguese, or Arab? Was there a possibility that the Chinese were trafficking certain types and nationalities of women back from Europe, Asia, and from the Middle East for the return trade of a labor force that was comprised for breeding stock and organ donors. In essence, were the women on Scully's farm tran-sitioning from the East into the US prior to redistribution and the farm laborers moving in the opposite direction?

Sowles was amazed and excited that he could piece together such a fantastic theory, although it made him question his own sanity, a form of introspection that was not new. But the conceived plot was at least good material for the novel that Scully had suggested Sowles was writing, a book that he was now seriously considering, or perhaps reconsidering. He silently racked his own memory—*where is my damn Coach bag, an' my pens an' notebook? Did I only 'magine them too?*

As he anxiously waited for Ron to return for their final good-bye, he glanced again at the steel containers on the parking lot. He felt like he was behind the wheel of a careening downhill tractor-trailer as it headed for the emergency escape ramp. Again, his mind raced—

*Freight mostly be delivered in a one-way direction, but any damn truck driver know, most streets and highways run both ways, and in truckin' a man need a backhaul. Seem that Scully got his two-way trade business all figured out.*

Sowles's past study of history was finally useful. Scully was reharnessing the fundamental concept of Chinese barter. They had invented and controlled two-way trade routes centuries before European and Western civilizations existed.

It seemed at first glance that the current transaction of making payment for the weed in fentanyl was a method to avoid traceable cash. Scully then took the secondary step of forwarding the gel caps because the profit was multiplied six times beyond simply selling the weed. But it was conceivable also that an experimental trade model for international human trafficking had been established as Scully's worldwide drug trading had allied him with the many appendages of the slave trade network.

Sowles wanted to fly out the warehouse door, jump in the rig and run it over a cliff, but he maintained his composure and sat waiting for Ron to return. His studies of high school history and the Bible raced across his mind. His thoughts were coming fast—

*That nasty fentanyl put Scully in a European and Asian network that introduce' him to the human traffickin' markets of the Middle and Far East. Drug trade is the perfect way into gettin' deeper with the international gangsta' game. Tradin' dope is fo' real, but to trade one class of folks for another class is a hella idea, an'a ancient practice even written about in the Bible.*

The landmasses of Canada, Eastern Asia, Russia, Northern Europe, and Africa are accessible from anywhere in the world, but Eureka California and its old harbor were outside the U.S. port network. And except for a diminishing and non-replenishable redwood forest, the region no longer played a major part in US logistics. As such it was essentially obsolete for monitored shipping. Yet it offered entry to the Pacific and to Alaska and then into Russia and westward, providing further access to all of Eurasia and its smuggling cartels. In turn, the El Paso, Texas/Juárez, Mexico border entry point was also all but ignored by both bought and sold corrupt police agencies and disempowered or disenchanted federal agents on both sides of the border. These factors made the entire corrupt logistical effort a feat that could only be conceived by a global architect as Finn Scully was proving to be. But to Sowles, this brainstorm seemed as complicated and confusing as a Chinese kaleidoscope, and yet it also made sense.

Furthermore, marijuana is a hearty, weedlike plant that succeeded with very little maintenance. Sowles had seen the multitudes of stragglers on Scully's farm. That quantity of laborers was not needed for technicians or farm workers.

Aaron had often slipped the words "Middle East" and "Afghanistan" into their conversation. This was where he had lived while in the US Special Forces. Aaron knew the Middle East. It undoubtedly played its part, and between the Arab money, China's wealth, Scully's affluence and connections, there was immense influence and fortunes for buying and selling any commodity on the face of the Earth.

Sowles dug deeper into his theories—*'sides weapons, what are the most in demand an' profitable illicit commodities on the Earth? Drugs an' human bein's. People! That's it*—Sowles thought—*Scully is a lawless mastermind!*

Scully was a mastermind, far more evolved than any typical international drug dealer, and seemingly more influential than any known sex trafficker. Finn Scully could run a developing, two-way drug, human trafficking, and trading empire from his dining room as if it was a video game, moving every imaginable illicit commodity throughout the globe, all under the guise of being a legal weed farmer.

It then began to make sense to Sowles that Scully's cannabis and its transportation across state lines could just be an innocuous front that had been mostly ignored since the passage of California's propositions legalizing weed. It was regulated and as long as he kept his nose politically clean, the rest of his dealings went unnoticed.

Then who really was Dr. Finn Scully? Where had his seemingly limitless power, money, talent, charisma, and influence come from?

In his video, he claimed that he had witnessed forfeitures, seizures, and the arrests and prosecutions of numerous people. Maybe he was simply getting even. But why? He was still a great mystery. There were no brothers, no lineage, no family history, and as described by Aaron, Scully was somewhat of a nonentity.

"*Who is he?*" Sowles asked himself. He felt a familiar chill run up and down his spine.

Scully was a liar. Scully was deceptive. Scully was a manipulator. Scully was a tormentor.

Sowles's mind raced back to his mother's many Christian admonitions and then he thought of Reverend Persons' sermons. *Was there a fit?*

Was Scully the perfect example of a lost man in need of finding salvation? Sowles tried to answer that question as he thought of the comic books from his youth, the fantastic plots and intricate schemes, the demonic influences on humans.

Sowles realized that his mind had taken a dangerous, wide turn. *Had the monitoring chip malfunctioned?* He asked himself.

# Twenty-nine

## A LOCALE OF SORTS

Sowles felt nauseous when Ron returned. "You're not looking well," Ron said, smiling.

"Yeah, Ron, sure, man," Sowles said. "I'm coo', man. Ready to roll."

"Good!" Ron said. "Then I have a request."

"What?" Sowles asked.

Ron smiled warmly. "Please discard the gray uniform."

Sowles seemed dumbfounded, in fact, insulted. "I know they needs a good dry cleanin', but damn, man, y'all is a candid dude, Ron."

"Please do not take this personally, Mr. Sowles," Ron said, forcing a thin smile. "The Chinese have highly sensitive olfactory glands, but more to the point, our CSP agents are from an earlier generation with very old-fashioned values. They will be offended by a Negro wearing the party uniform from the Mao Zedong era. Most are not fond of Negroes and believe that all Blacks are subversives and terrorists. Let's not fuel their opinions."

"That's 'nother good reason t' leave them dudes at the restaurant in Frisco," Sowles said.

"No, Mr. Sowles." He handed Sowles a small slice of crisp cash. "This is for you, one thousand US," he said. "Please do consider some nice jogging suits perhaps. Two more things, get rid of the Ebonics. They make you seem just too Negro…and do not forget my father's bird."

Ron quickly turned away from Sowles. He walked toward the rear of the room and stood where a fan was blowing. Within minutes, the pistols were back in the glove box, both the scattergun and ammo were back under the bunk, and Sowles was back in the driver's seat, roaring west on Interstate 10.

"Goddamned tight-assed, prejudiced Chinese foo's," Sowles said. "Too Negro, and my damn clothes stink?"

He repeatedly banged both fists on the steering wheel. "A nigga jus' ain't gotta chance! Nobody got no respect fo' a Black man. A thousand bucks, an' I'm haulin' a hundred-an'-fifty-million-dollar dope load! An' top it off, the Chinamen think I'm a stanky nigga! Tell that booshit to Obama an' Michelle!"

He was pissed that he had sat inside the warehouse for five hours, drank Fanta together, and cut a deal that would get their shit up the road, and they still considered him to be an inferior nigger. The thought that he was lucky to be alive only briefly crossed his mind.

It was four in the morning. Worn out and depleted from the events of the past many days, it was time to unwind, recreate the paper Hours-of-Service logs to plan his northwest run, get some sleep, and buy fuel and clothes in the morning. Then he would have to answer the biggest questions of his life: to continue with the plan that he and Rong Ying had agreed on and return to Scully, or get his ass and the truck back to the Oakland yard, give the DEA the dope, and tell everyone his entire crazy tale?

In the predawn, opaque darkness of New Mexico, he drove just beyond the weigh station that was under construction and stopped in a gravel turnout that had three other major companies' rigs parked for the night. All three semis were illuminated from front to rear with their amber-and-red running lights. The parking looked safe enough and apparently legal. He rolled alongside a late model Freightliner with a clean-looking dry van and shut his rig down.

Flopping on his bunk, he had a lot to think about. He had survived the bullshit at Scully's and had successfully made the weed delivery, fulfilling the first leg of the mission that had been assigned under Aaron's watch. He also had a fortune of illegal drugs in the trailer that could make him a multimillionaire, or get him fifty years in prison, or get him tortured and killed. Yet to that moment, he had done it all unscathed except for his sore backside and ass which mysteriously felt like the wounds had never been inflicted.

"You good, Mr. Sowles," he said. "But yo' ass is headin' back to the white boy who kidnapped yo' ass, had y'all beat down, and hosed ya like you was marchin' the streets with Dr. King back in the day."

He was exhausted. Days of adrenalin pumping through his bloodstream had enabled his body and brain to work overtime and kept him moving forward, but it had also depleted his core. Yet, he was newly obsessed with determining what had really gone down with Aaron. *Had Aaron really boogied on Scully and Rong Ying with the two-hundred-and-fifty thousand dollars?*

*Was Mary involved? Was she the driver of the SUV that had been following them just north of the weigh station when Aaron had gotten ill? Could she be part of a Western European trafficking link?* She was old country Irish, and Ireland was not a country of leprechauns, clover, and jolly, red-faced crooners. It had many port cities too, and had long been a major crime and trafficking center.

As Sowles began to drift toward sleep, he thought about Rong Ying—*The dude be cool 'nough, but aren't the members of the Chinese Communist Party ungodly folks an' atheists? Who cares 'bout their damned 'peccable manners an' 'fficiency? Why give a fuck 'bout the cash the Ying family lost an' rebuilding their honor an' that ol' man's foo' ass glass bird?*

*And what about Scully? Who could really know who or what he was, or what the extent of the crime was that he was up to?* Sowles knew that even if he followed the plan and delivered the pills, the chances of

Scully giving him an outright pass back to the free world was slim at best. A more likely conclusion would be to continue in Scully's service under duress, as if he was a sailor shanghaied by pirates, and try to fit in as the official freight hauler or next idiot sidekick, like Winnie. Either that or be sent to a labor camp and then who knows where?

But the only valid emerging issue seemed to be how to walk away clean with Anna before she ended up in a Washington DC or Vegas brothel, or on an island of serving nymphettes, or worse, in a container on a ship to Europe or Asia! But how could he achieve that? How could he break free? He knew far too much, and just as Ron had suggested with the Aaron matter, Aaron needed to be interrogated and downloaded before processing. Why? because Aaron also knew far too much. *That's me now*—Sowles thought as he again was alone in the empty night. "I know too much." he said softly as he began to feel old fear perching on his shoulders.

"It's bigger than dope, or guns, or computer chips." Three people had dropped the hint. The words repeated inside Sowles's mind as he drifted off into a restless, dark void of sleep.

"You can run, but you cannot hide," he said, as Anna's young face glided through his muddled dreams. He felt her. She was a vivid light in the darkness and mayhem that Scully seemed to have authority over. She was also in the light of the sunshine that forced Sowles's eyes open four hours later when he awoke.

His rig was the only semi still parked in the gravel. He was very much alone, except for an occasional owl or hawk soaring overhead and the sounds of the screaming diesel engines on the interstate as they sped past.

His thoughts were of Anna, the beautiful, youthful, Native American, mixed-race woman—a princess, maybe, a damsel in distress, he hoped. Where had she come from? Why had she helped him? What was Scully doing to her, or with her?

Sowles knew that he needed to make contact with Anna again, see her at least one more time, talk to her, learn about her. He was committed to returning to the Emerald Triangle only to take her away from Scully and set her on a new path, not one that involved him as the man in her life, but as her friend or maybe a father figure. But he had to pursue the connection with her, as it felt right to him, natural, as if she was the daughter that he had never been able to know or had the chance to love.

And yet, on the other side of that whimsical vision, he realized how silly, stupid, and dreamy his plan was, as in reality, he was approaching seventy years old, a Negro truck driver living on borrowed time from a reprieve for his life given by a white madman. Even as Anna's friend, how could he help her? Let her stay at his parent's museum in the ghetto of Oakland with its eighty-year-old furnishings? He had nothing to offer anyone. He never had.

He realized that he was musing over the same familiar insecurities and fears that he had always had. They had been ignored or suppressed while he endured Scully's torture, argued with Aaron, stayed on point with the load to El Paso, and while he bantered with Rong Ying, yet when the stress was reduced, again the dread that had always represented his life flew in his face, like moths from an ancient trunk that had been reopened to the light.

His thoughts melded with unintelligible visions of a shadowy male figure somewhere in a distant void, a man separated from humankind itself, maybe banished to something or someplace that was neither life nor death, but instead a locale of sorts, a place, yes, but also a sensation of isolation beyond understanding and more remote than any human perception of the far side of the most inaccessible planet of the galaxies.

He assumed that the sinister figure was Scully, but then he realized it was himself, Noah Sowles. But what the isolated setting was, he truly feared to speculate on! He considered at that moment that either he was crazy or he was inspired, but his choices were either to run fast and far or to return to Scully, subordinate himself, and then try to get Anna and get away.

In either case, it was a struggle between black or white, right or wrong, good or bad, the dichotomy that had always propelled his life and had actually led him to Scully.

"How did it get so fucked-up in a few days?" he asked aloud, but he answered his own question. "It has not been a few days," he said, knowing that his struggle had been for years.

Regardless that he had slept, he was still exhausted, and it was half past nine in the morning in eastern New Mexico. He had to roll. The familiar feelings of anxiety and craving were returning in anticipation of the wheels spinning and humming on the highway.

"It's time to face the music," he said, thinking of one of his father's adages.

The eastern morning desert sun beating through the front windshield made it impossible to sit any longer stewing in his shit as if he was in a pot of his mother's ham hocks and beans. He stood up and splashed some water on his face from a plastic gallon jug that was under the bunk that along with the lone flashlight, had been ignored by Scully's crew when they ransacked and repainted the rig.

He reminded himself then of his need for food, fuel, and cleaning himself. That would first require rolling farther west and finding a major corporate facility that had a restaurant and truckers' showers. After forty-five minutes of seventy-five mile an hour racing on the 10 West, he stopped in Deming at a big, national truck stop chain.

Inside was a fancy restaurant with soothing background music, nice tile showers, and a combination gift shop and convenience store, all supported by very overpriced diesel fuel. He reluctantly fueled two-hundred gallons, more than enough to get to the East Bay area and Oakland, but just enough to get to the Emerald Triangle and then get back out. "Why not fill it up?" he asked himself. He knew the answer: he might leave it on the farm.

Inside the store, he paid $1450 cash for the fuel, two pairs of overpriced blue jeans, two thin flannel shirts, underwear and socks, and another shower.

After drying his tired body in the small enclosure and dressing in the new clothing, he studied himself in the mirror, immediately hating the attire.

"What up, Forrest Gump?" he said, frowning at his image in the mirror. But he knew the clothes were the right attire for a Black man in the truck trade who wanted to look as if he belonged. They made him appear as an unassuming, southern Black Bo-Bo trucker, and not a man hauling $157M dollars' worth of illegal pharmaceuticals, three serious weapons, and a cache of high-powered ammunition.

He was more encouraged by his unshaven face, which had given him a new, masculine look. He liked it. He planned on keeping the beard. Again, Marvin Gaye came to mind. So did Sheylinn. So did Anna. He hummed one of Marvin's tunes under his breath as he headed into the restaurant.

Sitting at the counter, he stared at the plump arms on a dumpy, white waitress and the thin, muscle-deprived legs of a Native American women as both raced back and forth trying to satisfy a few white, hick drivers.

This was the life he knew. The life of a Negro blue-collar worker. In that moment, his mind wandered backward to Mannie Patel and Rudy, and he asked himself again what he had done to get himself in the situation he was in?

He understood that he could soon be facing the retribution of two serious criminal organizations or the laws and police of several states and the federal government, but he was also in the catbird position of sitting on over an eighth-of-a-billion-dollar fortune, with three guns and enough ammo to face a rifle squad of infantrymen, at least for a few minutes.

Maybe a bigger part of him liked the game more than the rest of him wanted to admit. Maybe it was what he had always needed. *Ain't crime what we niggas do?* he wordlessly thought.

He had the "lumberjack's breakfast" with his very own pot of coffee at his very own place setting. When he was finished eating, he tipped the Indian waitress a five and wished her a good day, again thinking about Anna. He then stopped back in the store and grabbed half a dozen Rockstars, each with 240 milligrams of caffeine, and four big cans of peanuts.

He paid with one of Aaron's fresh fifties and walked out, singing in the fresh morning air of New Mexico about eating peanuts from a can. The memory of booming rhythms from a bass guitarist and drummer pounded in his head. The tribal beat was a huge relief from the thoughts that had plagued him since he awoke.

Six minutes later, he was again speeding through New Mexico on his way west. He kept the hammer down on the truck all day, getting a pass at every weigh station, and leaving the driver's seat a few times only to piss out phosphorescent-looking urine from the energy drinks.

That evening, he was in Quartzsite, Arizona, on the border, looking at the local vendors' dusty rock and souvenir collections. He could be in the Bay Area by the following night if he followed the California speed limit. But if he played with the paper logs, he could also make the Triangle early the next day.

After he realized that he had no use for a box of rocks or a dried scorpion in a plastic bag, he pulled over to a sleepy-looking, all-night diner's parking area. SWEET SUE'S. As always, he parked in back, where he would be ignored. He slept fairly well, with the exception of dreaming that he was trapped in a dark, wet cellar with walls extending in four directions for miles.

The next morning, he decided to meet Sweet Sue face-to-face. The diner was one of those retro re-creations put together by the class of diehards who restore 1950s hot rods, listen to oldies, and attempt to revive the Americana that had existed on the old US, two-lane routes of yesteryear. But Sweet Sue didn't look so sweet. Her grill had been usurped by a fat, white, aging cook. He wore a stained apron with his name hand-scrawled in Magic Marker on a plastic badge that was pinned near the shoulder strap: MIKE.

The guy kept a menthol cigarette burning constantly above the grill on the stainless-steel shelf. When the ash reached about an inch in length, ready to drop into the scrambled egg mix, he would grab a puff, put the smoke out, light a fresh one, and repeat the process.

Mike wasn't the only thing indelicate about the joint. Sowles sat at the counter near a pimpled white kid about twenty-five. He was nursing black coffee and ice water and picking at an unfrosted doughnut with his dirty, too-long fingernails. He looked like a meth user who had been up for days. Sowles smiled, thinking about Ron's four pallets of fentanyl. The kid needed at least one gel-cap.

Sowles ordered the "Trucker's Special." At twelve bucks, it was overpriced for two medium-sized, over-easy, pale eggs, white toast painted with butter-flavored oil, and a skimpy portion of processed, pre-frozen, soggy hash browns, undercooked and cold in the middle. He had skipped the meat. The menu read "sausage patty," but from what he gathered by viewing the stack of gray, meatloaf-looking meat mush next to the grill, it looked like pure crap.

While he ate, he viewed the metal reproductions on the walls. The first one read: *Esso! Put a Tiger in Your Tank.* There was one from Texaco with a big red star and an offer of "Free Air." But it was the plaques with the Southern Pacific locomotives, their black, cylindrical-shaped boilers or modern, colorful diesel engines pulling passenger cars through desert cactuses that broke his heart.

He felt the tears forming in his eyes. *Where was his father now?* he silently asked himself. *Dead,* someone answered in the back of his mind. He wanted to scream aloud for both parents.

He tried to forget by becoming engrossed in the meth head kid at the counter. He had long, stringy, mouse-brown hair and a wisp of a foolish looking goatee. He half-ass reminded him of Aaron, except Aaron had a more robust, dark, Jewish look, and from all evidence it seemed that Aaron was a downer cat rather than an upper dude— opioids and fentanyl, not crystal or crack.

"I'll have some of that coffee there our friend's drinkin'," Sowles said, motioning to the freak. He drank his coffee black. That alone made him smile. "Black like my women," he said under his breath. *What women?* He thought. *I haven't been with one in so long, I got blisters on both palms.*

"What's that?" Mike the cook asked.

"Nothin', we good. Just black coffee, and drop two a them plain doughnuts inna bag fo' me, please, eh, Mike?"

"Comin' up, sir," Mike said.

Sowles thought about the sloppy, white cook. The man had never once suggested in his speech or actions that he was anything near a white supremacist, the current common description for all Caucasian Americans who looked like they came from any generation prior to the Obama era. Sowles felt pity for the man, for the kid, for himself. He knew that each of them was lost, and not one of them, especially him, knew how to be found.

"Thanks, man," Sowles said.

"You got it."

Sowles felt a profound sadness. He worried about the world, the country, the people, Americans. Where had it all gone? The list of political blunders, societal regression, and overall degradation of the US culture and the American Dream was apparent in every element of US society. Corruption and bigotry were endless. It seemed that people like Scully or Rong Ying ran the world and people like Mike, the doper next to him, and he, Sowles were their subordinates, the poor, the downtrodden, the lost. He was glad he was aging. He would not have to watch the country implode into further social division and chaos, or live in the world as it killed itself.

All he had ever wanted was to be a cop and then be able to love Sheylinn, or at least be with her, or maybe someone like her, but he had always been a common nigger, a second- or even third-class citizen, someone trying to measure up to someone or something that was above him in education, status or recognition. Yet now, in that moment in Sweet Sue's filthy dive, he saw for the first time that he wasn't alone, that his issues were not unique to being Black. The two white men in the diner had their own obvious sufferings.

"Just make that coffee to go, Mike," he said. "I gotta get rollin'."

"You betcha, pal," Mike said.

Sowles wanted to talk to Mike, even talk to the kid, find out who they were, where they had been, what made them tick, but often when he would meet any white person, not even necessarily an educated white, like a doctor, or a technician, or a teacher, but even a fat cook, or a meth head kid, he would feel the typical inadequacy that most Blacks felt when encountering any Caucasian. When he found himself in those situations, and someone got to talking about life, times, politics, economics, or really anything of interest, he would check out of the dialog and apologize for himself by saying that he was "old, born so long ago that the cars were round."

That was always good for an uncertain laugh, but people didn't always get the joke. He was from a different time. He was old and tired, and, regardless that he had survived, he had long ago accepted that he was a nigger who only wanted to fit in but didn't know how or really what he was supposed to even fit into. He had lived on a ship and then in a truck for decades. He still didn't know what to do about much…maybe open the trailer and take a bottle of the shit.

He left a ten, a five, and three ones on the counter and took his white bag with the two wrinkled plain doughnuts.

"Thanks, Mike," he said holding back the tears in his eyes.

"Stay safe," Mike said.

# Thirty
## THE PINPOINT OF LIGHT

As Sowles returned to the parking lot, he remembered the trailer seal. Rong Ying, his associates, and he had all fucked up. No seal. It was not a crime, not required by law, but as he had told Aaron, when the trailer is sealed, if a driver is stopped by law enforcement, the cops will rarely break the seal. Maybe that was because law enforcement couldn't break any seal without probable cause or a court order, and probable cause was hard to suggest, as was a court order, if there was no specific evidence or lawful suspicion leading to the trailer.

A second thought made him retract that theory. "Probable cause don' mean shit if y'all's Black," he said aloud as he climbed inside the truck and got a seal from the glovebox. Noticing the handguns, he briefly considered tossing them and the scattergun, but he decided he might still need them. He wasn't able to decide specifically what for, but getting Anna off the farm had finally become his only real motivation, and for that he might need help.

As he sealed the trailer doors, he thought of Aaron and the lesson in sealing trailers and having proper paperwork. But there was more on his mind regarding Aaron. Despite all the shit that Aaron had said and done, Sowles still missed the banter and even the excitement of threatening each other's lives. So, after telling Rong Ying that he would search out the truth about Aaron, he felt like Pat Garrett chasing down Billy the Kid.

Popular folklore suggested that Garrett and Billy had been friends or at least associates, but they found themselves on the opposite side of the politics and new laws of the expanding West and Billy went his way perfecting his skill of gunslinging. Garrett then supposedly stalked him and killed him, but then rode off alone, sad and unresolved. Sowles realized that he too really hadn't ruled out killing Aaron. That possibility interested him and disturbed him greatly.

It was time to roll. He glanced back at Sweet Sue's, wishing he could stay there and just sit with Mike and the kid, but he mashed the fuel pedal and headed back into the Colorado Desert Region. Soon enough, he would again pass through the Palm Springs area, then San Bernardino, and then catch the 210 toward Pasadena and Interstate 5 back up the Tehachapi Mountains.

"Damn foo's!" he said aloud. His patience was thin. In only a few short days on the road, he had become responsible for the entire operation of the Scully-Ying dope cartel. Each day and event since he had been hijacked had been leading him further into that same realm of isolation and darkness that he had seen in his visions and dreams at night.

Hours later, when he reached Pasadena, Interstate 210 was a parking lot of idling vehicles. Each car, SUV, truck, bus, and van appeared to be part of a mass exodus of steel and plastic, all seemingly running to nowhere. The angry, upset, anxious, or mesmerized vehicle occupants were as thorny and willful as any described in any writings or depicted in films about the zombie apocalypse.

As did many people who either lived in greater Southern California or observed it from a safe distance, Sowles anticipated a soon-to-be apocalyptic end to the area, but he also expected the same pandemonium and prospect for numerous urban areas he had driven in. He had seen that America's cities were essentially in ruins, with the suburbs following close behind, in an apparent unstoppable race to extinction. It did not seem to him that any group or political party, and certainly no individual, would ever put all the pieces of Humpty-Dumpty back together again.

He had harbored these fatalistic doomsday thoughts for decades, recognizably since the many years earlier when Sheylinn had left. He was only beginning to understand that both his relationship with her and then their emotional separation and divorce had been the true, significant turning point in his life. Nobody or nothing else had left its mark as she had.

"Yeah, baby girl, with you, I lost all hope for the future," he said aloud. "I been hidin' in a truck, drivin' the highways, and not findin' a damn bit a love."

It was only since encountering Scully and coming to an actual agreement with Aaron and Rong Ying that he had begun to embrace his manhood, but it was with Sheylinn that he would have wanted to happily live the middle-class life of a husband and father. It was with Sheylinn that he would have taken their children to her uncle's church. It was with Sheylinn that he believed he would have realized his true full potential.

"Stop it, Mr. Sowles," he said aloud. Or did he? Maybe he just heard the words. He hurt inside. He knew too well that the truck, any truck, any big rig with a sleeper, had become his lover, his home, his shelter, his church, a bubble to shelter inside of, to hide the man he never was and suspected he would never become.

He had hoped often for a pinpoint of light from somewhere, for a recognizable future for his lost life, and yet, he asked himself—*was that light now being revealed in the form of Finn Scully and the Ying family?* They each had directly and inadvertently offered him their path, an opportunity to find a profitable life promoting their efforts.

In essence, he really was Scully's guy now, and Rong Ying and he had come to an understanding. Maybe they were his answer.

"Maybe," he said, whispering while shaking his head. "But, Anna. I gotta get Anna outta there," he said, as he saw the traffic clearing.

He began moving toward the hills of Flintridge and got closer to dropping into the San Fernando Valley. He would then be heading up the tall Tehachapis to Castaic and beyond.

*Is Aaron still there in Castaic? Is he in a hospital?* he thought.

Maybe it was all horseshit. Maybe Aaron really had pulled a swindle, just as Rong Ying had surmised. If he had, how had he done it? How in the fuck had that little bastard managed to get two-hundred-and-fifty grand in his britches when the guy couldn't even hang onto his mud, not to mention a cellphone? In fact, how could the kid even be stupid enough to eat a rancid California roll to begin with?

Then it hit Sowles in the head harder than Aaron's shotgun butt had.

# Thirty-one

## BEDBUGS

"The bag! The damn bag! Aaron's travel bag. The money is hidden somewhere in that bag!" he said aloud, remembering that the bag had felt thick at the bottom. "Why didn't yo' ass see it when y'all was with Rong Ying?" He laughed heartily for the first time in a long time, as he downshifted and began climbing up the long hill. He knew exactly where he would stop next.

Locating the spot where he tossed the bag required having to drive north to Castaic and then exit Interstate 5 and then drive back south to find the rarely trafficked exit ramp next to the abandoned paintball range. He pushed up the hill, his heart throbbing noisily, as if it was pumping in unison with the thumping Cummins engine.

Turning around in Castaic, he tried to avoid looking at the few hitchhikers sitting on the corners, hoping that none of them were Aaron. Once back on I-5 South, he quickly found the exit and was soon off the highway and under the viaduct, immediately recognizing the exact dusty shoulder where he had dumped the scattered pieces of Aaron's clothing. The majority of the items were still there, a grim reminder of everything that had gone down in the prior few days.

He pulled the rig over and shut it down. Having to use one of the weapons was not a choice he wanted to make, but he stuffed the Glock in his waistband for reasons he wasn't entirely sure of, maybe an interloper, a tourist, a drive-by rubberneck, or some other trucker looking for a spot to take a piss. It would be another situation entirely if a California Highway Patrol officer or some smart-ass deputy from the LA County Sheriff's Department happened to roll by. He would have to explain how he had lost his gym bag upslope in the underbrush a few days earlier.

"Nigga don' get to explain shit durin' 'routine stops'," he mumbled as he tapped the pistol.

Scrambling up the incline in the thick brush to begin the search wasn't as easy as he had hoped. In only a few days, the bright-yellow mustard plant and fuzzy California buckwheat had grown taller, thickening in every direction, and there were bugs, flies mostly, and some yellowjackets, all of which did not welcome human invaders of any skin color. The bag itself was nowhere to be seen.

His heart rate increased. Again, he tapped the Glock with a finger to make sure it was there.

Aware that his two-hundred-pound frame could easily twist a knee or ankle, and deciding that he had tossed the bag farther than he remembered, he dropped to his knees while swatting away the bees. The small stones ground into his kneecaps. Peering between the stalks, the bag was still nowhere in sight. It took a half hour of crawling and tramping the brush before he spotted it, a mixture of military camo colors, like Aaron's Bic lighter.

Sowles realized then that he had flung it much farther than he thought, so he still had to wade another twelve feet through the sticky plants while being buzzed by green-and-gold shitflies living off the range dung left by small animals. The odor was foul. Finally, the bag was within reach. Panting and perspiring heavily, he allowed his heartbeat to lessen before making the anxious decision to crawl the last few feet to what might be the answer to his future.

Nervous about reaching or touching the bag, he took some time to rest his heartbeat, while surveying the area for three-hundred-and-sixty degrees, spying for anyone who might be watching from even the distance of the next range of hills. He couldn't take chances. Anybody could interfere—a cop maybe, or a hiker, or some mystical observer who just happened to be a mind reader. All he spotted was the freeway far below him, with its screaming big rigs heading to their stops and motorhomes pulling boats to or from Castaic Lake, but there was no visible human afoot.

Crouching deeper onto his knees, he rotated his large torso onto his ass and sat in the dirt, pulling the heavy, rock-filled bag onto his lap. He dumped the stones and instantly discovered that he had previously overlooked a zippered compartment below the upholstered carboard panel that made up the inside base of the sack. It unzipped completely around the entire bag, exposing the bag's foundation.

Inside were twenty-four bank-strapped stacks of brand spanking new hundred-dollar bills. They were neatly packed next to one another like perfect sardines in a flat tin. On each currency strap, stamped in purple, was the amount: $10,000. Next to them were two bundles of fifties, one still bank-strapped, the other thinner and rubber-banded. It appeared to have the exact few thousand dollars missing.

It was still a fifty-fifty guess whether Aaron had been planning on replacing the fifties and bringing it all to Rong Ying, or if he had planned to take the cash and disappear. It appeared to be the latter, and, if that had been the case, he would have had to deal directly with Sowles and the load prior to getting to El Paso. Maybe that was the reason for the SUV following them. Maybe there had been a plan to hijack the load also.

*But then why had Aaron been so willing to train me on the Glock?* Sowles thought. His stomach spun. He knew that he had been close to experiencing an even more dangerous situation. There had been no way that Aaron could have taken off with the money, let Sowles stand by and watch, and then allow him to live.

As nausea and dizziness seemed to overtake him as if whatever malady Aaron had experienced was now plaguing him also, he remembered that Aaron had said he was a Scorpio. Aaron was capable of anything, including a complete transformation of his personality.

For Sowles there was no immediate sense of pleasure, no smiles, no jumping up and down. Instead, he forced himself to control both his excitement and fear and calmly zipped the compartment shut and secured the upper part of the bag. Then, feeling for his handgun again, he stumbled down the hill, concocting various stories that he might tell the police if they rolled up.

Within seconds, he was back inside the rig. It had worked. There were no problems. It was as simple as that. He concluded that it all went down as it was meant to. He had a little less than two-hundred-fifty-thousand dollars in unmarked cash and the throaty diesel was running again.

"Mr. Sowles, y'all done made yo' fortune," he said, laughing. "Sacrificin' yo' flesh an' blood for they money. They paid yo' ass, motherfucker!"

He put all the guns and ammo into Aaron's bag and neatly stashed it under the bunk, covering it with the extra shirt and pants he had bought. Then he threw Rong Ying's pretty Chinese cloth sack out the window, where Aaron's tattered clothes were flapping in the breeze, smirking that all of the debris was a commemorative marker for the site that had just made him rich.

As he crept the truck back onto the rough pavement, he thought about Aaron's camouflaged bag stashed in the truck and Rong Ying's pretty Chinese sack then newly on the road. The thoughts jogged his memory—*my Coach bag really is gone! So's my notebook. I didn't dream it. I was writing a book!*—Then he tried to dismiss it all from his mind as his next immediate concern was having to again use valuable time driving in the wrong direction on I-5 to be able to find an exit that had an on-ramp on the opposite side that would take him northbound again. But he knew then that he had to finally yield to the truth of his entire situation.

There was no avoiding the fact that he had been abducted and forced to run the weed, but he had knowingly gotten himself deeply involved in the entire illegal and corrupt escapade when he got rid of Aaron. It was then that he had dismissed the opportunity to turn back to Oakland and tell the story while it was plausible.

"I'm just like all them crooks," he said aloud, well aware that he had delivered the weed, allied with Rong Ying, and, while in possession of illegal firearms, driven fentanyl across three states' borders. The bag of cash finally confirmed his overall culpability.

"Y'all out there fuckin' 'roun' with white people will get yo' ass in jail soon 'nuff."

His father's fatal words still hurt and yet had proven correct. "Y'all was right, Pops," he said.

He knew then however that he had no intention of aborting any plan. He would continue north up I-5, stop in Oakland, and stash the money in the old family home surrounded by the spirits of both parents. But only in that split moment did it occur to him that keeping Aaron's bag in the truck was a major oversight.

He continued north for another one-hundred-ten miles to Lost Hills, California and stopped at a small, off-brand truck stop. Inside, he purchased two, two-and-a-half gallon plastic gas cans and some dark brown cigarillos similar to what Aaron smoked. He paid for everything at the counter, including five gallons of gasoline. Then, grabbing a large handful of matchbooks as he reached for his change, he nodded to the young clerk. "These matches free with the smokes, right?" he asked.

The clerk shrugged his shoulders. "I guess, man," he said.

"Make sure y'all turn on the damn pump, boy," Sowles said as he walked out.

Outside the store, he scrambled up into the cab and transferred the guns, ammo, and stacks of cash from the bag into his pillowcase and then to a spot under the bunk. Then he quickly filled both of the gas cans with premium fuel and loaded the containers on the floor of the passenger side of the rig.

He cautiously drove the rig around to the rear of the station where the parking lot ended in a gravel lot. Outside the cab, he soaked the bag with fuel and ignited it with a full book of flaring matches. The bag roared with flame, spewing a swirl of oily black smoke into the immediate area. It attracted the attention of two men, both shabby and street worn. One was mixed race, maybe Native-American and Negro. The other pureblood African American. They ambled over to Sowles and stood near him, staring at the bag.

"Whacha cookin', boss?" the spokesman asked.

"Ain't cookin' nothin'. Bag's got bedbugs or some kinda damned insects," Sowles said as he pulled Aaron's woolen cap out of his pocket, sniffed it for a few long seconds, and then tossed it into the flames.

"Can't deal with that, eh, boss?" the guy said, leaning closer to Sowles. "Hey, boss, can ya help a brothah out?"

Sowles calmly backed away, placing his feet in a casual stance, his left foot slightly forward. He adjusted his balance but kept his hands at his side. The guy seemed surprised.

"Man, you's jumpy," the guy said.

Sowles chuckled. "I been through a lotta shit today, man," Sowles said.

"Me too, man. My old lady, dig it now, ho gotta bring her ass on down t' the courts, man, fo' smokin' a blunt inside a damn CVS pharmacy. Then she get her mouf all up in the judge's face an' shake that big ass in front a the motherfuckah, and the big-time bitch got fo'teen weeks."

"That there's an absolute fact," the other guy said. "Motherfuckin' pigs."

Sowles handed the first guy a twenty. "Get yo'selves a coupla six-packs."

The guy nodded, and the two of them began walking away.

"Chill, bro!" Sowles said. "After I drive away." He waved them back.

The two men turned around and stood with him. The three of them silently watched the bag smolder into a puddle of melted plastic and ash. When Sowles was satisfied that the bag was unidentifiable, he kicked some dirt on it, bumped fists with the derelicts, and jumped in the truck.

Three hours later, he was on the 580 headed west toward Oakland. In Livermore, he was pulled into the westbound scale and quickly weighed and released. Up to that point, he hadn't been giving the DOT much thought. The caffeine and money had increased his confidence.

He rolled through the late-day, dusky traffic in Dublin and was soon in the hills, headed toward Castro Valley and Hayward. In San Leandro, he caught the 880 and ran northwest, with the San Francisco Bay on his left shoulder. After a few minutes, the Oakland Coliseum, the former home of the once-revered Oakland Raiders was on his right.

He finally pulled off on Exit 39 at Fruitvale Avenue, the epicenter of the inner East Oakland ghetto, near where Oscar Grant had been murdered on the Bay Area Rapid Transit platform in 2009, another grim reminder for Sowles. He felt an extra wave of depression sweep over his mind. This was also the general neighborhood where he had grown up and where he and Sheylinn had bussed to school.

Making a left onto International Boulevard, he headed toward 23rd Avenue, a narrow thoroughfare of aged, dumpy two-stories. Immediately he caught a whiff of the familiar smell of a large commercial bakery that bordered the old neighborhood. Memories of his youth again flooded his mind as he realized that he was nine blocks north of where the wide avenue intersected with East 23rd Street, where his family home had sat vacant for decades waiting for him to dispatch a wrecking ball.

*You basically fulla booshit, Sowles*—he thought as he tried to avoid looking at his old neighborhood haunts. *What the fuck you doin', foo'?*

The area had always been tough and primarily Black. It had changed. Hand-painted murals depicting the social ills of numerous migrant races that lived in the area adorned wobbly fences and stucco walls. Gang graffiti was scrawled on every available surface except the sidewalk and street. There also seemed to be fewer small bars and barbecue pits, replaced by check-cashing services, payday loan hustlers, and numerous small liquor stores.

International Boulevard had come into being in the mid-1990s as a liberal civic response to the high population of poor ethnic groups in the general neighborhood. In Sowles's youth, the street had been known as East 14th Street, a shabby assemblage of old, stained, and littered sidewalks, an occasional pawn shop, and cheap hotel rooms for the streetwalkers and heroin addicts. At that time, a mile south of where he was, a multistoried Montgomery Ward dominated the boulevard. His father had loved that store, especially the garden department.

The wide street had also added a spectacle of greasy-smelling chicken take-out windows, open-air auto polish shops, and a few abandoned storefronts that had been taken over by various oddly named Christian groups that advertised their Saturday night or Sunday morning services on hand-scrawled signs. These bastions of faith primarily attracted homeless Negro men.

For the ladies of the neighborhood, International also had a plethora of Black-owned, one and two-chair beauty parlors with year-round Christmas tree lights in their windows, and a few Vietnamese nail salons that dared to defy the local Black gang youth with their Asian presence.

International Boulevard at 23rd Avenue was too congested for parking the rig and too far to walk the nine blocks to the Sowles family residence, and because 23rd was narrow, he could not get the rig in far enough to access his street anyway. He would have to find an open curb for a parking spot, maybe on Foothill Boulevard. That would shorten his distance by two long blocks.

Assuming the thugs weren't too heavy on the streets and he didn't run into someone he knew or a gung-ho Oakland cop cruising in a tactically armed black-and-white, he would walk the six blocks and keep it as low-key as possible.

He figured he would blend into the black-and-brown landscape, as long as he didn't run. A Black man running anywhere, at any time, in any neighborhood, even during a major building or block fire, was a suspect.

# Thirty-two
## THE FLAG OF SURRENDER

He found an open curb on Foothill, in front of a couple of run-down, classic, old Victorian-styled Oakland homes that were fenced in and undergoing total demolition. When they were razed, they would add another vacant lot to the decaying street that at one time had flourished with grocery stores, dry cleaners, car lots, and hardworking Blacks and poor whites.

It was now fully dark and the workers at the demolition site were long gone. He removed a few cones, parked, and then reset the cones. The rig looked like it belonged in the spot. He shut it down and then sat and waited, counting the minutes, while cars and delivery vans whizzed by.

There were two issues. He had no padlock for the trailer. He might be quick enough that the trailer would go unnoticed, but it was a target, especially for any juvenile criminals on the street. The other problem was that without the bag, how would he carry twenty stacks of cash? Carrying it in his pillowcase as if he had stolen the bishop's candlesticks guaranteed a trip to the Alameda County Jail.

He tried to stuff the money inside his recently purchased hillbilly denims and then hide it under his flannel shirt, but it competed with his nuts, making that effort hopeless.

"Prob'ly a nigga wearin' Chairman Mao clothes ain't even gonna get noticed in this foo'-ass neighborhood," he said aloud, deciding that the cops, nutcases, and gangbangers would pay no serious attention to him in the gray fatigues.

He quickly changed back into the dirty gray uniform. With plenty of deep cargo pockets and Velcro fasteners, stashing and securing the money was feasible, two stacks of hundreds in each of the three pockets and all the fifties in the fourth pocket. He hitched up the trousers around his waist confirming that the thick stash of currency was safe, providing he could survive the walk through the edgy neighborhood.

Things seemed low-key at that point of the evening, but he still grabbed the Glock.

Then the moment of truth. It was what he imagined a soldier's moment was before an attack. Waiting a few more minutes for the motivation to move, he finally locked the doors and slipped out of the rig. On the sidewalk, he walked quickly, with the 9mm in his belt, his right hand resting on the grip. His first thought was quickly getting back to the truck before the boys in the hood or the Oakland PD saw that the rig was a new addition to the neighborhood.

He was lucky. Except for two young, Black, smart-ass punks who yelled at him from a lowered Lexus, suggesting he was a "crazy nigga lookin' fo' some wine," it worked. In seven minutes, he was safe in his family's dark, musty home in the shadowed light of the lamp pole that sat out front, the same one he had knocked out with a rock several times in his youth.

The house was ice cold and felt slanted as if it had slid partially from its foundation. He shivered, not certain if it was from fear or the cold, but leaving the lights off, he tiptoed past numerous dusty family photos and portraits of his parents when they were young, a few stained embroidered pillows, and various other family artifacts. When he was in his childhood bedroom, he quickly unloaded the cash into his chest of drawers, where he had kept a few firecrackers and cut-out photos of Mary Wells from when he was a teen. He covered the money with crumbling bath towels from the hallway linen closet.

There seemed to be no reason for further delay. He headed toward the front door, but then his anxiety created a strong urge to pee. He turned back.

Lighted by another streetlamp atop a wooden pole, he saw that the hall bathroom conditions were deplorable. The toilet water had calcified against the bowl, creating a thick ring that looked like concrete, the tub seemed to have regurgitated black sewage that was at least three inches deep, and the bar soap had degenerated in the dish, leaving a filthy stain. But it was the white shower curtain that struck him. It was stained with brown blotches like those in Scully's dungeon and had decomposed. It barely hung from rusted hooks, resembling a battled and shredded flag of surrender.

"Everything rots, Sowles," he heard an unidentifiable voice say.

Fear immediately blocked his ability to piss as if his peehole had an overlay of new grown skin. He zipped up and decided to check all the locks in the house, but the emotional impact of being near his parent's bedroom finally broke his momentum. He could smell his mother's stale talcum powder. His stomach rolled in conjunction with a wave of dizziness that forced him against a wall in the shaded hallway struggling to catch his breath.

It was as if his parents were still there, alive and sleeping in the master bedroom. He felt stinging tears drip from his eyes, making his cheeks itch. Wiping his face with the back of one hand, he instinctively reached for the Glock with the other. He yanked it from his britches.

With the gun in one hand leveled in the blackness and using only the fingers of his other hand, he fired up a book of matches and then slowly descended a narrow, rickety flight of wooden steps that led into the street-level cellar and one-car garage. He was instantly confronted with his aged Volvo P1800. The once vibrant, fire-engine red sports car was gray from a filthy covering of thick dust, with its four tires flat on the floor as if they were an elephant's feet.

Memories of Sheylinn and the rare moments they had shared in the car forced him to stop to regain control of both his mind and his breathing. When he felt that his heartrate had slowed to normal, he checked all door and window locks, crushed the matches and tiptoed silently up the dark, creaking stairs. Returning to his bedroom, he opened the drawer and stared at the money for a few seconds, but then grabbed over a thousand dollars in fifties and stuffed them in a pocket. Then checking all the upper-level windows and doors he slipped out the front door and bounded down the brick steps as if he was nine years of age running from one of the ghosts that had haunted his comic book collection.

Surveying both directions of the street for slow-rolling gang-bangers' cars, thugs on foot, or nosy neighbors, he began a brisk walk to the corner and then back down 23rd Avenue. He was beginning to feel a desperate fear. He needed to reach the truck without any type of encounter or incident, anything that would draw even a small crowd; two or three Black people gathering with raised voices would bring at least one Oakland squad car and a minimum of two cops.

It was a crazy, seven-block race against time as the streets got darker and the boomboxes in the trunks of the lowriders began their evening raps and chants, but he succeeded. He was soon back in the truck with the doors locked. He fired the engine and shifted his mind into truck-driver mode. It was time to write a new chapter as he faced the next round of shit, but then he remembered again that the notebook was gone.

"Fuck it," he said, as he crept away from the timeless concrete curb, crushing the tall, rubber cones. He then rolled into already racing, one-way Foothill Boulevard traffic, found a left turn, and reversed direction back onto International Boulevard and 23rd, this time heading southwest to where he caught the I-880 ramp.

The sector was a washed-out industrial area replete with dilapidated, World War II vintage factories, hollow looking from having most of their windows punched out, and the remnants of ancient, two-story, shack houses that had been uninhabitable for decades. Their wooden staircases beckoned to local crack users and on the lam gangbangers.

It was also where the old Southern Pacific Railroad had once staged miles of freight, fuel, and hopper cars, and where the union workers like his father caught the passenger trains long before Amtrak emerged and rerouted the railway through the trendy, gentrified shop and animated film studio area of Emeryville, a few miles northwest.

Relieved to get back on the freeway, within minutes, he was passing the big cranes in the Port of Oakland, not long after rolling by the duck pond, where the cities of Oakland, Emeryville, and Berkeley began to intersect. He soon saw the Golden Gate Fields racetrack, where he believed his father had sacrificed the part of his life that was not given to the railroad. Just beyond, the San Francisco–Oakland Bay Bridge stretched across the water, leading to the sparkling lights of the skyscrapers in the infamous city across the bay.

Passing by the freeway ghetto areas of Albany and Richmond and the refineries of Martinez, he was soon crossing the bridge into Vallejo, now another Black ghetto, but previously known for its contributions to the naval efforts of the Second World War as a ship repair yard and training facility for submarines.

The Emerald Triangle was only hours away, but he wasn't quite ready for what lay ahead. He stopped six miles north of where Sheylinn and he had lived in Rohnert Park. Parking behind a large Safeway store in Santa Rosa seemed safe enough. He pulled under the dock floodlights in such a manner that anyone observing him would assume he was delivering in the early morning.

With so much caffeine and tension over the previous hours, he struggled to sleep, but finally drifted off. His last thoughts were about being rested and prepared for dealing with Scully and seeing Anna. Heavily armed, he had no intention of being intimidated, not to mention imprisoned again, and he was committed to taking Anna wherever he decided to go.

At 6:00 a.m., he was awakened by other trucks coming and going in the Safeway yard. It was a typical morning for freight unloads, so he relaxed among the familiar setting of other drivers making their deliveries. He took his time getting ready to roll, even going so far as to walk around to the front of the store to look for a coffee outlet to buy another small sack of doughnuts.

The sign on the door of the Starbucks in the lobby of the grocery store offered the same apologetic message as the sign at Scully's fuel stop:

SORRY, WE'RE CLOSED.

He waited. At 7:00, a collegiate-looking African American kid opened the door. He smiled warily at Sowles, still dressed in filthy gray fatigues.

Sowles decided to splurge on several frosted, old-fashioned, cake-like doughnuts. As if he was a child with a dime in his pocket, he bashfully pointed them out to a very cute, short-haired, pixyish-looking blonde woman behind the counter. She was about thirty. His heart sank, as he longed to relive his youth, start over, and find the love of his life and his place in the sun.

For an over-the-road truck driver, buying doughnuts was as routine as breathing, but after all that he had experienced, it felt uncomfortable and strange, as if it was an abnormal act. He knew that it was because in that coffee outlet in the early morning hours, he was the archetypal, unknowable, too Black, dangerous looking, strange nigger within the boundaries of a classic, old tree-lined, well-established white neighborhood.

Walking back to the rig, he nibbled on the doughnuts and wondered if he would live through the day.

After finally boring himself for another thirty minutes, watching other drivers fight their way to the docks, he started the big engine and headed east on a wide city street in the west part of the city, until he reached the US 101 on-ramp.

Still not certain what he would do when he reached his destination, he turned north and merged into the traffic. He was five hours from showtime.

# *Thirty-three*

## RED-PAINTED TOENAILS

Driving north during the day on US 101 in California, above San Francisco, offers one of the most scenic routes in the country, but it did little to diminish the anxiety Sowles felt. It was unlike any apprehension he could remember from recent years, except for the first few days of being held in Scully's mansion, when he began to realize that he was slated to be tortured and indoctrinated.

Part of the anxiety was a creation in Sowles's own mind. He was as drawn to Scully as he was fearful of him. And as manipulative and deceptive a man as Scully was, he and his lifestyle were also as pleasant and inviting as Sowles's wildest fantasy of what success and fame were.

At the same time, Sowles knew that Scully was capable of anything. He was a hypnotic and devious man, and far more influential and notorious than it seemed anyone in his immediate circle of government or his business associations knew, except for possibly Aaron and Rong Ying.

Sowles's revelations about the entire Scully-Ying alliance while he was wrapping up with Rong and his subsequent vision of the blackened, alienated void were reminiscent of the emotional terror he had experienced when he was facing being sent to Vietnam. He knew then, at age eighteen, that either being able to live his life to its normal completion or dying prematurely in a rice patty would have been determined strictly by others' Machiavellian decisions.

With Finn Scully, Sowles realized that the machinations the man was capable of may even be more perilous to his life than that horrific now long-ago war.

Big questions remained. How to maneuver around Scully's sharp mind? How to overcome Scully's magnetic power? How to overcome Scully, maybe even kill the charismatic young man?

Anna's solution to trick Scully with flattery was viable when he was locked inside his compound, but what did that look like when face-to-face with Scully in some form of emotional or psychological combat?

Sowles knew that he had only survived the challenge of the US Army by confronting his anxiety and then facing down the empowered officers and intrusive onlookers at the induction center, but his response had been far out of character for who he was back then. Speeding through a hostile forest toward a different frightening destiny to confront a man of boundless financial power and some form of captivating control over people left Sowles with a vision of himself facedown in a farmer's irrigation ditch, his body concealed with mud.

As he drove past the opulence of the recently harvested vineyards of Alexander Valley and the imperial manors built to resemble medieval castles that lorded over the various grounds, he mused over Scully's statements in the town hall meeting, when he compared the Wine Country to the "weed country." Who among that meeting or the government of the state actually knew the truth about Scully and his many cloaks and disguises? Sowles believed he had only seen one layer of his personality exposed at that point. As Anna had said, there really was more to be revealed.

He was soon in the redwood groves of Mendocino County. The woods thickened when he reached Humboldt County, the hub of the Emerald Triangle. At half past noon, he approached the turnout for Scully Brother's Fuel. He pulled in and was greeted by the same potholes.

Controlling his feelings in the light of day was easier than it had been the fateful night when he was low on fuel, but the dreadful sensations still manifested. As tranquil as the property seemed by day, it still projected a fiendish atmosphere, a consciousness of something ethereal, threatening, like being scared shitless in an overly realistic amusement park horror house and only assuming it wasn't real.

He asked himself repeatedly—*how would he handle himself when face-to-face with Scully? Was all of his own fresh knowledge about the young man and his criminal campaigns, and the three weapons in the rig with a cache of ammunition enough of a defense?*

Sowles didn't believe it was. Would he be found rotting in an irrigation ditch or in a container on a ship routed to the Far East?

He felt his shoulders quiver. He was happy to sit tight for a few hours to see if Winnie would show with whoever his new sidekick was. That could still be Aaron or Mary.

If someone from the farm didn't pull in, he planned to drive the thirty-five miles on the rough road into the isolated backwoods. But he didn't expect Scully to greet him with open arms and another gourmet meal when he discovered he was there only for Anna.

As the day passed, the midafternoon sun had begun to dive behind the tops of the giant trees. He had to roll. He was soon slamming the truck's suspension over hard-to-see potholes and cutting the muddy curves on the dirt road, as he had done with Aaron on the first day that they encountered each other.

Time seemed to have sped up. In the short forty-five minutes it seemed to have taken to get to familiar landmarks, there was barely enough remaining daylight to guide him on the rough, unpaved road. As the shadows formed and the draping trees created a cavernous whirl of foliage, he hammered the truck's throttle, taking bigger risks, speeding with the rig, jeopardizing the equipment and his life at every sharp, dark, muddy turn.

How had an hour's drive turned day into twilight? It no longer mattered. He was a crazed big rig driver. The engine roared into what had become night as he entered enemy territory.

His first break came when he discovered there were no armed guards riding ATVs at any point on the road. Then, as he got closer to the manor, the usual throngs of tents, aimless people, and laborers milling near the roadway or in the perimeter of the growing fields were also not visible. It seemed as if they had pulled up tent stakes and moved on like a bunch of gypsy carnies.

That could mean they were shipped out, but if so, the farm still needed to run. Where were the replacements?

After another fifteen minutes, he parked about a football field's length from the massive home. The sky was black and starless; even the moon seemed to have been stolen, and yet there was flickering firelight in the large windows. It allowed him to see the distinct outline of the Land Rover sitting near the house. The Jeep was nowhere in sight. He could also see that the garden had a slightly unkempt appearance, possibly explained by what was becoming very apparent—there were no workers!

Irritated over losing his ballcap, as it had given him the masculine appearance of a pure mug, he grabbed the SIG, adding it to the Glock under his belt. He was a modern-day gunslinger, packing two semiautomatic handguns, their grips accessible above his beltline.

Exiting the truck, he trod softly in a wide arc around the side of the immense home into the area where he had been battered by the hose. There was no response and no visible activity in or near the house other than what he thought might be the lavish drapes fluttering in the great room. Someone could be peering through the windows, or it could a breeze inside the home, but didn't Scully hate the cold? Then recognizing the familiar odor of woodsmoke that seemed to drape the area, he glanced up at the stone chimney and saw a wispy gray haze drifting upward into the dark sky. Scully had to be watching.

He rechecked his weapons, and, much as he had done when he recovered Aaron's bag, he gave thought to whether he would actually use the guns as he continued poking around outside, unsure of whether to simply go to the door as if he was a returning hero with a tale to tell.

After surveying the back and other side of the general yard area, he finally tiptoed around to the front and onto the large wraparound porch. There was still no response. Standing on the wide veranda, quietly adjusting his stance on the welcome mat, preparing to either run or knock on the door, he had a momentary feeling of foolishness, as if he was a door-to-door salesman preparing to offer his wares. He then decided again that if he was selling anything, it was a plan to get Anna away from Scully.

"Please, help." It was a whisper, perhaps a squeal, a tormented cry. It sounded like an animal in pain. It came from the grass near the rows of hedges and flowers. He turned in the direction of the sound. In the scant light escaping from one of the widows where Scully's hearth fire roared, Sowles could see movement. It was maybe a distance of forty feet. As he focused his eyes, he saw that it was a woman with the small figure of a child sitting alongside.

"Anna?" he said softly.

"Help me," she said. "Please."

He jumped off the porch and ran toward the figure. "Anna?"

"It's me. Erika, she said as the child whimpered.

"Erika?" he asked. He knelt down. It was obvious that she had been hurt badly, maybe hit by a vehicle, or very possibly she had been severely beaten, maybe by more than one assailant.

"I'm injured," she said. Her militant persona was gone. Even in the darkness, Sowles could see that she was unarmed and was wearing both a dark colored pair of tight Wranglers and a matching cowboy cut denim shirt. Then he realized that they were actually blackened with soaked-in, dried blood.

Sowles examined her face. It was far from plump and rosy as he had remembered it, but horribly bruised and bloody.

He fired up one of the books of matches and examined her face holding a palm against her disfigured cheek. "It's okay," he said. "I'll help you."

Her nose seemed twisted and broken, and her blonde hair was matted with blood and dirt. One eye was swollen shut, and the other was bloody and stared off-center, as if someone had beaten her face to the point of dislodging her retina. Both wrists had severe rope or chain marks on them. It was obvious that whatever had happened, she had been taken by surprise and had not been able to dodge the power of her attacker or fight back with any form of defense.

"Who did this to you, girl?" he asked, as he gently took her head in one big palm while still holding the burning matchbook in the other hand.

"I don't know," she said, whimpering like a small animal.

"Scully?"

"No. Maybe," she said, barely able to speak. "I don't know."

"Who?"

She didn't answer.

"Aaron?" he asked.

She moaned. "Aaron is gone," she said. "Nobody knows where."

"Were the Chinese here? Did they do this to you?"

"I don't know," she said.

"Where's Scully?"

"Europe, maybe, somebody said." She moaned. "I can't talk. It hurts so much."

"Please Erika, just a few more questions. I need to know. "Where's Winnie?"

"Winnie was also hurt badly."

"Is he dead?"

"He was trying to crawl when I saw him," she said. She began to fade, her eyes closing. The child began crying loudly.

He held the bleating child's hand as he focused his gaze on Erika's face. "Please, stay with me," he said. "Can you tell me about Anna? Is she alright?"

"I don't know," she whispered. "She disappeared when it happened."

"What exactly happened? Can you remember?"

"I don't know. It was light and then it got dark."

"You mean you were unconscious?"

"No, I was running and then all of a sudden, I was on the ground, and then it was dark but I was awake."

"I'll get you out of here," he said, as he tried to soothe her, rubbing his palm along the side of her face.

"No, it's too late."

"I'll take you to a hospital."

"No, please. Just stay with me." She took his big hand. "I'm sorry I treated you the way I did. He made me do it. I'm so sorry. I'm so sad."

"Let me get you out of here. Please, let me help you."

"I can't walk," she said. "I can't feel my legs. I don't know. I think I'm dying."

"No, you can't die."

"Just know, please, I am so sorry for hurting you. Please, understand, many things are wrong. It's as if the whole farm is wrong...I don't know...I couldn't see what hurt me so badly. Something overwhelmed me, but I never saw what it was."

"You mean it was nighttime?"

"No, it was daytime," she said.

Sowles felt his heart leap. "Daytime?" he asked. "How could you not see who hurt you?"

She didn't answer. Sowles then examined her legs and back. "Can you feel my hands? Does it hurt?"

"I can't feel anything down there. I only feel the pain in my face, head, and neck."

"I'll carry you," Sowles said.

"No, please, just stay with me," she sobbed. "Listen, please. Something went wrong. People were screaming. They put the workers, every one of them, on buses," she said between sobs. "They loaded everyone into black busses, like old school busses. They rounded up everyone and questioned them. They put them on the busses."

"Who did? Who?"

She didn't answer. "I'm just so grateful I could tell you that I'm sorry, Mr. Sowles. Please forgive me." She closed her eyes. "I'm so sorry," she whispered. "Please protect my child."

In that moment Sowles realized that the child was the little girl that had served him the lobster. "I will. Be calm, Erika, please. Stay with me. Look into my eyes," Sowles said. His face wrinkled. His tears clouded his eyes, the stinging itch dripping onto his cheeks.

"Find Scully," Erika said weakly, her eyes flickering. "He is called among the wicked."

"Who calls him? I don' understand."

She seemed to be fading. Sowles soothed her face with his hand. "Where is he?" he asked. His sadness was replaced with teeth-grinding anger.

She didn't answer. There was no sound. Erika was gone. Her frantic eyes finally at rest.

"Erika? Erika?" Sowles pleaded as he unflinchingly crushed the still burning matchbook in his hand.

He then carefully laid her head on the grass and then lifted up the sobbing child and sprinted back to the truck. Still holding the little girl, and feeling his own strength for the first time in years, he climbed inside the tractor and grabbed the blanket and uncased pillow from his bunk. Then he ran back to her lifeless body, and straining his eyes to see her in the dark, he blanketed her small, bare feet and tiny red-painted toenails and then covered what had instantly become the lifeless, empty shell of a human being, a young woman not much older or taller than a high school teenager. When he reached her face with the coverlet, he touched his lips with his two fingers, then his heart, and then placed the same fingers on her lips. After covering her face, he carefully put the pillow under her head.

Standing tall, he raised one arm and a clenched fist, and then yelled into the starless sky. "NO! NO! Scully, come and get me now! Come and get me, you blue-eyed white devil!" His voice echoed in the night as if it was the call of a great animal announcing its territory.

"Come on! Fall out, Scully! I'm here! Come and get some!" he said, convinced that he felt the black bear roaring inside his abdomen.

There was no response. The entire property was as silent as a nighttime cemetery.

# *Thirty-four*
## MY ONLY SON

Still holding the now silent child while she rested her face on his shoulder, Sowles checked both handguns, making sure they were chambered and ready to fire. Taking first the Glock, he crouched close to the ground and very carefully moved in the direction of the Land Rover. Trying the driver's door, he discovered that it was unlocked.

Climbing inside, he set the child in the passenger seat as he spoke very softly, "You must wait here, I'll come back for you." She nodded and smiled, but avoided his glance. He then touched the push button ignition. Instantly, the computer detected the presence of his hand, and a tiny, amber-colored message came on the dashboard screen:

NO KEY PRESENT

"Damn!" he said.

"Noah, my friend. What a surprise." The voice came from the car's sound system. "I've been waiting." Again, it bellowed from the car's speakers. Sowles turned the volume knob higher. "I'd wager you want this," the voice said.

Sowles felt the presence of something nearby. He quickly turned his head. Scully was standing outside the passenger window, waving a key fob. "No key, my friend, but do come inside, Noah. Come in, please. We must get caught up," Scully said, as he opened the door and lifted the little girl into his arms. "I'll take this," he said turning toward the house.

Sowles stuffed the Glock further inside his waistband, slowly opened the door, climbed out of the car, and then as if a lamb being led to the slaughterhouse attached with an invisible cord, he dumbly followed Scully into the home and down the familiar hallway into the dining room.

The room was hot, at least fifteen or more degrees higher in temperature than the hallway. The flames in the hearth lapped into the stone chimney. Sowles's legs felt weak and rubbery.

"It's a long ride back to civilization. Sit!" Scully said, directing Sowles to the dining chair he had sat in before. Scully then set the child on her feet. She bolted from the room.

Sowles fell into the upholstered dining chair. In the short minutes he had been around Scully, he could feel that his energy had been drained. He struggled to sit upright.

Scully paced the room. "How is my shipment?" Scully asked. His voice was firm.

Scully's hair had been prepared, as if he was going on stage. It was a glistening, golden hue. The dreadlocks were tightly wrapped behind his head just above the base of his neck, forming a large, braided knot. It was tied with a feminine, thin, purple ribbon.

As Sowles gradually regained some of his senses, he noticed that Scully was wearing a purple running suit that matched the ribbon. It was the same style of clothing that Rong Ying had suggested Sowles buy. Scully was also wearing a pair of feminine-looking, leather bedroom slippers that slipped on and were open at the heel.

"Nice threads," Sowles muttered drowsily.

"Thank you, Noah. Now, what is the status of my shipment, Noah? I have asked you once already. Don't irritate me, please!"

Sowles thought he saw a deep, emerald-green color flash very briefly across Scully's face. He remembered the comic books in his youth.

"I know who you are, Scully," Sowles said.

"My shipment, Noah?"

Sowles felt a surge of power. He was also becoming visibly irritated. "How the hell d' y'all think it is, Scully? Everything is out in the trailer, all stacked up right where Rong Ying put the shit," he said.

"The mission is not complete, Noah. The trailer needs to be backed into a warehouse and unloaded and you're the trucker, right?" Scully said. "After that, we need to talk about you."

"Fuck me. Fuck you. Y'all ain't directin' the show no mo', Scully! I ain't yo' driver fo' y'all crazy-ass Scully's Feed and Seeds. I'm done with y'all. Yo' own ass can back the shit in an' unload it yo' own self. This nigga done did his part."

He pulled out the SIG and pointed it at Scully.

Scully grinned warmly and then began laughing. "Give that to me, Noah," he said, glaring at Sowles. "Don't be ridiculous. You'll hurt yourself, and remember, your heart is bad."

Sowles felt the strength in his arm fade as if it had been drained out of him like water from a cracked decanter. A hot pain shot across his chest. He barely had the strength to hold the gun. It dropped on the table.

"Relax, Noah!" Scully laughed. He examined the weapon. "Aaron's, wasn't it? Nice choice, the SIG," he said. "Schweizerische Industrie Gesellschaft...yes, the Swiss, lovely fools."

"I don' need none a that booshit, Scully," Sowles said, as he struggled to breathe. "Jus' tell me where Anna is!"

"Oh, my dear Anna," Scully said. "She is probably wild dog shit by now, Noah."

"You a damn liar," Sowles said, half whispering while he struggled to fill his lungs with fresh air in the stifling room.

"Yes, I am indeed." Scully laughed. "But I'm aware of how fond you were of each other."

"Did you kill her?" Sowles asked.

"I don't like the word 'kill.' I never really have. It's a bad rap," Scully said.

"You killed Anna!" Sowles said. His face collapsed.

"Anna made choices. Everyone makes choices, Noah. Then, *finis*. End of story. Case closed!"

"I wanna know where Anna is," Sowles said.

Scully laughed. "Anna? *comme ci, comme ca*! Mary will attend to you now. I did retain her just for that purpose—her and a few others." He chuckled bashfully.

Sowles was visibly shaken when Mary entered the dining room.

"Aye, our nigger returns, an' so good t'is thet the fire is right hot tonight, eh, Doctor Scully?" She saddled up next to Scully and gave him a deep kiss on the lips.

"I never let an attractive, capable woman get too far, especially redheads and blondes," Scully said to Sowles.

"That's booshit too, Scully. You killed Erika," he said, as he suspiciously eyed Mary, again contemplating whether she was somehow allied with Aaron, and remembering Scully's statements about things never appearing to be what they seem to be.

"Oh, Noah, such a fool you can be." Scully laughed. "Erika? Come here, darling."

Within short seconds, Erika walked into the room.

Sowles heart raced. He studied the young woman. She was perky, her face radiant. Her hair was pigtailed and golden, and she was dressed in the same Wranglers and denim shirt, but without any trace of blood.

"What kinda booshit game is this?" Sowles asked.

"Oh, Noah, you know the game," Scully said. "Now, friend, look at my Erika. Isn't she so very attractive with her eyes bright blue, her hair and pigtails perfect, tied at the ends with the same color ribbon as my hair knot?" Scully asked and then laughed until he coughed. "We're married," Scully said solemnly, but then again burst into hyenic laughter.

"What kinda trick is this, Scully?" Sowles asked. "Erika's dead. I held her. I know!"

"I thought you listened more carefully, Noah. Surely either Anna or I told you that things are not always as they seem. Correct?"

Erika giggled as she sat on Scully's lap. She and Scully laughed together while Erika nuzzled the inside of Scully's ear.

"Go back to your hole, Scully. You're a trickster and a liar," Sowles said. "Your whole game is phony, man. It's pure-ass booshit, done with damn mirrors."

"I'd say, Noah, my good friend, you're finally getting it." He laughed again.

"Just tell me where Anna is, and I'm gone. That's all I care about. Tell me an' I'll go, an' you can forget all about Noah Sowles."

"It's not that easy for you, Noah; remember, my friend, we have another hearing to examine you again? Especially since you got rid of Aaron. You do realize that decision was not listed on my manifest?"

"What manifest? Y'all's amateurs, man. Yo' asses didn't even have a manifest. I don' give a damn, Scully. I know what the fuck I'm doin' in a truck. I am the driver. I made the damn decision t' drop that California roll, sushi eatin', white boy foo'."

"That decision cost two-hundred-fifty-thousand dollars, Noah."

"Like you need the bread? Fuck y'all, man."

"Noah, this bravado of yours impresses me…finally!" Scully said.

"Like I'm sayin', Scully, tell me where Anna is, an' I'll roll my Black ass down the road."

"I regret to say that Anna went her way in the woods. Of course, she is skeletal remains by now. Such a waste…or not." He laughed.

"You are pure-ass evil, Scully."

Scully's perfectly white teeth flashed. "I'm certainly not that pale-faced redeemer that the pedestrian fools dream of, Noah. But you among all are very clever, and yes, you finally do know exactly who I am."

"So what? Yeah, I know who you are an' yo' ass got no damn further hold on me, no way, no how."

Scully laughed again. "Is that so? I've had a hold on you for decades."

"You ain't had shit on me, Scully. An' that booshit you an' Rong Ying are up to ain't gonna happen!" He pulled out the Glock.

"Go ahead, Noah. Fire the weapon. I dare you! Shoot us! Please!"

"I am not a killer, Scully." Sowles said.

"Yes, you are! Kill or be killed, Noah! Fire the weapon!"

Sowles squeezed the trigger once. The round went straight into the wall behind Scully. Then as if he was overtaken by a blinding compulsion, he clenched his teeth and fired repeatedly at Scully and the two women. He emptied the clip. But it was as if he had fired blanks. All three just continued to sit casually in the chair together and giggle like children as they each played and fondled one another.

"Are you enjoying yourself as much as I am, Noah?" Scully asked. "Care to join us now that you shot your wad of rounds? Come shoot another wad. Erika likes you, and I can include the children. We'll get the camera."

Sowles ran for the door, but he was instantly stopped in his tracks and thrown across the room. His two-hundred pounds slammed hard against the wall, knocking the wind out of him as if he had been hit by a professional football tackle. He was unable to stand.

"Whatever would make you think you could kill me, my dear Noah?" Scully asked. "Where is all this courage of yours coming from?"

Chuckling, Scully and the women went to Sowles and stood over his bent body. "Hurt?" Scully asked, laughing like a crazed wax woman in a carnival fun house.

"Y'all is some sick honkies," Sowles said as he writhed in pain. "But I know your game, now. I know who yo' ass is, fo' sho', Finn Scully."

"Yes, Noah, you do," Scully said. "But better that you hadn't!" He pushed the two women away and walked around Sowles several times, forming a circle, as he had done in the hearing. With each revolution, the room seemed to become hotter.

"Now that we understand each other, my Noah, let me tell you about my European travels."

"Go to hell, Scully!"

"Really?" Scully laughed again. "I dined every night, saw a few shows. You know, Noah, a vacation, my millionth or so, but it was pleasant." He smiled warmly at both women.

"Fuck your booshit," Sowles said, whispering, his voice almost inaudible.

Scully ignored him. "Now, you'll be interested in knowing that I was also in Scandinavia, China, Russia, Ukraine, all of those forsaken, frozen shit-bergs with their emotionally starved, lascivious denizens. Big trouble coming." He sighed. "We had plenty of business there."

"I don' care, Scully. Go to hell!" Sowles said, managing a vocal outburst.

Scully roared with laughter again. "I'm here, Noah, with you. Let's just be together, and we shall share a pleasant bottle of Chardonnay, and the four of us can chat about your travels with Aaron and Rong Ying. Then, perhaps we will also share a little fun, maybe a four-way."

"I understan' y'all's game now—the weed, the dope, the people here on the farm, the women, yeah, Rong Ying, the sex, the kids, everythin', man! Y'all's game ain't fo' me, Scully."

"But it is for you, Noah. That is why you're here, still here, in our moment, in the now, but I must remind you my friend, you owe me a lot of money."

"You wrong, Scully. I call down on you, Scully."

"Oh, Noah, you little novice of a human. What could your Black, insignificant life possibly call down upon me that would even cause a pimple on my white ass?"

The fire grew more intense. Scully laughed again and kicked Noah in his ribs repeatedly. "Does that hurt your feelings, Noah? Did you think I was really your friend?

Sowles grimaced in pain as he watched the flames licking at him from the hearth. It was the same feeling as watching his life drain down the scupper when he was hosed. He tried to stand but was unable. He tried crawling away from the heat.

Scully stepped on Sowles's spinal column with both feet and began jumping and giggling as if he was a child on a mini trampoline. It felt as if the small man actually weighed thousands of pounds. Sowles screamed with pain while the two women chuckled and Scully's laughter echoed against the walls of the big room.

"I'm merely suggesting that you stay and we visit together," Scully said, as he jumped higher and came down with more force on Sowles's vertebrate. "I want to commend you on your effort on the road and in Texas. Good work on Job One, eh?" He laughed. "Now, let's celebrate together. Just us. We'll chat and reacquaint," he said and breathlessly soared across the room to where the women had resumed sitting.

"No!" Sowles said, groaning with pain. "Not now. Maybe when you're indicted, I'll visit *your* cell at night with a big bag of dry ice."

Scully frowned nervously. "Oh, Noah, my child. Let's not be rash. I'm indicted constantly, every moment of every day and night, but you do see me here, don't you, right in front of you? I'm still here just doing what I do, taking care of business, entertaining, living the dream. Now, be gracious, Noah. I've received you. I've extended you an invitation."

"Your invitations kill folks, Scully," Sowles said.

"As you should know, I rarely issue orders. Please don't defy me. I want you to stay and just chew the fat, so to speak. Your room is prepared."

"Which room, Scully? The dungeon?" Sowles asked as he struggled to get on his feet and stood facing Scully.

"I'll not answer you, Noah. I know not of what you speak of, but you know what I'm capable of," Scully said.

"Yeah, man, I know who you are," Sowles said. "I already told you." His voice became weaker as he tried to control the pain.

Scully laughed. "Good then, so we understand one another for the moment," he said and turned away from Sowles, but suddenly spun back around, his body flying into a series of kicks, rapid punches, and stiff fingered strikes to Sowles's face, eyes and ribs. "That's Shaolin Kempo, not that ridiculous Tang Soo Do! Hurts, doesn't it?" he said laughing, as Sowles collapsed again onto the floor. Scully then returned to the two women. He purred like a cat as they both fondled his hair.

"There my friend, you on the floor makes it so much easier to talk about progress and salvation, and your life, and other frivolities, and of course your future, or lack thereof. We are not done with that topic."

Sowles tried to speak, but he was unable to breathe. His mouth opened, but he didn't have the air in his lungs to form words. He gasped much like the dying salmon had on the deck of the fishing boat that he had sailed on in the mouth of the Columbia River many years earlier.

"Ah, Noah, you are such a frail, ill-fated soul," Scully said. "I was only here to help."

Sowles could only purse his lips about the size of the hole in a soda straw as he made a weak attempt to suck in breathable oxygen while Scully and the women chuckled. "Perhaps I was incorrect, Noah. Maybe you are not a man who can lead legions. We will soon exercise the sunset clause in your contract."

"No, Scully!" Sowles finally said, blurting out the words as if he had been holding his breath while drowning. He began coughing.

"Your heart, Noah!" Scully said. "Remember your heart and your mother's heart murmur! An inherited flaw. Six decades, give or take, is about all it's set for. And you're getting on toward seven decades!

Not a good thing, old boy…and let's not forget those kidneys!" Scully again howled with laughter.

Scully picked up the spent Glock from the floor and examined its perfect machine work. "Excellent quality, but worthless." He then took the SIG from the dining table. "Same! Swiss, Germans. All crap. Who needs handguns?" He threw them in the fire.

Sowles rolled over onto his knees. He began mumbling.

"Do you want to live, Noah?" Scully asked. "Then say my name, Noah! Say my name!"

Sowles didn't answer. Scully grabbed his head with both hands and twisted it as if it was rubber while lifting Sowles off the floor. "Should I break it?" He said laughing. He then tilted his own face and examined Sowles's beaten face with incredulity, as if Sowles was a bug in a jar. Scully then threw the lifeless man's head and body to the floor.

"Say my name, Noah, and you'll feel so much better, invigorated, in fact."

"Tell me where Anna is and I'll say your name," Sowles said. His voice was just a groan.

"Oh, Noah, have you not learned the lesson of listening to a woman? Don't make that mistake again. She will mislead you for sure, my friend, just like the others."

"So, she is alive, then," Sowles said barely able to speak.

"Alive, dead, it's all the same, Noah."

Remembering the preacher's sermon on the radio, Sowles curled into a fetal position and clasped his hands together.

"What are you doing?" Scully asked. His voice had softened. "Stop, please."

"Father in heaven, in the name of the Lord Jesus—"

"Stop!" Scully said.

Sowles continued. "Father, remove me from this wickedness. Forgive me for my sins and errors. Takes this evil from me!"

Both women ran from the room. Scully turned his back on Sowles for a moment. When he turned around to face Sowles, the wounded man had again struggled onto his knees while continuing to pray aloud. Scully screamed a series of unintelligible words in Latin and at the same time he instantly transformed into a greenish-brown amphibious looking creature that towered over Sowles. The entity was covered with spines and appeared to be wearing a hood or helmet that resembled the head on some odd type of prehistoric creature. It seemed to have external lungs that rapidly inhaled and exhaled with a raspy sound and produced the horrible stench of decaying flesh. Its appendage like limbs resembled arms. They extended almost to the floor; at their ends were webbed hands that had the sharpened, long claws of a vicious carnivore.

Sowles remained on his knees, struggling not to stare at the horrible presence, while continuing to call out the name, "Jesus! Jesus! Jesus! Forgive me! Help me!"

With each of Sowles's utterances the lapping fire in the hearth shrunk. Almost in unison, the entity became smaller, gradually transforming back into a frowning and mournful looking Doctor Scully.

"Just say my name, Noah, please!" Scully said. His demeanor had softened. He seemed to be pleading.

Sowles only continued to pray more fervently. "Lord Jesus, forgive me, save me."

Scully seemed to be dazed. "Go, Noah. Go," he said. "You are free to leave. There is no need to cause a further scene. You may leave, my friend. You are free to leave," he said, as he sat in his chair and held his face in his hands. "Go, please."

"Sowles weakly pulled himself onto his feet. He appeared to have regained some strength. "Your chip didn't work, Scully! And now in the name of the Lord Jesus Christ, I say, get the hence, evil one."

Scully tried to laugh but instead he began coughing explosively as if he might spew his own lungs.

Sowles raised his arms to the ceiling as if he was a Black Moses. "You're the father of the lie, the great deceiver. Go back to your dwelling," he said.

"This is my dwelling!" Scully roared. You are free to leave now, Noah, but I offer no promises," he said. "Take your Christ with you and go," he said. "But this is not over. It will never be over!"

"It's my turn to laugh now, eh Scully?" Sowles asked.

"Remember, Noah," Scully said. "I cannot make you do anything you don't want to do, but I can make you wish you did." Scully chuckled again, but his voice was weak. He then turned toward the wall.

"It's no more use, Scully. Don't try that ugly monster stage trick again, foo'. Get behind me in the name of Jesus Christ." Sowles said as he edged toward the front door.

"Wait!" Scully said. The flames in the hearth rose again. He turned back around. It was Sowles's father. "Noah, my boy, I've missed you so much. Please, let's talk."

"No," Sowles said, barely able to speak. He fell again to his knees. "You are not my father! Get behind me!"

"Get up from that floor, you worthless, simpering representation of mankind," his father said. "You were always a coward of a nigger, a mama's boy, a damn weak-ass draft dodger, a man who couldn't keep a woman."

Sowles shut his eyes. "Lord, Jesus, please make it stop!"

"Look! I make all things too." It was Scully speaking again. He seemed reenergized by his transfiguration. He watched Sowles curiously, the way a wayward child examines a small, defenseless animal he has tortured. "Speak my name, Noah, say my name! Seek your relief and say my name!"

"I know your name, Scully," Sowles said weakly. "But I won't speak your name."

Sowles stared blindly at Scully. The Reverend James Persons flashed through his mind. The old man was standing at the pulpit. His hands were in the air, his palms upward. He looked down and smiled directly at Sowles and Sheylinn sitting in the hard pew.

"We shall be taught the words of the Gospel of the Lord, Jesus, by the Apostles John and Peter," Persons said.

Sowles felt the perspiration under his starched, white, Sunday-go-to-meeting shirt as Persons moved closer on the platform and then bent forward in front of Sheylinn.

From his position on his knees, Sowles glanced up at Scully. He was examining his nails.

Persons again flashed through Sowles's mind. The pastor was holding his arms outstretched over the congregation.

"Your adversary walks about like a roaring lion seeking whom he may devour," Persons said. Then Persons raised his voice. The church room vibrated. "Praise the Lord Jesus!"

Scully bellowed with laughter. "Do you think fairy-tale mantras upset me?" he asked.

Sowles appeared emboldened. He stood and moved closer to Scully until they were four feet apart and toe to toe, as if they were facing off in a three-point martial arts match.

"You heard the words, Scully! You heard the testimony!" Sowles said. "The words did not come from my mouth, but you heard them!"

Scully's face again flushed with anger. The fire in the hearth increased, blazing into the room. "I heard them, yes. I've heard those words many times. Go to hell, Noah Calvin Sowles!"

"Resist him! Now!" Persons yelled inside Sowles's head.

"I know who you are, Scully, an' I know you ain't long fo' our world! Get behind me! We're done, man. Go back to where you came from. Get behind me in the name of Jesus Christ, the savior of the world!"

"Hell no!" Scully said.

Scully cursed and babbled expletives in ancient Latin and then German, Russian, Polish, and again in English. "Come back to me!" Scully yelled as the heat in the room increased, and the fire surged out of the hearth. The paintings began to melt and drip, running onto the floor and sizzling into the hardwood as Sowles fell again to his knees. He then clasped his hands together. "Mother!" he said, crying as if he was a boy.

Scully spun in a circle. "I'm here, son," his mother said. She was dressed in a pink chenille robe. The same bathrobe she had worn every morning when she made her coffee.

Sowles sniffed the strong odor of her talc above the scent of the burning wood. "I love you, son. Come with us," she said, but she quickly was gone. Scully had transformed back into himself. Then without using his hands, he lifted up one end of the massive, wooden dining room table and flipped it over on its top, breaking it and the chairs into pieces.

Sowles crawled toward the door. "Lord in heaven, help me," he said. In the name of Jesus."

Scully screamed like a dying animal as Sowles stood and hobbled out into the dark evening. "No! This is not over, Noah. It will never be over!" Scully said.

When Sowles reached the rig, he stopped and looked up into the heavens—the same sky that had been pitch dark only minutes or hours earlier had become filled with twinkling pinpoints of planetary light.

"We have a journey ahead. Are you ready to cross over the gulch?" A woman's voice seemed to be speaking to him.

Anna? Is that you?" Sowles asked. "Mother?"

"Yes, dear. You called for help."

"Why did you die, Mom? Why did you give up?"

"My kidneys, son," she said. "They were gone, barren. I could not maintain my blood pressure no matter what the doctors did."

"I smell your powder, Mom." His voice had become childlike for the first time in many years. "Where are you, Mom? I can't see you."

"Yes, Noah, my boy, my powder. Please never forget that scent, Noah. It will guide you. The comic books are gone. Go to church. Go to pray. Go to repent. Go to be baptized," she said. "Always do the next right thing! But, my son, I must go now."

"I'll go. I'll go," he said, as the tears poured from his eyes. Through the blur, he looked at the behemoth truck and trailer. Sitting on the dark road, it resembled a tired, beached whale.

He ran back to the truck and hastily separated the air hoses and electrical cord from the trailer and then pulled the release that detached the trailer from the truck. First cranking the landing gear down to the ground, he then quickly jumped inside the cab and started the rig. The noisy motor invaded the otherwise silent evening, forcing him to pause and bury his face in his hands, but within only seconds he grabbed the shotgun, all the ammo from under the bunk, and both gas cans from the front passenger seat area. While holding everything in a bundle in his arms, he then dove out of the rig and ambled to the rear of the trailer.

"Help me, Mom. Help me Anna," he said softly as set the bundle on the paved driveway and then tore away the plastic seal on the trailer, painfully remembering the discussion with Aaron about the seal. Then opening the two heavy doors he stopped and stared at the pallets of fentanyl sitting neatly in the nose of the box. In that moment he was reminded of his commitment to Rong Ying. Shaking his head as if to forget, he loaded the armaments and gas cans onto the floor of the trailer. Pulling his body up inside the dark cavern, he disappeared inside. In a fraction of a minute, now empty handed, he jumped out onto the pavement, quickly dashed back to the cab, and climbed up into the driver's seat.

Slowly the tractor pulled forward and dropped the trailer. As he rolled ahead, behind him the massive trailer exploded in a fiery ball of orange as if it had been hit by a missile. Oily clouds of smoke quickly engulfed the area and began boiling upward into the night sky.

He drove forward, toward the gravel road that led back to the highway. "Where can I find Anna, Mother?"

"You must hurry!" It was his mother's voice responding. "Go to any church where you see a plaque out front that reads, 'VISITORS WELCOME.' He will be there waiting for you."

"He? Who?"

"The Lord," she said.

"I'm afraid, Mom," he said. "I feel like I'm in a movie, like none of it's real."

"Listen, my only son. You have been through the worst. You must go forward now. Then later, you will go to the reservation, to a place called Covelo. You will search for her. When you find her, she will join you to the grandfathers, and the many fathers of the grand-fathers, and the many bears, and the many cousins, and together you will learn other things of Him and all of His covenants."

"I will find her," he said. "I will find everyone, Mother."

"I love you," she said. "*Vaya con Dios*, my son."

Driving only the vulnerable tractor, he rolled as quickly down the mushy, earthen road as the dark mud would allow. Within short seconds he felt an unusual sense of peace. It was a new feeling, a foreign feeling, something akin to an awareness of comfort. He felt an urge to listen to some music. "Motown," he said aloud as he remembered Aaron criticizing his affinity for the sixty-year-old rhythm and blues. "No, Mr. Sowles. Soul, Mr. Sowles, soul music," he whispered as he pushed the power button on the radio. The sweet, melodious voice of Lionel Richie instantly filled the cab.

He smiled and glanced in the outside mirror. "That fire oughta keep Scully's white devil ass warm," he said.

# Epilogue

Rudy Mendoza sat in his office with his feet on his desk, playing with his mobile phone. The owner, Mannie Patel entered with his wife, carrying a small, white poodle. Rudy quickly put his feet on the floor. Patel shook his head.

"So, Rudy, you're saying that Sowles's trailer was spotted out of state? Where was this?" Patel asked. "How can this be? Where is the tractor? Where is Sowles?"

"Yeah, Mr. Mannie," Rudy said. "But it don't make lotta much sense to me. I means, the cops, man, like they sayin' now I'm off the hook. But Sowles, man, his trailer was like in some place like Ohio or some place, maybe they sayin' Iowa, I dunno.

"Slow down," Patel said. "How's that? He was lost in Humboldt County."

"They's sayin' it was burned up, melted to the ground, like nothing left, like some fire happened or something, like they now saying, arson, and they ain't gots no dead body, but they sayin' it's his trailer, but they ain't for sure, you know, like cops, they ain't got it right, maybe, you know…but I don't get it, Mannie! Ohio? Iowa? They sayin' a lotta boolshit. And, man, that's like a lotta miles, right? Like far away, man. I don't know, man, that Sowles dude. That ain't like him, man. He'll be back, man, I'm sure, I mean, who knows?"

END

Made in the USA
Las Vegas, NV
16 September 2023

77559189R00196